I0819667

RASPUTIN

SWIMS

THE

POTOMAC

ALSO BY BEN FOUNTAIN

Devil Makes Three

Beautiful Country Burn Again

Billy Lynn's Long Halftime Walk

Brief Encounters with Che Guevara

RASPUTIN SWIMS THE POTOMAC

A Novel

BEN FOUNTAIN

FLATIRON
BOOKS
NEW YORK

This is a work of satirical fiction set in an alternate reality in the not-too-distant future. All of the names, characters, organizations, places, and events portrayed in this novel are either products of the author's imagination or used fictitiously, and nothing herein should be construed as real.

 For information, address Flatiron Books, 120 Broadway, New York, NY 10271. EU Representative: Macmillan Publishers Ireland Ltd., 1st Floor, The Liffey Trust Centre, 117–126 Sheriff Street Upper, Dublin 1, D01 YC43.

www.flatironbooks.com

Designed by Leah Carlson-Stanisic

Library of Congress Cataloging-in-Publication Data

Names: Fountain, Ben, author.
Title: Rasputin swims the Potomac : a novel / Ben Fountain.
Description: First edition. | New York : Flatiron Books, 2026.
Identifiers: LCCN 2026004090 | ISBN 9781250776549 (hardcover) | ISBN 9781250776556 (ebook)
Subjects: LCGFT: Fiction | Novels
Classification: LCC PS3606.O844 R37 2026
LC record available at https://lccn.loc.gov/2026004090

First Edition: 2026

10 9 8 7 6 5 4 3 2 1

For my sisters: Stephanie, Claire, and Susan
"Don't make me stop this car"

And, as always,
for Sharie

The Neverland had always begun to look a little dark and threatening by bedtime. Then unexplored patches arose in it and spread; black shadows moved about in them. You lost the certainty that you would win.

—Craig Paulenich, "Maps of Neverland," *Old Brown*

RASPUTIN SWIMS THE POTOMAC

1

THE DALLAS DAILY

▇▇▇ Declares "No Stopping Us Now"

First Rally Since Supreme Court Decision
Celebration Turns Ugly
Weeping Sickness or Saboteurs?

By Clarence Thomas Jr., National Affairs
Correspondent of The Dallas Daily

COLUMBIA, S.C. POSTED JUNE 22, 11:55 P.M. EDT —

In his first rally since the Supreme Court's decision clearing him to run for a third term, President ▇▇▇ entered the Sports Line Arena tonight to McFadden & Whitehead's power ballad "Ain't No Stoppin' Us Now" and roaring affirmation from 20,000 newly energized supporters. Praising his hardcore loyalists for "keeping the faith" while his challenge to the 22nd Amendment worked through the courts, the president roasted "the doubters" in the Republican Party who have so far refused to support his bid for an unprecedented modern-day third term.

"They said it couldn't be done," ██████ gloated to raucous cheers. "'Don't even try,' they said, 'you're gonna rip the party to shreds.' Well, they were wrong and we were right, and we're standing here stronger than ever tonight."

"This Is Our Home!"

Congressman Hite Schimzer, R-S.C., whose recently introduced bill outlawing the Democratic Party has further vexed an already highly contentious Congress, opened the evening with a series of no-holds-barred attacks on the president's Republican and Democratic opponents, pausing frequently for crowd chants of "██████ for life!" and "This is our home!" As has become the norm at ██████ rallies, a large contingent wearing "Murder the Media" T-shirts took up position in front of the press bleachers, where they proceeded to taunt and insult reporters with a vigor not seen since President ██████ blamed the media for ██████ Jr.'s abysmal showing in the New York City mayoral race. But all eyes swung to the front when the president made his entrance, shimmying to the music with the awkward aplomb of an aging celebrity judge on "Dance Fever."

"That's right, my friends, that's right," he boomed into the microphone. "Not gonna be any stopping us now, am I right?"

He was answered with an ecstatic roar. Tonight's rally drew a smartly dressed swath of suburban electorate in which polo shirts, khaki slacks, and designer jeans predominated. Southern youth was well represented, although the several acres of gray hair reminded this reporter that the plurality of ads on Fox News offer cures for the contemporary scourge of erectile dysfunction. And because The Dallas Daily reports what other media outlets are too sissy and squeamish to tell you, here is another demographic fact, but you know it already: The crowd was 94.8% white.

████ on the Attack

On this hot, humid South Carolina night, the folks were primed to see their candidate in fighting form, and the president did not disappoint. He began by slamming the dissenting justices in the 6-3 ████ v. United States Federal Election Commission decision, calling them "very bad, very partisan judges who've always had it in for me."

"You know, we've got ways of dealing with those people," ████ mused. "Dealing with them in our third term, that's definitely going to be a priority for us."

Next the president embarked on a freewheeling monologue about his Republican opponents, characterizing his rivals for the nomination as "very small, such weak people." He mocked low-flow toilets and energy-efficient light bulbs, praised the hard-line tactics of the National Security Brigades, and described the latest "General Ludd" attacks on data centers as "Marxist Democrat terrorism."

"We're making America great again, but the other side, those very bad, very evil people standing in our way, they're more determined than ever to stop us.

"That's why I'm running," the president declared. "That's the only way we're going to beat those people."

Tears, Then Trouble

But tonight's rally would bring even more drama than the world's reigning reality TV star might have wished for. Some 27 minutes into his remarks, Mr. ████ paused as cries of distress rose from the seats directly below him. Distance and chaos thwarted firsthand discernment by this reporter, but subsequent review of news and social media video would reveal the extraordinary sight of weeping, wailing, apparently helpless rally goers, many of them decked out in MAGA gear, being punched and shoved to the floor by their MAGA neighbors.

The video record shows it plainly: Here, front and center at █████'s first official rally since his Supreme Court triumph, was the latest outbreak of the so-called weeping sickness, a phenomenon recently reported from a handful of locales around the country. As has been noted in previous outbreaks, the victims appeared to be completely undone by emotion, their personalities dissolving in fits of violent tears.

Even more remarkable to witness in these videos is the rage the weepers inspired in their fellow rally goers, and the savagery of the physical attacks.

"Get 'Em Out of Here!"

"Do we need some law enforcement down here?" █████ asked, let us assume rhetorically, and he added, "I think we've got some agitators here tonight." As the turmoil intensified, it was this reporter's impression that the president relished the spectacle of his supporters beating the snow out of the alleged "agitators."

"Right, okay, I get it," Mr. █████ continued. "We've heard about this lately, this crying thing. I guess this is the new Democrat hoax, right?" The rally faithful responded with full-throated boos. "That's right," the president urged as helmeted, black-clad officers from the Secret Service's Civil Disturbance Unit waded into the melee, followed by local police. Chants of "U-S-A!" and "█████ for life!" accompanied the security forces as they escorted approximately 20 people out of the arena. But no sooner had the president resumed speaking than a second fracas erupted several rows behind the first.

Rally Cut Short

"Can you believe it?" ██████ vented as boos rained down. "These people, I'm telling you, they're relentless. You've gotta beat 'em down and beat 'em down and beat 'em down till they just can't get up anymore. I'm going to ask our wonderful law enforcement—and they are wonderful, right?"—at this the boos instantly flipped to cheers—"we love you, our beautiful law enforcement officers, I want you to take these people in for questioning. We need to get to the bottom of this, okay? 'Cause, folks, I really don't think they're with us."

Even as the black helmets and police gained control of the melee, more clashes were erupting across the arena. As if appreciating that the situation was spiraling out of control, ██████ made several appeals for calm, to no effect. Then what can only be described as a kind of blast or shock wave ripped through the crowd, an energy that this reporter experienced as a blow to the solar plexus, followed by breathlessness and tingling arms and legs.

My colleagues on either side were similarly affected. We were left with the conviction that something genuinely uncanny had just transpired. Proof, for anyone who needed it, was as close to hand as the Murder the Media contingent, most of whom sank to their chairs and wept hysterically.

"Relax, everybody," ██████ urged from the podium. "Please, let's just take it easy for a minute." The president paused as he was surrounded by security personnel, then disclosed that he had to leave, prompting a fresh outburst of boos.

"Just for a minute," he promised. "I'll be right back. Stay calm, people."

President ██████ would not reappear this evening. In the tense atmosphere that followed his departure, the press corps was advised to leave, but not before this reporter was subjected to insults of an epidermal nature, "globalist n*****" being the most original.

The numbers: 20,300 in attendance; over 100 detained; 17 hospitalized with non-life-threatening injuries. As for what actually happened tonight, and whether it was a phenomenon psychological, chemical, electromagnetic or supernatural—To Be Determined. At present, all this reporter can say is that he experienced an evening that has so far outperformed his brain's ability to comprehend.

2

So now only everybody, literally *everybody* in the world is waiting for a statement on last night's clusterfuck, and Himself is bunkered in the Oval chugging Diet Coke and ripping people's faces off. First thing this morning Faith reached across the pillows for her phone and checked the president's SonicX feed. He'd been silent for slightly over three hours, resuming flamethrower operations at 5:16 a.m. Mr. President, please! Give yourself a break! "████ cuts and runs" was trending into the red-zone millions, along with "Italy tarantula dance" and "demonic possession theory." From there she scrolled to video of the rally meltdown, janky shots of ostensible ████ers weeping like tear-gassed lefties while being whaled on by other ostensible ████ers. Either there were some hella good trauma actors in Columbia last night, or a bunch of ordinary Americans lost their minds.

Now she and the other junior comms aides are standing in Harvey's office watching the TV wall and lashing their phones with veritable thumbs of fire. "What's a medical sociologist?" someone asks as CNN, MSNBC, RT, CBS, Fox, BBC, ABC, and CNBC pluck various flavors of brain doctor from their obscure and specialized lives to expound on a behavioral deviation of batshit proportions. "Mass psychogenic illness" is how the head of the International Federation of Clinical Neurophysiology explains it on CNN, an essentially psychosomatic affliction—picture a short circuit in the nervous system—that jumps from person to person in "tense and hostile environments." On *Good Morning America*, some baldy in a white coat and bow tie is talking about "conversion disorder" in the context of unraveling social norms. "What we saw last night," opines a lady expert on MSNBC, "is the symptom of a mass mental health crisis."

"Yeah, it's called Democrats," cracks Marty Weiss, raising a laugh.

"Shut up, everybody, this is important," snaps Susie Grumman, who nobody likes. The vibe is not so much high alert this morning as bomb-squad taut, everybody tiptoeing around the nuclear device in the Oval. "A psychic contagion may act very much in imitation of a pathological contagion," the president of the British Neuropsychiatry Association is saying on BBC. "And in this case I would posit line of sight as the vector of contagion."

But what about the beatings? Why would the sight of someone crying prompt another person to attack?

"Mania is not rational," responds the doctor. "I would point out that this is the very nature of mania."

Faith's phone is blowing up—a string of texts from Christie, and nonstop taps from dear friends in the mainstream media, Statement soon? and Throw me a bone and, from CBS's star flirt Steve Toler, Buy you dinner tonight?, which makes her laugh. Nice try, she texts back, and notes the time. She hangs a left out the door, then a right, and in twelve strides arrives at the suite of staff offices attached to the Oval. She enters with a mercilessly chipper "Good morning!" but they are not in the mood. Everyone is gathered around Madeleine's desk in postures vaguely suggestive of prayer. Eavesdropping, and not a smidge embarrassed at being caught. The president's voice reverbs through the wall like a dance party bassin' it in the apartment next door.

"How is he?" she asks, though she can guess well enough. But these things are always a matter of degree.

"We're all about to be fired," says Caden Roebuck.

Faith is the only one who laughs, and this in itself strikes her as funny. "We're scheduled for an Oval shoot at eleven," she reminds them. Madeleine, the president's secretary, aka executive assistant, raises her brow, then looks warily toward the Oval.

"He just had a plasma boost."

"Better and better," Faith says, and leaves them to it. She continues her recon of the West Wing, passing through the reception area for the Oval Office and down the south hallway. Senior staff are nowhere to be seen; they're all in *there*, getting their heads shredded. The vice president's office is, as usual, deserted, and Faith envisions actual cobwebs growing in there. As she turns the corner, someone calls from the top of the stairs.

"Faith!"

"Harrison." She waits while he descends.

"Were you there last night?"

"I was."

"What the hell?"

"Pretty much."

He flutters the sheaf of papers in his hand. "Now I've gotta go in there and tell him online money's tanked the last twelve hours."

"I wouldn't be in any rush" is the best she can offer. Last night was a one-two punch to the softest parts of the president's ego: full-frontal disrespect, in public, on camera, coupled with events he plainly did not understand. A double-barreled humiliation guaranteed to flip him out, and how he raged backstage, he bellowed and lumbered around like a wounded bull. *You guys set me up! How could you let those people in!* Faith had never felt fonder or more protective of the president than at that moment. The thing is, she gets him, and not just the good parts. She appreciates the primal muck at the bottom of his heart and isn't afraid to put it bluntly to herself, that he is a sucking black hole of insatiable need and simultaneously its inside-out inverse, both black hole and ever-expanding protoplasmic blob absorbing everything in its path, money, people, cheeseburgers, countries, the office of the presidency itself.

The primal in him activates the maternal in her. His is the plumpest, pinkest, most vulnerable of all infantile flesh, like the stuff you find on cracking open a crustacean's shell. Of course he's an ass and a total son of a bitch too but she can handle that, having spent her most formative teenage years in the viper pits of reality TV. All the scumbags, jerks, and psychos she encountered in that world were excellent training for working in the West Wing.

She completes her tour of the halls and retreats to her "office," a windowless eight-by-ten slot in the warren of offices attached to the communications director's suite. She has a no-frills desk and desk chair, one visitor's chair, a government laptop, bookshelves lined with binders on protocol and branding strategy, and two wall-mounted whiteboards, one with the projected three-day and seven-day shooting schedules, the other with potential and developing storylines limned in her own private code.

Here at the interface between the White House and the TV-entertainment industry, a less grounded person might be tempted to think she's running the world. Sometimes Faith smiles and says to herself, *not quite*. She pulls up the news on her laptop and fields incoming on her phone. There's a text from Kendra, ETA 10:45, more texts from her mother, more begging and wheedling from the press corps. Then a text from producer Bob in LA—my, aren't we up early!—essentially asking WTF. Faith forwards him the link to a breaking news story comparing the weeping sickness to the Tanganyika laughter epidemic of 1962, whatever that is, then another story referencing "the bin Laden itch," mass outbreaks of skin rash among US schoolchildren after 9/11. Now she pulls up a story on the detainees from last night's rally. Their statements and online histories indicate they are exactly what they claim to be, die-hard █████ers.

Her desk phone dings; it's the switchboard. "Miz Spack, your mother's on the line. She says she's been trying to reach you."

Faith sighs. The operator emits a gentle chuckle. Christie Spack is well-known to the White House switchboard, maybe *infamous* would be the better word. On several occasions Faith has sent them flowers.

"Thanks. Put her through." In the empty moment that follows, she braces.

"Baby!"

"Mom."

"Omigod, I couldn't believe it! Me and Muffin were on the sofa watching your rally and having our little Jesus juice and all the sudden it's like, what? What *are* those people doing? Then I started sort of losing it, thinking my sweet little honey-bunny's right in the middle of all that! And the president, omigod, is he all right?"

"He's perfectly fine."

"Well, I've been praying."

"Mom."

"What!"

"Did you go to bed last night?"

"I know I know I know but I just couldn't with all that going through my head! Faith! The truth is there for those with eyes to see."

"I'm sure."

"I do it for you, baby, these are things you need to know! Okay, so what I've found so far is back in the eighties the agency came up with this new kind of nerve gas—"

"Wait. The CIA?"

"We ain't talking Peace Corps, baby girl. Anyway the spooks invented this stuff they call chloropactrin, google it, it's a kind of nerve gas that knocks people out but doesn't kill them. Then a few years later Bill Gates gets the formula and modifies the molecular structure, which, you know, his people can do, all the work they've done on quote unquote vaccines. Long story short, it looks like some of his people were at your rally last night and released a bunch of it into the crowd."

"Mom—"

"There's video!"

"There is?"

"Of course there is, we just haven't found it yet!"

Her mother didn't used to be this way; or at least not so unrelentingly.

She used to be—okay, she'd always brought a hyper adolescent's energy to everything, but that was froth, fluff; she was always basically sane until the branding beast took over. When they were cast for the first season of *Nashville Next Gen*, she legally changed her name from Kristie to Christie as a symbol of her Christian faith. She retroactively ascribed her daughter's name to the strength of that faith, never mind that the daughter was born outside the Christian sanction of wedlock.

"Are you writing all this down?"

"I am." She actually does write *chloropactrin* on her notepad.

"There's an antidote out there somewhere, you don't cook up something like this without the antidote. You guys should be looking into Bill Gates for sure, and I'd put George Soros and Sean Penn in that same category. They're—"

Chase Piercey, "Chase like the bank," glides into Faith's office and flashes his phone at her.

"Sorry, Mom, gotta go. The president wants me." An excuse only a handful of daughters on the planet can plausibly use. "Promise me you'll get some sleep?"

"I promise! I absolutely will. Later."

"Mom, please. Love you."

"Love you more!"

Faith hangs up and glances at the news on Chase's phone, and with him hovering at her shoulder she turns to her laptop and brings up the latest. Weeping outbreaks are being reported at a high school pep rally in suburban Columbia, a large-section statistics class at the University of South Carolina, and a Shriners convention several blocks from the state capitol. They watch cell phone video of big, beefy men in tasseled Shriner fezzes doubled over in their seats, bawling. Another Shriner enters the frame and starts punching the nearest weeper. Chase giggles. Faith gives him a scolding look.

"Sorry, it's just funny. All those fat old guys in their hats."

"Three outbreaks," Faith says, keeping the focus. "All in the Columbia area."

"It's like it's almost, you know. A real germ."

"A real germ," she echoes. "And asymptomatic carriers, apparently."

"I think I feel a Covid flashback coming on. Wait." Chase retreats a couple of steps. "Weren't you there last night?"

"I was."

He's out the door like a shot. Her phone buzzes; it's a text from Kendra: Here. Faith texts back There in 5 and burns several minutes scrolling news. Nobody really knows anything beyond the bare facts, but a Clemson psych professor proffers an "excitation transfer" theory to explain today's outbreaks. She's debating whether to fetch Kendra and crew when Harvey Gladding appears in her doorway. He's been doing this lately, dropping by as if her office is his secret safe space, a break in the battle. She spins her chair around to face him.

"Are we fired yet?"

He puffs a cough-snort sort of laugh. His suit jacket is double buttoned, and he has a legal pad in one hand, fountain pen in the other.

"How is he?"

Harvey shrugs.

"He got plasma this morning?"

"He was due. It's been two weeks."

"Right. So how are you?"

"The state of my emotions isn't relevant."

"Harvey, you're weird sometimes. Come look at this." She turns to her laptop and tilts back the screen. His face looms past her shoulder like the rising moon.

"Yeah."

"You know already?"

"Chase told me."

"Does *he* know?"

"Not at the moment. We're letting him . . ."

"Right." She rotates her chair to face him. He reflexively backpedals to office-appropriate distance. "Harvey, what the hell is going on?"

"The bureau's looking into it."

"Yeah, no, I mean besides that. Like, why. What. Existentially speaking."

"Faith, we live in very strange times."

"Dude, my whole *life* has been strange times. But this"—she nods at the screen—"this is next level."

He nods, distractedly unbuttons his suit jacket, then remembers his paunch and holds the legal pad in front.

"Come on, Harvey, I know you've got an opinion."

"My current opinion is, I don't know enough to have an opinion."

"Is that what you told *him*?"

Harvey grunts. He'll take a pass on that.

"People are saying it's some sort of hysteria."

"That seems feasible," he concedes.

"Or hypnotism."

He winces.

"Poison gas?"

"Let's not go there yet."

She ponders for a moment. "Will there be a statement?"

"Jagger and Lucas are working on it." Now he's looking over her head at the storyboards, seemingly taken with all the pretty colors of boxes and arrows looping everywhere. In a White House overrun with hacks, grifters, sleazebags, and monomaniacal ideologues, Communications is one of the few functional offices in the West Wing, all credit to Harvey. He emerged from the Darwinian sump of North Jersey politics to rise steadily through state and national ranks, proving his ultimate mettle as head of messaging for █████'s third impeachment proceeding. Physically and demographically he is your average middle-management schlub, a chronically stressed white American male with a slack dad bod, mulch-brown hair, a wife, four kids, two dogs, two cars, and a big fat mortgage. The horror. His only evident superlative consists of his eyes, which are basically the kindest brown eyes Faith has ever seen. The yearning she sometimes sees in those eyes when they light on her—is this a random function of midlife fatigue, or is he crushing on her?

He is also scary smart, and rarer still in the pimp parade of White

House personnel, wise to the uses of mildness and modesty. Lately Faith is having fantasies of ambushing him with an affair, and how satisfying it would be to pump some life into that sagging middle-aged body. An affair with Harvey wouldn't be all that demanding, she tells herself, except for listening to the loads of Catholic guilt he would heap on himself. She suspects she'd spend a lot of the time watching him sleep.

"Earth to Harvey."

"What? Oh." He smiles and tips his chin at the storyboards. "Sometimes I think you're moving us all around up there like a bunch of chess pieces."

"You give me way too much credit. I'm just logistics." Now they're both staring at the storyboards. "You aren't up there, by the way."

"Good God, I hope not. Even my mother thinks I'm boring."

Faith gives him her brightest smile. "Not to me. You're a hero."

He cuts her a shifty look, alert to facetiousness. How long has it been since someone gave this man an actual compliment? Maybe he's simply too decent for this business. She wonders if in his heart of hearts he was hoping the Supreme Court would quash the possibility of a third ██████ term.

Her phone buzzes. It's another text from Kendra, a single question mark. She looks to Harvey.

"The crew's here. We're supposed to shoot the president this morning."

"Okay."

"But I'm wondering if we should? Maybe there's too much . . ." She gestures at her laptop. "And what if it's, you know."

"What."

"Contagious. In some way."

"Come on, Faith. If it was contagious we'd all be foaming at the mouth right now."

"I guess that's true."

"It's a blip, nobody's gonna remember this a week from now. It's nothing compared to most of the shit we deal with around here."

"Uhm, also true."

"And how do we deal with the shit, Faith?"

"We keep working. We power through."

"Good girl. Call in your crew."

Dan'ae Jones, makeup genius, can take ten years off the president with the subtlest layering of foundation, a few deft strokes of concealer around his eyes and mouth. A young Rembrandt of the cosmetic arts, she's been imported from LA solely to dress the president's face for the number one reality TV show in the land. *The Real West Wing* is currently shooting its third season, the product slated for broadcast next spring. All considerations of jurisprudence aside, the Supreme Court rescued this season from a lame-duck waddle into the post-presidential sunset. *TRWW* has just been gifted the world's most killer A storyline, the plot brimming with tension, intrigue, the highest stakes known to man—who will have their finger on the nuclear button? From the hot core of the A story all kinds of B lines and subplots are spinning off, rivalries, vendettas, blood grudges, the most deliciously petty Machiavellian ratfucks, and that's just the in-house stuff. The plot thickens exponentially when you stir in the doomed delusionals hoping to snatch the Republican nomination from the president, then there's the bonus of the goofs and weenies lining up on the Democrat side, though the Dems are mostly for later. The general election will be showcased in season 4.

Dan'ae has draped a barber's shawl around the president's shoulders, and at the moment she's enhancing his forehead and brow. He seems soothed by her attentions, or maybe it's just the natural mellowing that follows a twelve-hour tantrum. He does love a woman's pampering, and Dan'ae—pretty, petite, black, haloed in effortless LA cool—seems to have that extra-special touch. The president's notoriously crab-assed father always gets the starring role in the legend of his character formation, but Faith is more curious about the Scottish-immigrant mother. Did she love him enough, her blond, blue-eyed, probably ADHD middle son? The troublesome one they shipped off to military school, far from the harbor of his mother's tender regard. Faith wonders what "enough" even means in this context. How is it measured, assessed?

According to what scale? Are even the best-loved ever truly satisfied with their share?

She stands off to the side of the Resolute Desk in classic aide position, binder clasped to her chest, stance relaxed but alert. Crew setup is a balletic whirl of blue-collar grace, hushed, synchronized, smooth—Kendra hires only the best. There are three cameras, one mounted and two roving handhelds, the rovers for profiles and the low-angle shots that endow the president with Mount Rushmore majesty. Kendra hangs back near the Churchill bust and observes, ready to direct if the crew needs her, which they don't. Just before shooting she'll take up position behind the stationary camera.

█████ rouses from his somatic lull. "Faith, darlin'."

"Yes, Mr. President."

He clears his throat, runs his tongue around his lips. The plasma boosts—harvested from his sons and grandsons—tend to dry him out. "You were with us last night?"

"I was at the rally, yes sir."

He coughs, mentally recalibrates. "How we doing this morning?"

"We're taking care of business, Mr. President."

"Attagirl, that's what I like to hear. Yeah, Faith's a goer," he announces to the room. "Some days I think she's the only one holding this outfit together."

"Mr. President, you're too kind."

"I mean it! She's a spitfire, you're a spitfire, aren't you Faith, you don't take crap off anybody. Except me"—he favors her with a wink—"but I never do that. You know I'd never do that to you."

"You've always been very good to me, Mr. President."

"Well, I try. I try to take care of my good help. Hey, Van!" he barks, not nicely. "Van! You're getting hold of thingamajigger, whatsisname? The fancy shrink guy—"

"Dr. Rathshimbaripari."

"Yeah him, swami guy. Ooo, I guess I'm not supposed to say that, am I. Swami guy." The president cracks an impish smile, if an imp could weigh 280 pounds and have a face like a Buick.

"We're tracking him down." Van Mulligan, the president's chief of staff and unofficially the second-most-powerful man in the world, is standing at the center of the presidential seal rug. He's tapping his phone. Asher and Twister, two of his junior aides, are furiously tapping theirs.

"Well hey, it's only the president of the United States trying to reach him. You'd think this guy's people—"

He stops as Dan'ae goes to work on his mouth. Madeleine cracks open the side door for a peek, withdraws. Faith checks her phone. Two more weeping outbreaks have been reported in the last few minutes, one in Hilton Head, the other at a truck stop outside Valdosta, Georgia. Three children have died of heat stroke at the Territorial Control Center in Del Rio, Texas. The Dow is down 2,500 points in heavy trading, wiping out all the tentative gains of the past few months. The ACLU has filed new lawsuits against the National Security Brigades and Rapid Support Forces, alleging use of excessive force and unlawful detention during the most recent round of insurance protests.

Dan'ae removes the shawl from ██████'s shoulders with an *olé* flourish, the sound man's cue to step in and clip a lavalier mic to the presidential lapel. "I guess we're ready," ██████ says, pulling his chair up to the desk. "One two three four testing, testing, we're good? So last night"—he's off and running, no prompt needed—"what we're thinking about this morning is all those people crying at the rally last night, I see the crying and I'm saying to myself, What is this? What is it? Sometimes it happens, people feel so strongly about the country, they love their country and they come out to see their president and sometimes it's just too much for them, they're overwhelmed from all their feelings, right? I get that, they can't help it, such strong emotions they have for their country, but last night, I don't know, what was *that* about? They're crying like a bunch of babies out there, and I'm saying to myself that doesn't look like tears of joy to me! And we're doing so great, the country's doing better than ever, everywhere I go people are cheering and thanking me so much, so what's up with the crying, the sobbing, all this crybaby business?

"So I don't know. We'll have to get to the bottom of it. We've got top people working on it, the smartest people, right now they're saying it might be some kind of psychological thing, power of suggestion or some such thing, or maybe sabotage? The left got their people in there spreading their chaos, that's what they do, that's what they do, and it's shameful, frankly. The Supreme Court gives us the ruling and right away this happens, I mean come on, it's obvious! Then the Secret Service comes up to me and says, Mr. President, sir, we have to get you off the stage, and I told them no, I'm not leaving, I don't wanna leave! No, Mr. President, sir, they're saying, you have to leave, it's too dangerous for you out here. Okay look, maybe I'm in danger but I'm not leaving, but they're insisting, they're insisting so much, finally I tell them okay, but I'm coming back as soon as you guys get this under control. But they couldn't! I was waiting a long time back there, I don't know, maybe they were being too soft on those people? And you can't do that, you have to be very strong with them, if they think you're weak they'll run right over you, and then what? Like what we had last night, which was disgraceful, frankly. But we're gonna correct that. We know what's coming now. You're going to see a very different result from what we saw last night."

The president is on a roll. The friendly cameras always lift him up, and he has achieved his most engaging self, garrulous, candid, charming, a verbal creature who does his best work in the out-loud mode. Faith gathers in the goodness and hugs it like a pillow to her chest, but last night is a hangover in her mind, a bad dream layered into her waking life. The weeping seems to portend catastrophe, a distinct next step on some terrible continuum toward—what? She can conjure nothing more original than a horizon boiling with black storm clouds. An omen. Or maybe more than an omen, the thing itself. Flying home last night on Air Force One there were no hijinks in the aft staff cabin, none of the usual banter and buzz. Shell-shocked, the lot of them. Collectively freaking out. The loudest sound that Faith can recall was Helen Rausch bawling in one of the restrooms.

But that was then, she tells herself. Today is a brand-new day. A sunny day, the Rose Garden resplendent through the Palladian windows, the bushes in star-spangled bloom without a canker or blemish in sight. The president is in his office and all is right with the world. They are fine. He is fine. Everything is going to be fine.

3

Clarence's theme is trending metaphysical this morning. Dams crumbling, weirs and dikes giving way, the great inland sea bottled up in the country's back-brain is loosed and flooding all over the place. Mass incontinence of the tear ducts, millions of pounds of per-square-inch pressure have finally bested all the tired old infrastructure that limited truth to the occasional squirt or tinkle, orderly little outflows whereby nothing and no one was greatly disturbed. But even the stoutest materials break down over time. People know what they know even when they don't want to know it, and he'd be happy to put a name to it for them. Perhaps large numbers of Americans really do care about their souls? As distinct from the outward-looking, if not to say empathetic, function of owning up to four centuries of riot and ravage. Grief, he would call it. Historical grief. You might ask how long before the grief gets to its rage stage, except the rage has been with us all along.

At the moment he's sitting in a front corner booth at Ertha's Diner demolishing the #3 breakfast special and studying video on his phone. The #3 is his coming-home treat to himself, two scrambled eggs, bacon, scratch biscuits with gravy, side of grits, and a bottomless cup of coffee. Five days on the road covering the nervous breakdown of

America, now he's back in Farmers Branch supposedly taking it easy, except he isn't. Act III of his working life has become all-consuming, which might be a problem if he had anything else going on. Early retirement, parents gone, Covid widower, no kids. Family is three sisters who worry about him living alone, and a slew of nieces and nephews who, now that they're grown, think he's actually pretty cool. A faculty colleague once said he looked like Trotsky. A black Trotsky, presumably, and that was okay. Clarence is a medium-brown black man with rimless spectacles, a goatee and mustache going gray, and a graying Afro high and wide enough to trigger any co-citizen so disposed. Their problem. He's fine with looking like a black Trotsky, just don't go sticking any damn axe in his head.

The videos show what he thinks he remembers seeing in Columbia the other night. Strange, nobody else picked up on it? Nothing in *The Washington Post* or *The New York Times*, which he read at the kitchen table over his predawn pot of coffee. He watches four different versions of the weeping in Columbia, then several versions of an outbreak at a monster truck rally in Spartanburg. Next he clicks on an outbreak at a debutante gala in Charleston, but a few seconds in his screen freezes, and he's reaching for the phone when the silence hits him. He looks up, and there follows a moment of mental freefall, his mind dropping through a trapdoor in the cosmic terra firma. The world has stopped. Everything is frozen in place, waitresses, customers, the traffic outside, he sits at the center of a three-dimensional still life from which even sound has been vacuumed out. There's an *oh shit* moment of thinking he's having a stroke, or maybe he just this second had a massive heart attack and died, except he can feel his racing heart inside his chest, air moving in and out of his lungs. And, oddly, a gratifying lack of alarm, no urge or impulse to fight it.

He clears his throat as a test, "umh-hmmm." He decides to lift his hand and does, it moves. "What the hell?" he murmurs, his voice tinged with a subterranean echo. He doesn't think he's losing his mind. This feels like something else, phenomenological, ineffable, and now he thinks without trying to think, *About damn time*. Like he's been waiting for this his entire life and didn't know until now.

Mind, body, sentience, all his systems seem intact. The freeze lasts long enough for him to accept that it's happening, then there's a kind of grinding smear like audio of a gravel crusher played too slow, and abruptly time resumes, the diner comes to life, and traffic is moving again out on Valley View Lane.

Okay. Okay then. It takes a lot to rattle Clarence and he is duly rattled, not that the average onlooker would notice. He fixes the certainty of the freeze-up firmly in his mind. He knows he'll be doubting himself soon, start sorting through the various medical and psychical explanations. He takes a deep breath and detects the scent of ozone high in his nose, a vaguely metallic, vanilla smell that reminds him of Covid. A déjà vu sort of smell—did it happen then too? He takes a bite of biscuit to prove he's still here.

"More coffee?"

"Sure. Thanks."

"How's breakfast?"

"Pretty much heaven."

"Shhh." The waitress smiles, taps his shoulder, moves on. He pushes his phone to the side and lets it be; in fact regards it with suspicion, as if the freeze-up started there and enlarged at light speed into the wider world. Something revealed, a glimpse, a teaser. A preview of sorts. Truth, it's not much weirder than a lot of things happening lately, but now it seems he's seeing the world with fresh eyes. And what is there to see? Daily life in all its ordinary splendor. Eggs, coffee, summer sun flooding the windows, the homey clatter of the diner at the slack end of rush hour. So tender it all seems, everyone so intent and purposeful as they go about their business, as pure in their focus as children at play.

He eats slowly and takes it all in. The eggs are good, the bacon and grits just this side of transcendent. After the waitress clears his plate, he resolves to sit with his coffee and think about what just happened, but *The Dallas Morning News* is at his elbow, tempting him with its "█████ Lifts Rules on Leaf Blowers" skyline. He holds out for a few more seconds, then reaches for the paper. Ukraine's president-in-exile Zelensky meets with EU leaders to urge solidarity in the face of Russia's "soft" invasion of Lithuania and Latvia. US inflation dropped to eleven percent last quarter, and Elon Musk is suing the Sonic fast-food chain for its takeover of the app formerly known as Twitter. Medicare and Medicaid are still reeling after the administration's attempt to put their payment systems on the blockchain. Weeping outbreaks are reported in Pittsburgh, Birmingham, and Atlanta, and the Cleveland Orchestra shuts down mid-concert when the entire string section falls out sobbing. No mass shootings in four days, this is newsworthy, but electrical substations are machine-gunned in Kentucky and North Carolina, knocking out power to thousands. Human Rights Watch reports that over 12,000 federal detainees are currently unaccounted for, 300 of whom are US citizens.

"Professor T?"

He looks up. "Fernando," he says, and wonders if the freeze-up shows in his face.

The youth grins. "I thought that was you. How you doin'?"

"I'm doing well, young man. How are you doing?"

Fernando gives a soft chuckle and looks down at himself, suddenly shy. Dirty jeans, beat-up work boots, a grimy blue T-shirt with a triangle logo, *Fire, Water, Storm* tracking the sides of the triangle. Bright, inquiring Fernando, who was aiming for law school when Clarence last saw him. Who sat in Clarence's office one golden fall afternoon and asked, "Do you think I'm smart enough?"

He's got a ponytail halfway down his back that Clarence doesn't remember. So it's been that long. He invites Fernando to sit, and the younger man does, saying he has to leave shortly.

"We're doing a double shift," he says, nodding at a nearby table of more blue shirts. "We're working an office building over off Renner Road, pipes busted and they got three floors flooded out. We were there all night."

"Fernando, that sounds a lot like work."

The younger man nods, gives another soft chuckle. "Yeah, and they cut off the AC on us. It's like ninety-five degrees in there, and half the time they got us in hazmat suits. We switch out every forty minutes so don't nobody pass out."

"Well, I hope they're paying you decent."

"Hardly. Time and a half's all right, like today. I take all the overtime they give me. I got a little girl now, you know that?"

"I didn't. Congratulations."

"Yeah, thanks. She's my sweetheart. Kids, you know. You do it all for them."

"You still thinking about law school?"

Fernando briefly meets his eye, looks away. "I think about it. I was still taking classes for a while, but man, school and working full-time, and a little baby at home? It was a lot."

"It is a lot."

"Too much for me, I ain't gonna lie. It was burning me out." He glances over at his crew, all of them young, male, haggard. "So, lately, me and my girlfriend? We're thinking of moving to Canada."

"Wow. I didn't see that coming."

"They need workers up there, you know that? Yeah, and after a year you can sign up for health care, and my girlfriend could go back to school. For free, they don't charge you nothing up there. When she found that out she was like, we're outta here. She wants to be a nurse."

"Good for her."

"We're trying to think, um, strategically about all this. I mean"—he looks around again and lowers his voice—"we sure ain't making it here. She works, I work, we're working all the time and we're living with her parents and *abuela*, and we still ain't making it. And we got thirty thousand in student loans, and those people are coming after us, *hard*. They're sending people to the house, and I'm like, how'm I gonna pay you with money I don't have? So it's like, okay, let's get outta here and make a fresh start somewhere else." Fernando pauses. "You warned us, Professor T."

Clarence nods. For all the good it did them. "You got any family up there?"

"Nah. We'd be on our own." His eyes meet Clarence's, skip off and back. "You think we're crazy?"

"Not at all. You've got your reasons."

"It's like you always told us, be an acting person. An acting person. I think about that a lot." He blinks, looks down at his hands, then back at Clarence. "You still on the city council?"

"Oh no. I served one term, they voted me out."

"The fuck they voted you out!"

"No, it's okay. I'm fine with it."

"Aw man, listen, that was about the coolest thing I ever did in school. It was like being on a presidential campaign or something, it felt, like, big, you know? Real. Not bullshit. Everybody was so pumped for it, and you *won*, Professor T. That was crazy."

"We did have an experience."

"Hell yeah. And they voted you out?"

"It's okay. It's democracy. You win elections, you lose elections."

Fernando meets his eye, and they share a laugh over Professor T's most fervent lesson. "Doe" someone calls, it's his crew, they've finished breakfast and are moving toward the door. "I guess I gotta go," Fernando says, pushing back his chair. "It was really good seeing you, Professor T."

"It's good seeing you too, Fernando. Good luck with . . ."

Fernando nods, and they leave it at that. Through the windows Clarence watches the young men saunter across the parking lot. Canada. He'll have to think about that. He lays down cash for his check and sits there for several minutes, waiting for something else to happen, and presently it does. His phone buzzes with a text from Renfro, founder and editor of *The Dallas Daily*.

Renfro: You back?

Clarence: Yep.

Renfro: Coming in?

Clarence: Yep. Got something for you.

Renfro: █████?

Clarence: Better.

People in this country need to calm down. Problem is, there's a market for losing your mind, a vast system primed to churn the raw material of insanity into great heaping gobs of money and power and fame. Sanity is for suckers, apparently, but there are still a few ways you can mess with the system. In times of despair Clarence summons up the Arthur Ashe mantra: Start where you are, use what you have, do what you can. What he had: world-class name recognition, not that he asked for it, and twenty-five years teaching government and poli sci at Brookhaven Community College. Where he was: Farmers Branch, a close-in Dallas suburb of thirty-five thousand souls that had achieved national fame for enacting an openly racist, anti-immigrant housing ordinance. What he could do: run for city council, both to fuck with the system and give his students a live experiment in electoral politics. He filed on impulse, on a Friday afternoon thirty minutes before the deadline. Driving home from work that day, Gayle heard the news on the radio and marveled that there were *two* Clarence Thomases in little Farmers Branch, two! Who'd have thought!

Well, after a lifetime of confirmed bachelorhood, he was still learning how to be married in those days. The coincidence of his name sent Caucasia into convulsions of rage and loathing, and naturally the frenzy spilled over to her. That was the regret. That he put her through a ride she hadn't signed on for. They thought they had a fair idea of what was coming, but the sheer depravity of the abuse surprised even Clarence, a congenitally contrary black man who'd been talking back at America since first grade. The proportions were all wrong, for one thing, the maniacal energy they devoted to destroying one little candidate for city council in a small, politically negligible North Dallas suburb. It felt deep. *Old.* The whole scene made him tired. Didn't it make them tired too? Doing the same song and dance for four hundred years, you'd think Caucasia would be bored of itself by now, and the hating didn't seem to make them happy, he noticed. Pretty much hilarious was when they accused him of "misleading voters" with his name. Excuse me, folks, that's my *name*, had it since the day I was born, and as for that other Clarence Thomas, I don't know him, don't endorse him, am not his friend, family, relation in any shape, way, or form, and the only voters who might confuse me with the Supreme Court justice are either too lazy to do their civic homework or functionally brain-dead.

More convulsions—oh, now he's insulting voters! He never denied or admitted that his name was what got him elected, but four years later they made sure the fine citizens of Farmers Branch equated their incumbent councilman with the second coming of the Mau Mau. Losing hurt, more than he expected. Ruptured-appendix hurt, compound-fracture-of-the-femur hurt, but for solace he had the words of that famous political philosopher Pancho Villa: The defeats, they are battles also. And now, surely, the death threats would stop, but no, they wouldn't let it go. They seemed to miss him. Certainly they cared enough to track him over to *The Dallas Daily* and harass him there. Maybe you haven't heard the 'noose,' read a recent email, we know how to deal with NEGROS in Texas. He has lately been advised to watch your back, and we know where you live, and, most charming of all, your wife is going to die with my throbbing white cock down her throat.

No question America is losing its grip, but is he? Driving downtown he wonders how it would work if a freeze-up were to happen now, booming along the Tollway at eighty miles an hour. He eases off to sixty-five and wonders if he should worry that he's not more worried than he is. Could be a mini-stroke he had at Ertha's, a fugue spell, some sort of neurochemical event, but it felt too external to be a purely personal thing. It seemed more, well, *structural*, some sort of kink or tear in the natural order, or—here's that troublesome thought again—something uncanny going on with his phone.

If it happens again he'll call up his doctor, meanwhile he's fortunate to have more interesting things to do. *The Dallas Daily*, locally known as "the geezer paper," occupies the second floor of the old pie-shaped KLIF building on the edge of downtown. Renfro won't hire anybody who doesn't have a self-sufficing income stream—Social Security, a fat 401(k), a lump-sum severance invested in annuities and blue chips, or, rarest of all, the lucky stiff with an honest-to-God pension. Mailbox money, the workingman's lottery ticket. Renfro himself took a buyout after thirty years with *The Dallas Morning News*, waited out his non-compete, and started his nonprofit, online-only newspaper on the one-year anniversary of his de-employment.

"I can't pay you much," he said in their first phone call. *The Dallas Daily* refused ads, ran on subscriptions and donations. He was familiar with Clarence's foray into Farmers Branch politics; somehow he even knew about Clarence's brief postcollege career stringing for Reuters and AP from Central America.

"How much?" Clarence asked.

"I'm embarrassed to say."

"How much?" Clarence repeated.

"Sixty-five hundred." Renfro paused. "A year."

Clarence barely heard him. "What do you want me to write about?"

"What do you want to write about?"

"Politics, I guess."

"State, national, or local?"

What the hell, Clarence thought, and said "national," and so he became the *Dallas Daily*'s national affairs correspondent. In the two years since then he's reported on the long tail of the Flash Crash and the ensuing Musk Riots, the reinvigoration of the Comstock Act, Democratic Party fecklessness, Schedule F reclassifications and the firing of thousands of federal employees, the anti-AI "General Ludd" movement, the National Security Brigades, the patently unconstitutional Administrative Detention program, inflation, the Biden trials, and more. With his good Spanish he gravitated to the border and came back with livid stories on the Territorial Control Centers, i.e., mass detention camps, and the federal "work release" program that delivers cheap immigrant labor, on demand, to any sector of the economy that needs it. Problem was, the cops down there kept throwing him in jail. He kept going back, poking the dragon, so to speak; a kind of compulsion, testing himself against long-ago evils. Unfinished business could get you into all kinds of trouble, apparently. His last trip cost the *Daily* $4,500 in attorneys' fees, and Renfro suspended all excursions to the border until further notice.

At the moment they're sitting in the editor's office. Clarence taps up weeping-outbreak videos on his phone and hands it across the desk, Renfro watches and hands it back. This goes on for several minutes.

"Notice anything?"

Renfro waits. He is secure enough of ego to handle being schooled.

"It's all white people."

"Show me again."

Renfro takes another tour through the videos while Clarence considers the view. Renfro's office sits at the very tip of the wedge, big plate-glass windows all around. Clarence knows they present crisp silhouettes from outside, easy targets for any nut job with a gun and a grudge. Back in the early days of rock 'n roll, kids used to drive by and honk at the DJ spinning records in the wedge, got a kick when he waved back.

"Okay." Renfro hands the phone over.

"White cries. Black and brown just go on."

"What do we do with it?"

"I was thinking maybe a story on the one-drop rule. Does being even just a little bit black immunize you."

Renfro looks vaguely perturbed. He is pudgy, white, Protestant, polite to a fault. The perfect straight man.

"Ren, buddy, I'm messing with you. I don't know what we do with it."

"Oh. Well. Has anybody reported it?"

"Not that I've seen."

Renfro slides out his jaw, clamps his lip under his teeth. By the end of the day he might have a red line across his upper lip.

"Okay, so that thing at the end, the shock wave. Tell me about that."

"The shock wave. It was like," Clarence strikes his fist to his chest, "*that*. You can see it in the videos, everybody reeling back."

"But nobody else reported it."

"Of course not. Shit's way too spooky for *The Washington Post*."

"All right, what could it be? This spooky thing that nobody's reporting but us."

"God only knows." Clarence ponders for a moment. "Something got loose in there? ████"—again he pauses—"he's got some kind of voodoo going, psychological voodoo. You get all that crazy energy going in one place—I don't know, maybe you could explain it on the molecular level. Secretions, pheromones, they set up a charge in the air, start colliding with each other, get a chain reaction going. Critical psychological mass."

"A kind of hysteria."

"Maybe." Clarence wonders if his freeze-up falls in the same general category. "I'm just thinking out loud here."

"Clarence, you know I like the way you think."

"Like I said, it was a crazy night. Crying, fighting, you got the feeling anything could happen."

"In a way it did, I guess."

"In a way it did," Clarence agrees.

"And now he's running. Officially, legally."

"He is most definitely running."

Renfro sighs. With his big belly, the settled capaciousness with which he fills his chair, he could be the great white Buddha.

"So why are they crying? White people. Tell me why the white people are crying."

Clarence shrugs. "They're scared? Worried. They can't afford their lives." Even as he talks he's reordering his historical-grief thesis to account for the abject pathos of the weeping. "They're scared for their jobs. Their kids. How they gonna put the kids through college without breaking the bank? The crazy weather freaks them out, and they're scared what AI's doing to their jobs, all the jobs—gonna be any jobs left in five years? And what are they supposed to do if they get sick, their kid gets sick. Right now they can't even afford being well."

"And ████ was supposed to save them. Excuse me, *us*. White people."

"Uh-huh, so maybe they're starting to feel it in their bodies, how well that's working out for them. But even then."

"Go on."

"I suspect a lot of people would rather die than change how they think about the world."

Renfro looks past Clarence to the newsroom. It's an open floor plan, checkerboard of slate-blue cubicles filling out the middle. Aside from Renfro and Duncan, the managing editor, there are rarely more than a couple of people around.

"People are saying this thing could nip the recovery in the bud."

"Maybe. Yeah, how bad you wanna buy that new car when everybody down at the dealer's bawling their eyes out."

"You know, you could write it up just like you told me, 'American Fear,' something like that. People are panicking. Their nerves are shot. But . . ."

"It's a theory. We aren't *The New York Times*."

Renfro nods. "You know what they're saying over at First Baptist. We are witnessing the beginning of the end of days."

"Like they've been saying for years. Decades. Centuries. You want me to go over there and talk to them?"

Renfro allows a smile. "I think we can leave them alone for now."

4

As a precocious fifteen-year-old, Faith quickly learned the main job of the producers on *Nashville Next Gen* was stirring shit. It could have been a good show if they'd let it be about the music, but America being America they had to go low. Baiting "the kids," amping the rivalries to fever pitch, but worse was how they stoked the parents to near-murderous ruthlessness. Millions of dollars on the line, fame and fortune, set up the family in high-style luxury for life; *L.A. Next Gen* (pop and rock), *Atlanta Next Gen* (hip-hop), and *Miami Next Gen* (Latin) had proved the formula, no reason why the latest offering in the Next Gen franchise should deviate. Whereas Faith, she just liked to sing. Singing in church was a way not to be bored, and putting pen to paper she'd revealed a knack for turning out catchy, country-inflected lyrics. The audition video had been Christie's idea, but Faith was game in a what-the-hell sort of way. Here was a shot at getting out of Dallas for a while, lottery odds, about the same as your chances of being struck by lightning during a shark attack. Then the miracle.

"Your voice brought us all to tears," the great Mark Burnett himself told her over the phone. She'd sent in church songs, a cappella renderings of "Down to the River to Pray," "I'll Fly Away," and "Softly and Tenderly," and her own composition, sung to the only five guitar chords she knew, "Momma and Me." Twenty minutes of homemade video launched her into the *NNG* whirlwind of recording sessions, marquee mentors, and small-venue Nashville gigs where the contestants could "hone their craft," in the cornball phrase of the show's host, a slick sleazebag named Kenny Akins. The Taylor Swift comparisons started day one. Same general physical type, Faith a younger, blonder, tinier version of the megastar; all the more astonishing, then, how the slight youngster easily ranged half an octave lower than Tay-Tay's lowest register.

It didn't have to be mean and cynical, and that, as Faith saw it, was the tragedy. Something that could have been so good was played for kicks and cruelty, and her growing disgust made her a fan favorite, the smart, sassy kid who's wise to the grown-ups' jive. Her eye rolls and smirks furnished some of the era's most popular memes. Fan blogs endlessly listicled her top ten or twenty put-downs, mostly sotto voce comments on the aggressions and acting-out of the adults. She became the audience alter ego, the vessel for their presumed superiority to the material, and thus gave them permission to keep watching such blatantly tawdry crap.

As far as she's concerned, the whole production was an exercise in child abuse. The first season she rolled out a string of winning songs—"Doncha Feel It Going Down," "Big Blue Lonesome," "Rancher's Wife, Rancher's Life," and a thinly veiled slag on Kenny Akins, "I Don't Know Why You're So Annoying (But You Are)." She made the cut for season 2—it didn't hurt that "Rancher's Wife, Rancher's Life" was picked up as the theme song for a new Taylor Sheridan show—then her song "Daddy Dadgum Gone (and Momma's Crying in the Kitchen)" got the rumors churning about who her father was. Not Lonnie, the man Christie divorced when Faith was nine, but her biological dad, the fornicator and sperm shooter. Someone rich and famous, this much was known. Various names were floated. Bill Clinton, Steven Tyler, T. Boone Pickens, Gary Busey, all these and more, men whose orbits, according to charts and timetables constructed by obsessed fans, conceivably overlapped with Christie's in the correct month and year.

Stupids! All you had to do was skim the Dallas papers for any week of the past twenty years to find her dead-ringer male version staring back at you. But she wasn't saying and neither was Christie, not with Faith's NDA-contingent trust fund on the line. Not that the *NNG* team didn't try. Now *that* was child abuse for sure, the producers tried every trick and wile to get Faith to spill, but the kid would not crack, not for love nor money. Certainly not for the piddly $15k she and Christie were being paid for the entire season's work. And keeping the secret, she discovered, was her own private superpower, knowing she could blow up not just the show but the entire city of Dallas with two words.

The bastard princess of Dallas refused to yield, but Christie waffled. She was building her own brand as a diabolically perky stage mom, and missing the finals would nip that trajectory in the bud. They argued.

"Mom, don't even think about it."

"Well excuse me, I'm the parent and you're the child. I'll decide what's best for this family."

"Mom, you say his name and I'll sabotage us right out of the show."

"Oh really. And how do you propose to do that?"

"I'll call in the cameras and slit my wrists, that's how I'll do it."

The Real West Wing is a walk in the park compared to *Nashville*. She's never on camera, for one thing. Anonymity suits her. And thanks to an emotionally volatile White House staffed with vicious idiots, there's no need for shit stirring. These people would gouge out their mothers' eyes to climb one millimeter higher up the ladder, and crisis mode has everyone's reflexes at fight-or-flight pitch. The sad fact of the matter is, █████ World is flailing. Fundraising is flat, the trigger for daily battle royales about whose fault it is. Every week brings a staff purge of some kind, bodies in and bodies out, these same bodies shuttling on a loop between the West Wing and campaign headquarters. Vice President Greene continues to troll the White House, and █████ continues to rail on everyone about the Columbia rally. The slide started there, the bad polls, the stock market slump, the insufferable gloating of the Russians and Chinese. America has become the world's laughingstock, and nobody has a clue what to do about "the Weeps," as the

New York Post has christened it. The thing continues to spread at pandemic rates, except minorities—bizarrely, inexplicably—seem largely immune, with only a handful of cases reported among people of color. Blacks, Latinos, and Asians are increasingly supplanting whites in the media sphere, sparking fresh waves of grievance among the America First base. Mr. President, do something! Those people are taking over!

█████ himself is grumpy, morose, a lion in winter, except July temps along the East Coast are shattering all the records. He refuses to do rallies until the Weeps go away, and defensive crouch, needless to say, is not his forte. With so many people staying home—it's like Covid all over again—the fragile economic recovery has tanked, but Faith knows the president still has one thing going for him, the main thing: In a world full of bullshit, people crave something real, and █████, for huge swaths of the electorate, is as real as it gets. If he says the weeping sickness is a liberal plot to destroy America, that's good enough for them, regardless of whether the tears are "real," whatever that means. Privately she suspects that the Weeps boil down to mental toughness, steeling yourself against the distemper whirligigging across the land. Scientific opinion has coalesced around a range of variations on suggestibility theory. What it is, essentially, is a psychological contagion in the air, a nervous condition homing in on susceptible hosts. A psychosomatic phenomenon, in other words, which in Faith's understanding makes it sort of not real? Attacks generally last no more than fifteen or twenty minutes, but some cases persist for hours or even days, leading to life-threatening exhaustion for the victims. So far some 1,300 fatalities have been ascribed to the Weeps; elderly persons, for the most part, or people with preexisting conditions. Attacks seem to confer no immunity against future attacks. And, as of the present moment, there's no cure or natural end in sight.

Officially no one at the White House has been infected, but officially doesn't count what Faith hears in the bathroom stalls. Regular monsoon in there some days, she just does her business and scrams, no questions asked. Tonight she's on the dessert course of a meh first date when the switchboard calls: You are needed at the White House, stat. Sorry, fella, whatever your name is? Gotta go! She Ubers over to the White House, passes through security, and walks alone up the driveway to the North Portico. It's a brutal steam bath of a DC night, like being stuck in a sauna with a giant meat-soaker pad. Sirens wail in the distance, the city's eternal call to prayer, while frog and insect racket rivals the unholy roar of a 747 taking off. On such nights one is reminded that the nation's capital sits on an actual swamp, and to swamp it may eventually—inevitably?—return. Hark Grabel meets her in the entrance hall and they elevator to the second floor.

"What's up?"

Hark grins. He's barely out of college, the product of the third marriage of an old fraternity brother of the president, or something. As if the place needs yet one more supercilious twerp.

"You'll see."

Fuck you. "Is he mad?"

"I don't think so. At least not when I left him ninety seconds ago."

She's never been in the First Family's private quarters, and, as expected—this very old house is far grander in the mind than reality—is underwhelmed. Wall-to-wall blue carpeting, decorative vases on side tables, grandmotherly sofas and matching chairs, it's all very nice in the anodyne way of an oh-so-tastefully decorated funeral home. And underneath the odors of furniture wax and cooking, that barely discernible but ever-present White House funk, ashy, sour, musky, like the smell of moldering bodies buried under the foundation two hundred and however many score years ago. She follows Hark through the formal reception area and living room into the inner sanctum of the den. A big-screen TV tuned to pro wrestling is the only light, flickering, garish; man-cave light. The AC is set to deep freeze.

"Mr. President," says Hark, "Faith Spack is here."

"Hey Faith!" ██████ calls from the sofa nearest the TV. "Hey, looking good there, kid. Hey fellas, check her out, doesn't she look nice?"

"Good evening, Mr. President. Hello ████. Hello Jojo."

"Faith," says Jojo Parwellen, barely looking up from his phone. ████ Jr. smiles and sits up straight. He ignores his phone for the moment.

"So, Faith," █████ is saying, "all dolled up, eh, got a hot date? Lucky guy, whoever he is. You want anything? Soft drink, beer? Something to eat?"

"I'm good, Mr. President, thank you."

"Here, sit, come sit by me." He pats the cushion next to him. "Hey Hark, bring her a Diet Coke. Listen, Faith, you a wrestling fan?"

"Not really, sir."

"No? Hunh. Well, I think we might turn you into one tonight. Jojo, wind it back, start from the beginning."

Jojo sets down his phone and goes to work with the remote. Years ago he was a pothead college dropout in charge of washing █████'s cars, now he's point man for the president's social media accounts, thus joined at the hip with the Chief Executive body. Bald as a turtle, built like a bodyguard. ████ Jr., on the other hand, has let himself go since losing his girlfriend Kimberly and the mayoral race, in that order. Could be a roly-poly koala bear over there in the recliner, bushy haired, woolly faced, dressed in mismatched sweats and black socks, no shoes. █████ and Jojo are in golf-wear slacks and knit shirts. The rest of the █████s are nowhere to be seen.

"Okay," says the president, "this aired earlier tonight, they always tape these for me. This was—where were they tonight?"

"Atlanta," says █████ Jr.

"Atlanta. So this guy, you ever heard of the Russian Winter? Rasputin?"

"Well, I know about the Rasputin who was involved with the czars," Faith says.

"No, the wrestler Rasputin, huge star on AWW. I'm surprised you never heard of him."

Jojo hits Play and the screen erupts in a fantasia of purple-and-green strobe lights, jet flames, rainbow spumes of smoke billowing everywhere, all of it tracked to thick overlays of guitar-god vomit, SKRONKA SKRONKA SKRONKA. In-your-face sensory assault; Faith finds it impressive in a blunt force, dumbass sort of way. "Skip past all this," █████ has to shout, "get to our guy," and Jojo fast-forwards through a blitz of split-second freeze frames, it's like flipping through the gaudiest comic book ever made. "Stop!" the two █████s shout in unison, and Jojo stops, hits Play, and on-screen the wrestler Rasputin is making his triumphal entrance to a heavy-metal version of the theme from *Swan Lake*. He bears a middling resemblance to the historical Rasputin, a strapping man with long black hair, a lank pelt of black beard, close-set eyes, much nose; overall it's a rough-hewn but not unappealing face. He wears a gold pectoral cross over a shimmery black cassock, and a phalanx of sexy women accompanies him down the ramp to the ring, they're wearing white robes or togas that are supposed to signify, what? Then Faith gets it: vestal virgins. The crowd seems quite excited by it all, as of course they would, they have their own part to play. A tuxedoed and tanned emcee is standing center ring, and his booming delivery is so smooth, so synthetically perfect, that Faith thinks he might be lip-synching.

AND
now,
frrrrrrrommmm *RUSSIA*,
WITH
luuuuuuv,
RASSSSS-PUUUUUTIN!
the RUSSIAN WIN-TERRRR
and
the WRATH
OF
GOD

The crowd roars. The vestals lay hands on Rasputin and slide him out of the cassock. The cheering tails off as he takes the mic and closes his eyes for a prayerful moment. He raises his arm, and his first words seem to issue from the depths of an acoustically perfect cave:

"The wrath of God is a beautiful thing."

Belching flames, strobes, hits of metal guitar all stoke the crowd to a fine tizzy. They know what to do and do it with spirit and it's all great fun, which Faith appreciates, she knows a thing or two about trash TV. Rasputin commences a somewhat thudding diatribe against someone or something named Ono Olympo.

The president turns to her. "Whaddeya think?"

"Well, he really does look like Rasputin. And he's, uh, large."

"Large," ██████ echoes approvingly, and ████ Jr. pipes up: "Six-six, two forty-five. Eight percent body fat."

"Is he, uhm, does he ever lose?"

The men laugh. "Not much," Jojo answers, and Faith wonders how any mere mortal could take down *that*. "Is he really from Russia?" she ventures, and ████ Jr. chirps back, "Buffalo!" The guys break up laughing again.

"He played football for," the president begins, and stalls out. "Donny, who'd he play for?"

"Troy State," ████ Jr. answers briskly. "He dropped out after his sophomore year to join the Green Berets. Could've probably played pro, but he chose to serve. Four combat tours. He's got the scars."

It seems ████ Jr. is something of a fanboy. Faith is about to ask Rasputin's real name but hesitates, thinking the men will just laugh at her again. At the moment the wrestler is moving about the ring in solemn oratorical style, and his delivery—where has she heard this particular sound before, this earthy drone, the clunk-thud of an ox cart lumbering down a dirt road? Then she flashes on Arnold Schwarzenegger channeling Conan the Barbarian. A direct steal, except with Rasputin there's something extra, a faint slipstream of trills and tremolos, and in a second she locates the other movie reference. Borat.

"In these strange times," the wrestler is saying, "dark creatures come crawling out of their filthy lairs everywhere, ghouls, bats, snakes, worms, yes, every kind of filthy creature now lives among us, including that one who calls himself Ono." The crowd haws, hoots. "Yes, my brothers and sisters, Satan has been busy for a very long time, and now we see his work, and we know his servants are everywhere. But listen, brothers and sisters. We pray for Ono." *Noooooo*, the crowd bellows, *noooooooo*.

"Yes," Rasputin insists, lifting his non-mic arm, "it is our duty to pray for Ono. He is sick!" Big laughs now, razzing guffaws. "Yes, our brother Ono is very sick. Satan has afflicted him with that special perversion that leads to degradation and extinction." *Oh ho!* the crowd hoots, and Faith wonders if she's hearing what she thinks she's hearing. "Yes, we pray for his soul even as we battle his body in a holy and skillful manner. This we do in the name of the children, yes?" *YES!!! YES!!!* "In the name of the children, in the name of everyone who wants to live a healthy and normal life. Anything else is sin, sodomy, and darkness."

Sin? Sodomy? Darkness? Who even knows what sodomy means anymore, technically?

"She gets the idea," ██████ says. "Skip to the, you know."

Jojo fast-forwards again. Faith wonders why she's here, other than that ██████ is enamored of her TV past and thinks she's hot. She'd been on the job a few weeks when Stephen Miller casually mentioned that the president likes her.

"Nice to know! I like him too."

"But he wishes you'd lose about six pounds."

She considered for a moment. "I will if he will."

More important than anything is how she feels around him. Secure. Safe. Something about his bulk, the chthonic density of his body heat, pulls her in, and he in turn seems genuinely fond of her. This calculus of feeling counts for so much more than policy. She supposes it's all quite shallow of her, and she's fine with that.

After a few false starts Jojo finds what he's looking for and hits Play. Rasputin is right-angled on the mat with a blond, wavy-tressed, supernaturally suntanned man, they are chest to chest with Rasputin on top while his opponent—Ono Olympo, Faith assumes—is slamming his feet on the mat in desperation, and who wouldn't, his face is buried in the black forest of Rasputin's armpit thanks to the backward headlock Rasputin has him in. Faith swallows a little hiccup of a gag. Flesh, hair, glistening slabs of Spam-like muscle, it's all very elemental and somewhat disgusting, but on-screen the fans are lapping it up. *This might be it!* an announcer screeches, *Ono's toast* says a second voice as Rasputin raises his head and looks for the referee. *But what's this?* The camera cuts to the referee staggering around the ring. He lurches, bounces off the ropes, and collapses to his knees, covers his face with his hands. In a moment his body is racked with the telltale seismic heaves of the weeping sickness.

Rasputin looks stunned. He hangs on. Faith wonders how Ono doesn't suffocate. Cheers turn to boos as the crowd realizes what's happening, they sense a fix in the works, but the boos hollow out as Rasputin unwraps his arm from Ono's neck. Slowly, by stages—it's like an aircraft carrier standing on end—he comes to his feet. He steps over Ono and approaches the referee and lays a hand on his shoulder, bends deeply from the waist to speak to him. Ono comes to one knee and looks around as if hoping someone will tell him what to do. The announcers are babbling, *We've never seen anything like this!* Solo hoots and catcalls sail out from the crowd. All at once dozens of people in the front rows are sobbing. It hits without warning, they're fine one moment and the next they're not, it's like a bomb has gone off. Some double over and fall off their chairs with the force of it.

"They're faking," Hark says from somewhere in the shadows, but █████ shushes him. On-screen Rasputin lifts the referee to his feet and pulls him into a sweaty hug, patting his back, murmuring in his ear. After a few moments the ref raises his head and breaks into a smile. He gives a shrugging sort of laugh, clearly embarrassed, but there's a freshness about him, a look of peace on his suddenly relaxed features. Rasputin moves to the edge of the ring and motions at the front rows, leans over the ropes to speak to the ushers and cops swarming there. *Bring them here!* he can be heard saying. *Bring them to me!*

"Watch this," █████ urges Faith, as if she had a choice. It is, she will think later, like something out of the Bible, the column of weeping, wailing fans being guided along the ramp to the ring. Several hundred will process through before it's over, and they are every size, shape, and age of pale-complected human. Close proximity to the weepers infects many of the white ushers and cops, and their colored colleagues alertly step into the breach. Ono Olympo and the referee are doing their part, they escort the weepers one by one from the top of the ramp into Rasputin's arms. He hugs them, cradles their heads, speaks gentle words to them, and each person comes away cured, if that's the word. Smiling, starry-eyed, floating in a state that looks much like postcoital bliss. "Never seen anything like it," the announcers say a hundred different ways. They are "stunned," "amazed," "flabbergasted," "floored." "A unique moment in wrestling history, for sure." Presently Ono Olympo is pulled aside for an interview.

"Ono, what's going on down there?"

Ono has the mic in one hand, holds the earbud to his ear with the other. Waxy box-blond locks fall almost to his shoulders. His pecs are perfectly sculpted mounds of man-boob.

"You tell me, bro."

"Well, just describe for us your own personal experience of this moment."

"My own personal experience of this moment is it's freaking intense. I mean, guys, I'm standing right here in the middle of it and I got no idea. It's, uh . . ." He takes a breath, collects himself. "But it's just so great to see Ras helping our fans like this. Some of these people are really in a pretty bad way."

"What's he saying to them?"

"Uh, yeah, I don't really know about that. I think he might be speaking Russian to them."

"What else?"

"What else? I don't know, man, maybe it's some kind of energy he's giving them. We all know Ras is kind of a different guy, right? He must have something really special going on tonight, is all I can say."

"He was certainly doing you something special before you had to stop."

"Huh, yeah, he had it working for him, I guess. But we ain't finished, bro."

"Any discussion on when you'll resume the match?"

"Look, I'm just honored to be here for this moment, being able to help our fans any way I can. I'm not gonna lie, wrestling's my life, okay? But we've gotta take care of our people first."

████████ turns to Faith. "Powerful, right?"

"Yes sir, very compelling." She's intrigued, she must admit.

"We're thinking we need to get him to the White House and see what he's about."

It occurs to her that the president could be putting her on. If so, he does a hella perfect straight face.

"Yes sir, I can see that. Mr. President"—she pauses to hazard a glance at █████ Jr., hoping for a sign—"I can't say I know much about wrestling, but my impression is a lot of what happens is, um, planned?" The men stare, say nothing. Has she spoken the unspeakable? "I mean," she plunges on, "I've heard there are scripts these things follow. Or maybe I'm wrong."

"The scripts are more like guidelines," says █████ Jr.

"This isn't in the script," the president declares, but Faith knows that tone, belligerence standing in for factual basis. Jojo Parwellen barely looks up from his phone as he says, "Maybe we need to get Ricardo on the phone."

"Hark!" ████████ bellows. "Tell switchboard to get Ricardo! Tell 'em it's urgent."

Hark scurries over to a side table and picks up the house phone. Faith looks to █████ Jr., and the question is plain on her face. He clues her in with a stage whisper: "Head of AWW." On-screen Rasputin is working his cure on the last of the weepers. As the crowd catches on—perhaps their attention has wandered in recent minutes—a standing ovation builds, a slow, unstoppable freight train of sound that leaves the TV announcers gasping for superlatives. Someone hands Rasputin a mic, and he raises his arm for silence.

"All glory," he intones to the suddenly hushed arena, "all the glory of this night is to God the Father."

Another mighty roar rolls forth, giving it up for God the Father! "Fantastic," ████████ is murmuring, "amazing," "incredible," but Faith, never the most religious of girls despite her mother's best efforts, feels the clammy fingers of squeamishness in her gut. The God schtick strikes her as a bit much. It feels—well, *blasphemous* seems like such an old-fashioned word. Rasputin again raises his arm for silence.

"Why this weeping?" he asks in his interesting voice. "Why these tears? This grief? I tell you, my brothers and sisters, we all feel it, this poison rising out of the twilight into our souls, and we feel helpless, exhausted, God's grace seems far away. We are sad, so of course we weep! Many have died of sorrow, and we who remain, we wonder how long the wicked will triumph."

"Ahm," Hark cuts in, "Mr. President."

"What!"

"Ricardo's people say he's on his yacht somewhere in the Mediterranean. It's four in the morning over there."

"I don't care if it's goddamn four in the morning on Mars, get that lazy bastard on the phone, *now*. His president needs him! Jesus Christ," ██████ grumbles, settling back on the sofa. "What's he even doing in the fucking Mediterranean, American water's not good enough for him? It's a wonder we even have a country anymore."

"Dad, we'll get him," ████ Jr. says.

"You better believe we'll get him. I'll send the goddamn Navy after him if I have to."

From behind them comes the frantic murmur of Hark working the phone. Meanwhile there's the unignorable giant TV where Rasputin is holding forth, each word and phrase measured out like reps in the gym. "We think God has left us to the mercy of dark forces, but this we know in our hearts, we know our sins and lawlessness have done this. Everyone walks around so pitiful and ashamed of themselves, we forget that prayer can purify and protect us. We forget the evil are weak! They are like Satan, and like Satan they run from prayers. Prayer, true prayer, is victory without doubt. When we pray God is with us, the enemy is nothing, and our lovers' tears of happiness surround the throne."

"See," ██████ says to Faith, "they love him. They loved him before but now they *really* love him. You know, he's a very clean-living guy, doesn't drink, doesn't smoke, doesn't do any kind of drugs. He gets a headache, he won't even take an aspirin."

"Sort of like somebody else we know," says ████ Jr.

"Hanh, there you go, buddy. Me and Rasputin, we know a few things."

Rasputin's thing may be schtick, Faith thinks, but it's schtick with substance. As he is now, standing alone in the ring, she discovers a forthright intensity in him that holds the eye. He suggests an enticing combination of warrior and innocent, and it's the promise of innocence that seals the deal. His piercing, nothing-to-hide dark eyes, his endearingly clunky English, these are things that make you want to be on his side. You want to protect him. You want to know more. She's rather amazed at the response he rouses in her even as her TV-expert brain breaks it down.

Rasputin hands off the mic, and she realizes they're gearing up to resume the match. The crowd cheers and comes to its feet as the wrestlers stretch, shake out the kinks. Prayer, hope, healing, God's love and all that, now that we're cured we can go back to enjoying the spectacle of two people beating the living snuff out of each other. Oh, the irony. Ono looks none too happy about taking on Rasputin after he's saved the day, but he mans up for what Faith suspects will be a sound thrashing. They've just started grappling when Hark appears at ██████'s side with a phone.

"Mr. President, Mr. Levy is on the line."

██████ takes the phone. "Ricardo. Hard man to track down."

"_______."

"What the hell you doing over there anyway?"

"_______."

"How big?"

"_______."

"That's pretty good. Business must be good."

"_______."

"Nanh, I'm done with boats. Whadda I need a boat for, I've got friends with boats."

"_______."

"Hanh, that's right, I'm gonna hold you to it. Listen, your boy Rasputin tonight, that was quite a performance he put on in Atlanta."

"_______."

"Yeah he won, but that's not the point. I'm talking about that thing he did with the crowd. The weeping thing."

"———."

"You didn't see it. You don't know about this?" The president cuts a disgusted look at his audience. "Well then I'll tell you, Ricardo, that crying bullshit started going around and he stopped it cold. First it was the ref, like, I don't know, he put his hands on the ref, said some words to him, the guy's instantly cured. Then all these people in the stands started getting it, he had them come up into the ring and they get the same treatment, big hug, he talks to them, feels up their heads, just like that they aren't crying anymore. Very impressive. Made me think of Jesus curing the lepers."

"———."

"Lepers, I said *lepers*. Jesus, Ricardo, since when did Jesus ever cure any leopards?" ██████ looks to Faith and rolls his eyes. "Anyway, the point is what we're wondering here is what exactly the hell we saw tonight. Like was it a work or, um, you know, some sort of, uh, spontaneous, whatever."

"———."

"'Cause I know you're still involved with a lot of the storylines."

"———."

"Uh-hanh. Uh-hanh."

"———."

"Well, it looked pretty ad lib to us. And it went on for like, I dunno, half an hour? Pretty ballsy if it's a work, stopping the match that long so a bunch of people can come up and get a hug. Unless it's—yeah."

"———."

"Yeah."

"———."

"Uh-hanh."

"———."

"You do that, yeah. Call me back as soon as you know. Like, *soon*. Like in the next ten minutes, okay? We're talking about a matter of major national security here."

5

Two days later Clarence is in the passenger seat of his nephew's BMW heading west on Lyndon Baines Johnson Freeway. Destination, the residence of the professional wrestler Grigory Yefimovich Rasputin, a twelve-bedroom, fourteen-bath mansion in the uber-affluent Dallas suburb of Southlake. It's Saturday, a little after one p.m., and the dashboard thermometer reads 108 degrees. In today's *Dallas Morning News*, as well as *The New York Times*, *The Washington Post*, and a dozen more big-city dailies, there appeared a full-page ad paid for jointly by Americans for Prosperity and the US Chamber of Commerce urging Americans to take the optimistic view. "America has never been stronger or more prosperous," the ad enthused. "Our nation's best years lie ahead of it, and all Americans have much to look forward to." In other words, stop your sobbing and get back to work. Meanwhile the monthly meeting of the Federal Reserve Board abruptly adjourns when ten of its twelve members come down with the Weeps. The Major League Baseball season is in shambles, and every theater on Broadway has closed its doors. Fox News plugs the holes in its lineup with black and brown talent, and ratings dive despite the newcomers' ultra-hardcore right-wing rants. Lately the president has been giving impromptu press briefings where he gripes about "dark forces" and "foreign interferencers" in the land, and hints at yet-to-be-specified "drastic measures" in the works.

And now there's Atlanta. At the moment Nelson is explaining to his uncle about heels and faces, "babyfaces," and how Rasputin started his All World Wrestling career as a heel, then flipped to face, i.e., hero, good guy, white hat. But this was a while ago, around the time Nelson was aging out of his wrestling infatuation. Now he's the youngest felony prosecutor in the history of the Dallas County District Attorney's office, a fit, handsome black man of twenty-eight, clean-shaven, single, assured, with a wardrobe that reads rising professional. He has a badge of sorts, and a county-issued sidearm, a Smith & Wesson .38 that's currently stowed in the glove compartment above Clarence's knees. Always the straightest of arrows, by ninth grade he was wearing a coat and tie and carrying a briefcase to school, reading Angela Davis and Ta-Nehisi Coates on his own. "My little man," his mother, Dolly, Clarence's middle sister, would laugh as she waved his straight-A report cards around. Truth to tell, Little Man's precocity could be grating. The devotion to pro wrestling was one of his few age-appropriate interests, evidence that he was a flesh-and-blood kid and not some droning adolescent cyborg.

He's marginally looser these days, and claims no more than nostalgic fondness for the sport that consumed his middle-teen years, but it was Nelson who Clarence called for guidance into the world of pro wrestling. He knows next to nothing about it, and doesn't really want to know, but Renfro has put him onto this strange thing that happened in Atlanta the other night. A mass miracle cure, but really? Pro wrestling being famously "fake." Then Nelson mentioned that Rasputin happens to live right here in the Metroplex, his address readily available on any number of databases maintained by the Texas Department of Public Safety. But he wouldn't let Clarence make that house call alone.

"Key, there's too many ways for you to get in trouble out there."

"How so."

"Well, it's you. And there's the fact that they really don't like black people out there."

The BMW is a recent purchase—bought lightly used, typical of canny Nelson to work the depreciation angle. The car hums with Teutonic efficiency. Clarence messes with the AC vent, shooting jets of arctic air here and there while his nephew explains about schmozzes and kayfabes.

"So it's sort of like a soap opera, but with wrestling."

Nelson laughs. "I guess so. Or maybe more like Disney. You know, heroes and villains, a storybook in real life. But larger than life. The wrestlers take these very human qualities and blow them up to epic scale."

"Will I embarrass you if I ask him is it fake?"

Nelson bobbles his head yes and no. "The really good ones know how to blur that line. What's real, what's fake, they keep you guessing. But I can tell you this, the skills aren't fake, the athleticism. Those people do amazing things with their bodies. And they're some of the best extemporaneous speakers you'll ever see."

"What about the blood?" Clarence has been watching AWW YouTube all morning, crash-coursing on the sport.

"That's definitely not fake. Sometimes they secretly cut themselves with a razor to, you know, enhance the experience."

Self-mutilation, never a good sign. "Don't worry. I'm not going to ask him if it's fake."

"You know what, Key? You talk us in there, I'm fine with you asking him anything you want."

Point; their expedition is a long shot. Nelson seems determined to get them there in record time, and Clarence wishes he wouldn't. The freeway is slightly less clogged than on weekdays, but probably deadlier, given that traffic can pinball around at eighty miles per hour as opposed to fifty or sixty.

"Anyway, all I really want to know is what happened in Atlanta."

"Was it real."

"Was it real."

They've watched the video multiple times.

"You can ask him. I'm not sure he'll answer you straight. But."

"What."

"They'd need a hell of a lot of performers to pull that off. Weepers, cops, ushers, there'd have to be a couple of hundred people in on it. That's a lot of production even for AWW."

Clarence ponders. "██████'s a big wrestling fan."

"Yuuuuge."

"That guy. No telling where this goes."

"Uncle."

"Yeah?"

"Please don't get hurt."

"Nah. I don't do that anymore."

Mainstream media has so far ignored the Atlanta event. Too far out there, Clarence supposes, and of course everybody knows pro wrestling is, quote, fake. Nelson follows LBJ past the giant airport and merges onto State Highway 121, and coming off the ramp they're faced with miles of sterile freeway spooling into the haze, thousands of cars aligned in their lanes and the midday sun leaching color from the scene like a sheet of opaque vinyl stretched across the sky. The ugliness is breathtaking. For distraction Clarence pulls out his phone and checks the news. The phone behaves; reality follows suit. He has yet to have another freeze-up episode, but last night, checking his phone at two a.m. in the backyard, spikes of blood-red lightning lit up the sky. No thunder, no clouds, just a storm of red lightning that lasted for several minutes. This morning he checked the weather report for last night, then googled "red lightning." Nothing. As if it never happened.

Signs and wonders; either that or he's halfway off his rocker. GPS directs Nelson onto the eight lanes of alienation known as Highway 114 and then to the exit for Southlake Boulevard, and the town's mainline artery feeds them into a model consumer zone lined with name-brand retail and upscale-casual dining. Clarence is struck by the abundance of medical offerings, nearly as many for pets as humans. Low-rise office buildings and midsize megachurches conform to the wholesome visual vocabulary of upmarket commercial, the action punctuated by water towers, streaks and globules of lush green landscaping, artful stone portals marking the residential developments. The pattern repeats about every mile, each sector is its own elongated market square where every reasonable human appetite can be satisfied.

Clarence's gaze glides along the streetscape with no more friction than his tongue licking an ice cream cone. Everything kempt, smooth, orderly, no rough edges anywhere, and not a bookstore in sight. The algorithm couldn't have done it any better, he thinks. No, fool, he self-corrects, the algorithm *did* do it, you don't get discipline like this by accident, but into this beiged-out idyll of highly curated suburbia suddenly roars a delegation from *Mad Max* world. They hear it before they see it, a gurgital rumbling from behind that comes on fast. It's a MAGA convoy, mostly pickups and dualies with conspicuously armed Caucasians seated in the beds, flags flying, classic rock blasting, a political carnival on wheels. Custom-made scaffolds and tarps provide shade for the backriders, and all the vehicles, the trucks, the luxury sedans, the pseudo-military SUVs, are flying ████ flags of one kind or another. ████ as Rambo. ████ as bare-chested hunk. ████ as bewigged founding father. ████ and Jesus shaking hands, gazing soulfully into one another's eyes.

"Told you about Southlake," Nelson says.

"They do it in Dallas too."

"Yeah, but out here . . . it's the Wild West out here."

Everything trundles to a halt for a red light. A double-cab pickup idles in the lane to their right, and Clarence buzzes down his window to see what happens. The reaction is instant. The backriders shift his way, and several of them stand. They bring their AR-15s to present-arms position. Stunning, what the sight of his black face can do. They're in uniform, a kind of Afrikaner apartheid-militia getup—khaki shorts, khaki short-sleeved shirts with epaulets, red suspenders, bush hats. "Tactical" sunglasses. Web belts loaded with side arms and gear. The world does a little spin, and for a second Clarence isn't quite sure where he is.

"Uncle," Nelson murmurs. Molten heat pours through the window, bitter flatus of diesel exhaust. For Clarence it summons up smells from forty years ago: woodsmoke and jungle rot, gun oil, skank breath. Death smells.

"Key, come on now," Nelson coaxes. "No point picking a fight out here."

But Clarence knows there won't be a fight, not today. This is practice, playacting; dress rehearsal for a new reality for which the MAGAs may or may not have the guts, and what a secret torment that must be for them. That your nerve might fail at the critical moment. After all the tough talk, the dressing up, the domination fantasies. All the thousands of dollars you'd spent gearing up in the further pursuit of your happiness.

The light changes and the MAGAs roar out. Nelson goes slow, and the convoy pulls ahead.

"Did you know," Clarence muses aloud, "the Nazis had over a hundred and seventy different types of uniform?"

This rattles a laugh out of Nelson. "No, I didn't know that."

"It's true. Fascists tend to be very particular about their look." He has to stop himself from going into professor mode and enumerating all the signs that America has entered its Weimar phase. The racial chauvinism, the yearning for a white ethno-state, the fearmongering, and the willingness, even eagerness, of seemingly normal, neighborly, law-abiding citizens to submit utterly to the will of a violent strongman—most of the hallmarks of poor doomed Weimar are here. Not to mention, now that his mind has warmed to the subject, anti-Semitic conspiracism, hyperbolic hostility toward the press, the formalization of vigilantism and political street violence, and the trashing of democratic norms and institutions. But he says nothing. It's not his job anymore to lecture, and he's determined not to be that dreary old head boring everybody to death with his living history monologues. Instead he messes with the AC vent and thinks about the questions he'll ask Rasputin, assuming they actually meet the man.

"Uncle Key."

"Yeah?"

Southlake Boulevard is several turns behind them.

"Where does all the money come from?"

"Does make you wonder."

"And how do we get some of that?"

Yes, where does it all come from, for this. Mansion after mansion. They're on a narrow, countrified two-lane road lined with multi-acre estates, and the houses are enormous. The guest houses, the pool houses, the multilevel garages, they are enormous, too. Occasional sight-lines through the gates and fences reveal tennis courts, stables and riding rings, sapphire-blue swimming pools. Some estates feature ponds and their very own couple of holes of golf. This convergence of baronial lifestyle, proximity to Dallas–Fort Worth Airport, and generally competent city government makes Southlake the outer suburb of choice for centimillionaires, including an above-average percentage of pro athletes. Teen suicide and overdose rates are problematic, the collateral damage, perhaps, of a high-stress environment that consistently produces stellar test scores and powerhouse sports programs.

They pass a cop car idling in the turn-in to an estate. As soon as they're past, the cop swings in behind them.

"Hello," Nelson says, glancing in the rearview. The cop is practically on their bumper. "He's running my plates," Nelson says, and Clarence laughs.

"You think you have to tell me?"

"I—no. Sorry."

"You don't have to apologize either."

Out of nowhere a second cop car appears behind the first. Cop magic. For a while they have their own little convoy going, but Nelson drives cool and eventually the cops peel off. Several more turns and a winding route along a manicured greenbelt bring them to the purported house of the wrestler Rasputin, a spanking white pseudo-Italianate pile visible through the scrolls and curlicues of the wrought-iron gate. A twelve-foot-high stone wall bounds the property; an expansive circular driveway revolves around a rococo fountain depicting a frolic of dolphins and bare-breasted mermaids. Nelson pulls up to the intercom stanchion and hits the buzzer, waits a minute, and tries again. A voice erupts amid a sudden rash of static.

"May I help you." Brusque, borderline mean; don't count on any help here. Clarence leans toward the window and gives his name. "I'm a reporter for *The Dallas Daily* and I'd like to speak to Grigory Rasputin."

"He's not here. Yall need to leave." It's a rasping, high-pitched black man's voice, drawling sinks of small-town Texas in it.

"When will he be back? I'd very much like to talk to him about his Atlanta match."

"I don't have that information. Yall need to leave. Now."

"Wait a minute," Nelson murmurs. He sits up and speaks to the intercom. "Is this the Retribution?"

There's a pause, then a *tsssseee tssseee tssseee* sort of chuckling. "Now where you gettin' that?"

"Come on man, I'd know that voice anywhere! I was a huge fan of yours back in the day."

"Well now, I appreciate that. Been a minute, hatten it."

"The Black Thunder, man, nobody had a move like that. Black Thunder, the Closed Coffin, those were classic moves. You are missed, sir. Everybody's waiting for you to make your comeback."

"Too many bumps for that. No comeback for old dudes with metal hips. Look, I don't mean to be rude, but yall need to be getting outta here for real. Two brothers out this way"—Clarence has noted the security cameras—"somebody liable to come along and take a shot at yall."

Nelson glances at Clarence. "That's how it is?"

"Been known to happen," says the Retribution in a mournful voice. "People got some funny ideas around here." He clears his throat. "Who'd yall say yall are?"

Nelson explains he's a lawyer and lifelong wrestling fan, and this is his uncle in the seat beside him. A famous reporter hoping to speak to Rasputin about what happened in Atlanta. He pauses. For several moments nothing happens. Clarence is about to start pleading his case when they realize the gate is opening. No squeal or rumble issues from the mechanism, there's only the slow silent glide of several tons of metal. Classy, Clarence thinks. Classy, and vaguely ominous.

~~~

The Retribution, real name Herman "Bitsy" Bowman, once the pride of Palmer, Texas, all-American defensive tackle at UT, nine years in the NFL, two in the CFL, then a hard decade throwing what was left of his body around pro wrestling rings. Nelson has just enough time to brief Clarence while they pull around the mermaid fountain and park. Eventually the front door is opened by a bearded, char-black giant nearly as tall and wide as the doorway itself. Formerly famous for his catlike quickness, these days Bitsy Bowman moves at turtle pace, shuffling along on forearm crutches with ergonomic handles and padded wrist braces. He asks first thing for their phones.

"I apologize, gennelmen, but that's how we do things here. No cell phones in the house."

Clarence and Nelson hand over their phones, which Bitsy places in a discreet wall safe by the door. Then he leads them through the grand entrance hall, three stories high with a red-carpeted staircase curving to the left, a chandelier the size of a Prius overhead.

"It's very kind of you to invite us in," Nelson says. Little Man always did have perfect manners.

"Couldn't let yall just sit outside like that. My baby sister coming out to visit last week, two white fellas in a pickup nearly run her off the road. Gettin' so people can't even drive around here."

"That's sad," Nelson says.

Bitsy swivels around to meet his eye. "One word for it."

"We passed a MAGA convoy on the way here," Clarence says.

"Happen most every weekend," Bitsy observes. "People got to have their little hobbies, I guess." They are going at slow-motion Bitsy pace. Every step involves a heave-ho lurching of trunk and arms, the squeak of the spring-assist hardware in the crutches. They pass through a formal room decorated in chic minimalist style with baroque flourishes—plush daybeds, a giant gilt-framed mirror, an old-world icon in the corner whose eyes follow the mortals across the room.

"You stay here?" Clarence ventures.

"Stay here, work here." Bitsy wheezes and grunts with every
~~~

forward lurch. "He gone so much, gotta have somebody looking after the place."

He being Rasputin, Clarence assumes. "You known him awhile?"

"Ever since Japan." Bitsy slides forward a step. "Wrassling." Another step. "He was on the way up. I was on the way out." He stops and turns to Clarence. "So I'm gonna tell you right now, Mr. Reporter. We off the record."

"Okay."

"Yall even being here, off the record."

"Got it."

Twenty years as a professional athlete, the man would naturally have press savvy. Bitsy's small dark eyes drill Clarence a moment longer, then they're on the move again. The dining room is next, medievally themed with a long oak table and baronial chairs, and courtly-love tapestries ornamenting the walls. Bitsy leads them into a gleaming modern kitchen the size of a pickleball court.

"I imagine yall might like some refreshment on this blustering hot day. We got ice tea, all kind a soft drinks, sports drinks, fizzy water. I hope you won't be too cross with me when I say we don't serve alcohol in this house."

"No problem. Iced tea would be great."

"Same for me."

"And looka here," the big man says on opening the fridge, "that smart Bitsy Bowman just happen to have made a batch." He sets a pitcher of tea on the kitchen island and goes about collecting glasses, ice, lemons, moving with the submarine grace of a foraging manatee. Everything is immaculate, Clarence notes, not a crumb or grease streak in sight. The entire back wall is glass, giving broad views of the expansive grounds and pool area. Most striking about the view are the seven or eight attractive young women engaged in a spirited game of pool volleyball. A handful more are sunning themselves on the pool deck, and they are all, as best Clarence can determine, topless.

Nelson has seen as well. He whips around to his uncle with bulging eyes, fairly bursting with the whoop he holds inside.

"I make it kinda sweet," Bitsy warns, filling their glasses.

"That's okay!" Nelson yelps. To keep from staring at the women he moves around the island to where a glass of iced tea and a plate of sandwiches sit, along with a book. He checks out the title. "Pushkin," he remarks, then looks to Bitsy. "Yours?"

Bitsy squeezes a laugh between his tongue and teeth, *tssseee tssseee*, a hint of asthma in it. "You think an old baller don't read books?"

"No sir, I just—I don't know anybody who reads Pushkin. *The Captain's Daughter*," Nelson reads off the cover. "Good?"

"Some heavy lifting in it for sure, but yeah, man's got knowledge. Grishka told me the all-time champ Russia writer's a black dude, figure I oughta check him out."

He slides a glass of tea toward each of his guests and offers something to eat. They decline. Clarence has noted a void.

"You don't have help?"

"Plenty a help." Bitsy is making his slow way around the island to his lunch. "Weekends we send 'em home early, unless Grishka here."

"Grishka," Clarence echoes. A question.

"Grigory. Rasputin. The man you came to see."

"That's what you call him?"

"That's who he is."

"Okay."

"Is, has been, always will be." Bitsy sits, sheds the crutches, and pulls his stool up to the counter. "You can forget about whatever came before. He sure won't answer to it."

"Even at home he's Rasputin."

"Even at home you always Clarence, right? Clarence Thomas. Like the judge." Bitsy cuts Clarence a wry look; he's wise to the burden of that. "Look, Grishka's kind of a different cat. Best take him on his own terms, you just be wasting your time otherwise. He won't be rude on you or nothing, you just won't go very far with him."

"What does his family back in Buffalo call him?"

Bitsy nods, disappears a third of a sandwich with one bite. "Uh-huh, you done your research, that's good. Those people, let's just say they're real proud of Grishka. They accept him as he is. And they oughta, he provides real good for them."

Clarence becomes aware of the clicks and hums of high-tech appliances, the whoosh of the air-conditioning, the occasional splash and peal of laughter outside. "The Retribution," Nelson says. "I can't believe I'm actually sitting here with the Retribution. You were the Man, sir. Nobody was badder than you."

"Well, I thank you. I had me some times, I guess. Never did bring home the belt."

"And that's fuh—messed up. Everybody knows you were robbed."

"Just how it is, they got their favorites. Retribution only gonna rise so far." He turns to Clarence. "You wanna know about Atlanta."

"I do."

"You wanna know about him curing all those folks."

"Correct."

"Was it for real."

"That's what I'm wondering."

"I don't know, 's the honest truth. Might be, might not. Wouldn't surprise me, though."

"If it was real."

Bitsy nods. "Grishka's spiritual. Godly. It ain't an act, okay? I grew up in the church, I seen pew-hopping, talking in tongues, seen an elderly sister leap up to the ceiling, ten, twelve feet up, slap it with the flat of her hand. Grishka, he got the power like that."

"You've seen him do things."

"He got the power of God. I'm just gonna leave it at that."

"If he really did what it looks like he did—that could be a huge thing for the country."

Bitsy is solemn. "Yes."

"Have you talked to him since then?"

"We talk every day."

Clarence waits, but nothing follows. He senses that with Bitsy it's best not to push.

"Any chance he'd be willing to talk to me?"

"Folks at All World need to clear it first. Talk to the media office, that's gonna be your first call."

"In my experience it takes weeks to line up anything through people like that."

Bitsy laughs, *tssseee tssseee.* "You got that right, they always gonna be looking out for the brand. Grishka got his own person too you need to talk to. Charlie Cupps."

"Charlie Cupps." Clarence pulls out his notebook.

"Talk to him before you call the All World folks, maybe he can smooth the way. I'll get you those numbers."

They're exchanging information when the sliding glass door opens. It's two of the pool girls, but they don't enter. They've put on pool wraps, sheer little formfitting things that seem to make them more naked. "Bitseeeee," one of them calls in flirty singsong.

"Yes, Cinnamon." Bitsy barely looks up.

"Can we order sushi?"

"*We*, may, but as you see I am busy at the moment. You go ahead."

"You want anything?"

"I do not, thank you."

"Uhmmm. Bitsy?"

He sighs and lifts his head.

"Can we charge it to the house?"

He gives Clarence a heavy-lidded look; the patience of centuries in that look. "Yes, Cinnamon. You may charge it to the house."

6

The White House

Washington

LIMITED OFFICIAL USE

MEMORANDUM
TO: Russian Winter Working Group
FROM: Asher Simpkin
Twister Perkin
SUBJECT: Grigory Y. Rasputin

This memorandum is intended as briefing for all members of the Russian Winter Working Group in advance of GYR visit to Oval tomorrow.

Grigory Yefemovich Rasputin is his professional <u>and</u> legal name. Formerly known as Patrick Walsh Strickland, his name legally changed by court document filed in Erie County, New York, November 18, 20__.

Early Life

Born April 20, 19_ in Buffalo, NY. Father, David Debnam Strickland, Northwestern Mutual Insurance agent (retired). Mother (Doris Elaine (Anspach) Strickland is CEO and co-owner (with husband) of Doors-R-Magic, a closely held automatic garage door company in East Amherst, NY.

GYR attended the public schools of East Amherst, NY (suburb of Buffalo) grades 1–12. All-Conference in football junior and senior years of high school. Letterman in football and varsity track; co-captain of football team. Other honors include Eagle Scout; Boy's State; New York State Regent Scholer.

He attended Troy State University in Troy, Alabama on athletic scholarship (football). He is listed on the team roster for 20_ and 20_ seasons, and appears to have left school sometime after the 20_ season.

Military Service

Patrick Walsh Strickland was formally enlisted in the United States Army on March 1, 20_. He was assigned into basic training at Fort Bragg and was subsequently accepted to the "Q" course to qualify for the Special Forces (Green Berets), in which endeavor he was successful. Military records indicate he served at least five deploiyments overseas in Iraq (3), Afghanistan (1), and Western Africa (1 possibly 2). And for his Service was awarded the Purple Heart (three), the Bronze Star for Valor, the Silver Star, multiple campaign and good conduct medals. He received one reprimand for use of excessive force on an Afghanistan prisoner, who subsequently died. Honorably discharged on September 23, 20_ with the rank of Sergeant First Class.

The Russia Years

At this time little of definitive status which can be determined about GYR's years in Russia. It appears he traveled there shortly after his military discharge, and his stay was lenthy, perhaps as much as 5–6 years; a request for information from the Russian Foreign Office is pending. He has made frequent reference to his time in Russia "at the monastery," and/or his time there as a period of "pilgrimage," "spiritual seeking," "spiritual quest" and similar statements (all quotes in interviews). It was there that he attained fluent mastery of the Russian, and according to experts he speaks in a somewhat old-fashioned style, in somewhat of a "country" accent, suggestive that he spent most of his time away from major urban areas. In both pubic and private he testifies to having strong Christian faith, and expresses high regard of "the holy fathers" of the Russian Orthodox Church. Similiarly, he has been known to express high regard of the Czar and his family who were brutally murdered by the Communists Revolution. The Czar and his family were named "saints" in 2000 of the Russian Orthodox church. He has spoken in positive terms of President Vladimir V. Putin of Russia, and has stated the opinion that many Americans would like to have as their president someone like Mr. Putin.

Wrestling Career

GYR burst onto the wrestling scene as a virtual unknown in 20_ at the annual January 4 Tokyo Dome Show. This virtual unknown was substituted at the last minute for the injured Satoshi Tanahashi and shocked the wrestling world by coming out of nowhere to reach the finals of Japan's marquee wrestling event of the year. His winning of the IWGP Heavyweight Championship that year paved for his entry into the "big time" of the U.S. market, where he made his RAW television debut against Bash Daddy III in what is regarded as one of the truly all-time epic clashes of recent years, in a losing effort. In the nine years since then GYR has been established as one of the leading stars on AWW, and has won World Heavyweight Champion twice, the AWW Tag Team Championship twice (first with Wildfire Stevie Jones, second with Anaconda), the Ring of Honor Championship, and numrous regional champtionships. Pro Wrestling Illustrated frequently features GYR exploits, and magazine readers voted him Most Hated Wrestler of the Year in 20_, Most Popular Wrestler of the Year in 20_ and 20_, and Wrestler of the Year in 20_. He has won numrous Slammy Awards, including Most Eccentric, Most Extreme Moment, Beard of the Year, Catchphrase of the Year ("the Wrath of God is a beautiful thing), and the Humanitarian of the Year.

At this time it appears audience members who GYR cured of so-called weeping sickness in Atlanta do not appear to be "plants."

Religious Beliefs

GYR proclaims himself as a devout follower of the Russian Orthodox Church. He frequently states his reverence for the "Holy Fathers of the Church," and for "Holy Russia" and "saint Russia," which he has proclaimed is "the savior of the world." He has predicted the Second Coming of Christ will happen in the near future. He has often made reference to Satan's active presence on Earth, and other "Dark Forces," and frequently refers to himself as a "spiritual warrior" and "a solider in God's Army." He reportedly attends services at a private chapel as his Southlake estate.

Personal Life

GYR adheres to the "Straight-Edge" Lifestyle, and reportedly avoids alcohol, drugs, tobacco of all forms, and night clubs. He avoids all medications other than herbal teas, and quotes in one interview, "I trust my immune system because I have complete trust and faith in its creator, God."

There are certain unconfirmed reports of GYR as having "special powers" similiar to ESP mind-reader capabilities. Also the rumors he can cure illness thanks to the power of his Christian Faith, which would be consistent with his healing performance in Atlanta.

As best can be determined GYR has never been married and has no offspring. It does appear that he is heterosexually active, as inferred by the female entourage ("groupies") for which he is famous in the AWW realm and the "Maidens" who accompany him at all AWW events.

As noted above, he is fluent in Russian. While in the military he was trained in the language of Dari (Afghanistan) and Arabic (Iraq).

He is a resident of Southlake, Texas (pop. 32,000), a well-healed superb between Dallas and Fort Worth, where he resides on a 4.6 acres estate and a luxury mansion of some 31,000 square feet.

Politics

It is difficult to determine GYR's specific political leanings at this time, although it might be said that he "leans" conservative. He frequently advocates for "Christian morals" and "traditional values," and decries the moral degenerateness of many of his opponents. He has spoken in favor of the gold standard, and is reported to own a large stockpile of gold bullion that he keeps in a vault on his Southlake proporty. He has often expressed love for the deceased Czar and the Russian royal family, and his opinion Russia should reinstate the Czar form of government.

It appears he is not registered to vote and has no party affiliation. It appears he has not voted in any recent presidential election or otherwise.

Further research into GYR is ongoing.

AFS/TTP

7

11:03 a.m.

Ricardo Levy and Charlie Cupps are first through the door, followed by Rasputin, who does something Faith has never seen anyone do. The president has risen from his chair behind the Resolute Desk, all aides and staffers have come to their feet, the cameras are rolling and the majesty of the moment should carry everything along, but Rasputin stops a few steps into the Oval Office. He clasps his hands before him and solemnly, slowly, looks left and right. A Mona Lisa smile peeks through his beard. He cocks his head and blinks, and simultaneously with that blink Faith swears she hears the most dulcet little *ding* ring out, a chime like the burp of a baby angel. Did she just hear that? Did anybody? Rasputin's smile splits wide, revealing a mouthful of big white corn-chomping teeth, and he starts across the carpet toward the president.

10:58 a.m.

Van Mulligan,
Marks Robey,
Hoke Stebbins,
Ridge Thomas,
Jojo Parwellen,
Stephen Miller,
Harvey Gladding,
Ellen Biddle,
██████ Jr.,
Hans Ranlo,
Dr. Marlena Sepansky,
Valton Darwell,
Faith Spack,
Asher Simpkin,
Twister Perkin,
Smith Reynolds,
Paul Twiss,
Roy Nadler,
and Caden Roebuck
are assembled in the Oval Office, being, respectively,
White House Chief of Staff,
Deputy Chief of Staff,
Deputy Chief of Staff for Operations,
Senior Advisor for Homeland Security,
Special Assistant to the President,
Senior Policy Advisor,
White House Communications Director,
White House Press Secretary,
Son and Heir,
National Security Advisor,
National Security Advisor for Russian Affairs,
Senior Advisor for Political Affairs,

Assistant Communications Director for Special Projects,
Assistant to the White House Chief of Staff,
ditto,
Chief Operations Officer, Committee to Re-Elect the President,
Director, Committee to Re-Elect the President,
Deputy Director, Committee to Re-Elect the President,
and
Director of the White House Office of Presidential Personnel.

Senior staff get the cushy sofas and chairs, juniors are relegated to the cheap seats along the wall. The three visitor chairs in front of the Resolute Desk are empty. Faith takes the wall chair under the portrait of Andrew Jackson. She's budded into the camera crew's audio network, Kendra's whispers dropping into her ear like the murmurings of a phantom lover. *Kyle, pan the sofas. Carl, tight on POTUS's hands.* Except for Faith, all aides and staffers are head down in their phones, texting like it's the end of the world. Faith won't look at her phone for fear of freaking, thus she's free to watch the president survey his staff with that signature froggy moue of pride, impatience, and derision that only the ████ face can muster.

"Hey people," he calls out. "Remember, wrestling's not fake. And I don't wanna hear anybody asking him about it."

10:20 a.m.

"So we're gonna be meeting Rasputin in a little while, big wrestler, big star on AWW, been a huge fan of the guy for years. Russian Winter, one of the all-time classic moves—hey, is he in the Hall of Fame? Is he eligible? Caden, how about checking on that, I should know that, sheesh, I used to keep up with sports a lot better than I do now. Big guy, Rasputin. Bigger than Primo Carnera, maybe, and Primo was *big*, believe me. I met him a few times when I was a kid, champ boxer, heavyweight champ of the world, very sweet guy. A gentle giant, one of those. Okay, so maybe his English wasn't the greatest?" █████ flashes a naughty-boy smile. "He had a restaurant over in Astoria Dad used to take us to, very good Italian food as I remember. Some nights Primo was there greeting everybody, okay, I was just a kid, but he sure looked like a real giant to me! Anyway, what, when is he coming, eleven?" The president checks his watch. "Hey Van! Van! You said you had some papers for me."

"Right here, Mr. President."

"Well get over here! What're you waiting for, last time I checked we've got a country to run." █████ chuckles and hums a little tune, fairly fizzing with upbeat energy. The monologue segments always make him happy; they are the rhetorical equivalent of five-on-none basketball, guaranteed Team █████ will score every point. "Van the man," he merrily burbles as Van doles out documents for the presidential signature, "the Van man, the Van with the plan, ain't it grand. Did the Yankees win last night? Yeah? Who was pitching? You know," he continues, not missing a beat with the pen, "just thinking about growing up when I did, Primo Carnera, Mickey Mantle, all those great Yankees teams, that was such a great, great time to be a kid in New York. We had the whole city at our feet, and Dad, God bless him, he made sure we were out there in the middle of it. He took us everywhere, ball games, restaurants, job sites, that's how we learned about the city. About *life*, am I right? Later on, you know, he was older, not working so much, he'd come into the office and he always said the same two things. ████! he'd say, he'd of been looking around—████! he'd say. You got too many people working for you. That was the first thing. Second thing was always, How much money you got in the bank? That guy was tough! Old school, I'm telling you. All those guys who came through the Depression, they had to be tough, wouldna made it otherwise. I learned so much from him. Everything. And it's a good thing too 'cause no president has had more challenges than me. Covid, Gaza, the Flash Crash and all the Musk crap . . . and my own vice president, unbelievable. You heard what she said the other day? We give her the best job she's ever had and this is how she thanks us. Hey Faith!"

"Yes, Mr. President." *Kyle, on Faith*, Kendra whispers, and Kyle swings his handheld around to her.

"We all set for Rasputin?"

She wants to swat the camera away from her face. "Yes, Mr. President. We're all good."

"Super, good girl, Faith's one of the best we've got, I never worry about Faith getting it done. Anyway. Anyway. We're gonna see if we can get this thing off dead center in terms of the, um, crying, whatever that's about. Maybe Rasputin's the guy. Could be! Just based on what we saw from Atlanta the other night. You saw it, Faith, you know what I'm talking about. Pretty amazing, am I right?"

"It was, Mr. President. Very impressive." Kyle's camera is still on her, but no matter, she'll make sure she's edited out before the footage gets anywhere near production.

"And I—oh yeah, this." ██████ pauses over a document. "Ten-minute water breaks every four hours, how long does it take to drink a glass of water? Gimme a break. What some of these cities are doing with their rules, very unfair to the building trades. Everybody in construction knows—what's that? He's not in the Hall of Fame? He's not eligible yet, I figured. Well, he will be. He's a shoo-in. He's sure as hell gonna get my vote, I can promise you that."

9:58 a.m.

Faith: Is there anything in the Book of Revelation about red lightning?

Christie: "He is coming with the clouds." Don't recall lightning. Can check for you!

Faith: Red lightning. Anywhere in the Bible.

Christie: I'll check and get back to you! 😀

8:45 a.m.

Approximately twenty hyperactively jiggling bodies have crammed into Harvey's office for the comms staff meeting, Harvey and Ellen Biddle presiding. The air is an olfactory boil of perfumes and colognes and high-priced Arabica coffee, and breathing it seems to make everybody a little high. Of course by the end of the day the place will smell like a dumpster full of dirty socks. Harvey briefs everyone on the president's schedule and the day's messaging themes. Ellen keeps telling everyone to shut up and listen. The troops are restless this morning, antic, sassy. Maybe somebody at Starbucks made the coffee too strong.

June German raises her hand. "How are we supposed to characterize the Rasputin meeting as not a desperation move?"

"Because it's not a desperation move," ever-patient Harvey replies. "This is just the president doing his due diligence, exploring every possible option. All anybody has to do is watch the video of what transpired in Atlanta last Thursday, and it's clear why the president is following up with a meeting."

"Harvey," says Jagger Bomar, "it's pro wrestling. Everybody's laughing at us."

"Fine, they can laugh all they want. And if they've got something better, let's see it. Meanwhile the president is going to explore every possible solution to the, uh, this situation."

"Is he coming as Rasputin?" Holden Liston asks.

"I'm not sure I understand the question."

"Like, in his costume?"

"Will he be wearing his wrestling tights?" Jen Jensen asks brightly, and all the young comms women titter.

"Susie called in sick," blurts Marty Weiss. "She woke up crying this morning and can't stop."

"I'm sorry to hear that," says Harvey. "Keep checking on her. Keep us posted. Meanwhile"—his eyes meet Faith's, and he loses the flow for a second—"meanwhile it's important that we're all on the same page on this. The president wants to hear from Mr. Rasputin himself about what transpired the other night. That's all that's happening today. We made inquiries, and our information indicates that a meeting is warranted."

"It wasn't fake, in other words," offers Boomer Cawthorne.

"That is correct, Boomer. That is our information."

"Where's this coming from?" asks Britney Walton.

"Multiple sources. Top sources."

"Ricardo Levy?"

"Multiple sources," Harvey repeats.

"Don't forget 'top,'" chirps Lael Gardner, and Ellen tells him to knock it off. June German raises her hand again.

"Are we actually supposed to call him that? Rasputin?"

"*Mister* Rasputin," Chase Piercey chortles.

"Well, that is his name," Harvey begins, but he's cut off by lip blats, laughter, general razzing. "No, people, seriously, that is his actual legal name. He had it legally changed some years ago. As you would know if you'd read the memo, June."

Jagger Bomar raises his hand. "If Rasputin doesn't work out, is Madame Blavatsky available?"

Ellen crosses her arms. "You're too funny, Jagger. Hilarious. Now shut the fuck up."

"It's going to be ten times worse out there," Jagger says, pointing toward the press room.

"You just let me handle them," Ellen coolly replies. *Woooo woooo* go the troops.

"Look," Harvey says, and at this moment he seems to Faith like the hopelessly square principal of a high school for the children of movie stars, "there's just not a whole lot we need to say about the Rasputin meeting at present. Right now we're focused on yesterday's Ludd attack on the data center outside Wichita, and why we think the new GDP numbers aren't telling the whole story. And the new resort projects for Gaza. And when is the Fed going to start dropping interest rates."

"And California?" Johnny Freling pipes up.

"California, the wildfires, that too," Harvey confirms.

"I meant the governor."

"Sure, keep pounding the governor. All right, that's all for now, people. You know what to do."

Faith files out with everyone else and returns to her mini-office. She's coordinating today's shoot with Kendra via text, but holding the phone for more than a couple of seconds makes her dizzy and short of breath. A kind of simmering PTSD effect, which must mean she's traumatized? Between texts she sets the phone on her desk and sips Fiji water.

Harvey taps at her half-open door. "Knock knock."

"Hey. Come in."

"Are you okay?"

"Sure, fine. Why wouldn't I be?"

"Because you're white as a sheet, that's why."

"Well, I haven't had much time for sunbathing lately, Harvey."

"No, I mean *really* white. Like, sort of blue. The way skim milk is sometimes."

"Gee, thanks."

He steps up to her chair and puts his palm to her forehead, and she can't help but groan. So many people in this town, so little contact.

"That feels good."

He clears his throat, says nothing. "Just stay like that," she murmurs, and leans her full weight into his palm, which is dry, warm, slightly rough like toast. Her eyes are closed but she can feel him turn to see if anyone is passing in the hall. She suspects the only woman he's ever slept with is his wife, and only after they married.

"You aren't feverish."

"Mm."

"Kind of clammy. Are you sure you're okay?"

She opens her eyes, and his hand withdraws. Spell broken. "Maybe not my best day. I probably haven't been hydrating enough."

"If you need to go home . . ."

"I'm not going home, Harvey. Not today of all days. I'm fine. See?" She takes a swig of Fiji water and cheeses up a big smile. "The very picture of health."

"If you say so. Just don't pass out in the Oval."

"I'm not going to pass out in the Oval. But, Harvey."

"But, Faith."

"We're getting killed on this."

"We'd be getting killed no matter what. Look, we're basically dealing with some sort of mass psychosis here—a whole country that can't stop crying, when has that ever happened? And the smartest doctors in the world don't have a clue. So who knows, maybe one way to fight it is with religion? I'm willing to try anything at this point."

"All right. So say this guy really seems to have the, whatever, the mojo. What then."

"What then." He sighs, looks at his watch, tries and fails not to look at her chest. "The thinking is we take him out on the road with the president. And if we get the kind of situation we expect we're going to get, then we hope he's got more Atlantas up his sleeve."

"And if he doesn't . . ."

"Well, that is the risk, yes."

"That's betting the whole friggin' house."

"Maybe. Maybe we have to. This president has always been a high-risk, high-reward proposition. I don't know why that would suddenly change at this point."

"So what we're contemplating, just to clarify—we're talking about sending a, um," she coughs by way of clearing the mental hurdle, "a professional wrestler who calls himself Rasputin out on the campaign trail with the president. Like, *Rasputin*, one of the most maligned historical figures of all time. And when people start to lose their shit, he's going to heal them through the power of his faith."

"It's probably better not to overthink this. But don't forget, he's a combat-decorated Green Beret."

"Right! That makes it okay."

Her phone vibrates, an angry hornet in a jar. She turns it screen-up but leaves it on her desk.

"You need to get that?"

"It's just Kendra. She's got it covered."

"That's amazing. You just turned white again."

"What?"

"You were getting your color back and now you're white as a sheet. It's like somebody flipped a switch."

"I'm fine, Harvey, really. Don't worry about me. Worry about the president."

"Always," he says as his own phone buzzes. He has a look and clicks his tongue.

"What."

"Susie. Marty says she's hyperventilating and doesn't know what to do."

"Susie is indeed a very delicate flower."

"If that was the case I could understand. She's about the last person . . ." He ponders for a moment, then thumbs out a quick text.

"It's nice how you care about your people, Harvey."

He looks up sharply, sees she's serious. "Well, sure I do. Of course I do. Keep drinking water," he says, and heads out the door.

7:50 a.m.

Walter from tech security returns Faith's phone, hand delivering it all the way up from his lair in the West Wing subbasement. Mop-haired, smiley in a stoner-ish way, he's in his forties and has the affect of an overgrown skateboarder. "It's clean," he says with geek-pothead cockiness. "I ran a full diagnostic. The whole panel."

"Great," she says, "thank you. Thanks for the quick turnaround."

"No problem. You had some creaky old apps I cleaned out, but no Albanians or anything." He lingers. She wishes he wouldn't. Either he wants to flirt or fish for gossip, and she is not in the mood. Now he helps himself to an eyeful of *The Real West Wing* whiteboards.

"So this is where it all happens, huh."

"If you're talking about the show, not really."

He goof-laughs. "Hah, yeah, of course you would *say* that. You know, sooner or later everything comes through our shop. We're sort of like the ship's pharmacy down there, we know everybody's little secrets."

"Is that right."

"It can get pretty interesting down there. I mean, you wouldn't believe some of the stuff we see. Come on down and check us out sometime."

"I'll keep that in mind."

"And, hey, as long as I'm here I'd just like to take this opportunity to say you, like, totally killed it on *Nashville*. You were the best. Everybody knows you were robbed."

"Walter—that's your name, right? I really don't want to talk about that."

"Hah, yeah, I get it, fame's a bitch and everything. But a lotta people wish you'd kept on singing." Her dire look warns him off. "Ummm, right. So I'll just get out of your hair now. But you have any more issues with your unit, lemme know. I'm your guy."

"I appreciate that."

"But you said you hadn't been noticing anything weird lately."

"Nope. Just woke up feeling sort of paranoid."

"Oh yeah," Walter says, nodding sagely. "This place'll do it to you."

6:01 a.m.

Her phone alarm doesn't ring but she wakes up anyway. Maybe twice a year she forgets to set it and such a lovely way to start the day this is, pissed off and no one to blame but herself. She reaches over and swipes the phone off the bedside table and rolls onto her back to check ██████'s SonicX feed. Her brain refuses, that's the first thing that happens. There's an actual tempest in the screen—black clouds, howling wind, lightning, tiny thunder, but the lightning is red, needle-fine streaks of it are shooting everywhere. She squints, gives an exasperated scream, and bucks up to sitting position. Tapping the screen does nothing. The storm howls and booms in miniature, a cataclysm shrunk down to matchbox size, yet it exerts a peculiar psychic force, a long tentacular reach that seems to arc across her head and burrow into her brainstem. She has the sudden and absolute conviction that her phone has become a portal. This isn't a video, no. The screen is a sidereal judas hole into some parallel realm, the thing itself, live and direct and terrifyingly intimate. That *tck tck tck* she's hearing, that's the sound of the lightning hitting the underside of her screen.

At last she has the bright idea to shut it down. At least *that* works; the screen goes dark. She sits there panting like she just chased off a burglar. Sweating all over and static fuzz for brains, can't think her way to explaining what she's just seen. It's like she glimpsed some vast, annihilating force from beyond, and she wasn't supposed to see it? As her breathing evens out she tries to will herself into accepting what a more conventional personality would think was obvious all along. The Occam's razor explanation, sane and simple. Idiot, your phone's been hacked.

11:10 a.m.

Behold the *starets*: elegantly tailored black suit, white dress shirt with band collar, black ankle boots, gold cross dangling between his pecs, long hair gathered in a ponytail. *Starets*, holy man. Except for Dr. Sepansky, who already knew, this is the new Russian word they've all just learned, and the vocation to which Rasputin aspired when he entered the ancient monastery in V#%*kt$@)#r.

Wait, what, who?

Kyle, tight on Rasputin, Kendra murmurs.

"Verkhoturye," Dr. Sepansky repeats, and she and Rasputin palaver in Russian for a moment. "The Saint Nikolaev Monastery in Verkhoturye," she clarifies.

"That's a real place?" snaps Ridge Thomas, borderline fresh. Dr. Sepansky gives it right back with her whisk-broom voice.

"It's very real. And quite famous to anyone familiar with Russian culture."

"Verkhoturye, duly noted," Van Mulligan says with a smile, essentially telling these two to cool it. He turns to their celebrity visitor. "I'm sure that was a very formative place for you. Perhaps even the place where you became Rasputin?" He offers this with a sugary chuckle, pitching it as an inside joke. A way into the larger joke of the Rasputin stage persona.

"No," the *starets* calmly replies. "I have always been Rasputin."

There's a pressure drop in the room as everyone sucks wind. A few people laugh.

Manny, quick pan out from POTUS.

"You definitely make a very convincing Rasputin, no doubt about it," Van says agreeably, and again he tries to wheedle, joke, cajole the wrestler out of character. "But young Patrick Strickland, our war hero, what about him?"

"That boy died," Rasputin answers in the dreamy voice of an oracle. "There is that one man only, Rasputin. God's servant you see before you."

Nervous rustles burn through the room. The president leans forward and laces his hands atop the Resolute Desk, clearly intrigued.

"Okay," Ridge Thomas butts in, "I think we need to back up a minute. The record shows you are the Patrick Walsh Strickland who enlisted in the army, and the same Patrick Walsh Strickland who was discharged from the army, and the same Patrick Walsh Strickland on whose passport you traveled to Russia. I'm not trying to be rude, sir. I understand you have a certain image to protect as part of your, ahem, profession, but you're in the Oval Office now, in the presence of the president of the United States. And it's incumbent on all of us who the president relies on for advice to establish some baseline facts."

Rasputin is unperturbed. "It is true what you say about Patrick. But I, Rasputin, this man before you, I have always been Rasputin. I can see you are perplexed, but please put your mind at ease. These are the holy mysteries of the true faith. Someday, when the time is right, I will explain these things to you."

"Works for me!" [redacted] cheerfully brays. "You can back off, Ridge, we're gonna take him at his word. Nobody here intends any offense, Grigory."

Carl, close on Ridge. Good.

"None taken, Mr. President. And call me Grishka, please."

"Grishka, got it. Some things we just have to go on faith, right?"

"As you say, Mr. President."

"So listen, that was a very impressive performance you put on in Atlanta the other night, and I'm not talking about the way you handled Ono, though that was pretty impressive too! But the other thing, I think you know what I'm talking about."

"I think I do, Mr. President."

"You blew a lot of people's minds with that. And this guy here"—█████ tosses a backhand wave at Ricardo Levy, seated on Rasputin's right—"he told us it's the real deal, what you did for those folks. No kayfabing."

Rasputin nods. "The real deal, Mr. President. One hundred percent."

"So I guess what we all wanna know—and we all saw it, everybody here's seen the video—I guess, hm, how do I say this, I don't mean to put you on the spot or anything. But how did you do it?"

Kyle, tight on Rasputin. Manny, pan POTUS-Van-Ridge.

Rasputin takes his time, and there's fine showmanship in this, the ponderous breath, the way his gaze drops modestly to his lap, the meditative study of his meaty hands folded there. Not your everyday big dumb jock, Faith thinks. His deep voice, or at least the indoor version, is tempered and mild, not so much lumbering Conan this morning as the soothing submarine drone of Henry Kissinger. His skin has the phosphorescent glow of a saint, though that could be the expensive sheen that comes of top-shelf skin care. His eyes are a striking lake-water blue with glimmers of darkest violet, they alternate between twinkly seductiveness and the high-beam glare of a circus mesmerist. The couple of times Faith meets his eye she can hardly breathe, though perhaps it's just another sign that she's losing her mind.

Rasputin lifts his ponderous Easter Island head. "That was not me, Mr. President. The intercession in Atlanta was God's love flowing through me, His earthly vessel." The *starets* reflects for a moment.

"What happened in Atlanta recalls a saying we have in Mother Russia: 'Satan has been busy for a long time, but he finally flew out from under the porch.' That is what happened in Atlanta, we chased Satan out from under the porch!"

The president hesitates. "You think it was Satan," he ventures. Kendra is rapid-firing orders to the crew, her whispers crowding Faith's perspective with self-referential meta.

"The Dark One takes many forms in our world, Mr. President. Psychological, mechanical, electrical, animal, but he is nothing in the face of our Lord. In Atlanta we witnessed the invincible power of God's love."

"We sure did, and it was just a big-league performance in every way. But we're wondering how you, you know," █████ dips to his right, as if coaxing a putt toward the hole, "turn on the tap, so to speak. Is this basically an on-demand kind of deal, or what?"

"The key is prayer, Mr. President. For many weeks I have been praying about this very thing. So much weeping in the country, our brothers and sisters weeping—this is an affliction of the spirit more troubling than any material challenge God sets for us. I have been praying to the Almighty to favor us with His mercy."

"So I guess in Atlanta He decided the time was right."

"It was His will."

"It was His will. I just wish he'd done it sooner! Nah, just kidding, I'm not gonna get in the business of telling God what to do. But you know, Grishka, I don't have to tell you this, it's still out there. We're getting reports, just this morning we're getting reports—Ridge, tell him what we're hearing this morning."

Ridge Thomas refers to his notes. "We've got fresh outbreaks in San Francisco, Denver, Ohio, Pittsburgh. Charleston and Myrtle Beach. And now Newport, apparently. Rhode Island."

"Newport!" the president exclaims. "Can you believe it? Well, that crowd could stand taking down a notch or two. Anyway, the point is we're still dealing with it, I look around and I'm gonna tell you frankly,

Grishka, we don't know what the hell is going on. I mean, what is it?" The president raises his hands and sloshes his words like a Jersey mob boss down to his last nerve. "Whatizit? Whatizit? Whyzithappening?"

Rasputin nods. "Mr. President, America is trying to wake up."

Among the staff nervous glances fly about. The president frowns. "*Woke* is sort of a dirty word around here."

"No, Mr. President, I am speaking of a spiritual awakening. When we awake to the truth of God, no enemy can defeat us."

"Ah!"

"But we are trapped in the sleep of vanities. And those who are godless, they encourage this sleep so they can perform their mischief while our eyes are closed. But even sleeping, Americans are troubled. This is not the sleep of peace, for we know in our hearts we have lost the way. Following the Commandments, obedience to law and order, this is the truth of the real America. But we are lost! We are like children wandering lost in the woods, so of course we weep. We are desperate to find our way back home."

"That's what I've been saying! We've gotta be strong, we've gotta get back to all the things that made America great in the first place! And they're blaming *me* for what's happening, can you believe it? We're trying to get the country moving again, but everybody's so damn depressed they just sit at home and mope. You see what it's doing to the economy."

"It is a crisis, Mr. President."

"You're telling me."

"The gargoyles encourage the crisis."

"The who?"

"The gargoyles. The creatures in this city whose every breath and thought is to defeat you."

"You got that right, buddy. Gargoyles, I like that. I like this guy," proclaims to the room. "We did a smart thing bringing him here today. Ricardo, this guy is special."

"He's one of a kind, Mr. President."

"Listen, fellas, I'm gonna be frank with you, we need your help. If we're gonna get the country moving again we need Grishka out there doing more of his, whaddayacallit, interventions."

"Intercessions, Mr. President."

"Right, those. We've gotta get the campaign back out there and we need you with us, Grishka. So if people start crying and carrying on, you can step up and do your Atlanta thing."

"As God wills, Mr. President."

"God's will, I get that. So what we're thinking, Ricardo, we wanna borrow your star for a little while, just till we get the country back on track. Just for the good of the country, I'm not asking anything for myself!"

"Of course, Mr. President, we'd be more than willing to amend Grishka's contract. But the ultimate decision is really his and Charlie's."

"Very generous of you, Ricardo," Charlie says, crossing and uncrossing his legs, and it takes Faith a moment to tune into the sarcasm. Charlie Cupps is a jockey-small man in a baggy blue chalk-stripe suit, raw-skinned, with thinning ginger hair and a rutabaga bomb of a nose that seems the sturdiest thing about him. "Are we talking weeks?" he asks in a yappy, saw-fiddle Yankee voice. "A month? Six months? 'Cause I think it behooves me to point out that this man has to work for a living."

Van Mulligan barely deigns to look at Cupps. "Nobody is asking Mr. Rasputin to quit working. What we're proposing is to fly him in for rallies and high-visibility events, otherwise he can maintain his wrestling schedule. And I think it *behooves* me to point out that he'll be doing a vital service for his country."

Kyle, profile on Cupps, frame that nose. Carl, pan to sofas.

Faith shifts her weight from cheek to cheek. She's itchy, sweaty, can't get the waistband of her skirt to sit right. Harvey keeps glancing her way as if he thinks she's going to faint. Shaky, yeah; she might be tempted to go home and go to bed, except she'd have to be all alone with her phone. She becomes aware of a commotion in the Oval lobby. Voices, thumping, a scuffle of some sort. Someone sobbing? She thinks she recognizes—oh shit, they wouldn't. Surely they wouldn't. They would? She's trying to catch Harvey's eye when a hair-raising shriek penetrates the sanctum of the Oval.

Rasputin is instantly on his feet. "What is that? What is happening? Someone is in pain!"

"Right. That's"—██████ looks to Harvey, who nods—"that's a young lady who works for us, she's having a hard time this morning with the, you know, the thing. We were hoping you could do something for her."

"Bring her to me! At once! She is suffering!"

It takes three Secret Service agents to half-drag, half-carry Susie Grumman through the door. Weeping, slinging her head side to side, murmuring *no no no no* in a semi-delirious moan, she cracks her eyes just enough to see the president of the United States advancing on her with open arms. She throws back her head and wails, and her humiliation is truly awesome to behold, her bum rush into the highest office in the land wearing sweats and bedroom slippers, her hair a bedhead mess, no bra, no makeup, crying, hiccuping, snot dripping from her nose and only sleeves for wiping, it is a hideous variation on the age-old workplace nightmare, and for Susie the nightmare is real.

Her anguish is too much for ██████. He backs away, covering his retreat with a queasy smile. Susie has it so bad that she's infected the Secret Service. Rasputin gently detaches her from their arms and brings her into his own, and right there, standing atop the presidential seal with everyone gathered around in an impromptu circle, he bends his head to hers and murmurs magic words into her oil-slick hair. Susie Grumman is not a small woman by any means, but his size renders her childlike, and Faith feels a stab in her gut. To be held like that, cherished, heeded; to have your pain honored in this tenderest way. Watching them rouses longings from depths she didn't know she had.

Susie grows still. Rasputin motions the weeping agents forward and gathers them into a group hug. These big glowering guys rendered meek as kittens by his command, this in itself is a kind of miracle, and a collective sigh breathes out from the circle, *ahhhhhh*. Susie's earlier scream brought the entire West Wing running, and competitive staffers are jostling in the doorway for a look.

Rasputin lifts his face to the ceiling and closes his eyes, seems to mouth a silent prayer. Within moments the Secret Service are cured. They step back, smile, look at one another, and shrug. What just happened? Hell if they know. Hell if anybody knows. Susie is smiling too, then she's laughing, wide-eyed, seemingly stunned to find herself here. "Wow," she exclaims, looking around. "What was *that*?" And everyone cheers.

8

THE DALLAS DAILY

[redacted]: "We're on the Road Again"

First Rally in Four Weeks
President Tag-Teams with Wrestler for a Winning Combo
The Long Strange Trip Goes On

By Clarence Thomas Jr., National Affairs Correspondent of The Dallas Daily

SPIVEY, ALA. POSTED JULY 31, 1:27 A.M. EDT—

America does love itself some Jesus. Prosperity Jesus, Baby Jesus, Crossover R&B Jesus, Purple Jesus, Drop-Kick Me Through the Goalposts Jesus, America loves them all, and on this hot Saturday night in Alabama, the small town of Spivey got a double dose of the miracles-and-wonders version that we love along with the rest. Only a chump would call it coincidence that President [redacted] scheduled his first rally since the onset of the weeping sickness in the rural Deep South, home to that long, loud tradition of tent revivals, full-dunk baptisms and barn-burner preaching. Fertile ground for showcasing his new "secret weapon," the alleged healing powers of the professional wrestler who calls himself Rasputin, aka "the Russian Winter," aka "the Wrath of God." On this steamy July evening, neither man would disappoint.

All Roads Lead to Spivey, for One Day at Least

MAGA faithful began converging on this south-central Alabama town several days ago for the president's first rally in over a month. Some came from as far away as Michigan and Indiana to stake tents outside the Heath County fairground in hopes of being among the lucky 5,500 to gain admission on Tuesday night. Campaign officials deliberately chose this small town, and the limited capacity of the fairground, as a concession to the reality of the weeping sickness.

"A smaller in-person gathering seems advisable, just given the circumstances," campaign spokesperson Winnie Wainwright told reporters during an afternoon briefing at the Heath County Courthouse. She noted that portable screens were being positioned in the parking lots and fields surrounding the fairground, enabling many thousands to "participate virtually" in the rally.

Spivey would seem a safe location, given that the nearest outbreak of weeping sickness was reported five days previously in Birmingham, some 50 miles distant. When asked if Mr. Rasputin was invited on the strength of his purported "miracle cure" in Atlanta last week, Wainwright demurred.

"Mr. Rasputin is a strong supporter of the president, and his values align closely with the president's. I think his remarks will show much better than anything I could say why he's on the program tonight."

Wainwright refused to take further questions regarding the pro wrestler, nor would she comment on contingency plans for a possible outbreak of the weeping sickness. This reporter was left with the distinct impression of a campaign nervously hedging its bets.

Good Times, High Spirits, Plenty Guns

While Wainwright talked, the thick stone walls of this venerable Greek Revival, Jim Crow–era courthouse throbbed with the clamor of a small town bursting at the seams. Over 200 state troopers, along with law enforcement from seven nearby counties and several hundred federally deputized Rapid Support Forces, were on hand to help local police maintain order amid an estimated 40,000 visitors. Spivey's quaint downtown was transformed on this day into a multivalent street festival, equal parts Fat Tuesday getdown, Roll Tide tailgate party and politically themed biker rally. With a high temperature of 98 degrees and humidity like a hound dog licking your face, first responders and Good Samaritans stayed busy conveying heat-stroked rally goers to aid stations. The pungent smell of weed, illegal in Alabama, was omnipresent. The town's ordinance against public consumption of alcohol would be sorely breached as the day progressed. But the Second Amendment was honored to the fullest, enough armaments on display for the South to make a decent go of rising again.

Which, bluntly stated, is pretty much the point. A Black man in a small Southern town can't help but feel all too keenly the emanations of a corrupt and murderous past. Spivey's Johnny Reb statue stands proud on the courthouse grounds. In 1948, three Black veterans of World War II were assaulted and arrested on the courthouse steps for trying to register to vote. That same year, another Black man, James Shaw, was beaten and shot to death one block from the courthouse after attempting to vote. Today's colorful street festival could, with the slightest tweak of optics, take on the horror-house merriment of vintage postcards documenting lynching celebrations, and for anyone inclined to leave the past to the past, every few minutes the streets of Spivey breathed forth fresh visions from that unquiet history.

The white—as in Caucasian—militias were out in force, the latest iteration of an enduring American institution that began with colonial slave patrols, circa 1650. They came bearing arms—AR-15s, semiautomatic shotguns, handguns with high-capacity magazines—and carried themselves with the demeanor of people who mean business. One seemed well-advised to take them at face value, and having done so—having taken them as it seemed they wished to be taken—this reporter understood that violence was a live possibility today. Violence with the goal of influencing politics, it bears noting, being a classic fascist tactic. And, noting further, per the political science teacher this reporter used to be, that fascism in its classic European form offers three defining characteristics that seemed relevant to the day: white supremacy, Christian nationalism, and charismatic leadership.

The array of logos and legends denoted no fewer than eight distinct militias. The Southern League, the Average White Boys, Archangel, the Black Hundreds, Iron Hand, the Jebs, the Secret Seven and Blood & Soil were all present and accounted for. Most refused to be interviewed, but a member of Archangel who would identify himself only as "Cray, from Missouri," agreed to a short conversation, which follows verbatim in its entirety:

CT: I'm just looking over all your firepower and wondering if you and your colleagues expect trouble today.

CRAY: We're here to prevent trouble.

CT: A lot of people would say that's the job of law enforcement.

CRAY: That's for everybody else. We're here for █████.

CT: You're here to protect █████?

CRAY: To protect and serve him.

CT: Serve him in what way?

CRAY: Whatever he wants. Whatever he asks us to do.

CT: If he asks you to go to Montgomery and arrest the governor, would you do that?

CRAY: I'm not going to get into hypotheticals with you.

We Will Always Love Him, But . . .

Amid rock-solid support for the president, soft spots could be found. Several rally goers expressed reservations about any president serving more than two terms, while others had more pointed concerns. "I think maybe his ego has gotten the better of him," said Linda Badalementi, 50, of Covington, Louisiana. "I still support him, but I just wish it wasn't always so much about *him*." Her companion, Duncan Marvis, 47, added, "We love ██████████ and always will. But he's had eight years to get it done, and we're still dealing with so much of the same problems we had when he started. I think a lot of people would be okay with him passing the torch."

But with four weeks of pent-up energy to unleash, the vast majority of attendees were primed to show all-out support for the president. "He's so strong," Marjorie Hossler, 32, of Anniston, Alabama, said of the president. "We need protection in this country, and he's not afraid of anybody." Her friend Tina Glover, 31, affirmed her own unwavering loyalty to █████. "Of course we're going to vote for him, third term, fourth term, however many he wants. He's been called by God to lead. Who are we to question God?"

There was ample enthusiasm for the wrestler Rasputin as well, though many scoffed at the precautions being taken on account of the weeping sickness. Sentiment was widespread that the phenomenon is "a hoax." Mention of Rasputin's apparent healing feat in Atlanta last week reliably provoked laughter, and, toward this reporter, pity, as if only a fool would regard Atlanta as anything other than a slick All World Wrestling riff on a Democratic con.

"Get real, man." So I was advised by Thane Owens, 27, who'd come with a dozen members of his motorcycle club from Ardmore, Oklahoma. "Only tears you're gonna see out here is if any liberals show up. You might definitely see some people crying then."

The fairground gates opened at 5 p.m. in anticipation of the 7:30 start, and one might be forgiven for being amazed, even at this late stage of the story arc, that a born-rich brat, a New York City real estate developer, a certified Yankee of all things, could inspire thousands of sons and daughters of the Confederacy to bake for hours under the merciless July sun for a chance to be in his presence. And by 5 p.m. this crowd was well and truly parboiled. While thousands sought entry into the fairground, thousands more would be content to remain outside, many of them comfortably settled in elaborate tailgate encampments. With its vast array of luxury RVs, campers, party tents, grills, big-screen TVs and high-end sound systems, the MAGA army seemed well positioned to hold this ground for days.

King's Promise

To approach the press check-in, reporters had to walk a gauntlet of hissing, mocking Murder the Media youth, and it was here that your reporter received his first n-word aggression of the day. It would not be the last. Inside the fairground, the playlist, largely unchanged since 2015, was in full swing, "Tiny Dancer" serenading rally goers as they scurried for position close to the stage. The fairground's old-timey wooden grandstand backstopped a baseball diamond; a prefab stage was assembled over the pitcher's mound, the podium oriented toward the outfield and the grounds beyond, where Confederate flags were borne along like battle standards as their bearers jogged into position.

Some 60 years ago, Dr. Martin Luther King Jr. felt compelled to promise his people that they would encounter "arsonists, lunatics, and rampaging bigots" on the road to freedom. Yes, but still? One would hope we'd be further along by now. Hunting interviews amid the crowd, this reporter became the occasion for casual taunting. "Hey man, you lost?" "Yo waiter! We're ready to order now." "Obama's not your president anymore." And this, from an overheated elderly woman who planted herself in my path: "Are you even supposed to be here?"

For fans of symbolism, the bipolar mood was neatly encapsulated in the clashing aggregation of U.S. and Confederate flags. This crowd was joyful and surly, servile and mutinous, amped up and worn out, deadly serious and party your ass off. "YMCA" was shouting over the sound system when I was approached by a Heath County sheriff's deputy.

"Are you a reporter?" he asked, even though my credentials were plainly visible on the lanyard around my neck.

"I am."

"You're supposed to be in the press area."

"I'll be heading there shortly. Right now I'm just interviewing a few folks."

"No sir, you need to move on to the press area. You're upsetting people."

I laughed; a rhetorical laugh. "How am I upsetting people?"

"Yes, you are. Now you just move right on over to where you belong."

Reader, life is a never-ending choice between the battles we fight and the battles we decline. I pointed my feet in the direction of the press pen, and walked.

"He Will Slit Your Throat"

Among the subplots playing out this evening would be the state GOP's current internecine drama. Gov. Jarrold "Runt" Simmons has so far declined to endorse ████ for a third term, his neutral stance supported by the state party and its powerful chairwoman, Nancy Clapper. Others, notably Lt. Gov. Aubrey Reardan and House Speaker Strug Hovis, offered ████ their support within minutes of the Supreme Court's decision clearing him to run.

The old saw that all politics is local may or may not be true, but for sure there's no nastier kind than the family feud. Lt. Gov. Reardan came out flaming at the stroke of sunset, dashing young fellow, Harvard College, Rhodes Scholar, Yale Law, captain in the U.S. Army Reserve, former federal prosecutor, yes, the most industrious algorithms of the most advanced AI could hardly spit out a more perfect résumé. "He's here!" Reardan bellowed into the mic, his voice surprisingly deep for such a delicate neck. "Our president could be anywhere tonight, but he came here. We are honored, we are grateful, we are deeply blessed, and we sure as hell aren't going to disappoint him tonight!"

Big roar from the crowd, and half a beat later, an even bigger roar from the thousands outside the fairground, creating a kind of acoustical doughnut effect. Young Reardan—fair-skinned, smooth-cheeked, with a perfect head of auburn hair—proceeded to tick through his talking points with the ruthless efficiency of a metronome:

1. the unborn
2. immigration invasion
3. Woke
4. guns
    a. my guns
    b. my wife's guns

5. communists; “Marxist equity”
6. values, e.g., traditional
   Founding Fathers
   Judaic Christian
   law & order
7. GOAT POTUS part 1
8. Lord and Savior
9. take it back! country/faith/destiny
10. GOAT POTUS part 2

While Reardan talked, the sky was turning pastel seashell colors, creamy pink, sherbet orange, periwinkle blue. Swifts banked and wheeled over the fairground in dazzling displays of avian acrobatics, their pips and chitters faintly audible whenever Reardan paused. They were consoling messengers from the outside world, their breeze-borne grace suggesting how much richer our lives can be when we’re not consumed by politics. How a country in thrall to its own politics, its main energies turned inward like a stomach being eaten by its own biles, has that much less of improvement and possibility to offer its citizens.

Something is wrong with us if politics is the main point. As for Lt. Gov. Reardan . . . for all his years of expensive education, his speech offered nothing you couldn’t get from a small-beans county commissioner. One wonders what exactly are they teaching in those famous places, except there was this:

“What I love about our president is, he’s scary. He’s a very tough, a very resolved individual, he’ll do whatever it takes. Hey, he scares even me! And I’ve been tested in combat, I think it’s fair to say I don’t scare easy. So let me tell you, if you cross our president, he’s coming for you. You might as well get down on your knees and say your prayers, ’cause President ██████ is coming to slit, your, throat.”

The Wrath of God Is a Popular Thing

This ugly little fillip of macho posturing inspired the biggest doughnut roar yet. Of course Reardan was all but calling out Gov. Simmons, whose job he covets, naturally. By contrast, Grigory Yefimovich Rasputin—his actual name, let us note, legally changed from Patrick Walsh Strickland a decade ago—would be a model of restrained eloquence. He emerged from the home dugout looking like a 19th-century itinerant preacher, in a black suit, black boots, plain white shirt with a round collar, his long black hair and beard neatly combed. The bling was limited to a fairly gaudy gold cross hanging from his neck. He stepped up to the podium, eyed the microphone, then made a deft sidestep and whipped a handheld mic from his jacket, a stroke of All World Wrestling stagecraft that delighted the crowd. Wrestler don't need no stinking podium! He raised the mic to his lips and boomed:

"The wrath of God is a beautiful thing!"

They loved it. Big doughnut cheers for the hero of a thousand TV bouts, but this would be his sole concession to expectations tonight. The crowd was stoked for an AWW diss fest, and what it got instead were seven sober, thoughtful minutes of spiritually infused reflection. In the measured voice of a master of empathy, he spoke of losses: family farms, good-paying jobs, stable homes, nurturing schools. Friends and family lost to Covid. Regular seasons, predictable weather. A sense that fairness and justice prevail. And our government, a political system that works for the common good, not just for corporations and the rich—have we not lost that too?

"But we are not alone, my brothers and sisters," he counseled. "How well the road of our sufferings is known to God. He is our strength and our rock, and there is one among us who also knows this road, knows as a wise and loving father knows the trials of his children. And that one, you know who I am speaking of. Our most beloved president, ████████████."

The MAGAs cheered, but they sounded no more than dutiful. Something transformative seemed to have happened, some form of suspension or sublimation by which President ████ was temporarily rendered second fiddle. For these several minutes the crowd seemed entirely spellbound by the quiet authority of the man with the mic.

"The enemy tries to cast its weakness on the president," Rasputin continued, "but ████ is a fighter, he fights in a clever and holy manner for the country we hold dear in our hearts. And you know that country, my brothers and sisters. That great America of law and order, common sense, integrity, faith. America is the greatest country, but it is wounded, bleeding, and the hour is late. The hour is late, and we need our president, now more than ever."

Then a conceptual leap, and a change in tone. Rasputin was winding up for the payoff.

"Perhaps some of you believe that the Antichrist is an imminent possibility. You sense dark forces preparing the ground for him, and you know it is our sacred duty to take back the ground and sanctify it. I think this is why we are so happy when we see our beloved president. He lifts us up! He gives us hope! There can be only one explanation—God's chosen one is with us. The hope of the nation, the sanctifier. And that is why"—Rasputin paused and looked toward the home dugout, and our eyes followed his, and there was ████ in his blue Brioni suit and implacable red tie, and the doughnut roar went off like a tactical nuclear weapon—"by the grace of God the Father," Rasputin thundered, "I give him to you!"

Sweet Home Alabama

Some 100 years ago the German philosopher Max Weber described charisma as *a certain quality of an individual personality by virtue of which he is set apart from ordinary men and treated as endowed with supernatural, superhuman, or at least exceptional powers and qualities. These as such are not accessible to the ordinary person, but are regarded as divine in origin or exemplary, and on the basis of them the individual concerned is treated as a leader.*

Jesus of Nazareth might be the most charismatic human who ever walked the planet. At the personal level, his magnetism must have been literally stupefying, so much so that by the suggestion of his touch, his words, his presence, people believed themselves cured of terrible illness. Thousands flocked to him, in numbers so overwhelming that he had to escape into boats or up to mountaintops just to get a little peace. Supreme charisma could serve as the secular explanation for Jesus, not necessarily exclusive of the sacred. Complementary, then; one might construe charisma as an extra shot of the godhead, a rare quality or energy bestowed on the few, to the awe of the many.

The Charisma Club, let's call it. The wrestler Rasputin is a member. ██████████ too, manifestly, and as he sauntered onto the stage with Laura Branigan's "Gloria" crushing the sound system, the MAGA faithful lost their minds. The sheer force of the sonics sent a chill up this reporter's spine. And again, when ████ stepped to the podium and bellowed, "Sweet home Alabama!"

They were ready to cheer for hours, but the roar obediently died as soon as he started his remarks. "Beautiful! Beautiful. We love Alabama, always happy to come to the great state of Alabama. So we're on the road again, our first rally since all the crying business began," and off we went, dropped midstream into the whitewater froth of his thoughts as if we'd been there all along, the great man welcoming us into his world like our best and oldest friend. Great state, great crowd, so many people coming out for us, a line of cars on the highway 30 miles long!

"But your governor"—█████ makes a stagy show of looking around—"I haven't seen him tonight, anybody seen the governor?" BOOOO. "I don't know, maybe he's stuck in traffic, lotta traffic out there." Big laughs, happy boos. "In Birmingham they love the governor, isn't that how it goes? Great song, yeah, you know what I'm talking about, but maybe they're not loving him so much these days." Bigger laughs, even happier boos. "But anyway, anyway, we did bring a very special person with us tonight, the champ, and we're talking about a real world champion, folks. How about that, big night for Spivey, not only do you get the president, you get the world champion wrestler too!"

Big cheers, YAY!

"You like him?"

YAY! YAY!

"That's good, 'cause I like him too. Been a big fan for a long time, and the way he spoke just now, very impressive, am I right? So who knows. Who knows. I'm thinking he could make a pretty great vice president."

OH HOOOO, goes the crowd.

"Could be," █████ natters coyly, "could be a vacancy in that position we might have to fill, that other person's not working out so well." He offers this with a smile and a chuckle, an inside joke extended to 40,000 strangers, but can we be so sure? The cheers carry the charge of a new and intriguing idea, and █████ cocks his head and smiles, he's hearing it, this president who's known to spend hours listening to the counsel of top advisers, then he'll ask a passing waiter for his opinion, and follow that.

The Wrath of God to the Rescue

█████'s rap, like his playlist, is pretty much unchanged since 2015. There are the threats, veiled and not so veiled. "Your governor, I like your governor all right, but if he doesn't get on board with us soon he might not have much of a future in politics." The villainy of the media, "horrible people, totally disgusting, vicious people." The absolute evil of the president's political foes, who are, variously, "psychotic," "deranged," "insane," "totally corrupt" and "doing everything in their power to destroy our country." The through line of personal grievance and woe, so remarkable from a man born into the winning trifecta of whiteness, maleness and wealth. And, of course, his primacy among mortals. "Who else but me can you trust? There's nobody like me—nobody fights like me, nobody cares like me. That's why I'm running for this historic third term. I look at all those other people running, and frankly I don't see anybody out there who can finish the job."

The faithful were getting what they came for, it would seem. They came for raw, uncut ██████, and he was delivering, but it was only when people in the grandstand began wailing and keeling over that we were struck by the notion that maybe ██████ wasn't enough. Perhaps this, more than the president, was what we'd come to see, the same way that people go to car races for the crashes. The shocked, strangled outcry from the crowd on the field—maybe this was the sound of people getting some desperately wished-for thing that, until this moment, they didn't know they wanted.

Who would pass up the chance to see an honest-to-God miracle? It could hardly be thought without seeming traitorous, but ██████████ has been with us for a very long time. If we plumbed our hearts to their true depths, might we discover he's starting to wear a bit thin? Still our guy, still good for some chills and thrills, just not those searing serotonin highs that made life worth living for all these years.

Though all credit to ██████, he brought Rasputin, and it was ██████ who called the wrestler into action. With surprising quickness for such a big body, Rasputin vaulted from field to grandstand and over the railing in a matter of seconds.

Cops were converging as well, and a squad of Rapid Support Forces, and a good thing, too, otherwise the weeping MAGAs might have been beaten half to death by their suddenly furious neighbors.

"Attaway, Grishka," ██████ ad-libbed from the podium. "Look at him go, folks, he's on a mission. Amazing, right? I think he's got it under control. I think he really has God's grace in him, and you're going to be seeing a lot more of him. A lot more rallies we'll be having, and he'll be with us all the way, and no more crying, am I right? No. More. Crying. We're gonna get this country moving again."

He kept the commentary going throughout, the glib patter of the ringmaster, the emcee, the silver-tongued DJ. But perhaps it was all a little too perfect? The crisis conveniently delayed until the program nearly ran its course, and now came the finale, the fireworks, the Jesus action. Maybe trauma actors really do exist! Maybe ██████ was, yet again, three steps ahead of us. What a bummer for everyone if Rasputin came and never got the chance to show his stuff. Perhaps there was more bet-hedging afoot than this reporter suspected at the afternoon briefing. But what's clear beyond question is that an exciting new storyline began tonight, fresh blood to keep us glued to the ratings monster that began with "The Apprentice" back in 2004. And so the long, strange trip continues, destination yet unknown.

9

Andrew Mebane got it. Jagger Bomar got it. Jen Jensen, Sia Coppick, Zoë Haley, June German, they all got it. Trenwith Martens and Susie Grumman, multiple times, Susie so much that she's shuttled over to campaign headquarters and ends up taking medical leave. Outside the comms office it's mainly rumors. They don't know for *certain* that Stephen Miller got it, but that's the word around the West Wing. Somebody gets it, job one is to get them out of sight, the surest way to torque off these days is a weeper in the house. To him it proves weakness, lack of conviction; the truth of your traitor's heart shining through. Thus one enters the president's presence in a state of dread, wondering if today's the day your absolute devotion falls short.

Faith keeps waiting for it to happen to her, but so far nothing. Christie says it's because she's part of "the Light Occultic"—Faith doesn't ask—and the twice-daily prayers she sends up beseeching her daughter's protection. Headshrink consensus continues to focus on conversion disorder, while Christian evangelicals and right-wing media offer daft and frankly much more interesting theories. Variations on demon possession abound. Satan is the root cause, or if not him, vaccines, or fluoridated water, or slippage in the heaven-earth alignment, or a strain of African swine flu that found its way into American feral hogs. Microplastics, lymphatic acids, numerology, also big. It's all pretty whackadoo, but at least the right has the energy to offer up something, the left can't even try. As usual the Dems are hopeless, helpless. *Oh mother dear, we sadly fear! We're the party of little kittens who've lost our mittens!*

Contempt for Democrats is foundational to Faith's politics. Bunch of flakes and posers as far as she's concerned, the party of chickenshit sanctimony and woke bullying; so quick to get their tender feelings hurt, then they pounce like starved jackals. The flip side being her devotion to the president, an affinity she both can and cannot explain. So maybe this is her actual politics, not Republican and conservative or anti-Democrat and -woke but █████ himself, █████ the man, the physical being, flesh and heat and voice and the force field of his aura. His constancy in the life of the nation has been her comfort and safekeep for all these years. He answers a profound need in her, and she knows she is not alone, some eighty million voting Americans feel the same way. And as for his record, okay, maybe there's a lot that hasn't worked out so well, but is it really that bad? Best she can tell, people get up in the morning and go to work, then they come home at night and eat dinner and watch TV till their eyes blear over. How bad can it be when everybody's carrying on as usual?

She is in the West Wing, but not of it, and as for those days when the politics is all up in her face, it's soothing to remind herself that she's in the entertainment business. Lately she wonders if this means she's cynical. She's been doing this ever since the Biden trials, thinking, thinking about her thinking, and the externalities implicated in her career path. She gets that certain politicians and their families might deserve to go up on criminal charges, but the Biden trials disarranged her in ways she still hasn't sorted out. How pitiful the family looked on TV, hollow-eyed, hopeless, exhausted, and her horror on realizing that she might be an accessory to their destruction? Joe always struck her as no better or worse than your average Beltway sleaze, but what happened to that family seemed tantamount to a tragedy of war.

Faith has built her right-wing résumé largely on the back of her mother's

Christian conservative connections. The career path of least resistance, and it's funny how the doors have always opened for her. Summer jobs, internships, fellowships, all she had to do was ask, and sometimes not even that. She knows residual celebrity has something to do with it, and Christie's generous political giving, but she wonders if other forces are at work. Signals sent through channels: This girl is favored, special. The right people like her. It's not unlike all those royal bastards down through history being showered with preferments and princely estates, all due to their backdoor DNA. At Georgetown she majored in poli sci and international relations, thinking she'd like to be an international lawyer someday. Jetting around the world, doing whatever those people do, this appealed. She graduated magna and Phi Beta Kappa, thank you very much, and her plan was to work on the Hill for a year before law school. She landed a staff job with Senator Smoot, beating out only, what, about three hundred other applicants? And from there it's been a fast rise all the way to the White House.

People at parties, strangers in stores, they still come at her guessing who her biological father is, like it's even just a little bit their business. Do ghosts throw shade? This one does, he is the great white shadow over her life. For a fact he's donated millions to ██████ over the years, and last time around was honorary co-chair of the president's Texas campaign. In her squishier, drippier moments, Faith can be tempted to think bio-dad is smoothing her way, making sure his little girl is taken care of. Oh, he really cares, sigh, swoon. Such are the puerile fantasies of a sentimental twit. Much more likely is he'd just as soon see her dead.

She didn't strictly need to come, but Harvey asked. Producer Bob arranged for a second camera crew in Dallas, and Scottie P, a supposedly hot young MTV director, would fly in from LA to direct. They had it covered, but Harvey wanted her on-site poking around for bombs. As in: Is this guy going to blow up in our face? "Plus you'll get to spend some time with your mom," he added.

If you insist. She arrives at DFW midday and drives a rental out to

Southlake under a mango-orange sky. SMOKE EVENT IN PROGRESS warn the TxDOT electronic billboards, EXERCISE CAUTION. What, like don't breathe? She hasn't been in Southlake since her senior year of high school, driving over with friends for a football game. Trying to get back to normal life while the *Next Gen* universe spun on without her. Southlake's sprawl has bloomed considerably in the seven years since. Miles and more miles of same-same suburbia, and where have they all gone, her TV siblings of yesteryear? She read somewhere that Chastity OD'ed in LA, and Tristan purposely pilled himself right there in Nashville. Macon died in a motorcycle crash; Kimmie starved herself to death; Laney drowned swimming off Cabo with her Brazilian boyfriend. Faith wonders if the body count for reality TV is even higher per capita than football, all in the service of your nation's viewing pleasure.

America, it occurs to her, is a smiley, savage place. TV news trucks are parked outside the Rasputin estate. Cameramen scurry to film her while she waits for security to clear her through the gate. Rasputin blowing up mainstream, could get wild. Inside she meets Bitsy Bowman, who politely and promptly relieves her of her phone. Charlie Cupps is scheduled to give her an orientation tour of the house, and they find him on the back patio talking on one phone and texting on another, but naturally he would be exempt from the no-phones rule. He has an assistant, Belinda, a young, pretty Hispanic woman with long dark hair streaked with chestnut highlights. She's dressed like a nurse or dental hygienist, in brown surgical scrubs and spotless white Nikes, and carries an open laptop in the crook of her arm.

Charlie finishes his call and turns on Faith like a cranky old leprechaun. For such a slight frame he has weirdly broad birthing hips, and wears his business-casual slacks up to his navel.

"Your goddamn people won't give me approval."

"Sorry, but I work for the White House. Not the show."

"We spend years building his brand, now you're gonna come in here and film *my* guy, at *his* house, and I don't have approval over any of it?"

"I hear you, Charlie. But it's not up to me."

"Yeah, you only work for the president. Christ, I must be out of my fucking mind."

On that note, the tour begins. Charlie turns out to be as didactic as an actuary about the house, a thirty-three-thousand-square-foot extravaganza whose style he describes as "transitional Mediterranean." With Belinda trailing, he leads Faith through the two kitchens, the walk-in wine closet, the dining room fit for *Game of Thrones* royalty. Two "salons," one big enough for a disco, then moving along to the media room, the study, the two-lane bowling alley, the indoor lap pool, the cryotherapy chamber, the sauna. Two guest suites flare off either wing; the expansive home gym is not to be confused with the stand-alone pyramidal wrestling gym. They steer clear of the third-floor master wing, where master is resting from his recent labors. Tuesday's presidential rally in Spivey was followed by the two-day "Battle in Seattle" featuring AWW's biggest stars. He returned home at three a.m. last night, a very weary Rasputin indeed.

"I thought he doesn't drink," Faith says in the wine closet, eyeing rack after rack of bottles.

"He doesn't. They're investments."

For max energy efficiency, the house has twenty-four separate HVAC systems that can be turned on and off as needed. The nine-car climate-controlled garage gleams like a surgical ward. "Do you talk?" Faith asks Belinda. "Of course she talks," Charlie snaps. Outside—like walking into a wall, when did Texas get so hot?—Charlie's face flares up red as a desert sunset as he points out the regulation basketball court, the giant trampoline, the curvy saltwater pool and infrared hot tub. All around the pool are gazebos and trellises for shade lounging. A mini-castle of a stone cabana anchors one corner of the deck, deluxe shade featuring billiards and ping-pong tables and a fireplace nearly big enough to stand in. Charlie directs Faith's attention to the detached guest house, "sleeps six comfortably," and the pyramid wrestling gym.

"And this," he sweeps his arm toward the grass spooling out from the pool deck, "is the lawn."

"Is that . . ."

"Artificial turf, but not just any artificial turf, honey. That's from

Super Bowl 51. Tom Brady beat the Falcons on that turf. It still had confetti on it when we rolled it out."

"Kewl," she says. Charlie's voice takes on a reverent hush as he adds, "I beat the spread by one point. Made eighty grand that day."

Inside they join Bitsy in the breakfast nook and drink lemonade served by two nice ladies in khaki slacks and red polo shirts. The staff uniform, Faith infers. She briefs everyone on the plan for tomorrow. The crew will shoot B roll of the house and grounds and the staff at work, and candid footage of Rasputin doing whatever he does when he's home. The call with ██████ is scheduled for four p.m. CDT, and they'll have the shoot set up tight and right for that. Otherwise the crew will drift around shooting bits that will offer viewers an inside look at the life of the famous wrestler, avid ██████ supporter, and newfound "miracle man" healer of the Weeps.

Charlie reverts to turd mode. "No."

"No?"

"No fucking way. I'm calling it off. I've gotta have approval."

"Fine, call LA," Faith tells him. "This is way above my pay grade."

Bitsy speaks: "Grishka want this, Charlie. He already sign off."

"Well maybe he just better rethink that deal."

"That's certainly his prerogative," Faith says. "But we all know this is only going to enhance his brand. Charlie, think about it—is there a bigger show in America than politics? Look at his numbers since Tuesday, I bet he's gone through the roof."

Belinda slants her laptop at Charlie and points to the screen.

"Yeah yeah yeah, I still don't like it." He stews for a moment. "Whatever, Jesus. But I swear to God, if you people fuck us over we're coming after you with everything we've got. And we've got great lawyers, you just remember that."

"I'll be sure to pass it on," Faith says. "But nobody's fucking—who is *that*?"

A posse of beautiful women has appeared by the pool, dropping towels and tote bags and peeling off pool wraps, chattering happily among themselves.

Charlie is curt: "Those are the Maidens."

"The who?"

"The *Maidens*."

"Oh, right." She remembers the vestals from the Atlanta entrance. "What are they doing here?"

"They live here."

"Some of 'em do," Bitsy clarifies. "Maidens all over, not just Dallas."

The Maidens strip down to thongs and bikini bottoms, squeal fetchingly as they cannonball into the water. Friday Frolics have commenced; this could be straight from the vaults of the quaint old Playboy channel. Bitsy is seriously embarrassed.

"I don't want you getting the wrong idea," he says to Faith. "They're good girls."

"They seem very sweet," she assures him. And they do, they play well together.

"Been meaning to talk to them about those tops," he mumbles. Rasputin enters from the hall in a flowery silk robe, barefoot, sleep-tousled, holding a cold pack to his jaw. "Greetings, greetings," he says in furry Slav-inflected English, smiling as he fist-bumps the men. He steps around to Belinda and palms her head like a basketball he's about to dunk. She beams. Faith stands and introduces herself.

"Yes, young lady, I remember you in the White House. Welcome." At first he exerts no more energy than courtesy requires, but something about her brings him up short. Abruptly he's all focus, studying her features with an intensity that draws a massive blush to her face. His throat seems to catch, *akh*, then he's smiling at her. My God, Faith thinks, he sees. He knows.

He sets the cold pack on the table, takes her right hand in both of his, and bows to touch his lips to her skin. "Enchanté," he says in exquisite French. "La princesse, évidemment."

Muffin is in the kitchen, barking. Not *yap yap yap* nonstop, but a peremptory *yip* every minute or so. Faith and Christie are in the den drinking Chablis Jesus juice with Fox News on mute, Faith sprawled on the sofa with her feet in Christie's lap. This is their girlie time, two hardworking women unwinding after a long hot week at the office.

Faith is catching her mother up on White House gossip, but that dog is getting on her nerves.

Yip!

"Does she need to be fed?"

"I already did."

"Sounds like she's still hungry." Faith hopes her mother's borderline eating disorder hasn't extended to the innocent Maltipoo.

"Nope. She's just telling me it's time for cooking class."

"For *what*?"

"Cooking class. If I'm not in there by seven she starts barking. She knows it's time to cook."

"You're kidding."

"I am not. She's a very punctual dog." Christie does a quick check of her phone. The new Weekend Workout video dropped at five o'clock, and she's tracking the numbers. On the tube Laura Ingraham is reporting the news, baring her teeth and jerking her head like a shark tearing off hunks of flesh.

"Anyway," Christie resumes, "so █████ likes him."

"Loves him. *Yuuuge fan*," Faith says in her █████ voice, and they giggle.

"How about █████?"

"As far as I know she hasn't met him. She hasn't been around much this summer."

"Hmmm. And?"

"Everybody knows she's totally had it with Washington. And she is very *not* happy about him running for a third term."

"Then maybe she should think about the country and not just herself! We still need him, Lord knows we need him. Now more than ever." That phrase again, *now more than ever*. "Until the rally I was kind of losing hope, a little? But seeing him the other night I was like, hey, the old ████████ is back! And then Rasputin with the weepers, it's like, okay, we've got a way out of this now. I think he's going to give us a huge boost."

"He's definitely been good so far."

"Is ████████ serious about him being his running mate?"

"Who knows. But it's fun watching the Democrats lose their minds over it."

"He is a holy man," Christie declares. "He's got the power, the light. You notice how things have calmed down the past few days? No mass shootings, no bombs, no protests. And the stock market's up seven percent."

"Happy days, Mom."

"I think that man is a game changer. And when he talks about the dark forces? He gets it. He knows what time it is."

Yip!

"She sure is a bossy little thing." Faith doesn't ask what time her mother means.

"I like it. It's sort of like having you around again."

"Hey!"

"I'm teasing. Wait, this guy is good." She turns up the sound. Laura Ingraham is interviewing some crusty old wheeze from the Hoover Institution. Faith hasn't mentioned her moment in the breakfast nook with Rasputin, when he saw the paternal truth stamped all over her face. For sure he saw something—what else could it be? Her life dominated not so much by daddy issues as The Daddy Issue, and what a mindfuck it was growing up as the secret bastard princess of Dallas. She freely cops to having been a mouthy hellion in her youth; to basically being at war with her mother those years, the *NNG* era in particular, but Christie had a plan. Or maybe she made it up as they went along, Faith's memories of those years are mostly a fury-addled blur. Being cut from the show invariably sent the cuttees into emotional tailspin, but after several weeks of the requisite anger and depression, Christie went into action. She incorporated Christie Spack's Faith & Fitness, Inc. She rented twelve hundred square feet of flex space, transformed eight hundred of it into an upscale workout studio, and remade the rest as a TV talk-show set. Next she hired a videographer and a webmaster, and for the first year they got by with a workforce of three. Now it's a national niche brand with its own YouTube channel, a muscular social media presence, twelve full-time employees, and 28.3 million subscribers at a base rate of $39.99 per month, with an enticing stairway of premium and premier levels.

She actually pulled it off, rendering her know-it-all shrew of a daughter both humbled and proud. Miracles do happen, evidently, although God likes to see us put in the work. As the Christie's Crew mantra has it, Visualize First, Act Second, Pray Always. On the walls of her Turtle Creek townhouse, amid the crucifixes and sappy Christian art, are photos attesting to Christie's mid-tier celebrity. Christie with ██████. Christie with former President Bush. With Roger Staubach, Ted Cruz, Joel Osteen, various ██████ kids, Roseanne Barr, General Flynn, and so on.

The broadcast goes to commercial and she hits Mute. "Laura had a good one the other day. She said the Democrat platform for next year boils down to pot, porn, and Planned Parenthood."

"Better hope not. That sounds like most of America to me."

"Hey, whose side are you on?"

"You know whose side. But who doesn't use birth control these days—you think *she* doesn't? How many kids has she had?"

"I would consider that to be her private business."

"Right on, Mom. It's Friday. Let's not talk politics."

Yip!

On TV an ad for psoriasis medication is playing. Christie pours more wine, has a sip, and sits back. The ice maker flings a volley of fresh cubes across the freezer. Muffin's toenails tip-tap as she paces the kitchen tile. Christie clears her throat with a prissy cough, a sure tell for what's coming. Faith braces.

"How's your weight these days?"

"Oh, you know. Not bad. Not great."

"You look good! But it's time you started taking care of yourself. You're not a kid anymore."

"I know."

"I could do up a six-week program for you!"

"And I appreciate that, except I'm working twenty hours a day. I really don't have the time."

"Nobody does, baby doll, we have to make the time. One of the first things the Bible teaches us is time is sacred. The six days of creation, and on the seventh He rested."

Faith nods. There used to be all these Cialis commercials on Fox, what happened to those? Now it's happening again, the wine sip, the throat clear, the cough. Then the other shoe falls.

"You seeing anybody?"

"Not really."

"*Any*body?"

"I've had some dates. Not many guys interested in a girl who pretty much lives at the office."

"Then maybe you need to find someone at work!"

Faith flash-cards the options. "God, no way. That reminds me, I need to check in with Harvey."

"Oh Harvey, that dear man. Tell him your mother says hello. And thank you as always."

"Will do." Faith ascends the carpeted stairs to her second-story bedroom, gathering sufficient static charge that the doorknob gives her a nasty zap. With trepidation she opens her phone, but all functions are intact. Red lightning has yet to make another appearance, but now the phone is prone to random hot spells that make her nauseous, or maybe it's all in her mind. She flops on the bed and scrolls up Harvey's number. She's basically forgiven him for having Susie Grumman dragged into the Oval to be Rasputin's test case. I was only trying to help, was Harvey's line. I truly had her best interests at heart. If it so happened we could check out Rasputin's bona fides in the process, so much the better.

He clicks in. "Faith."

"This a good time?" She hears dogs barking in the background, TV blasting, kids shouting. A small child's inconsolable wail.

"Perfect. Let me . . ."

She waits while he relocates.

"Where are you?"

"Mom's. She says hello, by the way. And to thank you again for giving her daughter a job."

"Well, thank her for raising such a swell kid."

"You're sweet. So, I have been to the summer palace."

"And?"

"Quite the shack. He's got a nine-car garage, excuse me, 'auto gallery,' and has to park his Range Rover and G6 outside."

"He called it that?"

"Charlie, he gave me the tour. Rasputin was just getting up as I was leaving. He kissed my hand."

"He kissed your hand."

"You know, like royalty, lah-tee-dah *Downton Abbey*. But get this—he never broke character, right there in his own house. You could almost start to think he believes it."

Harvey grunts.

"And everybody just goes right along. I don't know, man, it kind of messes with your mind. Like everybody's in on the joke but you, but boy do they play it straight."

"Okay."

"And then the girls came out and I started wondering if I'd stumbled into a sex cult or something. He's got chicks all over the place."

"Oh God. Young?"

"Well, nothing like Epstein. These are grown women, definitely. Though I did meet a couple of Tri Delts from TCU. They said they're seniors."

"Where does he find them?"

"Who knows, maybe they find him. You know the women in togas who escort him into the ring for his matches? That's who these are, the Maidens. A bunch of them live there."

Harvey says nothing for several moments. An outer-space hiss fills Faith's ear.

"Well, is he sleeping with them?"

"To be determined. But, uh, of course he is? And would it even matter?"

"Point. We've come a long way since Gary Hart."

"Who?"

"Never mind. What else?"

"What else, okay. Charlie bitched and pissed and moaned about not having approval, and his weird assistant was there, and a big black guy named Bitsy who used to wrestle, and servants out the wazoo, and a ginormous saltwater pool. And turf from one of the Super Bowls in the backyard. And all those almost naked chicks."

"Got it." She can practically hear his jaw cramping. "You set for tomorrow?"

"All systems go. The crew's coming at ten, I'll be there at nine. They're giving us pretty much free run of the first floor and grounds."

"Faith, I want you all over that place. If he's got a dungeon somewhere, an arsenal, vaults full of gold, I want to know. If you can get into the rest of the house, do it."

"I'll try. Before I forget—you remember what Rasputin said at the rally, how we need [redacted] now more than ever?"

"Go on."

"People keep saying it. Like, it stuck. We need him now more than ever."

"Now more than ever. That was Nixon's slogan back in '72."

"Really."

"And he won in a landslide."

"Maybe it's time to bring it back."

"May be. I'll pass it on."

"Uh, Harvey? One more thing."

"Shoot."

"Are yall really talking about the vice presidency for this guy?"

"It's early days, Faith. We're nowhere near deciding anything like that."

In other words yes, they are talking about it. At this moment she appreciates as never before the magical properties of the president's brain. And then blows it.

"He does realize this isn't the real Rasputin, right?"

"I haven't asked. Good luck tomorrow."

He summarily clicks off, and Faith is left with the low feeling of having pissed off her boss. Idiot! Bad form for an underling to reference the president's limitations so directly. In the kitchen Christie is holding Muffin in one arm and whipping up a stir fry with the other. Faith opens another bottle of Jesus juice and they get properly tiddled over dinner. Christie starts trashing on Faith's father, as she's wont to do under the influence. Not stepfather Lonnie, good old Lonnie, deceased-for-over-a-decade Lonnie, but bio-dad, the very public mogul who lives less than a mile from where they sit. Swept me off my feet, the jerk. I was young and stupid and let him do it, I sure did. Shame on me, but I was twenty and just off the truck from Zanesville, for heaven's sake. I didn't stand a chance.

"It's okay, Mom. It was a long time ago."

"Do you know I was practically a virgin when we met?"

A standard in the bio-dad spiel. Faith nods.

"I thought he was going to leave his wife for me, how stupid is that! It hurts to think about now, but no regrets, baby doll. I got you, didn't I? The only thing I really hate him for is not having a relationship with you."

"Mom, it's all right. You don't need to hate him."

"No, it's not all right, a real man would own up to his child and have a relationship with her. And my God, look at you! You're beautiful! And smart and successful and strong. If he had any sense at all he'd bring you into the business."

"I doubt he knows the first thing about me."

"I can assure you he most certainly does, he knows everything about you. He knows everything that goes on in this town."

"Mom, I really don't want to talk about him."

"Well, I do. It's disgraceful the way he's treated you, *us*. His own flesh and blood, and he never reached out to you."

"It's not like he abandoned us."

"Oh no, he took care of his little problem by throwing money at it, how very *Dallas* of him. But how people *feel*, that's what I'm talking about. What it does to a person's *heart*. I know it's affected you in your relationships."

"Mah-ummm," Faith groans.

"You know it does! How could it not? What's the longest you've ever been in a relationship?"

"I've had plenty of relationships, just not one that's stuck. But that's true for a lot of women my age."

"But something's holding you back! I can feel it!"

"Then that's for me to work on. It's late, Mom. I think it's time for bed."

"I think it's not! We have to discuss this!"

Eventually she crashes and burns, as she always does. She's teary by the time Faith gets her into bed, not weeping-sickness teary but life-regrets teary, with lots of woozy mumbling and apologizing. Being a billionaire's mistress at the tender age of twenty, having his kid, dealing with armies of schmuck lawyers and similar horrors, who wouldn't spend the rest of their life getting over it? Probably she has some form of PTSD, her condition reliably triggered whenever the kid shows up. So she's allowed the occasional meltdown. Tomorrow she'll be okay. Purged. Contrite. Tomorrow comes and she's still in bed when Faith is up and out the door, hungover, dehydrated, lungs aching from the Dallas air like she smoked three packs of Camels yesterday. She arrives at the palace precisely at nine, relinquishes her phone to the smiling Hispanic lady who lets her in the door, and is deposited on the back patio. So they want her out of the way, fair enough. A smiling Asian lady brings out a silver coffee service and fine china cups and saucers, and returns a minute later with chilled orange juice and warm breakfast pastries. Things are looking up. Faith drinks juice and coffee, consumes a sugar bomb of a bear claw, and begins to feel semi-human again. Here in the shade with the ceiling fans it's reasonably cool. A cohort of Maidens is doing group yoga out on the Astroturf lawn. Several more Maidens are swimming laps. Belinda emerges from the house with her laptop and joins Faith. She's dressed exactly as she was yesterday, in brown surgical scrubs and blinding white Nikes.

"Good morning," Faith greets her. Belinda flinches, clicks her throat. Her eyes don't quite meet Faith's.

"Want some coffee?"

The girl shakes her head, fixes her eyes on the screen. She commences typing so fast that Faith wonders if it's gibberish. Her gaze drifts over the pool to the Maidens on the lawn. All those toned womanly bodies lined up in rows, moving in perfect sync. Faith can't decide if it's creepy or healthy.

Charlie steps out. "Ah, you're here," he says to Faith, and looks at his saucer-sized Rolex. "You're late."

"Actually I was right on time."

He scowls and returns inside. Belinda snorts. Something is funny? Her fingers speed along like they're on wheels. Bitsy emerges from the house with a noisy heave and ho of crutches.

"Good morning, young ladies, Miss Faith. You doing all right this sunny morning?"

"I'm doing great, Mr. Bowman. How about yourself?"

"Got out the bed, that's a start. I prefer you call me Bitsy."

"All right. And please call me Faith. Join us for coffee?"

"Maybe shortly. Still chasing myself around this morning. You got everything you need?"

"Everything's great, perfect. They're taking good care of me."

"Good to know. Grishka say to tell you he'll be down presny. Doing his meditation right now."

"No problem. I'm just going with the flow."

He returns inside. Belinda's mad typing eases into scroll and search taps. Faith eats half of a giant blueberry muffin, then fails to resist eating the other half. Perspiration tickles the small of her back. Out on the lawn the Maidens' sweat-slick arms and legs flash like blades in the sun. There's something Stepford-ish about them, she decides, a hive-mind aspect to their flawless voluptuosity.

"You ruled," Belinda says.

Ah hah, it talks. Though its eyes stay on the screen.

"Excuse me?"

"You ruled. On *Nashville*. You were radical."

"Oh, that. Thanks. It was all pretty much bullshit."

"That's why you ruled. You called it out."

"Probably not as much as I should have. Pour you some coffee?"

"You already asked me that. I don't drink coffee."

"Okaaay." Faith decides the younger woman is somewhere on the spectrum. The part that responds to the calling out of bullshit.

"So."

"So?"

"Is █████ going to pick him for vice president?"

"I honestly don't know. But what would you think if he did?"

Belinda shrugs.

"No opinion? Or just no comment."

No nothing. Faith hangs fire for a moment.

"So what's the deal with all the women?"

Belinda meets her eye for the first time.

"He likes women."

"Do they like him back?"

"I would say the answer to that is yes."

"Does he sleep with them?"

Belinda's lips crimp into the suggestion of a smile. "He calls it holy kissing."

"And what is holy kissing?"

"I wouldn't know, but they seem to do a lot of it up there."

"Up there."

"Third floor."

Faith hesitates. "More than one at a time?"

"God is love," Belinda answers tonelessly. "You're kind of nosy, aren't you?"

"I guess I am, yeah. It's sort of my job to be nosy."

"I think you want to fuck him."

"I—no. It really hadn't occurred to me." Belinda snorts from deep in her sinuses. Faith takes a calming breath and squares up to her. "How old are you?"

"Nineteen."

"Aren't you supposed to be in school somewhere?"

"They kicked me out."

"For?"

"Sleeping with my professor."

"They kicked you out for sleeping with your professor. Isn't it supposed to work the other way around?"

"Yes, but I threatened to kill his wife."

"Oh."

"I went to their house. With a knife. I think I was kind of out of my mind."

"Well, love will do that to you. And where was this?"

"Cambridge. MIT."

Faith wonders if she's being put on.

"How did you end up here?"

"Charlie found me on Craigslist."

"Charlie found you on Craigslist," Faith slowly repeats. She was working as an escort? "What happened to the professor?"

"He's still at MIT."

"Really!"

"He has a Nobel."

"Ah. Well. I'm sorry all that happened to you."

"Thank you for being sorry. If you want to know about holy kissing, you'll have to talk to the Maidens. I'm just internet girl."

Scottie P arrives an hour late. He brings three cameramen, a woman soundman, a gopher, a tech, and the driver. In about a minute Faith determines Scottie is useless, and she spends the next two hours getting everyone oriented and on task. By the time she sits down, it's 101 in the shade, and even indoors with the twenty-four air conditioners everyone is sweating. Word comes that Rasputin is heading to the pyramid gym, so she sends Scottie and two of the cameras that way. She knows she should go herself, but her nerve fails her. She's scared, she admits to herself, scared and enticed both. By what else his x-ray vision might see.

She doesn't do much actual spying. Pokes around a few closets, does a walk-through of the baronial study. No way she's going up to the third floor. She cools out for a while in the breakfast nook with Bitsy, who observes she's having a busy day.

"I guess I am. Though it's nice not being in the office."

"You work at the White House."

"I do."

"You see the president?"

"I do, yes."

"Every day?"

"Not every day. But lots of days, yes."

"Sounds high-powered."

"I'm very low level, Bitsy."

He smiles. "Modesty is nice in a young person." They're drinking iced tea and snacking on guacamole and chips. "I been there once."

"The White House?"

He nods. "We were national champs that year, they take us up to the White House to meet the president. Everybody get right in their suit, we're all looking real sharp except I'm shy about my pants being too short in the leg. Come on man, you at the White House! Country boy up in George Washington's house, ought to be enjoying himself and looking around so he can remember everything, and there I am worrying about my pants too short. Then it come time to shake the president's hand. We line up, I shake his hand and tell him my name, he smile and ain't even once look at my pants."

"Well, there you go."

"Silly, things we fret about."

"It is."

"He was nice," Bitsy says. "President Bush. Seem like."

"That's what people say."

"President Trunk, he seem like a different sorta man."

"That's probably fair to say."

Bitsy gives her a careful look. "A harder man, maybe."

"He definitely has his days."

With all the cameras around, the Maidens keep their tops on. The kitchen pumps out heaping platters of party food, and that's what this is, Faith decides, party central, tunes, babes, fun in the sun, all that's missing is the Jägermeister body shots. Presently she excuses herself and makes her way to the pyramid. Inside it's an open floor plan with tumbling mats, space-age weight machines, a wrestling ring, and a wall lined entirely with mirrors. In one corner there are heavy bags and speed bags for punching, as anyone who's seen the *Rocky* movies knows. Rasputin and a thickset older man, Coach Tarnoff presumably, are slow-motion choreographing a move on the mats while Charlie Cupps and a beefcake trainer type look on. The cameras are close on the action, all good. Belinda is seated in the ring with her laptop. Scottie stands outside the ring with his arm hooked over the lower rope, trying to chat her up.

Good luck with that, boyo. Rasputin does a ballet-worthy pirouette with hulking Coach on his hip, and coming around he spots Faith by the door. He smiles and waves. Her cue to leave. Crossing the pool deck on her way to the main house, she's hailed by a bevy of Maidens. "Hey you! Faith Spack! Get over here!" It turns out Belinda has been spreading the word about her; turns out further that these Maidens are fans not only of *NNG* Faith but also of Christie's postshow reinvention as the guru of Christian fitness. Faith sits among them in the shade of a jasmine trellis, crossfire of misters pocketing them in tolerable cool. Someone hands her a red cup of orange juice, and the first sip fizzes all the way down.

"Mimosa?"

Pealing laughter. It sure is!

"I thought alcohol's not allowed."

Judith, a statuesque, dark-haired beauty who, Faith will learn, is a physical therapist in real life, assures her it's okay. "We don't drink in the house," she explains. "And hey, if you wanna be forgiven, you gotta sin a little first."

Maybe she's stumbled into the Maiden bad-girl clique. She drinks her mimosa and spills eight-year-old *Next Gen* gossip. She agrees that, yes, Christie is a "hero" for going bigger and better after they were cut from the show. Several of the Maidens are F&F subscribers. "I wish my mom was strong like yours," says Katrina. "My mom's a wimp," says Emerald, laughing. "I love her to pieces, but she lets these men walk all over her." A cameraman comes sharking around and Faith sends him packing, and over more bootleg mimosas the intel begins to flow. They all have jobs, except for the two Tri Delts, whose job is college. They are paralegal, aesthetician, personal trainer, yoga instructor, radiology tech, retail associate/sometime ski instructor. Two are former Dallas Cowboys cheerleaders, and they all live here where it's fun and safe and rent-free, and Grishka's house has many rooms.

"What do your boyfriends think about that?"

Guy's got a problem, that's his problem, he's a nonstarter with us. They take turns doing "trips," it's a big enough group that work schedules and personal lives are easily juggled to supply a contingent of Maidens for every match. Yes, we travel on his jet. Yes we're all completely gaga for the guy, which they don't say in so many words, but Faith gets the drift.

"The first time we talked," Bethany tells her, "it's like he knew me. He told me things about myself I've never told anybody."

"He sees into your soul," says Katrina.

"He's definitely reached a higher spiritual plane," says Monique, "but not like in a high and mighty way? He's all about us, who we are. Where we're going on our life journey."

"He can just look at you and tell if you're hurting," Bethany adds. "I swear, I *swear*, if you've got a headache or cramps or a muscle ache, he puts his hand right there and it goes away."

"Yes!" they all cry. "It's true!"

"And none of us has gotten the Weeps," says Judith. "We already knew he had that under control. It's no surprise to us what he's doing out there."

Fine, but are you fucking him? But Faith can't bring herself to ask, there's just no version of the question that won't spoil the cozy vibe. The Maidens seem happier than pretty much anyone she knows, so who cares if they're all fucking. For sure America's not going to care, certainly not the part that's predetermined to go all in for you, and to hell with pussy-grabbing and sleeping with porn stars and every other dank ditch of moral turpitude.

She looks up to see Rasputin coming around the pool. His hair is wet from a post-workout shower, and he's dressed in flip-flops, baggy shorts, and a billowy Hawaiian shirt, a heatwave apparition of a bizarrely fit Lebowski. "Greeeshka," the Maidens lilt and coo, and casually hold their red cups below their chairs. "Grishka," says Judith, gesturing at Faith, "this is Faith Spack! She's famous!"

"I know Faith." He ducks under the trellis. "I think someday she will become even more famous. Sisters, if you please, I would like to speak to Faith alone."

The women withdraw with no evident jealousy, taking their red cups and pitcher of mimosas with them. Rasputin sits facing Faith and pulls his chair so close that their knees practically touch. A small gold cross is pillowed on the chest hair bubbling out of his shirt, and his eyes are kindly, soft, their blue depths shading to mysterious aubergine. Faith's heart is banging so hard she can feel it in her temples.

"I hope," he says in his sonorous Slavic voice, "everything has been satisfactory today."

"Yes! Yes it has been, great, yes, thank you, everything's been great! I think we got a lot of great footage today."

"Excellent. And you yourself, you are well?"

"Great, yes, thanks, super, couldn't be better!"

His gorgeous eyes are steady on her. "Do I make you nervous?"

She can't help her rubbery sputter of a laugh. "Well, sort of. I guess. A little?"

"But it is not your nature to be a nervous person."

"I guess that's true, it's not."

He solemnly takes her hands, his gaze so soulful that he could be about to propose. She swallows hard.

"Faith. God in his wisdom allows me to see certain things. But it is not my business to tell the world everything I see."

For some reason this brings tears to her eyes. She blinks as subtly as she can.

"The challenges of our lives, the uncertainties, these are all God's plan according to His perfect wisdom. They are the tools with which He tasks us to mold our truest selves."

She nods. A raggedy sniffle escapes her nose.

"Your life is the workshop of your soul, Faith. And you are working, I see this in you. Sometimes struggling, yes, the work is hard! But remember always who your Father is. Your true Father." He smiles and nods to confirm their secret understanding. "The Father who will never abandon you."

He squeezes her hands, then leans forward and kisses both her cheeks. His lips hit like bee stings, *pow, pow*, but these are bee stings of bliss. She seems to float right out of herself.

"Okay?"

"Yes, okay. Yes! Thank you, yes."

"Now—what is the time? President ██████ will be calling soon. But first there is a reporter who wants to interview me. Would you like to film?"

"Sure. If it's okay?"

"It is for certain okay. Go find your guys, and I will see you inside."

10

Spivey knocks him flat. The heat and travel and lack of sleep do a number on his sixty-five-year-old frame, not to mention the psychophysical exertion of breathing while black in the midst of forty thousand white supremacists. Wednesday he can barely move. Lying in bed half out of it, aching all over, missing Gayle so bad he thinks his heart might quit, fine, why is he still hanging around anyway. Freeze-up episodes keep hijacking his dreams. He'll be messing with his phone, texting or checking the news or whatever and *zuut*, the screen locks up and so does everything else. Which raises the question: Are these merely dreams of freeze-ups or the real thing, the disorder jamming him up even in his sleep?

Maybe these are death premonitions, a modern update on the screech owl. Thursday he starts pushing fluids on realizing he hasn't urinated in most of a day. Sits in the recliner in his bathrobe and reads, watches the news, makes some calls. Rasputin fever has gone mainstream, and the TV commentators—do they all go to stupid school? Everybody saying the same thing in the same way, the feedback loop just gets louder with every lap, and once again the Democrats are sandbagged by ██████'s latest wile. He can't be *serious*, please? A professional wrestler for VP?

Rasputin's not even *real*, he is a character, a made-up TV thing, you can't put a creature like that one heartbeat away from the presidency, and by the way, what about his time in Russia—might we please consider the national security ramifications here?

After all these years the Dems have yet to figure out how to counter ██████'s weirdo energy, now he's going for a third term and doubling down on the weird. Flash polls from Quinnipiac and *The Wall Street Journal* show big bumps for the president. Meanwhile there are fire tornadoes in the Sierras, algae blooms in the Great Lakes, and the Weeps are burning through California's Central Valley, jeopardizing the nation's food supply. This reminds Clarence to water his plants, which he does retiree-style in his robe and slippers, under a sky as chemical orange as the president's hair. As late afternoon bleeds into evening his mood darkens. He skips dinner, shuts down all his devices, and takes to bed. When did all the shit start, that's what he's pondering. The way way back, back to the beginning, the first preemptive murders by paranoid colonists. Night raids, sneak attacks, sabers and thunder sticks. Devils out there in the dark woods; devil drumming in the night made the English murder-crazy. Paranoia being the half of it, greed and avarice the other, the mania—no other word for it—for extracting kingly fortunes from a land that would have served just as well for a society of modest yeoman farms.

So there's your history, people: paranoia and greed. Not promising the lesson will set you free, but it might make for the occasional burst of clarity. He did the best he could for twenty-seven years, semester after semester of increasingly beleaguered kids and he didn't set a single one of them free. What does it mean when nearly thirty years of doing your best can roust a good man out of bed in the middle of the night to stare at his books? As if the answer might magically fall off the shelf. Back in bed his mind wanders to the detention camp in Tornillo, the soccer balls the kids kicked over the wall with their names and hometowns written on them. Political orphans, their parents hauled off elsewhere, the children left to the tender mercies of lightly regulated private contractors. Clarence walked the perimeter of the camp copying down names and places, then stood by the back wall and wrote every name the kids shouted over to him until camp security called the cops.

He did a night and a day in jail for that one, long enough for old memories to sink their teeth into him. He is the man, he suffered, he was there, now he's here and the children are still there, or deported God knows where, into whose arms one hardly dares to think. This is where his mind leaves it when he finally falls asleep. Sleeps hard and takes his time getting up, decides he's feeling decent enough to do what he has to do today. Nelson wants to go too, and picks him up in the Beamer after lunch.

"Welcome back."

"Yep."

"█████ goes to the cracker center of the world, and you've gotta go too?"

"It's my job."

"Why are people still listening to that fool?"

"They must like what he's selling."

"Uh-huh. Anybody give you a hard time?"

"Not as hard as they wanted to."

"Damn, Key. Next time I'm going with you."

"Nope."

"No?"

"You've got better things to do than follow an old man around." He pulls an audio recorder out of his daypack and starts tapping through the data screen.

"Whoa. Where'd you find that dusty old thing?"

"Office."

Nelson laughs. "I bet old Renfro is loving you lately."

"Spivey article got over six hundred thousand hits. We've never had numbers anywhere close to that." He tries to keep overmuch of his pride from showing through. What he doesn't say is that today's interview is an exclusive. The little *Dallas Daily* has snaked *WaPo*, the *Times*, *The Dallas Morning News*, every local and national heavy.

"Maybe time that man gave you a raise. You know what I think, I think you should write a book about Rasputin. Way he's starting to blow up, you'll make a fortune."

"Maybe. I've got to figure out who he is first."

"All right, that's our mission today. How about this, you stay inside with the Russian and do the interview, I'll be out by the pool working the girls."

"Well son, you just do that."

The dashboard thermometer reads 112 degrees. The sky is the oyster-ish yellow of spit-up bile, and the highway grass has the dull purplish tint that means the roots are cooked. Grackles the size of small children stand by the road with their beaks hanging open, stunned by the heat. Nelson is pushing ninety, but they're passed by a column of motorcycles cruising in two-abreast formation. Small Confederate flags flutter from the rear fenders, and long guns in leather scabbards are strapped to the sides like cowboys of yore. Nelson cuts a sour look at his uncle; Clarence grunts, flashing on paranoia and thunder sticks. In Southlake they see a new kind of flag flying from the MAGA patrols, a royal-blue cross on a white background with three crossbars intersecting the post. The lowest crossbar slants downward from left to right.

A dread feeling comes over Clarence. The flags are everywhere, too many too fast for it to have happened by chance. This took foresight, funds, logistics. He begins to sense a vast underground convergence at work, a massing of forces deep and powerful enough to smash continents. You get in their way, one little solitary human being, there won't be enough left of you to scrape into a sock.

"You know what that is?" he asks his nephew.

"What is?"

"Those flags. That cross." Clarence pauses. "That's the cross of the Russian Orthodox Church."

"Wait. As in, Rasputin?"

"As in Rasputin."

Nelson lets out a slow breath. "Uncle, I really think you need to write that book."

The city of news trucks parked in front of Rasputin's estate has shrunk the road to a single lane. An honest-to-God global media sensation, in vapid Southlake of all places. Off-duty cops and private security man the gate today. Tough guys, barely polite, but once Clarence gives his name they are polite guys, barely tough. A smiling Hispanic woman lets them in the front door and relieves them of their phones. Bitsy, lagging, crutches his way across the foyer.

"Gennelmens."

"Bitsy."

"Retribution."

Dap and handshakes are exchanged. Clarence thanks Bitsy for putting in a good word on his behalf.

"No problem. He like what you wrote about him in Spivey. Come on back and we'll get you set up."

Bitsy leads them down the marble hallway, which today is an amplifier for the happy racket issuing from the back of the house. Nelson mugs a look at his uncle, *You ready for this?* "Don't Stand So Close to Me" by the Police is booming over the outdoor sound system.

"I watched Seattle," Nelson says to Bitsy's back. "Our man was banging."

"He did all right," Bitsy answers with pro understatement. "Funk Fu give him a handful for a while. But he got over."

"Looked to me like he could've put Funk down in about a minute."

"Yeah, but how much fun that gonna be for anybody. Just so you know, we got the *West Wing* film crew here today. They say don't pay 'em no mind, just go on about your business."

"Some business," Nelson chirps back. "Sounds like there might be a party somewhere."

"You might have that right. Saturday crowd apt to kick it."

From the pool come screams, cheers, thumping tunes. "Stop it!" a man is shouting somewhere down the hall. "Stop it! Stop right now!" They follow Bitsy into a sunny room with full-length windows overlooking the pool. The room is an old-school gamer's paradise, with pinball machines, a ping-pong table, foosball, billiards, air hockey, and table shuffleboard. Rasputin is tipped back in a gravity chair while a little red-faced man jumps about waving his arms, trying to shoo away two guys with shoulder cams. A pair of giggling young women are perched on stools by the wrestler's feet, very industriously painting his toenails pink. Now the little man turns on them.

"You two! Stop it! You're making him look like a fairy!"

Rasputin laughs and wiggles his remarkably long toes. "Charlie, chill. It is okay."

"No it's not okay! People see your toes—stop filming, now! They're gonna think you're a pansy."

This, Clarence infers, is Charlie Cupps.

"They will not think I am pansy. They will think I am cool."

"Bitsy, tell him!"

"I think his toes mighty pretty, myself."

Now basically everyone is laughing. Charlie stalks out of the room, followed by a young, good-looking Latina in brown surgical scrubs. Rasputin tries to stand as his new guests are introduced, but the pedicurists shout him down. Chairs are fetched for the guests, iced tea is served. Through the windows they have a view of the all-female volleyball match roiling the pool. Contrary to plan, Nelson takes a seat next to his uncle. Once everyone is settled, Rasputin fixes Clarence with a dire forensic stare.

"You almost died," he proclaims. His voice is suddenly deeper, Delphic, with a gong-like reverb humming at its core.

"That's probably true of a lot of people," Clarence answers.

"But for you death was very close." Rasputin pauses, brings his focus to a finer point. "It was hot. Far away. Bad place." Again he pauses. "Bad people. This happened many years ago."

Clarence feels Nelson going all spooky beside him, and he shouldn't. Anybody with access to the internet can find the bones of that old story in about a minute.

"Yes, I think death was very close for you," Rasputin intones. "So much death where you were. But you do not like to talk about it."

"It's not necessarily my favorite subject. Anyway, we're here to talk about you today. Thank you for seeing me."

"Of course, you are welcome. Bitsy says you are good people. I trust Bitsy's judgment in all things."

Bitsy has taken a seat a few feet behind Rasputin's shoulder, so any time Clarence looks at the wrestler he meets Bitsy's eyes as well. More to that old country boy than he lets on, Clarence thinks. Rasputin leans forward and the chair rotates upright, inspiring protests from the women. He looks to his visitors and smiles.

"They take good care of me."

"You do seem like a fortunate man," Clarence replies. The two cameramen circle about with the languid stealth of aquarium fish. "Do you mind if I record the conversation?"

"As you wish."

Clarence sets up the recorder on a side table and places the table between himself and Rasputin. He has his pen and notebook, but these are mainly for his hands to have something to do. He activates the record function and states the time, date, and place with an eye on the volume levels. Then his name, and Rasputin's. He sits back.

"Have you always been spiritual?"

"No. Well, yes. The light was there, the longing, but I was always turning away from it. For many years I lived the life of a wild young man in the world—fighting, drinking, carousing with women, and all of those things. I was with the world, I loved what was in the world, until one day I realized that I was weary of this person and the life he was leading. God led me to take up the way of the pilgrimage, and my journey brought me to Verkhoturye, to the Holy Fathers of the ancient Nikolaev Monastery."

Charlie and the woman in brown scrubs have returned. They sit with Bitsy, but not before Charlie silently shoos off the pedicure team. A few moments later a striking young woman with blond hair enters and takes a seat well back from everyone. Nelson stirs and glances at Clarence, then settles back in his chair.

"Right, let's talk about the monastery. You got your military discharge in early 20_. Not long after that you went to Russia, and I'm curious about your reasons for that, the whole trajectory that led you to Verkhoturye."

"That was not me."

"Excuse me?"

"Rasputin has never served in the military."

"Uhm, okay. But my information is you served eight years in the US Army. Most of that in Special Forces."

"You are speaking of Patrick."

"Well, yes. I'm referring to the military record of Patrick Strickland."

"This is true," Rasputin says in a dreamy, lilting voice, "once upon a time there was Patrick. But that boy died."

"That boy died," Clarence echoes, processing. He notes that Rasputin's team has gone as still as a group photo of themselves. "Would you mind explaining a little more about that?"

"There is Rasputin only, and there has always been Rasputin. Patrick was Rasputin before he was Patrick, and he was Rasputin after he was Patrick. There has always been that one man you see before you today. That man they killed long ago in Saint Petersburg, he, too, was Rasputin. Three beings, one Rasputin."

"All right, I just want to make sure I'm following you. There's you, Rasputin, and there's Patrick, who is also you, and there's the first Rasputin, the original Rasputin, who died in 1916 in Saint Petersburg."

"Rasputin died, and yet he lived. He is the man before you today."

Clarence offers up an accommodating smile. "I know I'm probably going to seem kind of tedious getting all literal on you, but I want to make sure I understand what makes you you. I get that you're Rasputin, Rasputin the wrestler, the Russian Winter, Wrath of God, world champion several times over. Great career, by the way. But once upon a time there was that other Rasputin, the one who was assassinated by his political enemies in 1916. They poisoned him, shot him, and threw him in the freezing cold river there in Saint Petersburg. So I'm just trying to square up that Rasputin with the Rasputin I'm talking to today."

The wrestler projects the serenity of a man speaking from a great height:

"I am that man."

Clarence hesitates. He has no interest in following this character down his performative rabbit hole. Rasputin smiles. "You are skeptical."

"No, we're just obviously talking about two different things. If you don't want to go there with me, fine, I'm not insisting. You've made an amazing career for yourself as Rasputin, and I'm not here to slag on that."

"I thank you, Clarence Thomas. There are many things to explain, but the hour has not yet come. For now I say only that in my pilgrimage I encountered vast spiritual riches in the wilderness of the ancient Holy Rus. Such wisdom there is in those hidden little corners! And in the Nikolaev Monastery I was privileged to learn from the great elders who have attained moral perfection. The spiritual feats they are capable of—these are nothing short of miraculous! Above all, the ability to foster Christ in oneself."

Clarence sits with this for a moment. "Resurrection?"

Rasputin smiles, inclines his head. "Perhaps you doubt me, Mr. Thomas."

"No, actually I think you're pretty good at this."

"With God the Father all things are possible. Would you like to see the wounds?"

"The wounds."

"The wounds of Saint Petersburg, 1916."

Clarence tries not to seem too eager. "All right. I think I would."

With the ponderousness of a rocket ship lifting off the launchpad, Rasputin straddles the gravity chair and rises. The cameramen duck in and out as he pivots toward Clarence and unbuttons his hibiscus blossom shirt. Clarence, too, is standing, though he doesn't remember getting up, and Charlie Cupps skitters around them like a strung-out junkie.

Rasputin tosses his shirt onto the gravity chair. "Okay, you see here, first shot." He points to a starburst scar just below his heart. "The bullet came in here, went out there." He turns and fingers a blobby keloid scar on his lower back. "Second shot, here." He curls his wrist and touches a shiny splot of keloid scar just above his right kidney. "Now, third shot." He turns and stoops so that he's eye to eye with Clarence. "You see that?" He points to a faint starburst scar at the center of his forehead. "The coup de grâce, control shot. From eight inches. I saw the bullet come out of the gun."

"Okay okay okay," Charlie barks, "enough. This is just morbid, Jesus. Grishka, put on your shirt."

Clarence is not a squeamish man, but the gristly sheen of all those keloid scars has made him queasy. He sits and has a couple of swigs of iced tea, wipes the sweat off his brow. He recalls that Patrick Strickland is reported to have suffered no fewer than three combat wounds during his military service.

"I have no regret for that night," Rasputin says as he buttons his shirt, and his gaze sweeps the room to include everyone here. "The moment the first bullet enters my body, I realize something holy is happening to me. The pain, let me tell you, the pain was unbearable! But I felt God so close to me then. His spirit entered my flesh with the bullet, and that was when I understood the holy martyrs and saints and their sacred ecstasy. So much pain they suffered, extraordinary pain, unimaginable pain—and it was joy! Because they know Jesus by sharing His holy pain and suffering. In their pain they enter the realm of the blessed and are reborn as God's creatures."

Whatever of the absurd and sublime Clarence expected from Rasputin, this is more—more God, more skin, a more immersive performance on every level.

"Well," he manages, "thank you for all that. I appreciate your candor."

The wrestler sits. He offers Clarence a sympathetic smile. "You are perplexed."

"Who wouldn't be?"

Everyone laughs, Rasputin included.

"Just trying to make sense of all this," Clarence continues, scanning his notes, "should I take it you're describing some sort of reincarnation process? Because right now I really don't know what to make of it."

"Brother Thomas."

"Sir."

"My brother Clarence."

"Present."

"With God all things are possible. The mysteries defy us, this is true, but with humility and patience some measure of understanding may be granted. For me this required years of study under the guidance of the Holy Fathers of Nikolaev. You asked me about the monastery—that was my life in that place. Study. Prayer. Meditation. The devotion of all my heart and soul to the holy mysteries."

"The holy mysteries. Tell me about those."

"Someday. Not today. Another time."

"They seem to be at the center of everything you do. Who you are."

Rasputin nods once, slowly.

"What you're able to do with the weeping sickness, all the people you've helped—is this part of the holy mysteries?"

"In good time, Clarence Thomas. Everything will be revealed."

"Were you happy at the monastery?"

"Very happy."

"But you left."

"I was called."

"By God?"

"By God."

"God called you to become a professional wrestler."

Such is the moment that this doesn't sound like a joke.

"God leaves the personal details to us."

"Do you think God wants you to be political?"

"But Rasputin has always been political. When I go to Mass, when I wrestle and witness for my faith, these are social as well as spiritual acts. I am a human being, I live in a society among other human beings that is governed by a state with economic powers, industrial powers, administrative powers, and so forth. Whether the state governs well or badly—we ask this always with reference to God's law. His law is the measure of holy righteousness and the true foundation of an orderly state."

"Do you think President █████ governs according to God's law?"

"Absolutely! █████ is transforming America into a land where God's people hold sway. You see, he understands our recent history, not just the history of America but the entire West. He understands this is the history of a civilization killing itself through decadence, individualism, godless self-regard. Only by rededicating ourselves to God's true and holy church can the West be saved."

"The true church," Clarence begins, and falters. He knows he's out of his depth.

"Two Romes have fallen," Rasputin solemnly proclaims. "But the third still stands."

The flags, of course. In Clarence's brain the pieces snap into place. "The Russian Orthodox Church," he says, and Rasputin beams.

"It is the stronghold of everything that is noble and good! What began in Rome and continued in Constantinople now resides in the person of His Holiness Patriarch Kirill of Moscow and All Rus, Primate of the Russian Orthodox Church. This is the reason for the natural sympathy, no, more than that, the kinship, between the Athonite consciousness of the Russian church and the traditional West. President █████ knows this in his heart—why else his instinctive feeling for President Putin? They are kindred spirits, these leaders of the two great Christian superpowers."

"That would certainly explain a few things," Clarence offers in a neutral voice.

"This is the terrible tragedy of the Ukraine war, the wedge it drove between spiritual allies. Not only Ukraine and Russia, which are one, but Russia and America, the entire Christian West. It began with the signing of the tomos of autocephaly by Patriarch Bartholomew in 2019. You know this? No? The separation of the Orthodox Church of Ukraine from Moscow? For three hundred and fifty years the church is one, then this schism, this dagger in the heart of our holy unity. It could not stand, not if Christian civilization is to fulfill its destiny."

"Right," Clarence says, working hard on his notes. He knows he's going to have to up his game to hang with this guy. "Let's come back to that in a minute, but right now I'd like to ask you about the Russian security services. During your time in Russia did you ever—"

"White House calling," Charlie blurts, and steps out to the patio. Rasputin placidly turns to Clarence. "President ████████ and I are about to speak. Would you like to stay?"

Clarence blinks. Not a trick question. "Sure. Thanks."

"You stay too," Rasputin says to the camera crew, and there's a flurry of conferral and positioning led by the young blond woman. Charlie returns with a cell phone at each ear. He walks over to Rasputin and stands at attention by his chair. After a moment he speaks into his left-hand phone.

"Mr. Rasputin is on the line." He passes the phone to Rasputin, who switches it to speaker. Charlie tries to grab it back, but Rasputin easily fends him off.

"Please hold for the president," says an officious woman's voice. Then: "Mr. President, Mr. Rasputin is on the line."

"Grishka!" booms the president. "How are you, my friend?"

Good God, Clarence thinks, it's really him. He glances at his device to make sure it's still recording.

"I am very well, Mr. President. I hope you are well also."

"Great, tippy top, just shot a seventy-five, best score I've had all summer. You've seen the polls?"

"I have, Mr. President, but please first let me advise that I have you on speaker, for the benefit of the *West Wing* camera crew."

"Totally cool, Grishka. 'Cause I've got a *West Wing* crew right here with me too!"

"And Mr. President, a few other people are here as well, including a reporter from *The Dallas Daily* newspaper. Mr. Clarence Thomas."

"*Who?*"

"Mr. Clarence Thomas, of *The Dallas Daily*."

A moment of silence. "You're kidding me."

"Not kidding, Mr. President."

█████ erupts in a machine-gun sort of laugh, *eh-eh-eh-eh!* "Well, hey, lucky guy! With a name like that he can't be all bad, I guess. So, the polls, Grishka, I'm looking at the polls and we're doing the best we've done since this whole weeping business started. You're our breakthrough guy, my friend, I want you to know that."

"That makes me very happy to hear, Mr. President."

"We're gonna need you with us big-time while we get this thing under control. I know you're—hey, Seattle was awesome, you totally crushed it out there! The way you put away poor Funk, I don't know why he'd ever get back in the ring with you."

"Thank you, Mr. President. Funk is a worthy opponent."

"He looked more like a whipped-puppy opponent the other night. So, uhm, I know you've got your wrestling commitments, and your fans want to see you out there and everything, but as much as we can have you with us—you're still willing to help us out with some rallies, right?"

"Of course, Mr. President. Whenever you need me, I am there."

Clarence has gone queasy again. A kind of fog or film is clouding his vision, and for a minute he thinks he might throw up. Listening to █████ and Rasputin banter, it's as if reality has become too dense for normal processing. Or maybe he's getting sick, or there's too much gassy celebrity in the room. Or perhaps he's witnessing the beginning of the end of the world.

Breathe, fool. He wets his fingers on his iced tea glass and touches them to his temples. Time is running somewhat loose and rattly on its tracks, but it doesn't feel like the prelude to a freeze-up episode. This feels internal, his own private psychosomatic shock. Maybe it's what this black man does instead of weeping sickness? He realizes he's staring at the gold cross hanging from Rasputin's neck, the Russian Orthodox cross, same as the flags. For a moment he's convinced it's a mesmeric device, and Rasputin has put some sort of spell on him.

Fuck that, he tells himself, and *breathe*. He decides he will need to be extremely careful around this man. The rest of the call is mainly ████ talking about himself, and when it's over Rasputin sits back, smiles, and sighs as if he's just consumed a very fine meal. "The president," he says, a kind of verbal burp. Then people scatter. Charlie demands to see Rasputin "in the office," and charges down the hall with the girl in brown scrubs on his heels. "He is angry with me," Rasputin murmurs to Clarence, and winks. "He doesn't like that I let you stay. I will be back." Bitsy leaves with Rasputin, and a cameraman follows. The young blond woman motions the other cameraman to follow her out to the pool. Nelson shoots his uncle a wide-eyed look, *here goes!* and takes off in hot pursuit. Alone now, Clarence collects himself by going through the motions. Shuts off the recorder, checks the batteries, scans the data screen. Looks over his notes for what he'll ask when Rasputin returns. Behind all this tidy industry, boiling up like a massive storm front devouring the sky, is the certainty that something has happened. Is happening. About to happen. He doubts it's good, whatever it is, but maybe this is just the natural irascibility of an old man. For how many millennia have tiresome old men been predicting the end of the world? Our saving grace the fact that cranky old men couldn't pull it off on their own.

He circles and stars "FSB/KGB" in his notes. There's lots of noise about the wrestler being a possible Russian spy; highly unlikely he'll admit it, but Clarence intends to get him on record. Presently Bitsy returns and says, Come on, we need a snack. They sit at the kitchen island and are served lemonade, guacamole and chips, flautitas, queso con carne, slices of apple and fancy cheese. "No sabía que iba a cenar aquí," Clarence says to the cooks, along with his compliments, and they whoop. "¡Miren a este güey hablando en español! ¡Y sí, habla bien!" They chat for a while, and he learns they're from Guadalajara, Oaxaca, Tegucigalpa. He notes all the pots they have going. "¿Hay una gran fiesta hoy?" he asks, and the women laugh. "Cuando el jefe está en casa nos toca cocinar para diez o veinte personas. Nunca sabemos cuántos van a venir a cenar, así que preparamos mucha comida, porque nadie se queda con hambre en la casa del jefe." "Sí, les creo," Clarence says. "Si viviera aquí creo que me pondría como un marrano."

This gets a laugh and several rounds of back-and-forth about hogs and the fluidity of Clarence's accent. Bitsy sits quiet and attentive through all of it. "Where," he's finally able to ask, "you learn to speak Spanish like that?"

"Guatemala. Mainly."

Bitsy seems ambivalent. "Why'd you go down there?"

"College. I figured out I could get four semesters of Spanish in a summer and fall and do it for half what it would cost me at North Texas. So I went, and it turned out I liked it. So I went back after graduation."

"You have a job?"

"I was a reporter, stringer. Freelance, mainly for the wire services. A lot was happening in that part of the world in those days. You're probably too young to remember Iran-Contra."

"Can't say I do. Name rings a bell." Through the windows Clarence spots Nelson mixing it up with the pool volleyball crowd, grinning like an idiot who's just won the lottery. "That how you almost died?"

Clarence swings around to find Bitsy's eyes steady on him.

"I did get into some trouble, yeah."

"But you don't like to talk about it."

Clarence shrugs. "I was working on a story I really had no business messing with. In El Salvador. Certain flights in and out of a military airport there. Some people took exception to my activities, and they pulled me in."

"Jail?"

Clarence nods.

"Rough?"

"Rough enough. For a while I thought I might not get out of there. But eventually my daddy and uncle flew down and got me."

"How they manage that?"

"You know, I have no idea. Later on I'd ask Dad about it, he wouldn't say much. He and my uncle had never been out of the country. Barely been out of Texas—never been on a plane either. Best I can tell, they got themselves to the embassy in San Salvador and parked in somebody's office, and they just stayed until people started doing things."

"Well, that's family. They gonna find a way."

Clarence realizes he's talking too much. Bitsy flipped the script, got him talking about himself when it's supposed to be the other way around. Then something else occurs to him.

"He's not coming back, is he."

"Not today. He send his apologies. He say for you to come back another time, and for sure you can take him up on that. Grishka don't say a thing like that if he don't mean it."

"All right. All right, I will. Tell him thanks for me." Clarence pauses. "I guess it's time for me to leave."

Bitsy winces, cocks his head in apology.

In the car Nelson is all smiles. He copped a handful of Maiden phone numbers and has a lunch date next Tuesday with a beauty named Emerald. As for whether Rasputin is sleeping with them, to be determined.

"Careful," Clarence tells him. "We might be treading in very deep waters here."

"It's cool. You know that was Faith Spack back there?"

"I don't know who that is."

"Blond lady bossing the camera crew. She was on *Nashville Next Gen*."

"I never watched that show."

"Of course you didn't. She was famous back in the day, for about a minute. You know what she said when I asked if she was Faith Spack from *Nashville Next Gen*? 'Yes,' she said, said it all vague and drifty like when you asked Rasputin about Patrick Strickland. 'Yes,' she said, 'I used to be her. But that girl died.'"

11

The Russian Orthodox cross is popping up everywhere, on T-shirts, ball caps, bumper stickers, travel cups, on bills glued to utility poles at major intersections. Vice President Greene sees the writing on the wall and officially launches her campaign for president, the “Vice” on her vice presidential seal suddenly shrinking to small print. Following a late-summer lull that right-wing media labels the Rasputin Effect, the weeping sickness rebounds with a vengeance. Half the games in week one of the NFL get no further than the singing of the national anthem. The Weeps streak north along I-85 like a lit fuse, sending kinks throughout the national supply chain. Airlines are forced to cancel thousands of flights, and the Rolling Stones suspend their Tongue in Cheeks tour when the basic twelve-bar blues progression reduces Mick Jagger to a sniveling mess.

“None of my very good people get it,” proclaims at a rambling press conference. “I think it’s got a lot to do with breeding, in fact I think we’re going to see some data on this fairly soon, science data, genes and so forth.” In the same press conference, he muses that a vegan diet increases susceptibility to the Weeps, and cites the latest Covid vaccine as a causal agent, and depression, “which I never had a single day in my life." That evening the Democrats hold their first primary debate of the season, a host of hopefuls taking the stage in College Park, Maryland, to talk to an empty auditorium. They include Senators Tiplady, Scatterboo, and Packpaunch, Governors Headwall, Toeslope, and Munch, Ambassador Wigglesworth, Representatives Gimghoul and Scunthorpe, a Kennedy, and Billy Bush of *Access Hollywood* fame, median age around seventy-three. Clarence settles into the recliner, grits his teeth, and watches. The talking points remind him of 1997, and as for all the gray hair onstage, did the Dems burn up their bench for firewood? They seem to think they're being quite centrist and reasonable when what they are is stuck-in-the-mud status quo, that same sick status quo that's got eighty percent of America in the ditch, working too much and too hard for too damn little with the AI Death Star breathing down their necks.

What is needed, he scribbles before dozing off, *is the development of an entirely new political tendency*, and the next morning he'll wonder what exactly he was thinking when he wrote that. With the change of seasons come fresh waves of migrants at the southern border, and some of the weirdest weather on record. Tornadoes in the Northeast, hurricane-strength storm fronts stonking the Midwest, a forty-mile-wide band of softball-sized hail stretching from Boise down through Wyoming, knocking even mighty buffalo out cold. "Does anyone remember ice-nine?" an English professor at SUNY Binghamton asks in a *USA Today* op-ed, and she urges the nation to forgo social media for a week and use those hours to read *Cat's Cradle* by Kurt Vonnegut. The ██████ campaign rolls out its new slogan, MAKE AMERICA GREAT AGAIN. NOW MORE THAN EVER, and after a spate of minor infrastructure bombings in Georgia, the Carolinas, and Kansas, the president puts the National Security Brigades and Rapid Support Forces on alert and warns of civil war with "radical-left Marxists." Then the birds go crazy. Hawks and falcons (day shift) and owls (night shift) begin attacking humans across the Southwest, prompting citizens from Austin to Tucson to break out their umbrellas in the midst of a thousand-year drought.

Wherever he goes, Rasputin is besieged by fans seeking a prayerful laying on of hands. The first GOP primary debate takes place at the University of Nebraska, a "nothingburger," according to President ██████ (he skips it), that Faith and Harvey watch from Faith's bed in her Georgetown condo. ██████ lawyers Sidney Powell and Lin Wood produce documentation proving that the wrestler known as Grigory Yefimovich Rasputin, né Patrick Walsh Strickland, is in fact a natural-born US citizen, thus eligible to serve as the nation's vice president. "We have found the Godly man!" declares the Reverend Jenkins Gilchrist, CEO of the National Prayer Breakfast and forever ██████ fan. "████████████ put the Christian faith at the forefront of our politics. Now Rasputin will install Jesus Christ himself at the center of our national life."

Small-dollar donations pour into the reelection campaign, but the big money is holding out. For their second date, Nelson takes Emerald to dinner at Al Biernat's, plies her with wine and questions about life as a Maiden. Evenings when Rasputin is on the road, Bitsy Bowman retires to the study to read Pushkin, while Belinda sits outside in the early autumn cool and watches bats sweep across the saltwater pool. She sees red lightning in the distance; waits for thunder that never comes. Russian President Vladimir Putin declines to comment on the rising political fortunes of the wrestler Rasputin. "I do not get involved in the political affairs of other nations," he says, and seems to smile, though with his face so puffy from Botox it's hard to tell.

The Wall Street Journal is the first to report a grassroots "Draft Rasputin" movement stirring the heartland. "We still love ██████ ██████," says James Crutts of Algona, Iowa, a quality control manager at Hormel Foods and self-appointed president of the movement. "But we think it's time for new blood at the White House, and Rasputin's exactly the guy we've been waiting for."

Clarence has a feeling. It feels like money. He consults with Renfro, and goes into deep-dive investigatory mode. The *New York Post* runs front-page photos of Rasputin and ████████ walking arm in arm on the White House grounds, prompting a terse statement from the White House press office: "The First Lady regards Grigory Rasputin as a trusted spiritual adviser and friend. In addition to the bond of their shared Slavic roots, they also have in common their devout Christian faith." Brooks David, star columnist for *The New York Times*, graces the nation with weighty thought-leader thoughts on the Rasputin phenomenon. "Though the performative character of Mr. Rasputin's religiosity cannot be gainsaid, he increasingly presents an intriguing option for right-wing evangelicals who have grown weary, one would imagine, of apologizing *in perpetuum* for the ██████ian circus." Further and moreover, "the brand of muscular Christianity embodied by Mr. Rasputin seems to be striking a nerve even among our casually secular electorate."

"I don't want to hear it," Ellen Biddle huffs at the White House press when questions keep coming about Rasputin and ████████'s walks. "Anybody who thinks anything inappropriate is going on, I'm just going to say that person has a perverted mind, and leave it at that."

The second Republican debate is scheduled for Liberty University in Lynchburg, Virginia. "The nothingburger special," ██████ cracks. "That's the nothingburger with extra-soggy fries." In lieu of debating "the pygmies," he travels to Oakland for the AWW West Coast Throwdown scheduled for the same night. The stellar card includes Maximal versus the Continental Kid, and the tag team of Redbone and Tater taking on the Citadel and Texas Chainsaw, and women's world champ Lucinda Body squaring off against spunky upstart Toxic Shock. The grand finale will be a Nasty Nine Battle Royale with, among others, Rasputin, Fatal, the Saudi Prince, Thrilla Nilla, and Cody Crash all vying to be the last man standing. Watching from bed in her Georgetown condo, Faith is struck by the multitude of Russian Orthodox cross armbands in the crowd. Am I the only one who's seeing this? she wonders. Throughout the evening the broadcast cuts to the president sitting ringside with

Ricardo Levy and a penumbra of aging █████-allied celebrities, Herschel Walker and Robert James Ritchie among them. The undercard matches "don't fail to disappoint," in the words of one of the announcers. There's chair action, ladder action, barbed-wire board to the head action, and thousands of thumbtacks thrown into the ring by Chainsaw's manager. Redbone knocks out Citadel's trademark chromium-steel front teeth. Toxic Shock gamely takes it to the champ, but seven running turnbuckle head slams in a row finish off the challenger. Maximal schools the Kid with an exquisitely prolonged hangman-on-the-ropes showcase, followed by an elegant powerbomb for the coup de gracias.

I never liked wrestling, Harvey texts Faith. He's in Oakland, watching on TV backstage with the rest of the travel staff.

Faith: Dude loosen up. Its just good clean fun.

Harvey: So were gladiators in Rome.

Faith: Nobody dying. Pretend its cartoons. It sort of is.

Harvey: Cartoons for idiots.

Faith: Snob.

Harvey: That's real blood out there.

Faith: I agree its kind of gross. Remember they're getting big bucks for this.

Messing with the cell phone still makes her nauseous. In private, as tonight, she wears surgical gloves when handling the device, no idea if it actually helps. She's half-asleep when █████ is invited into the ring to serve as "surprise" guest emcee for the battle royale. Tilted back in his recliner at his Farmers Branch home, wearing the silk pajamas Gayle gave him on their last Christmas together, Clarence notes that █████ is greeted by the loudest roars of the night. Does anyone doubt he's still got it? After all the baroque sadomasochism of the past two hours, it's an obese, jowly, elderly, garishly tinted and tanned Caucasian who rouses the crowd to its bloodlustiest cheers. The noise coalesces into a familiar chant:

█████ FOR LIFE! █████ FOR LIFE! █████ FOR LIFE!

Standing center ring, █████ slowly rotates and soaks up the love. He smiles. He nods and waves. Clarence wonders if he has ever seen a fellow human so completely blissed. In fact he finds the president's happiness somewhat embarrassing. The pathos of it, the bottomless pit of puerile need and the bitterness built into it, the angst that inevitably comes of never getting enough. But for as long as it lasts, █████ is in his heaven.

"Are we having a great time?" he bellows.

YAY YAY YAY.

"What a great crowd, fantastic crowd—"

YAY YAY.

"—and what a great cast of characters we've got here tonight."

YAY YAY YAY.

"I'm a fan, you all know that, been a fan ever since I was a kid. And I mixed it up in the ring a time or two myself, right?"

YAAAAAY.

"Oh yeah, you know all about it, that haircut I gave Ricardo, Ricardo Levy, there he is"—█████ points at Ricardo ringside as the crowd haws and cheers—"yeah, admit it, Ricardo, you never looked so good as when I shaved your head."

Faith gets busy with the phone. He shaved Levy's head?

Harvey replies, Long story. They bet on a match. Ricardo lost.

"We had some weepy folks here earlier tonight," █████ continues. "But our friend Rasputin took care of that—"

YAY YAY—

"—he's quite a guy, I tell you, just an amazing human being, but you can say that about all the great wrestlers we have here tonight. They're all winners, all winners, anybody who fights like they do, every one of 'em's a winner. Because Americans *fight*, am I right?"

YAY YAY YAY.

"And that's the story of my life, my whole life has been one big fight after another, and now, what we're facing right now, the communists, the Marxists, the atheists, all the vermin right here in America that are trying so hard to destroy our country, we've gotta fight them with everything we've got."

YAY YAY YAY.

"This is the big one, folks. This is the ultimate. And if you give me four more years, I guarantee we're gonna make America greater than ever. But God forbid, if we lose?"

NOOOOO.

"We could. We could. Those people will do anything, they will lie, cheat, steal, murder, they won't stop at anything. Those people who want to take away your guns, your jobs, everything you fought so hard for, they wanna brainwash your children and turn them against you. They even want your trucks! Right here in California they wanna take away your trucks and make you drive those stupid little cars like they do in Europe, those little dink cars, it's ridiculous. Real Americans will never stand for that."

Faith drifts in and out. Carry on, Mr. President, I'm just going to have a little catnap here. She rouses to the sonic assault of Rasputin's heavy-metal *Swan Lake* theme and the man himself entering the ring with Maidens arrayed about him like teeth on a circular saw. The sight of him perks her right up. She gets tinglings on a tremulous line from her navel down to her crotch, as if the tautest, most delicate muscle in her body is being strummed. She has to admit she has somewhat of a crush on him. For sure it's different from the thing she has with Harvey, which is comfortable. Sweet. He is so grateful. Their first few times he said "thank you" afterward, until she asked him not to. Harvey is a relaxing bubble bath, whereas Rasputin is a ninety-foot tsunami bearing down on you.

But it's after two a.m. and she can't keep her eyes open. She nods out during the round robin trash talk, and by the time the match starts she's thoroughly zonked. Had she stayed awake, she would have seen the following:

Cody Crash and the Saudi Prince tie up.

Rasputin and Fatal tie up.

The Cousins Twins tie up with Thrilla Nilla and the Duke, and Mr. Natural dive-bombs them from the ropes.

Cody puts Prince on the mat, teams up with Fatal on Rasputin.

Duke goes after Fatal.

Prince revives, goes after Cody.

Thrilla Nilla goes barbed-wire board on Twins.

Fatal duplexes Duke onto prostrate Twins.

Rasputin pins Fatal, tosses him out of the ring.

Mr. Natural tosses Duke.

Twins toss Natural.

Thrilla Nilla barbed-wire boards Rasputin and Twins.

Thrilla Nilla tosses one Twin.

Rasputin tosses second Twin.

Cody and Prince toss Thrilla Nilla, gang up on Rasputin.

Rasputin in trouble.

Rasputin going down.

But!

Rasputin lays out Prince with a sunset flip, then Russian Winters Cody for the pin and tosses him out of the ring.

Prince, flat on his back, begs for mercy. Is answered with a swan dive bonecrusher off the ropes, then Russian Winter with all the trimmings. And so the Saudi Prince joins the body pile outside the ring. Battered, bloody, sweat-soaked Rasputin raises his arms, and from twenty thousand mouths the chant booms forth:

WRATH OF GOD! WRATH OF GOD! WRATH OF GOD!

U seeing this? Harvey texts, but Faith is out cold. She slumbers through Rasputin taking the mic and giving thanks to God. Rasputin dedicating the win to President ■■■■■■, "America's savior." ■■■■■■ entering the ring for the presentation of the championship belt, taking the mic and speaking of strength, resilience, fortitude, grit. Two thousand miles away in Farmers Branch, Clarence's throat clutches with an involuntary gulp, and an eerie crepitation prickles up and over his scalp as if his head has become a giant pincushion.

He's texting Renfro Turn on your tv when his phone freezes, and now it's happening again. The pendulum on his grandfather clock stops mid-swing. The TV sticks on the moment of Rasputin accepting the belt from █████. Everything, the TV, the house, seemingly the entire world has gone silent.

"Again?" he says out loud, his voice echoing as if piped through the twilight zone. He's simultaneously alarmed that it's happening and glad for the chance to study the thing in real time. He does a quick mental check of his body. All systems go. "You are not losing your mind," he says firmly, holding fast against the echo. "This is real. This is happening right now." He looks again at the TV, both █████ and Rasputin with their hands on the belt, the thing frozen between them. Is this what he's meant to see? A passing of the torch, material proof of some fateful cosmic turn?

He doesn't know how much time passes, or whether time passes at all; whether he's been shunted onto a sidetrack off linear time. Then it's almost insulting, the way things resume with the blithe *pop* of a vacuum lid, and on TV Rasputin takes the belt from █████ and lifts it over his head. YAY YAY YAY goes the crowd, and █████ is smiling and clapping, he and Rasputin beam for the cameras while behind them a groggily resurrected Fatal climbs into the ring with the barbed-wire board. The crowd roar takes on a throatier slur as Fatal advances on the pair at center ring, cocking the board for a mighty wallop at—who? In a flash three Secret Service agents leap into the ring with Tasers drawn, and the next moment Fatal is flopping and writhing on the mat.

The crowd goes insane. █████ turns to see Fatal twitching and jerking at his feet, and he laughs and does a little backward hop-step. He looks to the crowd and points at Fatal as if to say, Can you believe it? Laughing and shaking his head, oh my what a crazy night this is. Soon people will be asking if the Secret Service was a work, or did the show veer a little too close to the real? But Rasputin isn't laughing. His expression is dour, Russian. He brushes past █████ and barks at the agents, who kneel and pull their Taser prongs from Fatal. With the championship belt slung over his shoulder, Rasputin goes to his knees and lays his hands on Fatal, instantly stills his thrashing.

Right, Clarence says to himself. Okay then. He doesn't know what he's just seen, but he knows he's seen something.

12

Their first time was in Chicago, with Air Force One grounded by mile-high tornadoes scouring the region like the kicking and screaming tantrum of an angry god. President ██████ pitched his own pint-sized imitation—since when did Air Force One wimp out to weather?—but ultimately settled on spending the night in the penthouse suite of the Drake, then had to move five floors down when the windows blew out. So passed a wild and gulpy night at the Drake, windows bursting, walls shuddering, wind booming up and down the elevator shafts like neutron bombs, while very cozy at the bottom of it all a man and a woman bedded down in a small, airshaft-view room on the second floor.

With all their clothes on. Harvey insisted. They spent the night dozing and cuddling while the end of the world raged above them. Their second time went much the same as the first, a late-night necking session at Faith's condo with Harvey's erection striving bravely against his pinstripe pants. So their first time didn't technically happen until their third. Harvey had thought about it. He'd prayed. He'd made up his mind. She found his determination endearing, his damn-the-torpedoes intention to sin while simultaneously planning tomorrow's trip to confession. Were all Catholic integralist guys this much effort? They'd barely finished when he rose up on his elbow and looked her in the eye.

"I want you to know that I have the utmost respect for you."

She managed not to laugh, and waited a beat before deadpanning back:

"I totally respect you too."

Then she laughed. Dude, chill! The sex was nice. Basic. About as electrifying as a good ham sandwich, and maybe just slightly, cloyingly, too considerate. He was self-conscious about his lack of worldliness. "You're lovely," she assured him, and he was, in his oversolicitous, former altar lad way. Blow jobs seemed to be a new thing in his life, and this allowed her to bank up soothing reserves of scorn for his wife, Maggie. Woman! Here you've scored the all-American husband and father, and you're too primly hygienic to treat him to a stress-relieving gob job now and then?

"Why me," he asked one evening.

"What do you mean, why you."

"Because I'm old. Fat. Boring. And you are . . ." He choked in the clutch, as if saying it would break the spell.

"Young and hot," she finished for him.

He nodded. "You could have any man you want."

"I suppose I could, pretty much. Or woman," she added, just to see him flinch. "But you're special, Harvey. A rare man among boys."

"Come on."

"No, it's true. For one thing, you're not a jerk."

"Mm, thanks."

"You're honest, and you're thoughtful and smart. You're good to your people, loyal. And you know stuff."

"Stuff?"

"Like real-world stuff, important stuff. Politics. Power. Human psychology. You know how to take the hits and you don't back down."

"I back down all the time."

"Not really. Tactical retreats, more like. Flanking maneuvers. I've been watching. Plus you have the most gorgeous eyes."

He blushed. "Come on. My eyes are brown."

"Really, gorgeous, brown, eyes," she affirmed. So maybe she was fluffing a bit, but she can truthfully say she's really feeling it, mostly. He helps out with the loneliness, and he's safe, as in, safely married, which preempts possibilities of long-term messiness. And he gets her mind off Rasputin. Face it, the fake Russian's done a number on her. Having your deepest truth discerned so cleanly by a dashing stranger, how could this not be thrilling and terrifying both? Their paths cross regularly these days, at campaign events, the White House, and she always does her best to blend into the furniture. But Rasputin is cool. The power he has over her, he doesn't press it. A smile and a nod from across the room, a special twinkle in his eye, this is as far as he goes toward acknowledging their secret, and anyway he has bigger fish to fry. For starters there's an entire administration to charm, and he brings the charm like a one-man Oscars night. The ██████s get all groupie hyper around him. Men, cabinet secretaries, become shy and tongue-tied. Women grow flushed and telltale squirmy in that damp-panties way, and the effect is trending nationwide. In late September a CBS News–*New York Times* poll shows a ██████-Rasputin ticket beating all Democratic contenders by five to fourteen points. Subtract the wrestler from the ticket, and ██████-TBD drops ten points across the board.

Rasputin shaping up to be the X factor, assuming the president's ego can handle it, and that ego has wormholes Freud never dreamed of. With the Iowa caucuses four months away, the pygmies are already starting to fold, the initial field of twelve thinned to seven. Maybe now the big money will commit? Not to mention the RNC and all the fence-sitting state parties, may they get eight-inch splinters in the ass. For Republican debate number three, in Milwaukee, ██████ naturally abstains. Harvey and Faith rendezvous at her place for a two-person watch party, and by the time the show starts they've had sex and are sitting up in bed with cartons of Chinese. The cheesy aesthetics are good for some laughs, the zingy music, the high-gloss polymer surfaces, the chunky glow-light podiums (podia?) that line the stage. Excuse me, would this be the set for *Wheel of Fortune*? The walking-dead candidates emerge one by one as they're introduced. Senator Inchmeal, R–Goldman Sachs. Senator Jawfair, R-Citigroup. Governor Zipple, R-Viagra. Vice President Greene in a shiny space-age unitard and matching jacket. Senator Cruz, R-Cancun. Former Governor Bridge Bullock, whose girth brings to mind the adage, Never eat in one sitting what you can't lift. Silicon Valley billionaire Name-Nobody-Can-Pronounce. Five minutes in, ■■■■■ is sniping at them on SonicX. Harvey and Faith track him on their phones.

This crew gives low energy whole new meaning.

Lyin Ted doing what he does best. Can't say he's not good at something!

Valley Boy couldn't innovate his way out of a wet, paper bag. I did so many deals way harder than his fake products company!

For several exchanges Cruz and Inchmeal gang up on Bullock, then Bullock and Zipple go at Cruz, then Valley Boy and Greene go mano a mano, and Senator Jawfair spills his notecards all over the floor.

Voters, you have my permission to switch over to threes company reruns.

"Why is he even watching?" Faith wonders. "He should just leave it alone."

Harvey grunts. Shots of the audience reveal scores of Russian Orthodox armbands.

Bridge never got over I didn't ask him to be my AG. Sad!

"Yall should've scheduled a rally for tonight, a fundraiser. Anything to get him away from the TV."

Harvey nods, grunts.

Of course Valley boy loves AI. It's his only hope of ever saying anything inteligent!

"He's punching down. Not a good look."

Harvey is brusque. "A president always punches down, just by definition."

Well, he has her there. The pygmies are small, nasty, brutish, basically terrible people, but for all their awfulness Faith can't help feeling sorry for them. Their eyes have the glassy look of defeat, and now even the vice presidency seems beyond their reach. What's the point of giving your all in audition when the role is already taken? At the hour mark there's an extended commercial break, and cures for acid reflux, psoriasis, and incontinence cycle through. Then something different. Faith's expert eye knows even as her brain works it out, the tamped-down palette, the pebbly texture meant to signify a time outside of time. To the gentle twang of an acoustic guitar, a stately montage of stills parades across the screen. A white clapboard country church. A playground teeming with a diversity of adorable children. July Fourth fireworks over a small town square. Lady Liberty with the protean Manhattan skyline at her back.

"America," declares a reedy, richly weathered white-man voice.

Next up, a locomotive with the engineer framed in the window. A color guard amid the headstones of Arlington National Cemetery. Muddied football players on a humble high school field.

"Our America," the voice avows in the sonic equivalent of flannel shirts and rocking chairs. A small-time beauty pageant appears. Tugboats. Rocky Mountains majesty. A missing-man flyover.

"Our home."

Cowboys doing roundup. NASCAR. Two little girls at a vanity playing with mother's makeup.

"For two hundred and fifty years, the light of the world, the shining city on a hill. And from this land, the promise of a better future for all."

The next still is of Rasputin in his black shaman suit with the band-collar white shirt, the first in a series of candids that show him mingling with people, hugging people, praying with people, laughing with people. Outstretched arms held high as if to embrace and bless the people. That he's by far the tallest person in every frame seems like essential information.

"And now," intones the avuncular voice, "a man has emerged. A man for now. A man for the future. A decorated Green Beret"—

Here is a beardless, buzz-cut Rasputin in dress uniform, dwarfing the officer who's pinning a medal to his chest.

"A lifelong star athlete and world champion"—

Next is a teenage Rasputin in football uniform, followed by the sweaty, smiling, bare-chested adult version holding aloft the AWW Championship belt.

"A man of uncommon strength"—

Rasputin again, bare-chested, grinning or grimacing as he balances a not-small opponent over his head, about to slam him to the mat.

"Of uncommon compassion"—

Rasputin wading into a scrum of weepers, two already under his arm as he reaches for more.

"Of uncommon faith"—

Rasputin in his shaman suit, head bowed, eyes closed, hands clasped before his crotch.

"A man who has lived the American dream," and here is a smiling Rasputin in jeans and a Hawaiian shirt in front of his mansion, climbing into a jacked-out pickup truck, "who wants that dream for all Americans. The man for now"—

A back view of Rasputin rimmed in light, raising his arms to an adoring stadium crowd.

"The man for America. For a better future for us all."

The music jangles to a winsome fadeaway as the image cuts to bold white letters on a field of black—

Rasputin. For a New America.

It lasts long enough to stamp the retinas of millions of viewers, with a brief pop-up of mouse print at the bottom, Paid for by Citizens for a New America. Then an ad for Geico takes the screen.

"Holy shit," Faith murmurs. "What was that?"

Harvey is already tapping his phone.

"Did you know about this?"

"No."

"Where did it come from? Jesus. That was something!" The ad's got her all stoked and she senses she shouldn't be. "That was totally a campaign ad."

Harvey is grim. "Oh, you think?"

"Could be a great intro if this guy's gonna be on the ticket. Those production values—"

"No."

"No?"

"You see any █████ in there?"

The next second his phone is blowing up. First it's Van, then Ellen Biddle, then Van gets off to take █████'s call and is replaced by Stephen Miller, meanwhile Faith's phone is overheating with calls and texts from Kendra, her mother, producer Bob in LA, and about ten other people. She has a notion to call Charlie Cupps and is sweeping for his number when Harvey barks "█████!" and snaps his fingers at her. The president is calling. She mutes her phone, then stuffs it under the blankets for good measure as Harvey taps into the call.

"Are you gonna tell me what the fuck that was about?"

Harvey's phone isn't on speaker but might as well be.

"Mr. President, I'm just as surprised as you are."

"And that's supposed to make me feel better? What the fuck, Harvey, you didn't see this coming? It looks like that motherfucker's running for president!"

"We'll get to the bottom—"

"—and who the hell is Citizens for a goddamn New America? A bunch of commies?"

"I'm sure we can—"

"Dammit, you gonna let me finish?"

"Of course, sir. My apologies."

But ████ falls silent. Three, four, five, six seconds pass. At last Harvey is compelled to speak.

"Mr. President?"

"You really didn't have a clue."

"I'm afraid not, sir. I don't think any of us did."

"What the hell do you people do all day? Christ. You know how stupid this makes me look? This guy I've been promoting all over the place, I swear, you can't trust anybody these days. Where the hell are you anyway?"

Harvey coughs. "A friend's house. Friends. A couple. A married couple. Sir."

"Huh. Well." ████'s hardly listening. "Is Faith there?"

Faith buries her face in the pillows to keep from screaming.

"Nuhhhhnnno! I mean, no sir. Different friends. Married," Harvey adds nonsensically.

"Well find her, ASAP. She was down there at his place, she'll know something. Dammit, what am I supposed to do now? I've been posting all night, I can't not say anything."

"Own it, Mr. President. Give him your compliments on an effective spot. Let people think we're on board with it."

"Huh. Maybe. I gotta say something." He pauses. "Harvey."

"Sir."

"I'm not happy."

"I understand, Mr. President."

"No, Harvey. I am really, really, severely not happy, okay? If this guy's got it in his head to run, we've gotta nip this thing in the bud."

"Yes sir, Mr. President."

"And who the hell, citizens for a bullshit whatever, that's a million-dollar ad they just ran! Who the hell's putting up that kind of money? It was damn good, too, looked like one of ours. Find out who did it. If it's people we're using, I want them fired, now."

"Yes sir."

"And if we owe 'em any money, tough. They aren't getting another dime from us."

"Of course, Mr. President."

13

Six a.m., Faith rolls over with her eyes closed and pulls on surgical gloves, then reaches for her phone and silences the alarm. Harvey left hours ago but his smell lingers, mingling with odors of Chinese food and sex. She cracks one eye at the screen; no red lightning. With both eyes now she checks feeds and queues and sees an email from Scrub-Grrrl that niggles her brain. Who? Oh, her. Though she doesn't recall giving this person her email address.

> Hi Faith you remember this guy was here the day you were black dude IDK why he made me think of Spike Lee but he did. Does that make me a brown racist bitch? 😜 In sisterhood think you should like to be aware of this News story. Yr grrl Belinda

Faith sits up and clicks the link.

THE DALLAS DAILY

A Palace Coup Is Happening in the GOP

Rasputin Signals a Sea Change in the Base
Party Elites Seize the Moment
"Bible-Thumping Hunka Hunka Burnin' Love"

By Clarence Thomas Jr., National Affairs Correspondent of The Dallas Daily

DALLAS POSTED OCTOBER 4, 5:17 A.M. CDT—

Seizing on a groundswell of popular support for the professional wrestler known as Rasputin, Republican elites are covertly funding the nascent "Draft Rasputin" movement in hopes of supplanting President ██████ with a younger, less divisive Republican candidate in next year's election. A weekslong investigation by The Dallas Daily has uncovered a shadowy network of well-funded charitable foundations, political action committees and so-called social welfare nonprofits channeling resources into the pro-Rasputin effort. After enjoying well over a decade of unwavering support from the base, ██████ now appears to be vulnerable among the very voters who have been his bulwark against challenges from the establishment wing of the party.

"Rasputin's not necessarily the end goal here," said a longtime Republican operative, speaking on condition of anonymity. "But ██████'s like that bottle of ketchup at the back of the fridge. About two years past its best-by date."

She swipes down. And down and down. Man wrote a freaking book. She forwards the link to Harvey and Van, showers, fixes a big travel cup of coffee, and summons Monsieur Uber. It's a brilliant fall morning in the nation's capital. Crisp air jazzes her nose like a snootful of Dr.

Pepper fizz, and the trees are blinged out in sparkly reds and yellows and spend-hither Hermès orange. In the back seat she straps on the surgicals, *wap wap*—the driver glances in the rearview, says nothing—and resumes reading approximately where she left off.

> . . . a ragtag movement consisting of little more than a handful of social media posts and a smattering of "citizen leaders" around the country. But in a matter of weeks the movement has morphed into a nationwide effort with professional signature gatherers in at least seven states, a central website employing some 15 full-time staffers, and coordinated guidance on talking points, press releases, event planning and recruiting.

She skips down a half swipe.

> . . . national organizations funded by undisclosed donors, with boards of directors that feature some of the country's wealthiest, most prominent conservatives.
>
> "It's essentially a massive covert operation being run by a bunch of elites who feel like ██████'s reached the point of diminishing returns," said Edward Rompstall, a former Arizona secretary of state who now works in private equity. "He's been great for their agenda, but at this point the ██████ brand has so much baggage attached to it. So why not back a fresh face that everybody's excited about."
>
> Records obtained by The Dallas Daily show that the New Patriot Project, one of the nonprofits at the center of the Rasputin movement, has received $3.1 million in the past month from Anacostia Advisors, a for-profit consulting group that administers no fewer than eight politically active nonprofits. These nonprofits have regularly received funds in the past from major players in the conservative dark-money network, including Americans for Prosperity, Heritage Action for America, the Club for Growth, the Phyllis Schlafly League . . .

She swipes down.

. . . In each case, had the donors given directly to the super PAC, their names would have been publicly disclosed. But because the money took an indirect route through a qualified nonprofit, their identities remain unknown . . .

Faith swipes and scrolls, swipes and scrolls.

. . . whose physical existence consists solely of a post office box in Flower Mound, Texas. But public records list Alan Pogue Burbett, a consultant on the payroll of Koch Industries, as the organization's president. When reached by phone at his office, Mr. Burbett told this reporter, "I don't have to tell you who I work for," and hung up . . .

. . . leaked records of internal deliberations show that Burbett worked 35 hours a week for the nonprofit during that period . . .

. . . it's meant to have that grassroots, up from the bottom-type look," the longtime GOP operative explained . . .

. . . Another organization under the Anacostia umbrella is Citizens for a New America, a 501(c)(4) nonprofit that was reactivated in recent weeks after sitting idle since the last general election. Citizens for a New America is poised to release a wave of pro-Rasputin television ads in the coming days, the first of which aired during last night's GOP primary debate.

"You okay?"

She meets the driver's eye in the rearview, and realizes she just groaned.

"I'm fine. Sorry. Work."

"Problems?"

"You know it, man. Wouldn't be work without the problems."

Faith refrains from asking his advice. In her experience, cabbie wisdom is a crock. She goes back to the story.

. . . so anxious to be rid of █████ that they are willing to promote for the presidency a professional wrestler who performs 24–7 as Grigory Rasputin, the Russian monk who was assassinated by political enemies on the eve of the 1917 Russian Revolution . . .

. . . "Face it," said Rompstall, the former Arizona secretary of state, "the Republican brand sort of sucks right now. The economy's lousy, protests and riots are happening in every major city and we're hated all over the world. It's hard to make a rational case for another four years of █████."

Longtime Democratic strategist James Carville agreed. "Ain't enough lipstick in the world to dress up that pig" is how he characterized the GOP's plight in a recent phone call. "How the hell they gonna run on their record, right? So what they gotta do, they gotta sell the Republican Party as the party of Christian soldiers saving the country from flesh-eating Democrats and space monkeys and tax-and-spend meth heads.

"And lo and behold," Carville continued, "just in time here comes this big old Bible-thumping, Jesus-hugging, hunka hunka burnin' love that's gonna help 'em do it."

Faith swipes to the end.

In sum, dear reader . . .

Since when did reporters write like this?

. . . the Draft Rasputin movement is being brought to you by the same high-dollar folks who bankrolled a bunch of angry, confused, dress-up-playing white people into that fake-grassroots movement known as the Tea Party. ███████████ walked that Astroturf all the way into the White House, and if the dark-money billionaires have their way, he'll soon be walking that rug right out the back door.

Okay. All right then. She texts Harvey and Van, stows the phone in her purse, and slumps back in the seat, ignoring for the moment the stacks of texts and emails waiting for her. Tax cuts, deregulation, fossil fuels, abortion, █████ carried out the conservative program to the letter. For three years she watched the billionaires grease their way into the White House and the president's favor, the Davos crowd, the Allen & Company Sun Valley crowd, a slicker bunch of suck-ups you never saw, and now it suits the billionaires to kick him to the curb. He's too divisive. "Erratic." Crude. Self-serving. All of which were fine while he was delivering for them, but now that the deliveries have been made, they, the billionaires, this class of people that collectively has the ethics of a termite colony, are ready to be rid of him.

It's not right. It is so infuriatingly not right that she can feel her eyeballs vibrating. Between office buildings filled with lawyers and lobbyists she catches glimpses of the Capitol atop its hill, as pure and white in the morning sun as a fairy-tale wedding dress. The heart swells, naturally. O Congress! Then you remember all the hacks and grifters up there, and it's like, oh, Congress. Inside her purse the phone is buzzing like a baby wolverine, gonna be a hellacious day. Near the White House they pass three distinct scrums of weepers and beaters. This is, sadly, about par for the a.m. commute. At the White House she dumps her stuff in her office and makes straight for Harvey's, where a gaggle of comms aides is playing and replaying the Rasputin ad on the big-screen TV. They are a swearing, sneering, hard-critiquing bunch; Harvey himself is nowhere to be seen. On second and third viewing Faith begins to deconstruct the craft of the thing. The liminally muted colors. The visual traction in the grain. All the artfully packaged roughage that reads as authentic.

She asks, "Do we know who made it?"

"The Gabriel Group," Chase answers. "Out of LA. They made those Subaru commercials with the driving gorilla."

A secretary sticks her head past the door and tells Faith she's wanted in the Oval. The room goes silent. Toxic clouds of ambition and envy follow her out the door. In the Oval they're briefing █████ on the

Dallas Daily article, Harvey, Van, Twister and Asher, Ellen Biddle, Stephen Miller, Jojo Parwellen, Marks Robey, Hoke Stebbins, █████ Jr. The campaign honchos are patched in via conference call, Twiss, Nadler, a few others, plus Steve Bannon belching and grunting from far-off Ibiza. There's a printout of the article on the Resolute Desk, though the president doesn't really read these days.

"How did they get all this?" he grumps. "Why didn't *we* get it? Why the hell didn't *The Washington Post* get it?"

"Mr. President—"

"The fucking *Times*, why didn't *they* get it? Those people never come through when you actually need them." He glances at the printout. "*Dallas Daily*, is that the big paper down there?"

"No sir," Asher says, "that's *The Dallas Morning News*. *The Dallas Daily*'s, uh, small. Online."

"And *they* get it? Are you kidding me?" He deigns to have another glance at the printout. "Clarence Thomas Jr., is that supposed to be some kind of joke?"

Faith waits for someone to speak, but no one dares. "He's a real person," she offers.

"Faith! Good, Faith's here. That's right, you went down there. You didn't see anything that would indicate all . . ." He flaps his hand at the printout like it's on fire.

"I did not, Mr. President. But that was three weeks ago. Apparently a lot's been happening since then?"

█████ snorts and cracks a smile. Somehow she has this disarming effect on him. "You said it, kid. Those people," he ruffles a corner of the printout, "they've been busy. Van, I want you following up on this, see if it checks out. And I wanna know what else is out there."

"Of course, Mr. President."

"You people shoulda been way out in front on this. They've got a whole army running around out there and nobody here knew a goddamn thing about it? I mean, are we *trying* to be as stupid as possible?" The campaign crew and Bannon are silent, happy to let White House staff take the grief for this one. "But *that* guy, Clarence Thomas, *he* got it. What makes him so goddamn special? What is he, is he a, a . . ." ████████ turns to Faith. "Is he really this good?"

"I barely talked to him, Mr. President. We've got him on tape if you want to see it, him interviewing Rasputin. He's older. I guess it seemed like he knew what he was doing."

"Clarence Thomas. Too much." ████████ shakes his head. "I'm gonna have to tell Clarence next time I see him. This guy, is he white? Black?"

"Black, Mr. President."

"Perfect. Jesus. Of course he is. It's almost enough to make you believe in conspiracies, two black-guy Clarence Thomases."

As he's saying this Dan'ae Jones appears in the doorway with her folding stool and makeup kit. ████████ blinks, goes blank. Did he just say something racist? Dan'ae smoothly makes her entrance and gets to work. Staff pull out their phones and retreat while the film crew trundles in and begins setting up. Faith gets an earbud off the equipment trolley and taps in. She stands off to the side in ready mode, portfolio clasped to her chest, silenced cell phone in her pocket.

Carl, Kendra murmurs, *two steps left, let's get a sharper profile this morning. Manny, watch out for that glare over POTUS's shoulder. Uh, Kyle? Hello?*

Yo.

Is there a problem?

Nothing that can't be fixed.

Kendra rolls her eyes toward Faith. These guys. *Phone call?*

Phone call, Faith confirms.

Fireworks?

Could be.

Hear that, guys? Be on the ready.

Staff hustle in and out with their faces in their phones. It's a wonder nobody collides. Harvey meanders over to Faith, and she taps off her earbud. They confer in barely audible hums.

"More ads due to drop today."

"Great. Who gets to tell *him*?"

"They made big buys for all the networks. Cable too. So, uhm, you okay?"

She meets his eye, and her insides tootle like a merry-go-round. "Lovely. You?"

Harvey can't help smiling. He turns his face to the wall. "Amazing. I've never had, uh, you know. Not like that."

"I'm flattered."

Hot whispering in the Oval, naughty naughty. Not like it's a historical first. A clandestine office affair, Faith has learned, makes for invigorating endorphin blasts throughout your day. The loaded eye contact. The secret hallway smiles. Way better than coffee for pumping you up, almost as good as a raise. Harvey moves off, and she checks her news feed. Russian troops are doing maneuvers on the Estonian border, student-debt defaults have reached an all-time high, and eight percent fewer Americans had health insurance last year than the year before. "Okay," █████ says as Dan'ae folds up her stool and withdraws, "testing testing one two three, we're good? So we're gonna be talking to Rasputin about the ad that ran last night, that ad, looks like some people are really wanting him to run, like I haven't done enough for the country! And those people, a lot of them friends and supporters of mine for so many years, and it's disgusting, frankly. Disgraceful. No loyalty, those people. And look, I love Grishka more than anybody, why else would we be bringing him on board like we're doing? Just a special, special guy in so many ways, but we've gotta keep our eyes on the prize. This election's way too important to be messing around with amateur candidates. We've got enough pygmies in the field as it is, I mean, anybody who watched that debate last night, how pitiful was that? You see why I don't waste my time. And their ratings, oh my God, so pathetic their ratings, they—what? He's on the line? Already? Okay folks, here we go." █████ punches into his desk phone. "Grishka my friend, howya doing this morning?"

"I am well, Mr. President, thank you. I hope you are well in every way."

"Top of the world, my friend, top of the world. Listen, I'm gonna get right to it, we need to talk about that ad that ran last night."

"Yes, Mr. President. They just showed me." The wrestler sounds subdued this morning, weary, pooped. Maybe he just rolled out of bed, or perhaps it's an attack of the famous Russian melancholia. "This is the first time I am seeing this thing."

"Really! Interesting. So you didn't know anything about it?"

"I did not, Mr. President."

████ surveys his staff, shrugs.

"What about Charlie, is Charlie there?"

"I'm here, Mr. President."

"Did you know anything?"

"I certainly did not, sir."

████ screws up his face and mouths *liar* for the cameras.

"Well, guys, what we're hearing is some people, big money people, and a lot of these people are friends, used to be friends of mine until about an hour ago, they wanna use Grishka to stab me in the back is what it basically amounts to. Political assassination by my so-called friends, how low is that? And Grishka, buddy, I just don't think you're the kind of guy who wants to be a part of anything like that."

"You are right, Mr. President. Rasputin is not that kind of guy."

"But listen, you must've been hearing about this draft thing. It's been going around ever since our first rally."

"I hear some little thing, Mr. President, here and there some people saying Rasputin should run for president. But it is so silly. I never pay attention."

"I know you don't, Grishka, you're a stand-up guy. So look, this is how we're gonna handle it. My people are gonna write up a statement for you saying you disavow the whole thing, the ads, fundraising, all done without your knowledge and consent, and you're a hundred percent for ████, no ifs ands or buts. And you're calling on this whole draft business to stop."

████ pauses, and there's a breathless moment when Rasputin says nothing. *Steady*, Kendra murmurs to the crew. ████ leans over the phone like he might eat it.

"Grishka, you with me? That work for you?"

"Of course, Mr. President," comes the answer, and everyone exhales. "Rasputin is one hundred percent for that."

"Good! Good, 'cause we've got a really special thing going here. You've seen the polls, right? You and me are going all the way, buddy. Stick with me and the sky's the limit for you. I'm not going to be president forever."

"Oh Mr. President, it hurts me to hear that. Let us imagine some new and wonderful thing, first forever president in US history. Why not President ██████████?"

"Hanh, I like that. I like the way you think, friend. The way these plasma treatments are going you never know, I have to say I'm feeling better than ever!"

█████ relaxes with several minutes of wrestling chat, Rasputin verbally nodding along as the president airs his views. I agree, Mr. President, Ice Man is looking strong. Yes for sure, Mr. President, Yukon's woodchipper move is totally awesome. Everything is goodness and light between them when they click off. █████ sits back and brays:

"Has there ever been a bigger lying sack of shit than Charlie Cupps? Bullshit he didn't know about that ad, I bet he's right in the middle of it. It's like Elvis, Elvis's manager, you know, the guy, the fat guy, whatsisname in the movie."

"Tom Hanks," says Asher.

"No! The guy he played!"

"Colonel Parker," says Twister.

"Colonel Parker! That guy, what a fraud. Cupps, that whole RINO backstabber crowd, they're using Grishka to get at me and here he is such a totally sweet guy, but politically? He's just too trusting. Not in a bad way, just very spiritual, head in the clouds and all the Bible quoting and reading, I get it, that's what makes him so special, the healing and all the positive effects he has on people, but he's got a lot to learn about politics. Wrestling's tough, no question, but it's *Romper Room* compared to what I do every day. But he'll learn. No question he's a pretty bright guy."

Van calls an end to the shoot. The president has a meeting, something about fighter jets and Israel. "I've got twenty Jews waiting for me in the Cabinet Room," ████████ quips on his way out. Faith hangs around and confers with Kendra while the crew packs up, then heads to her office. Online and in the news Rasputin is trending, a classic hockey-stick curve that gives her shivers. She checks her whiteboards. Later this morning they're filming Ellen Biddle doing her daily dozens with the press. The afternoon will be for roaming, spot interviews, staying loose for whatever comes, but at the moment something's nagging her. She pulls up Belinda/ScrubGrrrl's email with the *Dallas Daily* link and notes the story was posted at 5:17 this morning. The email followed four minutes later. Like she knew it was coming. Like she was waiting for it.

Such a strange person, this Scrub Girl; this would-be stabber of faculty wives. Harvey taps at her half-open door and enters. There are moments, and this is one, when their affair seems utterly surreal to Faith. She sees the worry in his face, and as a mini-test of her emotions she pretends he's about to break up with her.

"Thoughts."

"About?"

"The Russian."

"Ah, the Russian." She ponders for a moment. "Did he or did he not know, and when did he not know it. I guess the only thing that really matters is he says he's on board. You?"

"I think we caught this tiger by the tail, now we're going to have to ride it."

"Could get wild."

"I think we're already there."

"But Harvey, you notice how logy he sounded? Like slow, off. Flat. Like he's coming down with the flu."

"Well, now that you mention it."

"Almost like he was drugged, except he doesn't do drugs."

"And people never lie about that."

"Maybe we got him up too early. Or maybe it's something else. Like, I don't know. Dread? Guilt?" She hesitates, as if saying the thing out loud will make it true, the truth that's been building inside her head but couldn't prevail until the moment of speaking it. "It's out there for him. Can't you feel it? All he has to do is reach out and take it. If it was you, the power was dangling right there in front of you, your name's on everybody's lips and all you had to do was reach out and take it—wouldn't you take it? Wouldn't you? Who wouldn't take it?"

14

He was well into researching the dark-money story when the audio file showed up. It came naked, no names, dates, places, just a fuzzy recording of two guys talking on the phone. White guys, vulgarians; they took form in Clarence's mind as degenerate former frat boys. After his first listen he emailed the sender, but the address was already defunct. He ran the file through the transcription app, reviewed and revised for errors, and in due course had the transcript.

GUY 1: —don't allow cell phones in the house.
GUY 2: What?
G1: Stop saying that, Christ, you sound like a fucking dick. Whot? Whot?
G2: Well, it's just weird. No cell phones, why would they do that?
G1: Security, I guess. Or maybe to keep people from videoing all his chicks.
G2: Ohhh. Yeah?
G1: Place is dripping in it.
G2: Prime?
G1: In-sane.

G2: We shoulda been wrestlers, man. Or rock stars.

[unintelligible]

G1: —trying to go all Jesus on me and I said save it, Charlie, take it somewhere else. 'Cause I know to the fucking penny how much you're skimming.

G2: I bet that shut him up.

G1: He didn't have much to say after that.

G2: He's a twerpy little shit.

G1: He's a fucking iguana is what he is. We'll drop him easy enough when the time comes. Wouldn't mind boning his assistant, though.

G2: I think you need to get laid, man. That divorce is starting to eat your brain.

G1: My brain is fine, asshole—

[unintelligible]

G1: —you can tell Wichita the levels are good for now. In two weeks we'll have a lot better feel for where this is going. If it's going. And if it does we'll need—

G2: Right.

G1: They know the ramp-up is coming. But right now we're getting plenty of burn for the buck.

G2: No worries. I haven't heard any complaints on that end.

G1: Well I would fucking hope not, considering it's their project. We'll need to start moving on Wisconsin and Michigan in the next—

[unintelligible]

G1: —DC on Wednesday. So set it up for Thursday, and I want Myron there. Chuck, Rita, everybody, this is a capital call. Tell them to bring their checkbooks.

G2: I was thinking briefcases.

G1: Funny.

He doesn't waste time trying to figure out who these people are. It's noise, chatter, essentially useless except for tone and attitude, the basic angle of attack. The lion's share of his material comes from non-sexy open sources: tax records, corporate filings, public interest websites. He finds enough people willing to talk, mostly fools or insiders with an axe to grind. He's thinking two or three more days' work will do it, but Renfro calls at 9:30 on the night of the debate.

"You watching this?" he asks.

"No." Clarence is reading Pauli Murray, as it happens. "Should I be?"

Renfro sends him a link for the ad, and as soon as Clarence sees it he knows he'll be posting before the sun comes up. He spends the rest of the night cranking words and emailing drafts to Renfro, and around three in the morning they hash it out over the phone, writer and editor butting heads like two punched-out boxers in the final rounds. Neither man is ready to think of himself as old, but they are definitely too old for all-nighters. The article goes live in the darkest predawn when law-abiding, clock-punching America is still snug in bed. Clarence flops out on the sofa and naps, is up with the first wave of leaf blowers on his street. Makes coffee, reads the papers, waters the plants. He's still in his robe when Renfro texts that producers from CNN and *The Rachel Maddow Show* are calling.

Once again Texas's best little online paper scooped the bigs! Mainstream's mistake was treating Rasputin as an absurdist sideshow; as if American politics hadn't gone full tinpot Dada some time ago, a nation of leaders with kitchen implements for hands and toasters for heads. Renfro, borderline giddy, herds the interviews Clarence's way. He talks to KGNU in Boulder, Radio Pacifica in San Fran, KUT in Austin, WAMC in upstate New York. A decent night's sleep and a clear head would be nice, but for twenty-seven years he mainly talked for a living, along the way his mouth grew a brain of its own. Late morning, Renfro and his tech-savvy grandson Drew arrive and set up the laptop in front of Clarence's most photogenic bookshelf. Is he nervous? Nah. Nervier by far were city council meetings with red-faced "citizen activists" howling for his head. At a little after twelve he sits down with the bookshelf at his back and goes live with Colleen Maguire of CNN, a stern, strong-jawed gunner with the most lustrous hair in television news. She ticks through her questions, he rattles off answers. It's not so different from being interviewed by cops.

Nelson has a family text thread going. Uncle Key hittin it nationwide! Everybody check out Maguire At Midday, Rachel Maddow tonight. Hey Key when you going on Fox?

Not likely, but if invited, sure. He would be delighted to scorch the circuits of Caucasia's white-supremacist news source of choice. He does more radio, and during the lulls gets out his notepad and makes some calls. It occurs to him—why only now?—that a freeze-up could strike while he's on the air. Well why not, and how would that work, exactly? Would, say, Rachel Maddow and her studio crew and all her millions of viewers freeze up while his own little reality puttered along? He takes short naps on the recliner. He puts on his windbreaker and walks laps around the block. All afternoon he's getting emails from old friends he hasn't heard from in a while.

> Just saw your coon ass talking on the Commie News Network. Suprised nobody's iced you yet.

> Hey fake Clarence Thomas you lost your election and now you're on CNN. I guess affirmative action is alive and well.

> You still ugly as dog shit.

Nelson brings in Italian for dinner. Clarence's sisters Dolly and Julianne swoop in and head straight for his bedroom closet to confer over his wardrobe for tonight. Renfro and Drew show up at 7:30 and review the setup, same bookshelf and camera angle as before. The show wants him on deck as of 8:00 CDT. "Don't blow it," Renfro says, trying and failing for deadpan, he can't stop grinning over the monster numbers the *Daily*'s clocking. "Think of all the groupies," Nelson says, which gets fierce shushes from his mother and Aunt Julianne. Clarence remembers to worry about a potential freeze-up, but he's too tired to give it more than a mental shrug. At eight sharp he banishes the entourage to a back bedroom. At 8:04 the tyro producer in New York gives him a thirty-second warning, then fifteen, five, and they're live, Rachel Maddow's famous face filling his computer screen. First thing after the lead-in she cheerily addresses the elephant in the room.

"So Mr. Thomas, sir, just to clarify here at the outset, just in case *annnny*-body out there is wondering—you are not the Clarence Thomas who sits on the Supreme Court, correct?"

"That's correct, Rachel, I am not." Her people told him to call her Rachel. "Justice Thomas and I just happen to share the same name."

"Okay! Now that we've got *that* out of the way." Then it's on to the seismic shift that seems to be happening in the Grand Old Party. She lobs him peppy questions about dark-money networks and the Tea Party antecedent, and the slimy underground world of campaign finance generally. She marks the many familiar names he's turned up and the conundrum of how the Draft Rasputin movement got this far while flying under the radar.

"What's your sense of how much of this effort is being driven by principle? A basic objection to the idea of *any* president being allowed to serve more than two terms."

"Well, I certainly heard that expressed among the people I talked to. But my sense is it's much more about █████ himself, the fact that a lot of folks are just plain tired of the guy."

"'█████ fatigue,' as you call it in your article."

"'█████ fatigue,' correct. So he's already wearing pretty thin, then along comes this intriguing new figure seemingly out of nowhere, and as far as a lot of folks in the party are concerned, he checks all the boxes."

"Right! And I can't help wondering, and I think a lot of people are wondering as well, just what to make of the entire Rasputin presentation. Whether Mr. Rasputin, the *wrestler* Rasputin, who, as we mentioned earlier, changed his name from Patrick Walsh Strickland early in his wrestling career—well, let me back up and note that you've spent time with him, you did an interview with him last month that was published in *The Dallas Daily*. And in that interview he insists—very emphatically it seems!—that he *really, is*, Rasputin, the famous Russian monk who was born in Siberia in I believe 1867, and died, was murdered, in Saint Petersburg in 1916. And that would be Saint Petersburg, Russia, not Florida, just to clarify. So my question to you, sir, goes to what we might call baseline reality. Because if he *really* thinks on any level that he's the actual Rasputin, I think that should be setting off all kinds of alarm bells."

Clarence nods. Right to the guts of it, good for her. "Well, we've got an interesting cognitive puzzle here, no question. What exactly is the psychology of the situation. Maybe the best way I can express my sense of it is, he gives a very convincing performance of a man who really believes he's the historical Rasputin."

"Uhhho-kay! So let's—just to unpack this a bit further, I guess we could say what you're describing is a performance within a performance? He's performing the role of a person who—oh wow. I just flashed on those Russian doll figurines, you know, you open it up and there's an identical smaller doll inside, and you open that up and there's a smaller one, and on and on. Anyway," she smiles and resets, "extraneous digressions aside, I'd like to dig a little deeper into this rather fascinating territory. And I'm wondering, based on your time with him, if you feel like there's possibly an element of delusion, of loss of reality, on the part of the performer here?"

"Based on the time I've spent with him, I would say no. In fact he strikes me as more dialed into reality than a lot of folks. I guess the best way I could describe it is to say that he is fully, and I mean *fully*, committed to the role he's taken on."

"The role, just to be clear, of a man who *really* believes he's Rasputin."

"That is correct."

"Interesting. Okay then!" She appends to this a run-on giggle that leaves her slightly breathless. "And just to add another layer to all this, there are quite obvious national security concerns raised by the six years he spent in Russia, six years that we really don't know much about."

"It's a serious issue, Rachel, no question. And as far as I can determine, nobody inside or outside the US government has much of a sense of his activities there, other than his own account of those years as a time of religious pilgrimage."

"His time at the monastery and so forth."

"Right, the Nikolaev Monastery. But even that's pretty vague."

"I have to say, sir, I'm finding all of this a bit surreal! That you and I are having this conversation about a potential contender for the presidency of the United States."

"I'm with you, Rachel. But this is the world we live in."

"It is indeed, sir. Strange days indeed."

"So it's incumbent on us to keep our wits about us."

She sputters, does a little corkscrew twist of the head. "I'm with you there! Absolutely, let's all hang onto our wits for all they're worth. And as long as we're delving into the strange and surreal, as it were, do you have any insight into his interactions with weeping-sickness victims?"

"Rachel, I do not. I'm as baffled by the whole business as anybody."

"I appreciate your candor, Mr. Thomas. And in turn I'll say what truly baffles me is the way he's garnered so much support, major donor support, without anyone seeming to know all that much about his politics. We know he's an avid supporter of the president, at least up to this point, and he professes to have strong Christian faith. But beyond that, most of what we know is in your interview that I alluded to a moment ago. And I would urge all our viewers to go to *The Dallas Daily* website and see for yourselves, but Mr. Rasputin made several statements in your interview that I think are worth highlighting here. Such as, in your interview he calls for, quote"—

The words appear on-screen to the right of Maddow's head.

—"'a grand alliance of the US and Russia, the world's two great Christian superpowers, to re-create Christ's kingdom on earth.' He also professed the belief that, quote"—

Again the words appear on-screen.

—"'homosexuality is a sin,' and, further, the movement for equal rights for LGBTQ people in Western societies is, quote, 'a suicide of civilization. In basic biological terms,' he goes on, 'if we are not reproducing according to the biblical model of Adam and Eve, man and woman, mother and child, we are dooming Western civilization to extinction.' And he goes on to talk about how recent generations of American men have, quote, 'been belittled and demeaned just for being men.'

"I also want to touch on—can we have the next panel, please—here we see he espouses the view that Satan is, quote, 'a distinct, physical presence here among us on earth,' and 'our spiritual war with Satan is quickly moving onto the material plane.' And he castigates Christians who are, quote, 'too timid to take back the kingdom of heaven by force.'

"And I could go on, there's so much here to absorb and digest, but just looking at all this in light of the performative aspect you've described, I'm wondering again how we're supposed to think about this. Are these statements part and parcel of the performance, as you've described it, or should we, or to what extent should we, accept these statements as reflective of the man's sincerely held beliefs?"

"Right. Well, your question's well taken, but I'm not sure the distinction matters. It could be that for our purposes, the persona, the character, is the most genuine thing about him. So if Rasputin, the persona, and I put that in quotes, 'Rasputin,' believes in something, that might be all that really matters. You remember how we started out all those years ago with the art of the deal, but maybe that's evolved over time into the art of the persona. Or maybe that's what it was all along, not so much a deal as a persona, a character, an act. An act that's so effective it's capable of bending reality to its will. And so reality ends up being just another aspect of the act."

"Whew! Wow. All right then! Again I have to say my head's sort of spinning. Okay, so as we know Mr. Rasputin released a statement earlier today endorsing Mr. ████████ and pledging his full support for the president, and he urged all Americans to, quote, 'pray for President

█████ and for our country.' But pro-Rasputin ads have been airing all day, and we're getting reports that the president might be just a *liiiit-tle* hopping mad for what the statement didn't say. That Mr. Rasputin didn't come out and explicitly disavow the draft movement. He didn't tell his supporters to cease and desist."

"Right. We may be having another stand back and stand by moment."

"Exactly, my friend. A non-disavowal disavowal, you might say."

"The people in the draft movement I've been talking to, they're still at it. They're working. Nobody's closed up shop and gone home."

"So it's your sense that this is all still very much in play?"

"Very much so, Rachel. I think if Rasputin really wants to stop the movement, all he has to do is say so in no uncertain terms."

"Which he hasn't," Maddow points out, and turns coy. "Not really. Sort of? Maybe? Still waiting for that other shoe to drop. But you mentioned the conversations you've been having with Rasputin supporters. So might we assume you're still on the story?"

"I am, Rachel. Still very—"

At that instant it crystallizes fully formed in his mind, the awful question he'll have to track in the coming weeks, months, perhaps—God help us—years. Is █████ the lightweight, the opportunistic, pick-and-choose fascist versus the hardcore true believer that Rasputin might be? █████ as precursor and prelude, and the brutal detention camps, the federal militias, administrative detention and hack judges and strategic street violence, they are all merely opening acts for the main event, the coming of the heavyweight champ of the world. That it took him so long to form the question makes Clarence want to slap his own face.

"—much on the story," he continues, his speaking self staying the course.

"Great, that's great to hear. And if we may, we'd love to have you back on the show as this story develops."

"That would be my pleasure, Rachel."

"Mr. Thomas, thank you for joining us this evening, and thank you for all the great reporting. You and your colleagues at *The Dallas Daily* are much to be commended."

"I do appreciate that."

And out. He sits back. Cheers and applause erupt from the back bedroom. Not bad, is his sense of it, but he's not satisfied. Not with so much work still to do.

15

This year's WrestleFest at the Indiana Convention Center in Indianapolis is a kaleidoscopic, multiday extravaganza featuring merch sales, autograph sessions, interviews, a sound stage, a car show, a gun show, a pop-up casino courtesy of the Pokagon Band of the Potawatomi Nation, and such a mother-loving load of actual wrestling that it takes five rings to hold it all. Arriving on day one for his contractual appearance and autograph session, Rasputin pauses on the red carpet to acknowledge the small army of political press on hand.

"My friends! I had no idea so many of you are wrestling fans."

Feathery chuckles waft into the hard city air. "Are you running for president?" someone shouts.

"Guys, I am here for wrestling. Wrestling only today, no politics."

"Have you spoken to President █████?"

"The president and I have not spoken in several days."

"Are you still interested in being his running mate?"

"Wrestling, guys, please, that is why we are here today. But because you came all this way to speak to me, I will say a few words. First, I have so much respect and admiration for our amazing President █████. He is a great man, great president, for sure one of the greatest businessmen of all time. For him to consider me to be his running mate, I tell you with all my heart this would be the honor of my life. But I must say also, I do not accept to be insulted by any man. Not president, king, senator, rich man, poor man—no, I do not accept this from anyone. We are all formed in God's image, does the Bible not tell us this? Each with his portion of dignity and self-respect, this is the human feeling of God's spirit in each of us. President █████'s harsh words of the past several days, saying perhaps I have deceived him, I am associating with shameful plots—no, this I cannot accept. I cannot accept a relationship demeaning of dignity and self-respect. And so for me to continue down this path with the president, I must humbly ask to receive a statement of apologies from him."

Twenty minutes later, appearing in the rotunda of the New Hampshire capitol with his state reelection team, the president is asked if an apology will be forthcoming. He glowers, turns the hot pink of a candy valentine. "He said that? He wants *me* to apologize?" At the next stop, Philadelphia, █████ gets off an impromptu rant about loyalty and betrayal and "scum of the earth backstabbers," although the only proper name he invokes is that of Julius Caesar. Watching from the wings, Faith texts Harvey, Can't somebody rein him in? Harvey is onstage with the entourage, buried deep enough in the pack that he can check his phone. No, actually, he texts back. You're welcome to try.

Today they're hopscotching around the country's northeast quadrant, doing "boutique" events to showcase the campaign's local efforts. Getting back to grassroots, summoning the scrappy underdog spirit of 2016. The small-ball approach may also have something to do with the special virulence with which the Weeps are striking the president's events; it seems the widening █████-Rasputin rift has triggered something fragile in the MAGA psyche. They're on Air Force One, en route to Pittsburgh, when the █████ story breaks. Reports have it that the First Lady was seen in Indianapolis around midday entering the JW Marriott through a rear service entrance, the hotel, coincidentally, where Rasputin is staying. With "Where's █████?" trending on social media, Ellen Biddle warpaths to the back of the plane to inform the press that the rumors are "sick," "absurd," and "totally unfounded," and for them to even consider reporting this garbage would be the lowest form of tabloid journalism.

She concludes briskly: "The president kissed the First Lady goodbye when he left this morning, and he will kiss her hello tonight when he returns. And I don't want to hear another word about it."

It would seem easy enough to snuff the rumors, but hours pass with the First Lady nowhere in sight. A somber, unnervingly tight-lipped [redacted] truncates the Pittsburgh event to a presidential hit and run. Faith can feel the pressure building. Loss of face of any kind is anathema to him, and sex is the fragile undercarriage of his macho soul.

I smell a setup, Faith texts Harvey en route to Buffalo. He's in the forward cabin with senior staff, she's in steerage with the peons.

Harvey: Discussing. Def a possibility.
Faith: Easy to solve. If she's at WH?

Harvey doesn't answer. Not good. She tries a different tack.

Faith: Arguendo she's in I'apolis. You know who's leaking this shit.
Harvey: Right.
Faith: Or even if she's not.
Harvey: Same difference.

[redacted], Faith will soon have occasion to reflect, is both the smartest man in the world and the dumbest man in the world. He takes the bait. Can't help himself. At his western New York campaign headquarters in downtown Buffalo, speaking to a packed house of campaign staff, precinct captains, door knockers, and local and national press, he begins reasonably enough by thanking staff and volunteers. "The best people, only the very best people work for us," the president says. Then he slags on the Fed for the high inflation "that's making us look so bad" and simultaneously for its refusal to lower interest rates. "Are they against us?" he wonders out loud. "The

Fed's not supposed to get involved in politics, but I'm not so sure, and we know, we all know what the deep state is capable of, and the Fed's as deep as it gets. Those people will do anything to sabotage us, including murder."

Heads snap back. Did the president just accuse the Fed of murder?

"That's right, folks, people that you've never heard of, people that are in the dark shadows pulling the strings, controlling the streets. I could tell you about those people, and the planes, that's part of it. The dark uniform guys, they're on the planes in the cities looking down on us, circling." At this half the crowd looks up. "It's all happening right now, that's what we're up against, and the people you thought were your friends, turns out sometimes they're not! And we're seeing it right now, we're seeing it with the, you know, you know who I'm talking about." ██████ puffs himself up, dangles his arms gorilla-style, rocks side to side and clonks his feet. Faith hears titters, a few gasps. Did he really just do that? "This guy," ██████ resumes, "I don't know what he is, maybe another one of their puppets, who knows. Was he even born here, we aren't even sure about that! 'Cause we're hearing things lately that really make you wonder about this guy."

Shit shit shit shit Faith hisses under her breath. The president's best bridge to reelection might be this very instant going up in smoke. She notes the preternatural focus of the press, no yawns or checking watches, no dicking around with phones, they are fully dialed into the moment. Lined three-deep along the wall at the president's back, senior staff are as poker-faced as prisoners facing a firing squad. Then somewhere amid the crowd, a woman wails. It is the cry of ultimate pain, a severed leg, a stab to the heart, then it's a whole chorus of weeping, wailing campaign volunteers, and a melee erupts. "See!" ██████ shouts, clinging to the podium as Secret Service swarm him. "See! Sabotage! What'd I tell you! Get those fakers outta here!" Cops and security move in before it gets too far out of hand. The weepers take a few punches, and there's some semi-comic sumo-style grappling and shoving. As these things go, it's no big deal, but every flail, punch, sob, and shove is captured on video, shortly to be available on the World Wide Web.

Is it tragedy? Farce? Both at once? Any way you cut it, not a great look for the campaign. On the flight back to DC, Faith sets her phone on the tray table, plugs in her earbuds, and watches for as long as it takes to confirm that Buffalo was a disaster. After a while she hunkers over the tray table and pulls up the AWW app. There's tape of Rasputin doing warm-up remarks earlier today, standing center ring in his shaman suit and coolly describing the annihilation he will visit on his opponent for tomorrow, Montana Mike. The fans eat it up, and shots of the crowd show there's a fanny in every seat, a full house just to see him talking trash in his Sunday best. Then she gets it. He's doing politics by not doing politics. Which is: Genius! In an era where politics polls lower in public opinion than hemorrhoids and head lice, this might be the only politics possible.

As soon as they touch down she texts Harvey.

Faith: Just watched Rasputin being brilliant in Indianapolis.
Harvey: Not what I need to hear.
Faith: He's running for president. By not running.
Harvey: If you say so.
Faith: I do say so and he's kicking our butt. What now?
Harvey: I have to get home.
Faith: I mean the campaign.

For several seconds her screen pulses, dot-dot-dot.

Harvey: Beats me.

~~~

They've been sleeping together long enough for Faith to start asking herself what she's doing. Okay, so what she's doing is messing around. Having a fling. Getting into a guy who seems very into her. For his part, Harvey's on the verge of tears sometimes. Lying under her, overwhelmed by the sheer epithelial shock of all her parts exposed, he swags
~~~

his head side to side and declares, "It's never been like this. Not with anybody."

"And son," she vows, "it never will be again."

She can lay on the Texas thick when it suits her. That he's riddled with Catholic guilt goes without saying. He's at pains to inform her that he still loves his wife. Their marriage is, well, they've been married twenty-one years, their marriage is old enough to walk into a bar and order a drink. And Harvey works *so hard*, that would be a strain on even the strongest marriage, but it's not like Maggie doesn't understand the zeal he brings to the job. She understands him fine, she's just not much interested.

"This is probably the worst thing I've ever done in my life," he tells Faith one night.

"Okay." She wonders if he expects her to apologize.

"It also makes me happier than pretty much anything. Except for my kids, of course."

Of course. They don't talk about the future beyond the next rendezvous, always at her place, evenings or weekend afternoons. She's always the one to prompt the planning; he's too squeamish. Evenings, if he's heading back to the White House, she'll bustle around the kitchen and fix him "breakfast," a wicked twist on domestic tranquility. It's never occurred to her to cook for a man before, and sometimes she tries to imagine what a future with Harvey would look like, a thought experiment that yields only hazy MLS thumbnails of two-story houses in the suburbs. No. Not what she wants. And yet. That he's so solid and low-key exerts a sly erotic appeal. Rock-steady, this guy, and despite the age difference they're scarily compatible. Their sweet spot is lounging in bed after sex and flipping around the news channels. Couple of political nerds. They're thus arranged one night when he says he has a confession to make.

"All right." Oh God, here comes another one.

"Sometimes at night, when I can't sleep, I'll go downstairs and watch old episodes of *Nashville* on my computer."

"What!" She bursts out laughing. "Why would you even do that?"

"It just makes me happy. You were so darn cute on that show. And the way you sang . . ." He trails off for a moment. "You were so good, Faith. I mean it. You've got a gift. You didn't have to stop singing just because they cut you."

"I'm aware."

"So why . . ."

"It was all such bullshit. All the mind games and lying and playing favorites, how good you were didn't have anything to do with it. You shouldn't do that to teenagers. Or anybody. But teenagers especially."

"The way they brought your father into it was pretty unconscionable."

"They should go to jail for that. My trust fund was paying out three hundred thousand a year, contingent on the NDA, but if we say that man's name it all goes away, for what? So the dumbass show can win the ratings that week, and we're getting fifteen thousand a season, and that's for the two of us. So, uh, let's see, three hundred thousand versus fifteen? I was young and dumb, but I wasn't *that* dumb."

"I assume your mother was on board with that."

"Well, for a while it was an issue. Until I told her I'd cut myself on camera if she broke the NDA. And she knew I meant it."

"That's brutal."

"Basic survival is how I saw it."

"You had to grow up fast."

"I guess so. Bunch of psychos we were dealing with, and those were the so-called adults. Just completely awful people."

"But you can still sing. For yourself. They didn't take that away from you."

She shakes her head. "That's all gone. Like Santa Claus, teddy bears. All in the past."

He sighs and takes her hand, gives it a gentle squeeze. "I think I understand you a little better now."

For no reason at all her eyes squirt freshets of fat, sloppy tears. Not once has she ever cried over the show, and suddenly her eyes are dishing it up like a soup kitchen.

“Oh gosh, Faith, I’m so sorry. I didn’t mean to bring up all these painful things for you.”

“It’s okay. It’s nothing. I’m being an idiot.”

He huckles up close and they have a good cuddle while Laura Ingraham jaws about the immigration invasion. It goes on longer than it should, the crying. Trying to hold it in probably makes it worse, but she feels pleasantly spent when it’s done, and dozes off in a post–pity party buzz. Barely rouses when Harvey unwinds from her and heads for the shower. Twenty minutes later he’s toweling off when she joins him in the bathroom.

“How you doing?”

“Fiiiiine,” she singsongs, and snuggles up to him. He wraps his arms around her, and she’s like, ahhhhh. Right now she loves him so much that she would gladly empty out her bank account for him.

“Rmrumphn-qmmlfth,” she mumbles into his shoulder.

“What?”

She de-suctions her mouth from his skin. He goes all pie-faced when she tells him who her father is.

“Oh. *Oh.* My God, Faith.” Suddenly his eyes get very busy. “You know what? I can totally see it now.”

Work has never been this intense. Drama is there for the filming with every walk down the hall. The Rasputin Effect is comparable to, say, a cyclone or volcano making a surprise guest appearance on *Survivor.* Kendra, producer Bob, everyone in LA says they have the makings of the best season ever, the show’s a shoo-in for slews of Emmys when awards season rolls around. From far-off Texas, meanwhile, Christie calls and texts her daughter multiple times a day urging her to *do* something. “Why can’t they just get along?” she pleads. “We love █████ and Rasputin both the same, they shouldn’t make us have to choose. You need to get in there and talk some sense into the president!”

Faith gets it, the heartrending trauma of the base, the pangs of catharsis as they come to grips with a mad love that may have run its course. Someone new and exciting has entered their lives, and they can’t help falling hard for Rasputin. He is the Super ██████, the fresh young thing who offers all the kicks of the old model and none of the hassles. Still, it's hard. Wrenching. Breakups always are, especially when love and loyalty are still in play. Lolling in bed one night, Faith and Harvey catch the Reverend Jenkins Gilchrist on Fox rationalizing the situation in biblical terms. "████████████ has been God's battering ram against the deep state of Babylon, and we praise him and love him for it. He has prepared the way. He has sanctified the path. The president is our modern-day John the Baptist, and he will always have a special place in our hearts."

"Okay," Faith says to the TV, "so if ██████ is John the Baptist, that makes Rasputin . . ."

"A man of the cloth should know better than to talk like that," Harvey grumbles.

Sometimes their pillow talk wends around to bio-dad. This is new, having someone besides Christie to discuss this major thread of her life with, but by long habit she's reticent. Have never met the man, no. Never reached out to him, her half siblings, nobody. Classic bastard-in-exile story, and is she angry sometimes? Bitter? Who wouldn't be, but $400k a year (the trust corpus keeps growing) somewhat soothes the sting.

"He's a huge supporter of the president," Harvey observes.

"I'm aware." She waits a beat. "I know what you're thinking."

"What am I thinking?"

"That's how I got the job."

"What?"

"Signals were sent. Winks and nudges. Back-channel stuff."

"I don't think that's the case at all. And I'm the one who hired you, remember?"

THEY HAVEN'T SLEPT TOGETHER IN MONTHS screams the *New York Post* headline, quoting an unnamed White House source on the state of the First Couple's marriage. The Indianapolis rumors have yet to be resolved. Where was ███████ that day? The █████s aren't talking. Rasputin asserts perfect innocence in the matter. Teffy

Birnbaum, ██████'s spokesperson, issues a peckish one-line statement: "The First Lady is under no obligation to account to the press for every single second of every single day." A photo floating around the internet purports to show the First Lady cloaked in a trench coat, head scarf, and enormous sunglasses entering the JW Marriott guest garage on foot.

Leaving the White House one night, Faith looks up and sees red lightning over the Lincoln Memorial, three identical jagged streaks in a row like the tines of a Salvador Dalí fork. When she pulls out her phone to summon an Uber the lightning's in there, jabbing her screen as if trying to break through. At scaled-down, heavily screened campaign events—the Weeps are more of a pain in the ass than ever—██████ fulminates against false prophets, foreign agents, faithless ex-friends. Predicts death and destruction if he's not reelected. An online chaos campaign against the Draft Rasputin movement collapses in chaos. A clumsy attempt at a birther smear gets even less traction, undercut by the fact that the president's own lawyers established Rasputin's natural-born-citizen status months ago. Each new day brings breaking stories about another big donor contributing to the draft movement. Evangelicals seem to be domino-ing for Rasputin, and he polls robust favorables among the black and Latino demographics. The 538 average of polls puts ██████ and the wrestler in a statistical dead heat, with the pygmies barely a blip on the horizon.

Is he running? Will he run? Rasputin plays it cool. He wrestles. He trains. He posts on social media about wrestling and training. "I see a new awakening in America," he says in a brief live appearance on Erin Burnett's *OutFront*. "America is rising from its long sleep, coming to a new and blessèd awareness of God the Father."

But are you running?

"I am praying. I reflect and I pray. Of one thing I am certain, we must put God's word at the center of our politics." And never an unkind word for ██████, Faith notes. Sean Hannity devotes an entire show to Rasputin, a sugary, soft-focus hagiography illuminating the life, the legend, the man, narrated in throbbing fanboy tones by Hannity himself. █████ demands equal time, is rebuffed. The next night he sics National Security Brigades and Rapid Support Forces on a Draft Rasputin rally in Chicago's Grant Park. The ensuing violence leaves two civilians dead and scores injured, and the next day a third rally goer turns up dead in NSB custody. Within hours the draft movement has collected enough signatures to put their man on the ballot in six early primary states. The relevant forms and filings are hand-delivered to Southlake, and there they await the potential candidate's signature.

"Have you ever lost?" Faith asks Harvey one night.

"Sure. Plenty." They're twined about each other in postcoital bliss, the blue firelight of the TV flickering over them. "You do politics, you lose elections. That's just part of the deal."

"I've never lost," she says, idly diddling his left nipple.

"Do it long enough, you will."

"What's it like?"

"What's it *like*? Well, awful."

"Awful, how."

"Well, like someone died. A good friend. Maybe not your best friend, but close."

"And?"

"Well, you go into deep depression. You obsess over all the things you should or shouldn't have done. But it passes. You get over it. After a while you pick yourself up off the floor and sign on for the next one."

It happens not with a bang, but a filing. Once more Rasputin is doing politics by not doing politics, with zero fanfare, not so much as a press release, forgoing all the cheap pomp and so-called media savvy of the politics we've come to know and loathe. The Wednesday morning before Halloween, two thirteen-dollar-an-hour employees from a deluxe courier service file the paperwork simultaneously in Iowa and New Hampshire, and with that he's in. The nonchalance of it sends the media into a blithering tizzy. That's not how you do these things! They hate it. They love it. Faith and the crew scramble to record the West Wing reaction, which might best be described as shock and appall. Like nobody thought he would really do it? With characteristic graciousness, █████ welcomes Rasputin into the race by calling him "a world-class freak job," and vows to send him swiftly back to All World Wrestling "with his tail between his legs." "That is if they'll have him," he adds. "After we tag him with a great big *L* for loser. He'll probably end up doing a bush league somewhere up in Canada." As for the traitors, dirtbags, scumballs, and backstabbers who have forsaken █████ for the wrestler, "they have made the largest mistake of their lives," says the president, and he dedicates his third term to their obliteration.

Nobody does grievance better than █████, Faith reflects. The blast area of his wrath subsumes every square inch of the White House. "He's never been this much of an asshole," Stephen Miller mutters one day as he's leaving the Oval. The day after Halloween she is summoned to a meeting in a small ground-floor conference room off the Card Room. Something to do with the campaign, she suspects, the location a nod to Hatch Act requirements, and sure enough Bret Mathers, deputy campaign director for operations, is there, along with a buttoned-down minion. Also present are Van, Harvey, Stephen Miller, Asher and Twister. All men. There's something wolfish in the way they watch her enter and take a seat. Steve Bannon joins them via speakerphone from a friend's yacht in Palm Beach. It takes her a while to get the drift. They're talking around and past the point of the thing, but presently she realizes she's being pitched. They want her to . . . no. No way. They cannot be serious. They want her to go down to Texas and . . .

"*Spy?* You want me to *spy* on Rasputin?"

"Well, yes," Van confirms. "In so many words."

"Is that even legal?"

"Of course it is. We would never ask you to break the law."

"You'll continue to get paid," says Stephen Miller. "Your salary equivalent will be funded by one of the PACs and go into a secure account."

"And whatever the Rasputin campaign pays you is yours to keep," Bret adds.

Bannon's ice-scraper voice chimes in: "Sounds like a pretty sweet deal to me."

Faith looks to Harvey, who's said nothing. His expression is vaguely tragic.

"So I'm supposed to just show up at his door and say I'm in?"

"Why not?" Van says. "You've met him, you've seen him in action. Just tell them you're disenchanted with the president and you think Rasputin's the guy. It's not like you're the only one, unfortunately."

"So I join up and start sending intel back to you."

"That's the idea," says Van.

"But, uh, what. What do you want? What are you looking for?"

"Anything and everything," Bret Mathers answers. "Anything that seems potentially significant. Especially anything we can use for oppo."

She doesn't like it. The smell of it, the snaky feel. And she'll be down there on her own, surrounded by enemies. Her every move tracked by Rasputin's perspicacious eyes.

"Okay, so what if they figure out what I'm doing? Will they kill me?"

Big laughs all around, except for Harvey. No, no, no, no, the men assure her. They'll just quietly send you packing. They'd look bad if word got out that a spy penetrated the campaign.

"You know, guys, I'm not so sure about that. This could be the Russian Mafia for all we know, the KGB, FSB, whatever they call it these days. We really don't know who those people are."

"Faith," says Van, "we'll be monitoring the situation closely. Your well-being is our highest priority. And you'll be doing the president a tremendous service. He needs this, Faith. We need it. Right now everything's going against us."

"Does *he* know about this?"

The men look at one another, confer by telepathy. Van turns to her and nods.

"Okay, look, you don't even know if I'm capable. I've got no skills, no training for something like this. If I blow it it's going to look terrible."

"Faith, you aren't going to blow it. You're smart. You know how to handle yourself. The president himself suggested you for this."

"Right," she snorts. She has a pretty good feel for when she's being juiced. But Van smiles.

"You don't believe me? I'll show you."

He picks up the house phone and punches in two numbers. "Put me through," he says, and after a moment: "She's having reservations."

"________."

"No, she's willing. She just has doubts about whether she's capable."

"________."

"All right, yes sir. Right away."

Van hangs up and turns to her. "The president would like to see you in the Oval."

The seeming inevitability of the thing makes it hard to breathe. Right away he takes her into the private dining room, the same place where Bill took Monica all those years ago. She has never been so alone with the president, but instead of hanky-panky he wants to show her—the hats! Several dozen different prototypes of the MAGA Now More Than Ever hat are strewn around the table, each one a variant of the iconic MAGA original. They spend many minutes with the hats. The president is loose, chatty; playing with the hats makes him happy. At one point he bends to reach across the table, and Faith glimpses pale scalp shining through his saffron bouffant. The pathos of it, that double whammy of old-man vanity and vulnerability, pretty much melts her heart. On the wall is a framed clipping of the Nielsen ratings from the week *The Apprentice* was the number one show in the land.

Eventually they return to the Oval, where he invites her to sit with him on the cream-colored sofa. Madeleine serves Diet Cokes on a silver tray, and ██████ tells her to shut the door on her way out. Faith and the president are seated close enough that when he rests his arm along the sofa's back, his hand extends past her shoulder blade. She can feel his body heat, or thinks she can. He seems bigger, denser, redder, and she's intensely aware of his smell, that manly bouquet of mentholatum, laundry starch, and metallic-mimosa hairspray.

"Faith," he says, her name emerging from deep in his throat. He leans toward her, and his fingers grazing the nape of her neck set off sparks all over her body. Is he going to seduce her? Rape her? Eat her up and burn the bones?

"Do you believe in me, Faith?"

She's sitting with both feet flat on the floor, hands folded in her lap. Church posture. Her pits are damp. Her pulse is a hot timpani number pounding her temples.

"I do, Mr. President."

"Good, I appreciate that. And I believe in you. You're one of the best employees I've ever had, and I've had a million of 'em. You're special, Faith. One of a kind, one of a kind. I mean it."

"Thank you, Mr. President. That means so much to me."

He nods. They're close enough that she could count the pores of his nose. He shifts, crosses his legs. This brings him a little closer, and she catches a whiff of his body smell, a musty-tangy pungence like sourdough bread.

"Texas. You're from Texas."

"Yes sir."

"Texas is special. Lotta great people from Texas. John Wayne and the Alamo, Audie Murphy, so many great, great people. And some not so great."

"Yes sir, that's true."

"Local girl, that's good, you know the lay of the land. We could really use you down there, Faith."

"I do want to help you, Mr. President. But I'm afraid of letting you down. I've never done anything like this."

"And I understand, believe me I do. Stepping out of your comfort zone, never easy." He leans a little closer, and for a second she thinks he's going to take her hand. "You know, Faith, there's something just not right about that guy. Don't you feel it?"

"He's definitely unusual."

"He's good, don't get me wrong, his act is really pretty good, he even had *me* going for a while. But who is he? Where did he come from? All those years he was supposedly in Russia, that's a big black hole when you get right down to it. Very mysterious, very dangerous for the country. Maybe the only way we're gonna find out is if we have somebody on the inside. Is he a spy? A plant? Is he working for the Iranians? 'Cause I'm getting a very weird vibe from all this. What was that movie, the movie with the guy, the brainwashing guy . . ."

"*The Manchurian Candidate*?"

"Right! *Manchurian Candidate*, that's the one. The one with Sinatra, then there was that other one, sequel or something, Denzel was in that one, right? But anyway. Anyway, Faith, this is a huge deal for our country, I can't trust just anybody with this. I need somebody I can count on a hundred percent. What I'm saying here, Faith, is your country needs you. Your *president* needs you. And you will be rewarded, believe me. You will be so rewarded."

She can't speak. The Oval Office, the historicality of the moment, the intimate presence of the most famous man in the world, it's all too much. For a moment she disconnects, becomes unreal to herself. Who is Faith? What is she? This stranger wandering in and out of her life?

"Hey, Faith. Faith. You with me?"

"I'm sorry, Mr. President. I'm with you. I guess my hesitation—I have to confess, that man intimidates me. He sees things. People. When he looks at you—it just seems like he knows everything about you."

"Oh come on, you're way too smart for that. I'm sure that's what he *wants* you to think, but it's an act, a con. Believe me, I've seen a million like him, and you can take him, Faith, I know you can. You're smarter, sharper. You know character. And you're *good*, you know that? That's your advantage with people like him, you have a good pure heart that sees through phonies like him. That's your superpower, Faith, your good heart. Now if I can just get you to believe it!"

She thinks she might cry, hearing the president of America talk about her this way, and for the first time she thinks she really understands him. All the deals he's done, the fortunes he's made, the beautiful women he's had, the hit TV shows, the historic elections, it's all because he gets us. He sees us, sees and understands the good in us. None of his extraordinary accomplishments would have happened otherwise.

"How about this," he says, "let's work through it together, we're gonna act it out. Hey, I mean it! Stand up, stand up right here in front of me, okay, so here we go, I'm sitting here and you're coming in to tell me you're leaving to go to work for that other guy. And that's you, Faith, that's very you of you, anybody else would be a rat and just slink out the door, but you're a stand-up gal, that's not your style. Okay, go."

She stands before the president and takes a deep breath. He looks up at her with what seems like genuine intrigue. If it's a game, it's one he takes seriously. She clears her throat with a ragged *ahem*.

"Mr. President, thank you so much for seeing me today. There's something I need to tell—"

"No, sell it! Sell *me*! Put more oomph into it."

She nods, composes herself, starts again.

"Mr. President, thank you so much for seeing me today. This is, uh, hard for me, I'm truly torn about this, but I have to tell you that as of today I've resigned my position here, and I'm going to work for the Rasputin campaign. After all you've done for me, I just feel like I owe it to you to tell you personally. Because, sir, working for you has been the most rewarding experience of my life. It's been a huge honor—"

██████ is nodding, coaxing her along.

"—but I just feel like with the country where it is, the challenges we're facing, Rasputin is the right man to lead us for the next four years. And please believe me, sir, this has been the hardest decision of my life. I have the most tremendous respect and admiration for you, and I think you are truly one of the greatest presidents our country has ever had. But with the problems we're facing today, the challenges of a whole new era, it just seems like this is something I have to do."

"Gooood. Good! You're getting there. Okay, again. More forceful this time."

She squares her shoulders and launches once more into the spiel. It's clicking. She's really feeling it now. President ██████ nods along like she's singing a snappy tune. Then it's as if his internal wires cross. His eyes bulge, and he claps his hand over his mouth as if stifling a blast of projectile vomit.

"Stop!" he shouts, holding up his arm. "You're kidding me, right?"

"Ahm, no sir. I—"

"Faith, I'm shocked! I'm shocked and frankly I'm very disappointed in you. I thought you were special. My golden Texas girl, and now you come in here—where's your honor? Your decency? And your poor mother, oh my God that beautiful woman who I admire so much, she raised you to be so much better than this. When she hears about this it's gonna break her heart!"

He goes on, berating, bemoaning, and suddenly she's crying. Not weeping-sickness crying, just regular-crying crying, just normal, gut-heaving sobs of devastation and grief. It's all too much for her, this room, the president, the shattering synergy of his anger and world-destroying-level powers, and in the crisis of the moment she realizes she would do anything for him.

"Faith!" he cries out, and stands, and now he's reaching for her. "You did it, see? You got me! And you saw what you did to me and you got even yourself! See, didn't I tell you? You're a champ, Faith." He envelops her in the chaste hug of a doting father, and in the same spirit of patriarchy he tenderly pats her on the head. "There, there, you did good, you did so good, Faith. Didn't I tell you? I told you. I know these things. You're gonna do so great for us down in Texas, I know it."

16

THE COUNCIL FOR NATIONAL POLICY, TURNING POINT USA, PROJECT VERITAS II, THE PUBLIC INTEREST LEGAL FOUNDATION, THE NATIONAL ASSOCIATION OF SCHOLARS, THE CENTER FOR SECURITY POLICY, UNITED IN PURPOSE, THE CONSERVATIVE ACTION PROJECT, MOMS FOR AMERICA, CONCERNED MOTHERS OF AMERICA, MOMS FOR GENDER SANITY PAC, HERITAGE ACTION FOR AMERICA, GROUNDSWELL INC., THE YANKEE INSTITUTE FOR PUBLIC POLICY, THE GREENWICH GRASSROOTS COALITION, THE CLUB FOR GROWTH, THE ZIKLAG INSTITUTE, AMERICA RISING PAC, CROSSROADS USA PAC, THE COMMITTEE FOR A RESPONSIBLE AMERICA, AMERICANS FOR PROSPERITY ACTION, THE CATO INSTITUTE, THE AMERICAN ENTERPRISE INSTITUTE, CITIZENS FOR A NEW AMERICA, THE NOVA ACTION NETWORK, THE NATIONAL TAXPAYERS COALITION, THE POLITICAL THEORY PROJECT, THE MID-AMERICA LIBERTY COUNCIL, CONCERNED AMERICANS FOR JOB SECURITY, THE ANTIOCH GROUP, THE LYNDE & HARRY BRADLEY FOUNDATION, THE NATIONAL RIFLE ASSOCIATION,

THE INSTITUTE FOR HUMANE STUDIES, THE CLAUDE R. LAMBE FOUNDATION, THE PATRICK HENRY TRUST, THE ORANGE COUNTY POLICY FORUM, COME AND TAKE IT PAC, THE CENTER TO PROTECT PATIENT RIGHTS, THE COALITION FOR PATIENTS RIGHTS, WATCHMAN USA PAC, THE ATHENIAN LEAGUE, THE FRIEDRICH HAYEK SOCIETY, CONCERNED VETERANS FOR A STRONG AMERICA, THE NATIONAL FEDERATION OF CORROSION ENGINEERS, THE FOUNDATION FOR THE STUDY OF ECONOMICS AND THE ENVIRONMENT, THE CENTER FOR FREE ENTERPRISE, CITIZENS FOR A SOUND ECONOMY, FAITH AND FREEDOM PAC, ELIMINATE PROPERTY TAXES PAC, US CHAMBER OF COMMERCE PAC, THE SAMUEL ADAMS ALLIANCE, VALUES VOTERS OF AMERICA, GO TELL THE SPARTANS PAC, THE PARTNERSHIP FOR AMERICA'S FUTURE, THE EMERGENCY COMMITTEE FOR CITIZEN RIGHTS, THE PHYLLIS SCHLAFLY LEAGUE, THE CIVIC ENGAGEMENT GROUP TRUST, THE NATIONAL ASSOCIATION OF MANUFACTURERS, AMERICANS FOR TAX REFORM, AMERICA FIRST POLICY INSTITUTE, THE JUSTICE LEWIS POWELL LEGACY TRUST, DON'T TREAD ON ME PAC, REGULATE THIS! PAC, AMERICAN PIPELINE ALLIANCE PAC, MAGA-PHONE PAC, THE TEXAS TEA PARTY ACTION GROUP, THE ASSOCIATION OF FORMER FIGHTER PILOTS, PRAY FOR AMERICA PAC, THE SILICON VALLEY INNOVATION TRUST, THE SUN VALLEY BLUE SKY TRUST, ANYBODY BUT ████ PAC, THE JOHN LOCKE SOCIETY, THE NATIONAL ASSOCIATION OF CONCRETE MANUFACTURERS, BAIN CAPITAL PAC, THE RICHARD MELLON SCAIFE CHARITABLE TRUST, THE NATIONAL RIGHT TO WORK COMMITTEE, THE BENJAMIN FRANKLIN LIBERTY COUNCIL, SAVE OUR CHILDREN PAC, CONCERNED CITIZENS FOR EMINENT DOMAIN REFORM, SECURE OUR BORDERS PAC, THE SEVEN MOUNTAINS ACTION

COMMITTEE, THE OAKMONT TRUST, THE PROJECT 19 COMMITTEE, THE SCIENCE OF ENLIGHTENMENT FOUNDATION, THE APPEAL TO HEAVEN FOUNDATION, THE HISPANIC LEADERSHIP FUND, and THE RED RIVER ALLIANCE

all give money to the Rasputin campaign.

17

Uh-huh, Clarence says to himself, looking over the list. What these names represent are all the years of bullying, bragging, trifling, taunting, mocking, scoffing, sneering, jeering, lying, whining, sulking, chiseling, and out-and-out lawbreaking, the entire twisted gallimaufry of antisocial behaviors that ██████ inflicted on his friends and allies. For years they sucked cock, ate shit, and took it up the ass for the sake of white privilege and the sacred bottom line, and now, at last, the full fury of their loathing is unleashed in an avalanche of money. Going for it, they are. The palace coup has entered its executive phase. Fine as it is to watch a once-in-a-generation asshole get what's coming to him, the pleasure is complicated by the fact that we're all going to have to deal with the what. Really, billionaires? You're so hot to dump ██████ you go all in for a circus act? Which goes to show rich people are just as clueless as the rest of us. They might be brilliant at one stupendously lucrative thing, they're generally dumb as stumps at everything else.

He does a follow-up to the dark-money story, though it's hard to keep his interest now that the fat cats are out of the bag for everyone to see. As soon as it's done he drives over to the Half Price Books mothership on Northwest Highway and buys every Rasputin book he can find. The more he knows, the more he knows how little he knows, and with it comes a feeling he remembers from forty years ago, that hollow in the gut of apprehending—too late?—that you're in over your head. Except now he's home, not in faraway El Salvador, like this means he's supposed to know better? Run the logic of that causal chain forward through time, it seems only natural that ways and means deployed by the US government in Central America would sooner or later find their way back home. Coups, oligarchs, militias, street snatchings and wild prisons; de facto police states where even to look a certain way—to carry a book, say, or wear jeans and sneakers—made you a target. The deliberate and systematic subversion of democracy abroad, for which he was present, for a time.

More and more he feels this part of his past tugging at him like the suction of a sinking ship. A so-called self-defense force, the White Guard, has coalesced out of the Rasputin movement, and for five nights running they clash with National Security Brigades in multiple cities. In Ann Arbor, three students participating in a free speech march have their kneecaps blown off at point-blank range by masked gunmen. The CEO of Southwest Airlines criticizes ██████ for goon-squad police tactics, and the FAA grounds all Southwest flights for thirty-six hours. The DOJ launches investigations into Senators Sanders, Wyden, and Booker, and in Baltimore, a combined insurance and labor rights march is fired on by unknown assailants, leaving five dead and twenty wounded.

Paging through one of his old common books the night of the Baltimore massacre, Clarence finds this: *Every foul bird comes abroad, and every dirty reptile rises up. These add crime to confusion.* Abraham Lincoln, letter of 1863. He's having bad days lately, thinking about the country, and now he adds one more item to his personal portfolio: the chill willies. Itchy neck, darters and floaters at the corner of his eye, invisible needles poking the back of his head. It could be clinical paranoia over and above the baseline black condition, yes it could, except somebody is stealing his trash. Municipal pickup on his street is every Thursday, but his city-issued receptacle turns up mysteriously empty every other day. Lately he's seeing too many big dark American sedans on his street, and driving he doesn't have to try very hard to find one in his rearview mirror. Craft tip: If you want to blend in around Dallas, drive an SUV, even better if it's a prestige foreign make. Considerably lower on the evolutionary scale is the can of beer that sailed through his living room picture window a couple of nights after the Rachel Maddow interview. A Colt 45 tallboy, yeah, yeah, he got it. They punched a hole in the side of the can for maximum spewage and pretty well soaked Gayle's good Konya rug. The next day he hands the can to the cops in a plastic freezer bag.

"Mr. Thomas, have you been involved in any personal disputes recently?"

Hard not to get hung up on that "personal" qualifier. He can tell they remember him from his city council days, and no he did not try to defund the police, though they are plainly trying to recall if he did. Lord, the complications do take a toll. Sometimes he fantasizes about going the expat route. Du Bois went to Ghana, Wright and Baldwin to France, though Baldwin picked France more or less at random, just get me out of here. Clarence thinks some cheap little Mexican beach town would be more his speed.

"Key, *now* will you get a gun?"

He's on the phone with Nelson. The cops left an hour ago. Since then he's talked to the insurance people, the window people, and the rug-cleaning people.

"I've thought about it."

"You've been thinking about it for as long as I can remember. How about if I take you to the store this weekend. We'll look around, maybe have a session on the shooting range. You don't have to buy anything."

"Maybe. I'll think about it."

"Uncle. Man. People know where you live."

Clarence says nothing.

"How many times has your house been hit?"

"None, since I got off the city council."

"You mean none until now. How many before?"

His house has been egged, had the n-word spray-painted on the garage door, and had a cross burned into the front lawn with herbicide. It seems stupid to have a gun, and simultaneously equally stupid not to have a gun. Gayle had been adamant: no guns in the house. Why spend good money on another way to die when there are so many ways it can happen for free? His own calculation was less pragmatic, more philosophical. The gun being in essence a murder device, ownership would necessarily entail a rearrangement of your moral furniture, a prioritization of self over the competing claims of eight billion of your fellow humans. And when they came for you, your fellow humans with their guns and ropes and gasoline, what a total fool for humanity you'd feel then.

Maybe it comes down to this: He just doesn't want to give his money to that triumphantly blowhard sector of the white-supremacist economy.

"How's Emerald?"

"She's good. I'm aware you're changing the subject, by the way. She came downtown last week to watch me in court."

"Sounds serious."

"We're just having fun. But I really do sort of like her. She's smart. Classy. Grew up tough. Put herself through school."

"And you said she's . . ."

"Radiology tech at Baylor. I think she makes more than I do."

"So how does it work. You go out to Southlake and pick her up, take her back at the end of the night?"

"She's got her own apartment in Richardson."

"Ah."

"She's also got a room at his place. A lot of them do."

"Okay."

"I don't really know what the arrangement is out there."

Clarence detects the hint of a plaint in his nephew's voice.

"Well, like you said. Yall are just having fun."

"It's not like I can just come out and ask her."

"Nope."

"But I do quite like her. I think she likes me too."

"That's good."

"We laugh a lot."

"Always a good sign."

There's a hard stop on Nelson's end. Clarence senses his nephew would like to keep talking about Emerald.

"Anyway, Key. Saturday. Let's go look at guns."

"I'll think about it."

Fall has the best colors. Tawny caramels and russets, splats of scarlet and auburn like pulsing embers, chrome yellow, flame orange, golden halos of amber shading to umber, sepia, the silvery ocher of cocktail onions. The air offers up earthy hits of loam and fermenting mulch, and with daytime temps well off their berserk summer highs, walking outside no longer feels like a sledgehammer in the face. The crickets downshift to a lazy, we're-almost-done-here drone. Bumblebees bounce off doors and windows like amiable drunks, and in the mornings monarch butterflies wreathe the limbs of his redbud tree.

It's his favorite season of the year; maybe someday he'll take the time to enjoy it. He does an article on the Democrats' latest debate and their slide into ever deeper irrelevance, they just can't stop huffing that 1990s neoliberal glue. The unstated moral of the story: You don't have to be stupid to act stupid, but it helps. Once that's done, he and Renfro spend an afternoon brainstorming next things. The click surge from the Maddow interview has turned Renfro into a numbers addict, he wants more, more, more. So here's a story: Is the wrestler running? Because he's not acting like a guy who's seriously running for president. Everyone can see he's killing it with the slick TV ads—the éminence grise who did the Willie Horton ad has joined his team—but there've been no rallies, no press events, no position papers, and his only campaign "speeches" are diss fests in the ring, statements of general principle delivered via put-downs of his opponents. Perhaps it's all an elaborate branding stunt, very meta given the ██████ 2016 precedent. Right now nobody really knows, but masses of voters are all in regardless. A Medianet flash poll shows him up by seven points over the president in Iowa, and as for the rest of the primary field—what's that faint insect whine in your ear? Honey, somebody shrank the candidates!

The press would seem obliged to have some idea of the Candidate's politics. Renfro notes they're still getting heavy traffic on Clarence's old Rasputin interview. So there's our market. Demonstrable consumer demand that's not being met.

"Ren, we just don't know a whole lot right now."

"Come on, give me your gut. A working theory of who he is, what he stands for. You've spent more time with him than anyone."

"A theory."

"I won't hold you to it. We're just talking here."

"All right." Clarence gathers himself. "My theory is Rasputin personifies a gnomic, tribalistic, chauvinistically Christian strain of hypernationalism that may well harbor deep-seated fascist tendencies."

Renfro bites his lip. Clarence goes on.

"██████'s like, fascism-lite. Opportunistic fascism. He picks and chooses the parts that serve whatever grift he's got going at the moment. Whereas Rasputin might be the whole program."

Renfro releases his lip. "Mmm-kay."

"You asked for a theory."

"So I did. And your basis?"

"Gut."

"You think he could be a Russian plant?"

"He could, but why. ██████ already does everything Putin wants him to."

The editor nods, ponders his belly like all wisdom resides there.

"You got enough to go on?"

"Hardly."

"You need access."

"I'm trying. He's got people around him now."

"What about the guy you told me about, his house manager?"

"Bitsy. He's not returning my calls."

"Maybe you need a new approach."

Fair statement. Clarence gathers up his notes and says he'll work on it. Outside it's a mild autumn afternoon, partly cloudy with a slight chance of sweat. He crosses the street to the surface parking lot, gets in his car, and sits for a while with the windows open. Skyscrapers rise around him like jumbled canyon walls, traffic sluicing through the cracks in orderly flows. Pedestrians stride or saunter by, depending on their business. A homeless raver paces the sidewalk on the far side of the parking lot, and flocks of pigeons wheel about like the internal workings of a watch. All in all, it looks like an average weekday afternoon in the heart of Dallas city. Clarence gets out his phone and taps Bitsy's number, waits for it to roll over to voicemail.

"Bitsy, Clarence Thomas. Brother to brother—should I be worried? 'Cause I'm pretty sure I got people tracking me."

He clicks out and sets the phone on the dashboard. He might be waiting, obeying a hunch, or maybe he's just letting it be. He supposes they're watching him. Fine, give them something to think about. What's that crazy old Negro doing now, just sitting there? Over to the west, about a nine-iron as the crow flies, is the old Municipal Building where Ruby shot Oswald, the murder that launched a thousand conspiracy theories. Per year. And ten or twelve blocks beyond that, Dealey Plaza. Sitting here amid the tidy grid of city streets, the earnest traffic, all the purposeful forward motion of a reasonably functional downtown, Clarence experiences a sudden intensity of awareness. Certain lines and textures push into high relief, and there's an immanence to things, a nervous charge that seems to make him a witness, no mere bystander. The effect isn't so different from a freeze-up episode, the isolation and vivification of a single moment. Then it hits him like a physical blow, just how monstrous that day was: the murder of a president, in broad daylight, in front of thousands, in the middle of a major American city.

Then and there, they should have called the whole thing off. *Every foul bird comes abroad.* How much clearer did the signal have to be? *Every dirty reptile rises up.* Something rotten and depraved at the core of it, the sin simmering ever since, oh, 1619 seems as apt a date as any. *These add crime to confusion.* Paranoia and greed at the root, chickens coming home to roost, violence as American as cherry pie; in other words, nobody's free and safe until everybody is. So call it off. Start over. Do better. How much clearer did the signal have to be?

The phone buzzes, and he takes his time reaching for it. Somehow he already knows.

The next day they meet for lunch in Southlake, at a barely integrated Applebee's on Kimball Avenue. Bitsy is twenty minutes late, so Clarence gets to watch him crutch across the parking lot, his deliberate lurch-and-slide an object lesson in patience. One of the hostesses rushes out to hold the door for him, cooing and smiling, touching his arm, resting her palm on his shoulder. Okay, so they know him here. A safe place. Both of the hostesses and a waitress walk him over to the booth, where he introduces Clarence as "a nice fella I know." He sits, stows the crutches. Catches his breath. A second waitress arrives with a glass of iced tea for him, sweeps away before Clarence can order one for himself.

"Sorry to be late. We got a traffic problem at the house." Bitsy has a drink of his tea and looks out the window. "You bring your friends with you?"

"I didn't look. Either they're there or they aren't, I just go on about my business."

Bitsy's small eyes study him for a moment, blink off.

"If they are," Clarence adds, "I guess they know you're here too."

"I told Grishka already. He send his regards. And he wanna know how you know so much."

"About?"

"Everything. The money."

"It's public records, mostly. No big mystery to it. You just gather all the raw material you can and start putting the pieces together."

"Like that, huh."

"Pretty much."

Bitsy considers. "You was a professor."

"I was."

"Professor of what?"

"Political science and government."

"What happen with that?"

"What happened was, I put in my twenty-seven years, and I retired."

"And then you go right back to work?"

"I'd go crazy just sitting around."

Bitsy mulls this over. "Professor. Like I said on the phone, we off the record."

"Off the record," Clarence agrees.

"You still working on the money?"

"I'm working on several different things."

"Huh. Okay." Bitsy takes the lemon out of his tea and sucks it dry with a smack, sets it aside. "I'm gonna tell you straight-out, buncha people at the house know your name. Wondering how you do what all you do. Your story make 'em nervous."

"Like I said, ninety percent of what I wrote's in the public record. It's not like I'm going around hacking into people's computers."

Bitsy grunts, watches him a moment. Looks away, looks back. He speaks slowly, as if to ensure Clarence fully understands.

"I am not entirely comfortable with those people."

"Okay."

"Not messing-around type people, is my impression. Like, cold. Hard in the face. Doubt butter would melt in their mouth."

"All right."

"I don't know if they the same people tracking you, hell, I don't know half a what they do all day, tapping and talking on their phones, having their very serious meetings. They take over most of the house, the guest house . . . this whole thing bigger than my mind. But what I do know is, sometimes they talking about you."

Clarence nods.

"So when you call yesterday, I think you might wanna know. Man to man. Not because I think we're best friends or anything."

"Understood."

Bitsy sighs. It's a physical event on the order of shifting tectonic plates.

"It ain't nothing to do with Grishka, I can tell you that. Sneaking around not his style."

"Have you told him how you feel about those people?"

"He knows my mind." Bitsy pauses. "Just between him and me, I call them the Pharisees."

"Then I guess he knows."

"Grishka got their number all right. But he figure if he running for president, they come with the package."

The first waitress returns and takes their order. Large Caesar salad with chicken for Bitsy, chicken sandwich and side salad for Clarence. She leaves. Bitsy starts to speak, and falls silent while the second waitress tops off his tea. As if expecting a third waitress, he hesitates a few more moments.

"You thinking you ought to be worried? Professor."

"I don't know what to think. Those people have an honest-to-God presidential campaign to run, and I'm a senior citizen reporter for an online paper nobody's ever heard of. I don't know why they'd waste their time."

"They sensitive about the money. Folks tend to be."

"Folks tend to be. Maybe that's it. Maybe it's something else." Clarence pauses. "So your man's really running."

"Oh yes indeed, and you watch. Grishka put his mind to something, he a very determine individual."

"He's taking his time getting going."

"Grishka got his ways."

"How you feel about him running?"

Bitsy shrugs. "He know his own mind." He has a drink of tea. "Better this way than teaming up with old Trunk."

"Trunk."

"That man always Trunk to me."

"I take it you're not a fan."

"We all know what that man about. He the president, uh-huh, what he really president of is white America. Way I see it, Grishka can be the president of everybody, white, black, brown, every color and kind. 'Cause I know he don't have any hate in his heart."

"How about gays?"

Bitsy's eyes give a little jump. "Nunh-unh, not getting into all that with you. You gonna have to ask Grishka yourself."

"I would very much like the opportunity to do so."

"Maybe you will. But Grishka speak for himself, always. He don't need me doing his talking for him."

The first waitress brings Clarence an iced tea, and shortly lunch is served. Bitsy's salad comes with extra dressing on the side. He pours it on, chuckles when he sees Clarence watching.

"If I gotta eat rabbit food, at least want it to taste like something."

"I hear that."

"How you stay so skinny?"

"Just how I'm built, I guess. I'm definitely heavier than I used to be."

"You ever play ball?"

"High school." He sees Bitsy is waiting for more. "Cornerback."

Bitsy laughs. "Man, you *look* like a corner. Slender. Speedy."

"Well. I'm definitely not that kid anymore."

"Truth." Bitsy flourishes a hand at himself. "I always thought corner one of the hardest positions to play. Gotta be so fast and quick to cover the pass, but on the run you gotta fight off the lineman, then some big old running back coming at you full steed."

"I do seem to recall moments like that."

"Come on now. You don't ever forget a game."

"Not really, I guess. Except the ones where they rung your bell."

"Had a few of those myself. You never play college?"

"Never gave it any thought. Probably because I wasn't good enough. Maybe D three, but I guess I just assumed I was done with it."

"Uh-huh. Some hardhead got to be told they're done."

"Well, you were really good at it. It's hard to walk away from something when you're that good."

"I guess so. I can tell you one thing, I do still love the game."

"Can I ask you something? But we can drop it if I'm getting too personal." Bitsy gestures: continue. "Would you do your career all over again? Knowing what you know now, how hard it is on the body. Any regrets, I guess I'm asking. But I'll shut up if it's none of my business."

"Naw, it's okay. Huh. You know, nobody ever ask me that, and here I am the way I am all these years." He ponders for a moment. "I think I would, yeah. That sound crazy? But that's who I am. Wouldn't be no Bitsy Bowman without football. And wouldn't be no wrassling either, and then I'd never met Grishka. Anyway, you know how it was back in the day. What else a big old black boy from Palmer gonna do but play ball?"

The first waitress comes by to ask is everything okay, and stays to chat. The second waitress comes by to refill their waters and iced teas, and stays as well. A third waitress comes by to say hello and feel Bitsy up on the arm and shoulders. One might be allowed to think he is the honorary mayor of the Kimball Avenue Applebee's. The waitresses leave, and Clarence and Bitsy look at one another. The social visit has wiped the conversational slate clean.

"Professor."

"Sir."

"You think Grishka got a chance?"

Clarence pulls in a breath. "The way it's looking, yes."

"*Real* chance?"

Clarence exhales, and it feels like he's been holding it in for weeks.

"To tell you the truth? Yeah, actually. We've been in uncharted territory ever since 2016, so sure, why not. He looks strong. Right now he's looking stronger than anybody, Democrat or Republican. He certainly has the country's attention."

Bitsy blinks. "Never studied politics much."

"I think you're about to get a crash course."

"Huh, may be. I do know the country in a sorry state. People falling out crying everywhere, people running around with guns in they funny little uniforms, about every week some fool go off and shoot up a school. Trunk keep sayin' there might be another civil war, what *that* about—so they can put us back in chains? I don't know, man. All this too much for my mind. And now my good friend running for president and you say he might win, nunh-unh, I can't process that. All I can do is stay to the job and run the house. And listen, all the new folks around, I had to hire extra help for the kitchen. Housekeeping too."

"Sounds like you're running a hotel."

Bitsy laughs. "They seem to think so. Seem to think I work for them, and they want a lot, too. These kind of people used to getting their way."

"Any blood in that crowd?"

"Just one brother, fancy fella. He don't wanna know my name." Bitsy takes a bite of salad, chews for a moment. "Trunk ain't gonna go easy."

"No."

"That man . . . how low he willing to go, you think?"

"Well, you know." Clarence pauses. "Low." Their eyes meet, and Bitsy turns mournful.

"That how it gonna be?"

"Who knows. A lot of dark inside that man. You push him to the wall, no telling what's going to come out."

"Uh-huh. Guess we all best be on our toes, then."

Clarence takes care of the check. Accompanying Bitsy out of the restaurant is in Clarence's imagining like escorting Troy Aikman as he bids farewell to Texas Stadium, a celebratory passage lined with cheering fans, or in Bitsy's case, smiling waitresses, busboys, hostesses, assistant managers. Outside, the two men follow the sidewalk down to the curb, and here they loiter. Bitsy checks his phone. Clarence scans the parking lot for anonymous-looking Buicks and Mercurys. A nearby patch of landscaping features three non-native river birches, their leaves gleaming copper and gold in the buttery autumn light.

"Pretty day."

"Couldn't ask for better."

"I thank you for the lunch."

"My pleasure. Thank you for making the time."

Bitsy nods, hangs fire a moment. "Professor. I found you on the internet."

Clarence waits.

"That was a bad deal you up in, back in the day. El Salvador."

Clarence shrugs.

"Man, how you get yourself in so deep? You go all the way down there, like, what for?"

"To tell you the truth, I think I was looking for the next revolution. See, I was dumb. I thought we'd already won here. So I had to go somewhere else to see it happen."

"Then you come back home and sue the US government."

"I guess I did."

"The government!"

"We knew we basically had no chance." He has to pause; what's remarkable is some days it still seems to have the power to crush him. "Mainly we were trying to bring attention to what was happening down there."

"So you sue the US government," Bitsy repeats in a wondering voice. Clarence can't tell if he's impressed, confused, or contemptuous.

"Where they had me on the base, in a cell—it was a Salvadoran army base, but I kept hearing Americans. I don't know if they were military, CIA, or what, but they were clearly involved in operations, and they knew I was there. Getting beat on every day. Basically starving to death. It all came out years later, hell yeah America was up to its ears in the shit. Drugs, weapons, death squads, all the people doing that shit were our clients. The same people who were about an inch away from killing me."

"Well, now people know. You gonna sue again?"

"No thanks."

"Done with it."

"I wouldn't get any further than I did back then. Anyway, people know. Could know. The history's out there for anybody who wants to know, but most people don't give a damn. Not then and not now."

Bitsy hears him out with a mild, measuring look.

"You have a fightin' past."

"If you want to call it that."

"They beat you down pretty good."

"And I got up pretty good."

Bitsy laughs. "And now I'm standing here outside the Applebee's, watching you. You wanna talk to Grishka?"

"Me and the entire rest of the world, Bitsy."

"Yeah, but you come around from the start. That count for something. And he thinks you're all right."

"Well, that's reassuring."

Bitsy chuckles. "Oughta be. That man." He pauses and shakes his head. "Some days I swear I think that man know everything."

18

Mornings in Southlake, first thing Faith tips her curtain aside and looks out the window. She scans the courtyard and fountain below, the grounds, the stone wall, the small army of security milling about, and thinks: The bastard princess has her palace at last. Beyond the wall, in the vacant field across the road, multitudes are already gathering. Every day it's a chicken-fried Woodstock over there, a freeform outdoor happening of music, praying, chanting, bug bites, sunburn, Jesus freaks, Porta Potties, and godawful traffic. Rasputinheads and miracle seekers are installed on the right side of the field, anti-Rasputins are shunted to the left, and the press, like so much mystery meat lumped between two slices of bread, is confined to the fenced-off middle section. Every evening the cops clear the field, and break of dawn every day it fills up again no matter the weather. It's late fall in north Texas, highs in the nineties one day, freezing your tush off the next.

Bunch of crazy people over there. Zealots. Fanatics. True believers. Faith sort of envies them. In much the same way she envies Charlie Cupps, a disciple of the world's oldest and largest religion, the Church of Money. The man is positively giddy these days. It's a great time to be a believer. Rasputin's NIL scale has gone stratospheric ever since he announced for president. Paid subscriptions for his YouTube channel are approaching ten million. Everybody wants a piece of the *starets* and Charlie is always on the phone, negotiating seven-figure fees for matches two and three years out.

"Okay," Faith proposes, "so should we assume you think he's going to lose?"

Charlie is curt. "What are you talking about?"

"The election."

"Only a fucking moron would think that."

Now she's almost scared to ask. "He'll keep on wrestling even if he's president?"

Charlie leans close and theatrically sniffs her breath. "What a question! Faith, baby, we're making history here! This is what everybody in the business dreams of, nailing that beyootiful sweet spot where people don't know what to believe. Is it real? Is it fake? They want to believe but in a way they sort of don't, if it gets too real that might spoil the fun. And right now our boy's killing it! Shit, half the time *I* don't know what to believe."

Running for president, *best career move ever!* Doctrine in Charlie's church is bracingly simple: Get as much as you can however you can as fast as you can, and devil take the hindmost. Every morning Faith troops out to the grand ballroom with senior comms staff for the day's first briefing. Most days it's Bardem Hayes, the campaign's communications director and (he claims) a direct descendant of President Rutherford B. Hayes, who mounts the podium and walks the press through Rasputin's schedule for today, a preliminary version of which they've already received on their devices. The Candidate's training regimen is detailed. The lineup of visitors and anticipated topics of discussion. Whether a statement or in-person appearance might be expected. His reaction, if any, to the latest attacks by President █████, who has lately taken to calling the Candidate "Fake Russian," "Lurch," and "Cro-Magnon Man." Days when Bardem's not available, Faith steps into the breach, and in this way she's become one of the more prominent faces of the campaign, with all the collateral online snark and savaging. They put down her clothes (frumpy, extravagant), her hairstyle (grade school, hooker), her body (too fat, too skinny), her accent (hick, faux hick), her makeup (too much, too little). Then there are the ██████ers, who, when they aren't threatening to rape and murder her, convey their sincerest wishes that she die of some slow and disfiguring disease. There's an AI-amended video circulating online that shows her as Queen Cersei on *Game of Thrones* making her walk of shame through King's Landing, naked, hair shorn, being spat upon and pelted with rotten produce. Small comfort in supposing someday the truth will out, then she'll get it from the Rasputinheads.

Every third or fourth night she spends at her mother's, and it's there that she calls in her reports on a specially dedicated phone. Ad strategy, ground game, digital, fundraising, she details everything without the help of notes—no way she's getting caught with incriminating papers on her person. Directors and senior staff—she privately calls them "the Muggles"—are based at the palace. The bulk of the headquarters operation is housed in a nearby office building, three floors' worth and they're about to lease two more. The billionaire money is rolling in, and the campaign website is clocking a very respectable $1.6 million a day, median size of donation $27. Which means the little people are coming over right along with the bigs. Evangelicals are trending Rasputin, and the Reverend Miles Frisbee, president of the Southern Baptist Convention, recently declared him "the true Christian in the race." The boogaloo movement has splintered, rival ██████ and Rasputin factions going at it like Crips and Bloods. Leading Republicans are starting to defy ██████ and tiptoe toward the *starets*. Senator Ballyhack is negotiating a possible endorsement. Governor Grumbles has already visited Southlake, as have Representatives Grindstaff, Tarball, Bitters, and Slaughter. Vice President Greene's people are making overtures, hinting that she's close to suspending her campaign and would like to meet with the Candidate to discuss her endorsement.

Everybody wants something. Endorsements are property, nobody gives it up for free. Let's see, what else does she know. The maniacs in digital are sending out two million micro-targeted texts and emails a day. The ad team is already working up a "suite" of Super Bowl commercials. Zuckerberg and Bezos are visiting later this week, and internal polling shows the Candidate cracking twenty percent across the board with people of color. All of this she diligently relays to her handlers in DC. Usually it's Dieter who picks up her call, but there's also Amity, Louis, Barb, and once a guy named Dale. They're campaign staff—she's forbidden on pain of death to contact the West Wing—and nobody ever asks how she's doing, how she's feeling. She thinks she'd feel a little better if only someone would. It's damn stressful out here behind enemy lines, keeping secrets, living the double life. Lonely. Works on your mind. Not even Christie knows her true mission. Faith does this as a mercy to her mother—keeping *that* secret would explode the poor woman's head—but now their every conversation, meal, and hug is a kind of lie. Faith senses all manner of damage being done, impossible to know how much until she comes clean.

For several days a weird, prickling edginess prevails at Southlake, as if a film of finely ground glass has settled over everything. Is she imagining this? The housekeepers, usually so sweet and cheerful, hurry past with pursed lips and downcast eyes. Bitsy keeps to his room, claims he's fighting off a stomach bug. Finally Belinda clues her in: ████████ *was here.* No. No way. But Belinda swears it's true. At the next call-in Faith duly passes along the story, and two minutes later the phone rings. She practically jumps out of her slippers. The spy phone has never rung before.

"Hello?"

"It's me." Stephen Miller.

"I thought we're not supposed to—"

"Forget that. Tell me what you just told him, about her. No names."

"Okay." *Him* being Dieter, *her* being the First Lady, Faith assumes. "The word around here—and this is coming from the housekeepers—is she was here. She spent the night. Well, she got here at night and didn't leave till the next night. All very hush-hush, obviously."

"It didn't happen," Miller snaps.

"It does seem pretty out there."

He chews tongue for a moment. "When did this supposedly happen?"

This thing that supposedly didn't happen. "I'm not sure. Sometime this past week? I just heard about it yesterday."

"From who."

"Belinda. She—"

"I said no names!"

"Dude, you asked."

"I said no names!"

She decides to say nothing while he gets a grip on himself. With twelve hundred miles between them, she's less inclined than ever to take guff from Miller, who junior West Wing staff snickeringly refer to as "Eeyore."

"Is that a housekeeper?"

"No, admin. On the business side."

"Well, what she's saying is just not possible."

Something in her is moved to take up for Belinda and the housekeepers. "If you say so. I guess the log would confirm that easily enough."

"I don't need to check the log."

"Fine. So you're saying you've been with her 24–7 for the past entire week."

"What exactly are you implying?"

"What I'm *saying* is you might not know everything you think you know. And the White House log would seem like a logical resource to check out."

"You know what? I'm starting to think you made this whole thing up. Just to fuck with us."

She spins on her heels, pulls at her hair. "Man, what are you even talking about? I'm down here for you guys, for *him*. Why would you even say a thing like that?"

"Because this whole conversation is repulsive. I hold that woman in the very highest esteem."

"So do I! Look, I'm just doing what you guys told me to do. If something seems relevant I pass it on, you guys do whatever you want with it." She takes a breath. "This isn't easy, you know."

"What."

"This. Being here. Undercover, so to speak."

"Oh gee, want me to send you a violin? Politics is rough business, in case you haven't noticed. Maybe you need to toughen up."

Right now she'd love nothing more than to punch his sourpuss face.

"If you hear anything else, call me. Call me direct. Nobody else."

"You sure about that?"

"Do I stutter? Yes I'm sure. And I want you going proactive on this. See what else you can find out, but be subtle. This is a, um, highly sensitive area."

Duh. "I think I get that."

"Contact me directly. Nobody else. Text me at this number, just text, ahm, 'flags,' and I'll call you back. And the next time you talk to the campaign, tell them there's nothing to it."

Copy that. Has a presidential candidate ever stolen a rival candidate's wife? Could be history in the making, scandal of the century unfolding here, but even if it is what the housekeepers and Stephen Miller obviously think it is, Faith wonders. Perhaps it's both more and less. There's something about the *starets*, some combination of his calm, deep voice, his cavernous eyes, his centered serenity, that she finds both soothing and stimulating, a harmonic buzz that begins in her pelvic region and radiates out from there. It's sensuous, but not overtly sexual. Or is it? Perhaps both more and less. She's starting to get why the Maidens are so avid to hang around. He knows how to look at a woman and make her feel like a woman, and it feels good, powerful. Fulfilling. Physical sex seems almost beside the point. She can see how the whole arrangement might really be innocent, no orgies, no threesomes or foursomes, no sex whatsoever in the material realm.

She's still a MAGA girl, she sure is. Her feelings for the president are one hundred percent unchanged, yet she's somehow acquired an extra hundred percent for Rasputin. She can feel her insides bending and twisting, something new and possibly hideous, possibly holy, taking shape.

The Candidate is unfailingly kind and respectful toward her. He makes a point of including her in all but the highest-level meetings. He solicits her counsel, and tells the Muggles to sit still and listen. Lately he's inviting her to work out with him. "Even women have muscles that must be kept in order," he gently prods her. Is she being groomed for something? Fattened up for the kill? The way he smiles at her sometimes, all twinkly and chummy, it's like he knows. Like he knows and finds it all very droll and human, and he forgives her. Whereas █████ would have her summarily tarred and feathered and dumped on Connecticut Avenue in the middle of rush hour.

After working out, they pray. This happens in the small, semi-subterranean chapel attached to the pyramid, a dim, compact space stuffed with a cathedral's worth of high-church accoutrement. Gold crosses, gem-encrusted censers, an ornate gilded altar with chalice and candelabrum, a battered and bloody Christ for an altarpiece. They kneel on the rough slate floor before the altar, and Rasputin prays a mumbly hocus-pocus of Russian and Latin. The first time he hits himself, iron fist to oakwood breast, she thinks the roof is falling in. *Thoom*, mumble mumble, *thoom*, mumble mumble, with every whack she feels the impact in her chest. It's in the chapel where he teaches her how to sign the cross, with two fingers, "in the Old Believer way." And it's down here where she's most frightened he'll confront her. Or that he's grinding down her nerves until she has to confess, and sometimes she nearly does, so overwhelming is this spooky claustrophobic cave with its sickly sweet air and vampire light and mournful icons staring from every wall. Some days she wants to tear her hair and run right out of there, other days she thinks she'll faint. Meanwhile Rasputin prays his monastic mumbo jumbo, maybe he's putting an old-world hex on her. She prays too, or at least thinks she does, she's never quite sure. After prayers one day he invites her to sit with him in the front pew. He smiles and gives her The Look, that sexy, soulful, world-without-end look, and instantly she's mush inside.

"Faith."

"What."

"Your heart is troubled."

She can't deny it, now that the organ has leaped to the top of her throat.

"There is a person. A man. For whom your feelings are very strong."

"Well," she clears her throat, "yes."

"But he is gone."

She nods. No point asking how he knows, he just knows. "He's in DC. He works for the president. And now I work for you."

"So you broke."

"Yes."

"Faith, this is true sacrifice."

She nods and modestly bows her head. Gazing at the slate floor she's suddenly sure that's where the gold is, right under her feet.

"Love, romantical love, is very difficult, yes? The world is so much with us! So many cares and troubles stand in the way, yet to seek this love is our very nature."

"I guess that's true." She turns to face him. "What about you?"

He coughs up a popcorn pip of a laugh. She seems to have surprised him, surprised and pleased him both. "What about *me*?"

"You seem so self-sufficient. No wife, no girlfriend. It's almost like you don't need that kind of love."

"Oh but Faith, my life is filled with love, overflowing with love. God's love above all."

"But what about *that* kind of love. Romantic love."

"I am surrounded by love. God's love, the love of my friends. The love of my fans for sure! And my dear Maidens. The love I share with them is very special indeed."

No doubt, she thinks, and instantly regrets the silent sarcasm. He watches her for a moment, then takes her hand. Oh shit, here it comes. He's making his move. She's been waiting for this since the day she arrived, dreading it, wanting it, rehearsing it, and she doesn't have the first clue what she'll do.

"Faith."

"Grishka." She's never called him this before.

"Yes."

"Excuse me?"

"Yes. She was here."

"Uhhhh . . ."

"The First Lady."

Faith opens her mouth, but nothing comes out.

"She is struggling in her life. With her marriage, her position as a leading figure on the world stage. Her very complicated feelings for her husband. And, in all honesty, for me."

Faith is nodding and gulping, trying to get a grip. An enormous air bubble has suddenly lodged in her chest.

"She is a remarkable woman, Faith. I have never known any woman like her. She"—he hesitates— "stirs me. But I want you to know, she has not broken her wedding vows. When the First Lady and I are together, this is not the usual way of passion. My bed is a place for the refinement of souls."

"Well," she says with stunned candor, "I've never heard it put like that."

"We are creatures of flesh, with all the lusts and desires of flesh. Is this lust the work of Satan? Yet if our lust is properly disciplined it can lead to holy love, a very wondrous love. The body is satisfied no less than the spirit."

The air bubble in her chest is about to explode.

"Perhaps you are wondering why I tell you these things."

"Uh, yes," Faith gulps. "Actually I am, yes."

He smiles. Those teeth! Huge glorious stallion teeth that could crunch through steel.

"I tell you because there is something special in you. God has a plan. And you, Faith, you have a very special role in His plan."

"Okay. So are you going to tell me what it is?"

"It is a mystery. But God will reveal all in His own good time."

Nights when Faith stays over, Christie pulls out all the stops: a home-cooked meal, candles, cloth napkins, a tasty Meursault or Montrachet.

They may have put each other through hell during the teen years, but nobody can say they don't love and cherish one another. Tonight they're having lemon sole, haricots with almonds, and wild rice, along with a fantastically expensive Bâtard-Montrachet. With prosperity Christie has left Two Buck Chuck far behind.

"Well," she says, maneuvering her knife and fork around Muffin perched on her lap, "I just want you to know I totally support your decision. We all owe the president so much. He got our country back," she pauses to inflict a brisk noogie on Muffin, "isn't that right, Muffy Wuffy! But if you think Rasputin is the right man for the job, you couldn't keep working for ██████."

"No." Faith has to go dead inside to get through these conversations.

"I just wish your former coworkers would see it that way."

"That would be nice."

"And even Harvey cut you off! He seemed like such a decent man."

"He is a decent man."

"And he was such a great mentor to you."

"He was that."

"Well, who knows. Maybe someday you'll work together again."

"May be."

"Oooo, ██████'s on! Let's listen." Christie unmutes the TV and watches while Faith ponders the mysteries of romantic love. Harvey, you tool, she thinks. Ever the goody two-shoes, he insisted on abiding by the no-contact protocol. It might seem a slick maneuver for extricating himself from their affair, except he nearly went to pieces when they said their goodbyes.

It's not for long, he said, as if she was the one verging on tears. The nomination would be settled by February, March at the latest. But now ██████ is threatening to run as an Independent if he doesn't get the nomination, which means her mission could conceivably extend into November.

"What if I call you anyway?" Faith said in their last pillow talk. "Would you pick up?"

"You know I can't."

"What if I left a message saying I was desperate. Would you call me then?"

"Faith, please. This is serious. We're talking about the presidency."

"What if I called and said I was dying?"

He squeezed his eyes shut and reached for her hand.

She knew it would hurt. That some days it would be a headache sort of hurt, other days like the flu, still others like a knife to the neck. And that's pretty much how it's gone, except worse, and now she *really* wants to talk to him about the First Lady situation. He might not know what to do, but at least he would sympathize.

On the tube ████ is doing his martyr routine. "You see what's been happening this week? All week long they're going to see Cro-Magnon Man, all the Google guys, the Silicon Valley guys, after all I've done for them. Whaddeya think, maybe those people don't deserve me?"

"Mom, please. Not during dinner."

Christie hits Mute. For several moments blissful silence reigns, then she erupts in her town-crier scripture-quoting voice: "'He came for testimony, to bear witness to the light, that all might believe through him. He was not the light, but came to bear witness to the light.'"

Muffin whines and paws at Christie's lap. Faith keeps her head low and forks in the lemon sole.

"That's in reference to the president. Bearing witness."

"I figured."

"A lot of people are starting to believe Rasputin is the light."

"I'm aware."

"And a lot of people believe he's just the opposite."

"Mom, I look out the window at Southlake and see them every day."

"I never thought anyone would surpass ████, and he's doing it without even trying! But sooner or later he's going to have to get out there and campaign. Really talk to the voters."

"He's sort of doing that now. At his matches."

"That's right, and it's quite brilliant! Getting *paid* to make campaign speeches, even ████ never managed that."

Faith has two phones by her plate, her regular cell phone and the spy phone. She texted Stephen Miller earlier and is waiting for his call. She's also waiting for Clarence Thomas to ping her with the link to the new *Dallas Daily* interview, due to drop tonight. She was point person for the interview, though why Rasputin chooses to talk to a puny online paper instead of the *Times* or *Wall Street Journal* is beyond her. He seems to like Clarence Thomas, for some reason. Faith finds the reporter civil enough, if aloof. Distant. Vaguely put-downish. It's a vibe she often gets from black people, who make her nervous.

She and Christie are clearing the table when the spy phone rings. "One second," she says to Miller, and goes bounding upstairs to her room. She shuts and locks the door, turns on Billie Eilish loud, and plants herself on the floor, on the far side of the bed from the door.

"Okay. I'm here."

"Talk."

She finds that she has to catch her breath. It's more than the sprint up the stairs; the fate of the country, no, the world, might hang on what she's about to divulge. Plus she feels like a rat, though Rasputin never expressly told her *not* to tell anyone. But wouldn't that just be assumed? As blatantly obvious as if you'd been given the nuclear launch codes.

You have a very special role in His plan. What, the Judas role?

"Hello?" Miller prompts. "Is there a problem?"

"No, sorry. It's just—okay, I'll just come out and say it. I have it on very good authority that she was here."

Over the line comes a long hissy gas leak of a sigh. Nobody does snark like Eeyore Miller.

"And what is this supposedly good authority?"

"The man himself. The Candidate."

"Bullshit!"

"Nope."

"Oh come on. You really expect me to believe that?"

"Well, that's what happened."

"Why would he tell *you*?"

"I don't know, because he likes me? Because I'm in the inner circle? Which by the way is exactly what you guys tasked me to do."

Miller emits a prissy cough. "So when did he allegedly tell you this, this, *thing*. Was he drunk?"

"He doesn't drink. And he told me today, in the chapel. Right after we prayed."

"You *prayed* with him?"

"Yes I did, St—" She stops before his name is all the way out. "I work out with him, I pray with him, and I help run his campaign. You guys gave me a mission. I'm doing the mission."

Miller stews for a moment. "You know what? I think he's onto you. You screwed up and he knows you're working for us, and he's feeding you this bullshit to fuck with us. Okay. Okay, we can work with this. As long as he doesn't know that we know that he knows you're a spy, we've got the advantage."

"Wait a second. You saw *The Americans*, right? It's entirely possible this guy is a Russian spy. Those people have training, skills. Really serious skills. I kind of doubt we're up to going head-to-head with a professional."

"Don't you worry. I've got this."

Great. It's not enough that he wrecked immigration policy, now he thinks he's James Bond.

"I'm not trained for this. Neither are you."

"I said I've got this."

"Okay, fine." For several moments she says nothing. Then: "I'm waiting."

"For?"

"Instructions."

"Oh. Well, you know, just keep doing what you're doing. Be cool. Smart. Don't let him know that you know."

"Thanks. Very helpful. But if he knows . . . sooner or later the shit hammer's gonna come down. On me."

"What hammer is that?"

"You tell me. But I'd really like not to end up in an unmarked grave somewhere in Boonfuck County, Texas."

"Now you're just being dramatic."

This guy. How did the ant climb all the way to the top of the flagpole?

"So I just keep . . . I guess you want me to stay in touch with you?"

"Of course. From now on you report to me and the campaign. But our little thing, that's strictly between you and I."

"That's not how it was set up."

"Yeah, well, situations evolve. We have to respond to the moment. We can't be rigid."

Says the biggest stiff in the administration.

"Okay. Well. I guess that's all for now. Unless you . . ."

But he's already clicked off.

19

THE DALLAS DAILY

Rasputin Calls for a "New Awakening"

OUR EXCLUSIVE INTERVIEW WITH THE CANDIDATE

Politics on the Slow-Drip Method
Magical Thinking or the True Faith?
"Let the Children Play"

By Clarence Thomas Jr., National Affairs Correspondent of The Dallas Daily

SOUTHLAKE, TEXAS POSTED DECEMBER 5, 9:48 P.M. CST—

In his first in-depth interview since officially joining the race for president, the professional wrestler Grigory Yefimovich Rasputin, born some 44 years ago in Buffalo, New York, as an all-American boy named Patrick Walsh Strickland, sat down with The Dallas Daily at his Southlake estate to discuss his still-evolving views on religion, abortion, LGBTQ rights and the spiritual and psychological state of the nation. Against a backdrop of daily attacks by President ██████ on the rival he calls "Fake Russian," an insatiable media clamoring at his door, and fresh outbreaks of political violence triggered in part by his candidacy, Mr. Rasputin insists on keeping his own deliberate pace.

"I am a new candidate," he says, even while acknowledging his candidacy is over a month old. "Running for president calls for careful contemplation and study. So I am studying, learning. And praying, always. Might this be better than dashing around saying the first thing that comes into my head? Perhaps we have too much of that already."

Chill in the Chill

On this bitter cold day of intermittent snow and sleet, with the thermostat set to a bracing 55 degrees, the candidate seemed quite at ease in a short-sleeved T-shirt, gym shorts and sandals. "We must all do our part to preserve the grid," he said of the interior chill. Earlier that day, the egregiously misnamed Electric Reliability Council of Texas (ERCOT) performed what has become a regular exercise in the Lone Star state, issuing emergency conservation alerts and warning of blackouts. Would a President Rasputin have any interest in absorbing Texas's fragile, stand-alone grid into the national infrastructure?

"This is something I would definitely explore," he replied. "If Oklahoma and Arkansas can have heat and light on the hottest and coldest days of the year, I do not see why Texans should be deprived of these modern things."

On this reporter's previous visit to Southlake in September, the Rasputin estate had the rollicking pool-party atmosphere of a tropical resort. Now it more closely resembles a luxurious business retreat. Most of the mansion's first floor has been converted to offices and conference rooms. Campaign staff, layered up in bulky sweaters and scarves, scurry about with the keen air of bird dogs and McKinsey consultants. Workers putting up Christmas lights tend to their tasks with similar high-minded efficiency. The only party happening this day is outdoors, where a contingent of the wrestler's famous "Maidens" alternates between leisurely soaks in the steamy hot tub and shrieking plunges into the ice-cold pool.

"Our campaign is working hard," declared the two-time world champion wrestler. "But it is crucial not to be hasty. We are too much in a hurry in America! Iowa is not for many weeks. There will be plenty of time to reveal my program to the people."

The Evolution of an Agenda

One might suspect that American politics is seriously ill when millions of people throw their support to a candidate whose actual policies they know virtually nothing about. In any event, it's not new; think Obama in 2008, █████ in 2016. Thus far Rasputin's political rhetoric (gleaned for the most part from his All World Wrestling monologues) stakes out standard Republican turf: strenuous neglect of the "well-regulated militia" clause of the Second Amendment, stalwart support for prayer in the schools, and reliably soothing conservative verbiage about free markets, law and order, national defense, stringent border controls, and cutting taxes. But in several key areas he indicates a willingness to depart from the hardcore party line.

"Abortion is anathema to me," Rasputin flatly declares. "And of course the church has long considered abortion a sin. But in the law, in a modern society, women must have access to the medical care they need to live healthy, productive lives. To deny our sisters, our mothers and daughters this basic care—is this itself not a sin?"

He shows a similar willingness to wrestle with nuance and complexity with regard to LGBTQ rights, walking back previous statements broadly condemning any deviation from conventional heterosexuality.

"Perhaps, in the past, I have spoken rashly," he admitted. "Unthinkingly. In certain highly commercial settings. But a candidate for president is obligated to think and reflect, to put full truth into his words, and we know these things happen in nature. Hermaphroditism, same-sex affinity, gender dysphoria and so on, these too are part of God's creation. A just society, a healthy modern society, makes space for the entire scope of God's abundant panoply.

"So that is one side of it. But there is the other side, the side we are seeing so much today, not just in America but everywhere in the West, the erasure of gender on a mass scale. And I say bluntly, this is not nature. The way of nature is binaries—male and female, yin and yang, electron and proton, this is the universal pattern. But walk down the street in any major Western city today and you see boys in dresses and women's hair and makeup, their frail bodies, the feminine way they walk—no. This is not nature. This is the symptom of decadence and decay, the pageant of moral exhaustion we have so much of in the West."

The Russia Riddle

According to Rasputin, the West's salvation lies to the East, and the moral and spiritual rigor of the Russian Orthodox Church. He urges us to think in "civilizational terms," and his own range of reference includes the Roman Emperor Constantine's conversion to Christianity in 312 A.D., the conquest of Constantinople by the Ottoman Empire in 1453, and the 1686 edict granting the Russian Orthodox Church authority over the Orthodox Church of Ukraine. His politics hew hard church, including his take on Russia's subjugation of Ukraine and its ongoing "soft" takeover of the Baltic states.

"The Slavic peoples have a centuries-old common history that begins with the baptism of Russia," Rasputin asserted. "At the heart of our history is the mission of the Russian church to strive for Christ's kingdom on earth.

"The breaking of the Ukraine church from the Russian in 2019 was a huge scar," the wrestler continued. "President Putin could not allow this schism to stand. To do so would have betrayed Russia's holy mission."

Rasputin insists that he is neither an apologist nor an agent for the Russian state, merely "a simple man" whose faith is anchored in the Russian Orthodox Church. He claims to have had no contact with Russian intelligence or military services during his six years of uninterrupted residence in the country. Some American intelligence experts find this hard to believe.

"A U.S. Special Forces veteran in-country, that would definitely flash red on the FSB's radar," said Dan Sullivan, a former CIA case officer, referring to Russia's Federal Security Service, successor to the Soviet Union's notorious KGB. "Russian military intelligence too, they would be all over an American with that background."

Sullivan, who spent most of his career in eastern Europe, thinks Russian intelligence would assume the American was a U.S. government operative. "They'd be keeping close tabs on him, through human and technical surveillance. They'd also have assets developing personal relationships with him, not just as a way of figuring him out, but also to bring him around to the Russian point of view."

Would they attempt to recruit him to the Russian side?

"I'd be highly surprised if they didn't try," said Sullivan.

To Save America's Soul

But Mr. Rasputin insists he was never approached by Russian intelligence, much less recruited. His admiration for Russia, and for President Putin and Patriarch Kirill, head of the Russian Orthodox Church, is based on his faith in the Russian church as a bulwark against what he calls "Western decadence and paganism."

"As I myself can attest, I found my path out of the turmoil of decadence by following the holy elders of the Nikolaev Monastery."

His personal experience and his historical perspective inform his call for an alliance of "the world's two Christian superpowers," the United States and Russia. "It is the only thing that makes sense!" he declares. "First, it is essential for the survival of the United States. Second, for the creation of Christ's kingdom on earth."

A heavy order, on both counts. One pauses at the audacity.

Must America become a Christian country in order to save itself?

Rasputin's answer is unequivocal: "Yes." But he's quick to add, "This transformation, this New Awakening, cannot be forced. It will happen through prayer, leadership, example. Over time, if our faith is true, the New Awakening will produce equilibrium on the material plane."

What about the millions of Americans who practice other religions? Not to mention agnostics, atheists and all other varieties of none-of-the-above.

"In the New Awakening, no one is forcing anyone to come to Christ. Let us be clear, faith by force is a contradiction in terms. Our movement will accomplish its work through love and loving persuasion, and history shows this can be done. For over a thousand years, church and state in Constantinople functioned as two parts of a seamless whole, in a condition of *sinfonia*, harmony."

What about our constitutional separation of church and state?

"'Congress shall make no *law* regarding the establishment of religion,'" he offers in gentle reproof. "Our *sinfonia* will be organic, flowing naturally from within. It will marinate all aspects of our government in the spirit of Christ."

As for what a Christ-marinated Rasputin administration might look like, the candidate demurred. "The time for details will come, but not now." When pressed on whether his admiration for Putin might suggest similar authoritarian tendencies should he take power, Rasputin was adamant.

"Of course not," the wrestler answered forcefully. "America is a totally different system, a system of laws and independent judges and so forth. We can admire President Putin's dedication to the church without endorsing all aspects of his regime."

When pressed again for specifics—this time on the most constitutionally dubious policies of the █████ administration—Rasputin again demurred. Would President Rasputin dissolve the semiofficial militias such as the National Security Brigades and the Rapid Support Forces? Would he do away with the so-called Administrative Detention program? Would due process in criminal and immigration proceedings be restored? Would the grossly immoral family separation policy be abolished once and for all?

"We are carefully studying all of these things," Rasputin said. "Has █████ gone too far in certain measures? This may be so. But civilization requires proper order and security at all levels of society. Violence, chaos, anarchy, these are the opposite of civilized order. We cannot achieve God's kingdom on earth as long as there is chaos in the land."

Of Egos and Antichrists

When he's not traveling, Rasputin sometimes ventures into the crowds outside his estate to perform what his supporters claim are feats of miracle healing. To all appearances, he continues to comfort individuals afflicted by the weeping sickness, as millions have witnessed on his televised matches. As for rumors of his cures of cancer, Parkinson's disease, paralysis and other maladies, the candidate dismisses this reporter's inquiries with a shrug.

"I help people as I am able" is all he's willing to say.

Did you acquire these powers of healing during your time in the monastery?

"I grew in the spirit," he says simply.

Some people claim your healing power is evidence of pagan magic or even Satanic influence.

"I cannot stop misguided people from saying what they will. But I can assure you, in this they are deeply misinformed."

With his recent claims that Rasputin is the "agent of dark forces" and a "fan of the Antichrist," President ██████ has put the mystical element squarely front and center in the fight for the Republican nomination. Until now, the wrestler has refused to respond, but on this gray, snowy day in Southlake, he decides the time is right.

"The president is wrong on many levels to speak this way," the candidate begins, mildly enough. "*Tyomnye sily*, as we say in Russia, the dark forces that are more powerful than a nuclear bomb—even to reference them out loud is a dangerous thing. So I caution him. I caution the president in the strongest terms, for the sake of his soul. But perhaps it is too late."

Reader, your reporter could do no other than follow up. Too late for . . .

"Well," Rasputin answers carefully, "I have seen the true face of ████████████████. I have seen him with these eyes that learned from the elders of the ancient Holy Rus. An entire millennium of grappling with the mysteries of faith, and I believe that █████████████ is infected with the spiritual disease of narcissism. And his is the most malignant species of this infection—he is the narcissist who has fallen into the abyss of nihilism. If he cannot be the sun and center of the world, then the world cannot be permitted to exist. His mind cannot conceive it. His ego will not allow it."

"The Proper Work of Children"

Rasputin may fear for the president's soul, but he reserves his most biting scorn for Vice President Marjorie Taylor Greene. Resurrecting an old proposal by her fellow Georgian Newt Gingrich (remember him?) from the 1990s, the vice president recently unveiled a plan whereby cash-strapped public schools would, beginning with first grade, require students to take over the janitorial duties of their schools. "Students will learn valuable workplace skills and life lessons about responsibility, hard work and self-sufficiency," the vice president recently enthused. "Not to mention they'll have the great satisfaction of knowing they're giving back to their schools and communities."

Rasputin says he has a better idea. Instead of "volunteering" children to work as janitors, he proposes a program whereby members of Congress and local legislators do five to 10 hours of service each week as public-school custodians. "Yes," the candidate muses, "I think our politicians can learn many valuable workplace skills and life lessons under my program. And they will have the great satisfaction of knowing they are giving back to their communities."

Seriously?

Rasputin smiles. "Why not? Better than children. Our children have much more important work to attend to."

Such as?

"Playing! The proper work of children is play. And, of course, going to school, which should be a place of excitement, joy, discovery—another means of play. Let the children play, and learn from their play, and grow strong in their minds and bodies. Soon I will be unveiling a comprehensive plan of physical culture for all schoolchildren. In America we sit around too much! We need to get our bodies moving!"

"A Glorious New Day"

Unlike his chief rival for the nomination, Rasputin refuses to demonize his counterparts on the Democratic side. "They are our fellow Americans, and I accept their patriotism at face value. But Democrats are misguided. Naive. They are blind to the presence of Satan in the world. Until they acknowledge this crucial truth, all of their nice words and intentions will be as straw in the wind."

Throughout our interview, the candidate maintained the Rasputin persona he has perfected over the course of his successful pro wrestling career. The "Russian" accent, the occasional Russian-language words and phrases, the malapropisms and jumbled syntax with which he sprinkles his English—not to mention the striking physical resemblance to his namesake—all of these create a credible rendition of the Russian holy man known to history as Grigory Rasputin, 1869–1916.

"I am that man," the wrestler insists. As for how the candidate could be that same Rasputin who was born in Siberia in 1869, our modern Rasputin is cryptic.

"All of these things I will reveal at the appropriate time," he promises. "But for now, let me say that the ancient mysteries are more powerful than our skeptical modern age can imagine."

An explanation that so far seems to satisfy the Republican base. A recent *New York Times*–Siena College poll shows 86%

of Republican voters hold either "favorable" or "very favorable" views of Rasputin.

"They get me," he says of his supporters. "And I get them. The New Awakening has just begun, but already we feel its power! A glorious new day is beginning in America."

20

This morning, Saturday, putzing-around sort of morning, Clarence moving slow in sweatpants and a Brookhaven hoodie, and the flannel-lined slippers Gayle gave him several birthdays ago. Cold outside, *cold*, wind chill in the low teens, and a scurf of winter cloud the color of dryer lint. Two drive-bys by the Buick boys this morning. He sat at his dining room table reading the papers and watched them pass, a pair of clean-cut men in dark suits, one white, one black. So either a very nice gay interracial middle-management couple has moved in down the street, or he's being surveilled.

At the moment he's settled in his recliner with the gas logs going, CNN on mute, a book in his lap, a mug of coffee on the table to his right, and on his left the remote, cell phone, and laptop. Life could be worse. He counts his blessings and decides he feels . . . scoured. Rinsed and racked. Mood in the key of medium blue. Last night he did his second *Rachel Maddow* appearance with all the attendant nerves and adrenaline, and this morning Renfro texts every few minutes with updates on their numbers. Once again, the best little online paper in Texas smokes the bigs! Truth, he's kind of aggravated. At himself. Or maybe not so much aggravated as frustrated, unfulfilled. He hasn't come close to piercing the Rasputin veil, though he's yet to really try. Stalking, is what he's doing. Taking care not to make his move too soon. Last night on *Maddow* he offered hardly a hint of his suspicion that the Candidate legally known as Grigory Rasputin is a secret hardcore fascist. He didn't spill for Rachel, much as he likes her. As seductive as her bright-eyed attentions may be. But hell, just on their face the wrestler's pronouncements put him at the gates of Christianist theocracy. Think *Handmaid's Tale*—Clarence does—only without the funny clothes or critically low sperm counts.

How to hit this guy so the truth comes out, this is the challenge going forward. Meanwhile he's reading a dense tome titled *The Rasputin File* and eyeing the latest on CNN. At last night's Democratic primary debate, the candidates earnestly called for reasoned discourse, mutual respect for our fellow citizens across the political spectrum, and harsher penalties for parole violators. Also during the past twenty-four hours: mass shootings in Chicago (five dead, nine wounded) and Dearborn (seven, thirteen). Weeping outbreaks in Philly, Atlantic City, Cleveland, the Knicks game at the Garden, and a classic car rally outside Birmingham. Street clashes between ██████ers and the White Guard in multiple cities leave four dead and scores hurt. With the polar vortex sweeping south, advocacy groups warn of potential fatalities at Territorial Control Centers along the border, where thousands of detainees are housed in tents. Four UK journalists with *The Guardian* and *Tortoise* remain in jail while their challenge to the Administrative Detention program creeps through the courts, and at a mini-rally last night in Jackson, Tennessee, ██████ claimed the White Guard is full of "Venezuelan mafias" and "leftist hit men." "What they're doing in the streets, the streets of our cities, these riots were planned years in advance," the president declared, and Rasputin and "his henchmen" are plotting a "Marxist revolution just like what happened in Russia." Then he mused about the prospect of civil war and vowed to declare martial law "if this keeps up."

Nelson texts, Snowing up your way?

Clarence glances out the window. No.

Nelson: You got power?
Clarence: Yes.
Nelson: Flurries here. Be there around noon with lunch.
Clarence: Sounds good.
Nelson: Where's the box?
Clarence: Dining room table.
Nelson: You crazy.
Clarence: I really don't think it's a bomb.
Nelson: Careful. Don't do anything till I get there.

He sets the phone aside and checks his email. His *Dallas Daily* queue has been stacked ever since the Rasputin story posted, and the *Maddow Show* triggered a second wave. A goodly number of these things are flat-earth crazy. One correspondent informs him that Rasputin is a shape-shifting reptile from the Alpha Draconis star system, the same race as the Rothschild and Bush families. Several emails assert that the wrestler is the illegitimate son of JFK Jr. Another claims the Candidate's telepathic powers caused the train derailment outside Vines, Louisiana, that released clouds of mysterious stinging yellow gas. Clarence's eyes toggle between email and the TV screen, email, TV, email, TV. It's all the same continuum, the continuum he mentally files under Loss of Reality. He's also received his normal complement of eat-shit-and-die emails, and then there's this, an anonymous audio file that arrived overnight from a now-defunct email address:

[Sounds of rustling, heavy breathing; intermittent slapping]
MAN'S VOICE: Like that. Like that.
WOMAN'S VOICE: You are God! You are God!
MAN: I am driving Satan out of you!
WOMAN: Oh God yes oh god I feel it! I feel it! Oh God. Oh God.
MAN: More?
WOMAN: Yes oh god yes. You are God. You are God.
MAN: Love is holy.

WOMAN: Oh yes. Oh God please yes.
MAN: Say it! Say it! Love is holy!
WOMAN: Love is holy!
MAN: Louder!
WOMAN: [shouting]: Love is holy!
MAN: Out! Satan! Out of this woman! Out!
WOMAN: Yes! Oh God yes!
MAN: Out! Out! Out! He is leaving! He is—[unintelligible].
WOMAN: Oh yes, oh God, you are God, you are—[unintelligible].

After a gap, the audio resumes. It is the calm after the storm.

WOMAN: —ever being so happy.
MAN: That is the Holy Spirit in you.
WOMAN: Yes, I feel it. I know it. Such peace. I—Grishka.
MAN: My love.
WOMAN: I can't go back. Please don't make me go back.
MAN: [unintelligible].
WOMAN: There is no marriage. Joke marriage. He only wants me to stay so he can win.
MAN: My love, we must think about the country.
WOMAN: I am thinking about the country! If he wins it is disaster for everybody! US, the world, everybody. And if I stay with him, I help him win? I will never forgive myself.
MAN: Da. But if we declare ourselves—do you think the American people will forgive us?
WOMAN: They will. I know they will. Americans are good, Grishka. They understand love. And they love you so much.
MAN: No, I think they love you more.
WOMAN: Silly! They adore you.
MAN: They adore you more. Come here.
WOMAN: I—oh! Oh goodness! You are—
[Audio ends]

So far he hasn't shared it with Renfro or anyone else. Whatever game this is, he's not sure he wants to play, even assuming the audio isn't fake. He puts aside the laptop and goes back to *The Rasputin File*. Apparently it's required that all books about Russia be over six hundred pages and have teeny-tiny type. Well, Russia is large. Vast. Too much to pack into a normal-size book, yet the original Rasputin very nearly swallowed the whole country, which at the time was shredding at the seams. Mysticism, crank ideologies, and get-rich schemes abounded. The czar was neurotic, the church a bejeweled and moth-eaten fool, a crazy aunt who refused to stay in the attic. In Moscow, Saint Petersburg, on the streets and in the salons, doom was in the air. That a charismatic Siberian shaman, cunning, earthy, with a healing touch for the czarevitch and octopus hands for the ladies, would rise to the height of power seems no less logical than the plot of a really spicy soap opera.

Clarence makes copious notes in the margins, refers often to the royal family tree at the front. Russia is old as well as vast, and it dawns on him why Putin might want to replace his current White House tool with a younger, fresher model. Well of course, Putin's playing the long game; very Russian. Clarence goes online to read up on the Russian Orthodox Church and discovers that the monks of the Saint Panteleimon Monastery, said to be the most pro-Russia monastery on Athos, have formed their own chapter of the Wrath of God Fan Club.

Nelson arrives amid snow flurries. With white specks in his hair and deli bags in his hands, he walks straight to the dining room and regards the large cardboard box on the table.

"So that's it."

"That's it."

"No name or address."

"Nothing. It was just sitting on the porch when I went out to get the papers."

"Damn, Key. And you brought it inside?"

Clarence shrugs. "Didn't want anybody taking it." In all honesty, he thinks there's less than a two percent chance it's a bomb.

"All right. Well." Nelson studies the box a moment longer. "Let's eat."

He's brought fancy food from an upscale deli, healthy stuff, nothing fast or fried. They unpack bags and containers in the kitchen.

"Man, you're such a yuppie."

"What! Yuppies are *old*. Yuppies are your generation. Ruppies."

Ruppies; retired yuppies, right. "Nobody around here I know's retired."

"You don't have to tell me. You killed it on *Maddow*."

Clarence grunts.

"Seriously, you're a natural at this. And she was clearly digging your mind."

"I did sense a constructive rapport."

"You really ought to think about getting an agent."

"For what."

"Get your name out there! Monetize that thang."

"I got all the money I need. And I'm already working harder than I want to. Where you wanna eat?"

"Den? Duke's on."

Nelson is a proud double alum, BA and JD. They settle in with their lunches, Clarence in the recliner, Nelson on the sofa. It's Duke versus Princeton in a nonconference battle of the brains. During commercials Clarence surfs the news channels.

"You're kind of a junkie, you know that?"

"It's my work."

"Aggghhh, Fox, stop it! You watch *them*?"

"I think it's good to check in and see what they're saying. Test your assumptions." Then, before he can stop himself: "Something's happening."

Nelson's head swings around. "You mean like now? Today? Or just generally."

"Well, generally."

"Okay. So you gonna tell me?"

Clarence resigns himself, to a point. "Fascism."

"All right, yeah, people are talking about that. But they never say what they mean by it."

"Power."

Nelson waits.

"Power over justice. Power as justice. Ultimate power as the justification of itself."

"There! See? I get it! Nobody breaks it down like you. You oughta do a story, lay it out exactly like that. So people will understand."

"I could do that story. I'm not sure about the second part."

He flips back to the game. Duke scores. Princeton scores. Go, team. Ever since Gayle passed, Clarence doesn't have much use for sports. The mystery box nags at the back of his mind like a guest he's rudely abandoned in the dining room.

"Emerald says she saw you the other day at Southlake. Talking to the man."

"She shoulda said hello."

"She was heading out to work. And anyway she didn't want to intrude." Duke shoots, misses. "She thinks you're cute."

"Very kind of her."

"We're going out tonight. Dinner, hit a couple of clubs. Dance."

"Sounds nice. Nobody gives yall a hard time?"

"Not the places we go."

"Not Southlake."

"Oh hell no, we stay downtown. Listen, uh, I still don't know what the deal is out there. With, you know—"

"Forget it. You got a good thing going with this woman, stay on that. Forget about the politics."

Nelson sets down his fork.

"You sure?"

"You really like this girl, right?"

"Key, I think I do."

"She likes you?"

"I think so."

"That's what matters. That's pretty much all that matters."

He can see Nelson is thinking about Gayle now. Pitying uncle for the great tragedy of his life. Apparently he spoke with a little too much heat.

"But what if he's a fascist?"

"I'll figure that out soon enough."

They finish lunch coincident with the start of halftime. Clarence takes his plate to the kitchen and Nelson follows. Time to deal, not that anybody has to say it. They go to the dining room and eyeball the box while Clarence explains the plan.

"Well hell," Nelson grumps. "Why'd you even have me come over then."

"So you can call 911 if it blows."

As instructed, Nelson stands well back in the den while Clarence carries the box through the kitchen and out to the backyard. The box weighs about eighteen, twenty pounds, the weight concentrated in a compact mass at the center. Clarence is painfully aware of how this entire rigamarole smacks of old-man antics, yet there's the ominous weight of the thing, and the undeniable fact that a lot of mentally ill people hate his guts.

"You stay back," he calls over his shoulder to Nelson.

"I am back!" Nelson stands just inside the sliding glass door.

"Open that door all the way. So if it blows you won't be cut to pieces by flying glass."

"Yeah, well," Nelson stage-mutters. "I guess he *was* in a war zone, once upon a time."

"Damn right I was. Flying glass ain't no joke."

Clarence becomes aware that he's sheathed in a microscopic film of all-over sweat. He borrowed his neighbor's burn barrel for the occasion, an old fifty-five-gallon oil drum that now sits in the middle of the backyard. In the barrel he's placed a round, heavy-gauge plastic trash can, and in the trash can a three-foot-high kitchen stool on which he now sets the mystery box. The box sits well inside the trash can and barrel, but within workable reach. He goes slow with the box cutter. Surgical. Pictures the box going boom in his face.

"You okay?"

"Peachy," Clarence murmurs.

"Key, if you really think it's a bomb . . ."

A few stray specks of snow settle on the box. Cloud dandruff. With his fingertips Clarence eases open the flaps to find thousands of styrofoam packing peanuts. After several minutes of gentle scooping he's uncovered the top of the thing, wrapped in layers of tape and coarse white pulp paper. He starts slicing the outer layer.

"Game's back on."

He cuts a glance over his shoulder. For some reason they both start laughing.

"Shut up. Trying to concentrate out here."

"You go, unk. Doing a heckuva job."

More scooping, more cutting and peeling. Gradually the thing takes form. Brass. Cylindrical. Ornate. Highly detailed piping and filigree, elaborate teapot dome, curlicue handles on the sides. A vessel or urn of some sort. He takes off the lid and leans over for a cautious peek. There's a note inside.

"What is it?"

"One of those Russian tea things, I think. A whatchacallit"—now it clicks—"a samovar."

"No shit. For real?"

He pulls out the envelope and slices it open. "*Hey Fake News*," the note reads in galumphing boyish scrawl, "*I appreciate you! Your friend Grishka, The Wrath of God*."

Now he's miffed. Not flattered, not one bit. *I appreciate you.* To Clarence this means he wasn't hard enough on him in the article. He brings the samovar into the den and sets it on the coffee table, and he and Nelson give it a thorough lookover. What it is, basically, is a pimped-out brass urn with an elaborate spigot at the base and matching tray and bowl, all in all the kind of eccentric antique one might find in the penthouse suite of the most decadent hotel in New Orleans. Amid the fine Cyrillic engraving the only thing they can read is a date: 1875.

"You know how to work it?"

"Come on, man. I'm a coffee guy."

"Well, I think it's baller. Can I have it when you die?"

"You can have it right now."

"Come on! Future president of the United States gifts you this, you can't just give it away. Might be worth something!"

"Well, I sure can't keep it."

"Why?"

"Why? And you're a lawyer? Don't they teach ethics anymore?"

"I think you're drawing way too fine a line on this. Man gives you a car, a trip to Hawaii, I get it. But this"—Nelson turns his fond regard on the samovar—"this is a gesture. A simple token of his esteem."

Nothing simple about it, is Clarence's feeling. They settle in and watch the rest of the game. Nelson drinks one of his uncle's beers and surfs samovars on his phone. He comes up with a value guesstimate of $3,500 for this one. Clarence manages not to flip to news during commercials and goes instead to the Weather Channel. More flurries expected for the DFW area, lows tonight in the single digits, cover your plants and bring in the pets. Duke wins; Nelson predicts hard partying in Durham. When they ought to be studying, Clarence thinks, a cranky old-head thought that's tiresome even to him. But with the apocalypse looming you might want to learn a few things that could possibly get you through it. Outside, the flurries have morphed into snowfall. Regular snow globe out there, very pretty.

"You doing anything tonight?"

"Got a bunch of reading I need to do. I'll get on that."

Nelson pooches his lips, says nothing. Common wisdom in the family holds that it's time Clarence got a good woman in his life. Nelson collects his coat, his daypack, sets them on the couch, goes to the bathroom, sits back down, messes with his phone, futzes some more with the samovar. Whatever it is, Clarence wishes he'd get to it. Finally he does.

"Uncle, I got something for you. It's, uhm—now, you don't have to keep it."

Clarence says nothing.

"Just think about it. Tell me you'll think about it."

"Let's see it."

From his daypack Nelson pulls a sleek, matte-black, absolutely evil-looking sidearm. Here, in this house. Clarence had his suspicions, and even so recoils a little.

"It's a Glock nine-millimeter," Nelson says, setting the thing on the coffee table next to the samovar. "Semiautomatic, seventeen-round magazine, easy to learn and maintain. You see I had them go ahead and put a trigger lock on it. Comes with an extra magazine, and I got you two training sessions with an instructor. Package deal."

"Nelson." Clarence is both touched and horrified.

"I know! I know. But we just worry about you over here by yourself. All the shit going down, and you putting yourself right in the middle of it. On national TV."

There's something pornographic about the object, fetishistic, taboo. Its sleek perfection exerts a kind of dark gravity.

"Well, thank you. I wish you hadn't. But thank you."

"I went ahead and reserved a session for you tomorrow afternoon. I'll go with you. I could use some time on the range myself."

"Nelson, I'm just not feeling it."

"Would you just think about it, please? The world's gone crazy, Key. And all those crazy people know right where you live."

"I appreciate all that. And I appreciate you. But I need you to take this with you when you go."

Nelson rolls his face toward the ceiling. "You are the most *stubborn* man ever."

"No, that would be your grandaddy. He never owned a gun either."

"Uh-huh. The world's changed a lot since then."

Well, there's something to think about. Both yes and no, for better, for worse. So much the worse for better not being better than it is, given all that we know, all that we've been through. Medgar, Malcolm, Martin, all the angels of history weep.

Nelson stows the Glock in his daypack, says he'll keep it for the thirty-day return period in case Clarence changes his mind. Clarence sees him off from the porch. "Check it out!" Nelson shouts, spinning down the front walk with his arms stretched wide like a helicopter winding up for takeoff. "Got ourselves a regular blizzard!"

"Not bad for Dallas," Clarence allows. "You and your girl have fun tonight. Be careful out there."

"*You* be careful."

Monday, ten a.m., he's at the palace for press duty, packed into the ballroom with his Fourth Estate colleagues. Bardem Hayes announces the official campaign kickoff will take place on January 2 at JPMorgan-Chase+Citibank Stadium, home field of the Dallas Cowboys. "Cheerleaders, hubba," someone woofs, setting off ripples of *hubba hubba* across the room. Who will be speaking at the rally? Will there be celebrities? Wrestlers? Cheerleaders? What's the plan if the Weeps break out? But most of the questions today are follow-ups to the *Dallas Daily* interview. The media want to know more about the Candidate's views on abortion, Putin, the New Awakening, the state of the president's soul, and the Antichrist as an imminent political possibility. Hayes, a balding, chubby-cheeked thirty-something who looks nothing like his presidential forebear, turns testy. "I don't have that information at the present time," he says, on repeat. Clarence hangs loose at the back and holds his peace. He had his turn, let them have theirs. As the briefing breaks up, a campaign intern finds him in the crowd. "Bitsy would like to see you," he murmurs, and Clarence follows the kid through the house to the kitchen. Dead center of the cooks' hurlabaloo Bitsy sits at the island drinking coffee and eating avocado toast. He invites Clarence to take a seat.

"You get it?"

"I got it." One of the cooks sets a cup of coffee in front of him. "Thought at first might be a bomb."

"You know, that did occur to me. Oughta shoulda give you a warning."

"It's okay. It's quite a thing."

"Grishka very proud of himself for thinking that up. You'll see him shortly."

"Great. I can thank him in person."

Bitsy chuckles through his teeth, *tsee tsee.* Clarence admires the whirling-dervish energy of the cooks. So this is what the inside of a tornado looks like.

"My friends are still hanging around."

"Mmm, sorry. But that ain't coming from us."

"Any idea who?"

"Lord knows. I don't think they mean you no harm."

Clarence gives him a look.

"No, I mean . . . nobody gonna touch you, I mean. I just think you make 'em nervous."

"Then I'd very much like to know who they are. Maybe I can reassure them."

"Uh-huh. Well, follow the money, I expect."

"Right, but there's so much of it these days. Billions and billions, where would I start?"

"I do hear that."

Charlie Cupps breezes through the kitchen with Belinda on his heels. He gives Clarence a comically frosty nod and keeps going. Then here comes Faith Spack tearing along like a blond bullet train. She sees them and veers their way.

"Did he get it?" she asks Bitsy, giving Clarence the sly eye.

"He got it."

Now she speaks directly to Clarence. "You like it?"

"It's very unique," he answers, and the other two laugh.

"You use it yet?"

"Still figuring out how to work it. Listen, you think you can get me a few minutes with Twiss or—"

"Have a great day!" she cries, and speeds off. For several moments the two men bob in her wake.

"I was going to ask if I could get a few minutes with Twiss or Nadler."

"I'll put out the word. You might wanna mention it to Grishka too."

"I'll do that."

"Professor, I got a question for you."

"Shoot."

"Martial law."

"Okay."

"That mean ██████ could throw us all in jail?"

Clarence hesitates. "Remember the protective custody roundups after the Flash Crash?"

"Best I recall those people got out, eventually."

"Mostly. Once everything started settling down. But you wonder what if it hadn't."

Bitsy nods. "All right then." He studies his avocado toast. "It start going down, you might better look for me in Canada."

The intern returns for Clarence; the Candidate will see him now. They troop past various grand rooms converted to office cubicles and arrive at what used to be the poolside rec room. The adolescent fantasy world of foosball and ping-pong has been supplanted by a computer-driven war room, with rows of long tables where youthful citizen-soldiers man their stations. Rasputin is ensconced within a semicircular command post with six or seven senior aides. He rises to greet Clarence with a grin and outstretched hand.

"Fake News! Welcome!"

"Russkie."

At this a number of heads snap up, but Rasputin is unfazed.

"Good day to you, my friend."

"Back at you."

Several top aides swing their chairs around to watch. Everyone else goes back to work.

"You are well?"

"Extremely well. And you too, I trust."

"Very well, very well. Snow always makes me happy! Invigorated! Like Russia!"

"Too bad it's starting to melt."

"And so much buzz from your excellent article, Clarence Thomas. Should I have talked to you sooner, I wonder. But I want my thoughts to ripen fully before I take them to the people."

Clarence nods. "Thank you very much for the samovar."

"You are most welcome! Do you like it?"

"It's amazing. I'm floored. A real work of art."

"It is Russian Imperial period. Very special." He says something in Russian, and smiles when Clarence shakes his head. He switches to English: "The time of the blessèd czars."

"Well," Clarence says with a straight face, "now it means even more. I know you were personally very close to them."

More head-snapping among the ranks; the top aides seem poised to leap out of their chairs, and Faith Spack is suddenly hovering near. But Rasputin only nods and briefly closes his eyes, clasps his hands before his chest as if in prayer.

"May I ask you something?"

"Of course, Clarence."

"Are you a *Khlyst*?"

Rasputin's eyes go wide, and he beams.

"Fake News, you are learning! Excellent! Am I *Khlyst*," he pauses for a chuckle, "no, but for sure I know of those people. Why do you ask—do I seem as one of them to you?"

Twiss swoops through the door—did someone alert him?—and tells the Candidate he's needed on a donor call. In the same breath he thanks Clarence for coming and says it's time for him to leave. Instead of going straight to his car, Clarence crosses the road and spends some time with the Rasputinheads. Not to be harsh, but their part of the field looks like a trashed-out homeless camp, and it's here that he encounters the scruffy, the sick, the sad, the lost, the chronically unemployed; Malthusian casualties of the American dream. Two things he's learned in the second act of his reporting career. One, the longer you talk to right-wingers, the angrier they get. Two, many of them, the men especially, seem to have only the haziest notion of how human reproductive biology works. Leaving Southlake, he swings by Costco for paper products, batteries, and Covid tests. He stows his purchases in the trunk with the samovar box and undertakes the death-defying freeway trip to downtown Dallas. Arrives intact, one of those everyday miracles we're always taking for granted. He parks in the surface lot across the street from the *Daily* office, carries the box up to the second floor, and presents the samovar to his editor like the head of an enemy.

"Um-umph," Renfro says.

"It's a gift."

"From whom."

Whom. Clarence knows how lucky he is to have this editor.

"Rasputin."

"He gave you this?"

"He did."

"Because?"

Clarence shrugs. "I'm donating it to the paper."

"Are you now." Renfro considers the thing. "You're thinking it might be a conflict of interest."

"Something like that."

"You sure? I don't have any problem with you keeping it."

In truth, Clarence would prefer to be rid of the thing. It's depressing. It gets on his nerves. He sniffs all kinds of corruption in the culture behind it, a fatal fussiness and obsession with protocol. Such a big-deal production for dainty little sippy cups of tea. Renfro orders in sandwiches for them, and while they're eating Clarence plays the anonymous audio file. And again. Then one more time. Renfro blinks rapidly through parts of it.

"It sure sounds like him."

"Yep."

"She calls him Grishka."

"She does."

"It sounds like her, too."

Clarence agrees.

"Okay. Well. Of course we can't do anything with it. Not without authentication."

"Of course not."

"But, hell." Renfro takes a deep breath. "We could blow the race sky high if we wanted to." He ponders. "If it's fake it's a pretty damn good one."

"Ren."

"I know." He's silent for a moment. "No idea where it came from."

"None. Not really. One could speculate."

"I expect one could. Till the cows come home."

Over lunch Clarence pitches his next story, a preview of how the Rasputin campaign is likely to unfold in January. Then a story on the increasing frequency and lethality of political street violence, and is the country becoming desensitized? With references to Germany in the 1930s. And he's got a third story simmering, much more in the nature of a think piece: a survey of the fascist continuum in America, from opportunistic grifter to hardcore ideologue. Renfro blesses all three. Clarence leaves knowing he's got his work cut out for him, and is all the happier for it; maybe feels an extra bounce in his step for having shed the samovar. He has his key fob out as he weaves through the rows of parked cars to his Subaru. He punches it twice as he draws near; the car blips, followed by a thump and a man shouting "Ow!" Clarence steps into his row—now he has a clear sight line—and sees a man's legs sticking out from under his car. "Hey!" he shouts, and the next moment he's pivoting as a second man comes at him from the side. He backpedals and feels himself trip, knows it's a parking bumper he's stumbled over, and he's falling, arms swimming in empty air. He experiences a tremendous *clunk* at the back of his head, and everything goes black.

21

Khlysty sex, is that what they're up to on the third floor? Clarence Thomas's question sent her tumbling down an internet rabbit hole as dank and labyrinthine as the New York subway system. The *Khlysts* appeared in seventeenth-century Russia and endured well into the twentieth, an ascetic Christian sect whose members abstained from alcohol, swearing, and sex, fasted perilously, and were into whips. They renounced priests and holy texts in favor of direct communion with God, and worshipped their charismatic leaders as living Christs. For their ritual "rejoicing," they stripped down to underwear and danced themselves into ecstasy, spinning, screaming, sobbing, chanting, speaking in tongues. According to popular belief, these rites concluded with "holy intercourse," i.e., frenetic group sex, on the principle that true forgiveness is possible only after sinning your brains out. They were brutally hounded by church and state. Their leading "Christ" was twice crucified, and twice rose from the dead. They had "utterly special eyes," according to one who knew, eyes that "burned with a sort of liquid, iridescent light, and sometimes the gleam becomes perfectly unbearable."

The most famous alleged *Khlyst* in the sect's three-hundred-year history being none other than Grigory Rasputin, the Siberian holy man and spiritual intimate of the Romanovs. Now reincarnated, or something, as a twenty-first-century sports entertainment star and contender for the US presidency. "He's got heat like I've never seen," Ricardo Levy says to Faith one day. At least once a week the wrestling mogul flies in on his ooo-la-la 727 to check on his star and give advice to everyone in the political operation. "Not even Hulk had heat like this, and Hulk was epic. But he wasn't changing history the way Grishka is."

Faith nods. Ricardo always stands too close, and right now he's breathing on her salad and trying to look down her blouse. She finds him kind of gross, this aging billionaire bodybuilder with the dyed-blond hair and matching eyebrows. She can't help wondering why his colorist never thinks to tint the wooly gray tufts sprouting from his ears.

"Ricardo, would you like some lunch? I'm sure the kitchen would be glad to fix something for you."

"Nah, I'm good."

She was quietly eating at her desk and minding her own when he just happened to come along. Or maybe not.

"Faith, I've been thinking about you."

Uh-oh.

"You're an extremely beautiful young woman, Faith, I trust you know that. Just exceptional in every way, you check all the boxes. And you've got a story, a ready-made brand just begging for leverage. So I've been thinking—hey, that's me, the entrepreneur, can't stop thinking about business!—and I believe you'd make a super appealing product for our market."

She laughs. Is he hitting on her? "Ricardo, I—"

"You seem pretty athletic. You do sports in school?"

"Well, field hockey."

"Chicks with sticks, I love it. Grishka says you're really strong, he tells me you've been working out together. I ran it by him and he agrees, this would be a totally natural next step for you, reality TV to AWW."

"I don't know the first thing about wrestling."

"Bah, we've got the best trainers in the world. In six months we'd have you super ripped and schooled on the moves. I see real star potential in you."

"What if I don't want to be a star."

"What! Everybody wants to be a star, you're *already* a star. Come on, Faith Spack from *Nashville Next Gen*? You've got a name, a brand. A ready-made backstory. The whole thing with your dad, everybody was gaga over that! Okay, let me put it to you this way. How would you like to make a million dollars a year?"

"Is that a firm offer, Ricardo?"

Firm, that one little four-letter word, that's all it takes to get him all hot and bothered. His neck bulges, his eyes go slightly bug. He's settled only about umpteen sexual harassment suits over the years.

"What I'm offering"—he has to pause and clear his throat, *aghm*—"is the chance to have one hell of a ride and make a ton of money in the process. Listen, Faith, I know this country. I know what it wants even before *it* knows what it wants, and I see you becoming a huge star in our business. You want to make a difference, right? I'm guessing that's why you went into politics, very admirable. But if you really want to make an impact in the world, come get in the ring with us. You'll have more power and influence than you ever dreamed of."

His phone pings, and he has a look. "I gotta take this. We'll talk. Think about it! We'll talk."

The no cell phones rule went out the door a long time ago. Now it's all phones all the time and Faith is glued to hers same as everybody else, and what a malicious little beastie it is, toxic, temperamental, just to function she's taken to wearing surgical gloves in public. "I'm allergic to certain metals," she tells people, whatevs, maybe it's true. The physical effects aren't so different from what she's heard of the first-trimester blahs, nausea, fatigue, feelings of all-over bloat. She switches it on first thing in the a.m., it might snap a bolt or two of red lightning at her, just to remind her who's boss. Sometimes in heavy usage mode she swears she feels a kind of ionized thickening in the air, some sort of electrical charge or cloud crackling around her. Or maybe it's all in her head and she's losing it. The double-agent life is clearly not for her, of a piece—so maybe she isn't *that* crazy—with discovering early in her sexual career that keeping two boyfriends at the same time seriously messed with her mind. Lately she's tried reading a couple of John le Carré novels, hoping for sane-making tips on the spy game, but they just angsted her out more.

On the news, continuing reports of hawk and owl attacks on humans. One day a hawk swoops low over the palace and bombs a snake into the hot tub, talk about precision strikes. Bitsy has one of the yard guys promptly fish it out, but for several days the Maidens won't go near the hot tub. One by one the pygmies suspend their campaigns; by Saint Damasus's Day, Vice President Greene and Senators Jawfair and Inchmeal are the only small fry still in the race. Rasputin keeps rising in the polls, and the president keeps railing about foreign interferences, or is it interferencers? Nobody knows, much like the bigly/big league conundrum of yesteryear. He urges violence on the weepers at his rallies, calling them "actors" and "infiltrators," and vows to run as an Independent if the GOP "betrays" him.

"I'm still the president!" he bellows at a rally in Portland, Maine. "And I'm going to stay the president!" He's turning Gothic, going heavier on the blood and gore. Call it the passion of ██████████████: It's as if he's already up on the cross, or maybe he's just "the whiniest little bitch who ever lived," quoth Charlie Cupps. "Martial law," ████████ muses to the crowd in Maine, "you know what that means, we're allowed to fire at will. At. Will. Just level down and blast 'em to smithereens, right?" Big roar from the crowd. "It won't be pretty, but I guarantee it'll get the job done. And when it's done, and I mean *done*, let their mothers cry for them, 'cause the rest of us sure won't be shedding any tears."

Faith wonders if the docs have upped his plasma doses, which reliably excite his aggression levels. She read somewhere, maybe it was *Cosmo*, that men whose wives are cheating on them have elevated sperm counts. More sperm, higher testosterone, is that what's happening here? She tells Stephen Miller to please convey to the president that his Rasputin-as-apeman act isn't playing well in the heartland. "*You* tell him," Miller replies. "*He* thinks it's brilliant." Rasputinheads are already camping out in front of JPMorganChase+Citibank

Stadium in advance of the January 2 rally. It promises to be huge. Yuuuuge. Only natural given the pent-up demand. The Candidate is on sabbatical from AWW while he prepares for the official launch of his campaign. Now even the flabby big middle of public opinion seems to be shifting his way. He polls strong favorables among Independents and self-described centrist Dems, and Brooks David, house sage of the *Times*, weighs in with a column headlined "Is Rasputin the Answer?"

> . . . Perhaps Mr. Rasputin can wrest Christian slogans and symbology away from the partisan zealots who for too long have promoted an ethnocentric, materially acquisitive version of the creed. Whatever favors this strident strain of Christian dominionism has done for America, they are much outweighed by the divisiveness and infectious rancor it has fostered. One hardly recognizes the Christianity of Jesus in the dominionist agenda, which lays claim to "real" American values.
>
> Even for non-Christians, a genuinely Christological approach could animate a much-desired reset, a polestar toward which we might orient the country and rediscover our true American roots. For ours is indubitably a nation founded on the genuine ideals of faith and freedom. We need only think of the Reverend John Winthrop's "city upon a hill" sermon of 1630, in which he pledged the neophyte Massachusetts Bay Colony to a covenant with God to become a beacon for "all people," invoking the words of Jesus from his Sermon on the Mount: "Ye are the light of the world. A city that is set upon a hill cannot be hid."
>
> Southlake, Texas, would seem no less improbable a place than the small, isolated settlement of Plymouth Bay in which to forge a new American covenant. But Mr. Rasputin, currently Southlake's most famous resident, does the country a great ser-

> vice by reminding us of our founding Judeo-Christian heritage. For all of his bellicose showmanship in the wrestling arena, his years of study and contemplation among the monks of the Nikolaev Monastery are borne out by his insightful commentary on the spiritual life. This is a man who thinks deeply and walks humbly, an authentically charismatic Christian spokesperson whose message, firmly grounded in the Gospels, of love and reconciliation is a welcome balm for rancorous times.
>
> Perhaps despite the ubiquity of Christian posturing in our politics, the sad truth is that America is not Christian enough. Mr. Rasputin's "New Awakening" movement might just be the harkening of a new era, offering the prospect of a refreshed, more united nation.

"I think he's a lightworker," Christie says one night over dinner. "At the very least. Maybe he's more than that."

Logy from wine and sixteen-hour workdays, Faith can barely muster the strength to mumble, "More, how." Though she has only the haziest notion of what a lightworker is.

"I think he could be the Light Incarnate."

Faith takes a moment to process. "You mean, like, Jesus?"

"Well, no. Not exactly. Different category. But it's all part of the Light Occultic Force. You'd need to study up before I could really start to explain it. I could give you some reading material!"

Maybe someday. Faith hardly has time to brush her teeth these days, much less grind through reams of badly written Christian cant. The next day Christie donates $50,000 to the New Awakening SuperPAC, and Faith hits the roof. Mom! The campaign's got more cash than it knows what to do with! Save your money, let the billionaires carry that freight. Indeed, the freight borne up on oceans of dark money, Christie's piddly $50k a mere drop in the seven seas. Millions and millions wash in every day, where does it all go? The digital operation, staff of two hundred plus and rising, soaks up millions. Ditto for data collection, broadcast and cable TV ads, polling, fundraising, ground game. The campaign has paid staff in every one of Iowa's ninety-nine counties, with robust budgets for leadership sessions, neighborhood meetups, door knockers, and phone bankers. Same for New Hampshire, getting there in South Carolina and Nevada. Around the palace Faith hears rumors of Rasputinic troll farms in Macedonia and Belarus flooding the e-verse with anti-█████ fake news, and for a fact social media is teeming with wacko stuff. What goes around comes around, maybe this is the iron law of karmic physics? She suspects the president is wigging out, and Stephen Miller confirms as much in their next phone call.

"Be thankful you're down there," he says. "He's popping off about twenty times a day."

The poor president. One of the parts of *The Real West Wing* he loved best was lording over billionaires and business titans in the Oval Office. Even more than being fawned over by hot women, it was the truckling of CEOs that fed his bottomless ego. For three years Faith watched them pass through the White House, and like some half-wit herd of wildebeests obeying the migratory laws of nature, now they're all turning up in Southlake, the weaselly shits. They're not even subtle about it, but why would they bother. We The People let them have it all their way for decades, then came the Flash Crash, and for about a week the People were ready to hang them from the lampposts. █████ saved the day with a slew of emergency orders, the arrest of a couple dozen cryptos and hedge fund managers, and the confiscation of all of Elon Musk's US-based enterprises.

Now Musk is lying low in eastern Europe and it's business as usual for everybody else, and here they come, the daily parade of money mutts to Southlake. It sort of makes her sick. Is nausea a political emotion? If so she's still a MAGA girl, except Rasputin fever is starting to burn her up. She aches all over, hips, back, boobs, scalp, the roof of her mouth. She needs his big hard body on top of hers, crushing the fever out of her bones.

"You think I should go into wrestling."

They're in the gym, the day after Ricardo made his pitch. Rasputin goes blank for a second, then smiles.

"Ah. He spoke to you."

"He said you said it's a natural next step for me."

Now he's chuckling. "Faith, do not believe anything anyone in the wrestling business ever tells you. I said I think you have potentials, because he asked. That is all."

Faith ponders for two reps, *oof, oof.* She's on the leg press.

"You think I could do it?"

"If that is your choice. If you commit one thousand percent."

Two more reps, *oof, oof.*

"I really don't like the idea of people beating on me."

Rasputin laughs and touches her wrist, and that entire side of her body tingles for the rest of the day. She can feel herself starting to crack. She needs help. A dose of tender loving sympathy and a good pep talk. The next day she goes AWOL and drives over to Southlake Town Square. She gets a Starbucks at the drive-through and parks in a middle row, just one more Lexus amid the crowd. On the seat next to her are her regular phone, the spy phone, and a burner she bought at a Get-N-Git a couple of days ago. She sips her latte and considers the handsome shops, the tasteful holiday decorations, contoured suburbia in all its comforting banality, except the Christmas spirit has everyone on murderous edge. Within minutes she witnesses three near-collisions, multiple honking spats, and a middle-aged white lady cussing out a black security guard. Two spotless high-dollar pickup trucks face off over a newly vacated parking spot. Screams, engorged neck veins, the works. Will there be blood?

And ye shall be as a city upon a hill. Faith sighs and drums her fingers on the steering wheel. The windshield frames a panorama of pitiless ice-blue sky streaked with feathery cirrus. Winter is coming, baby. Deal with it. She picks up the burner and punches in the number for Harvey's personal cell. Leaves a message, *I really, really need to talk to you. Call me back in the next thirty minutes. Please.*

Now she waits. Her mind pitches within a williwaw of perfect randomness, but there's the ache, always, that double whammy of physical and spiritual yearning all mashed up together like a twice-baked potato of exalted lust. Working out with Rasputin yesterday, there were moments when she verged on delirium. His pheromones or whatever, his musk, his funk, she might as well have been mainlining MDMA, then came that touch on the wrist. Even now she detects a residual buzz. So if she goes full *Khlysty* and ends up in his bed, wouldn't that be just the ultimate espionage coup? Except she wouldn't be working for ██████ anymore.

She nurses her latte and resists the urge to mess with the phones. Come on, Harvey. Give me a reason, man. As the minutes tick by it becomes too easy to dredge up old resentments. As in, for instance, how squirrelly he was when she addressed a glaring omission in their relationship.

"How come you've never asked me about birth control?"

He blushed about fifty shades of red. A full-grown man, and the two of them lying there naked as the day they were born.

"I, uh, just assumed that's your private business. I don't want to pry."

She snorted. "My *private* business? You seemed pretty interested in prying into my privates a few minutes ago."

"I—right. Well."

"Harvey. What if I got pregnant."

The jaw drop, the big eyes, it was cartoon comical. She managed not to laugh.

"I'm not. But what if I was."

He looked away and dragged his fingers through his hair. "Then I guess we'd have to talk."

"Well then I guess we would!" She waited for him to say something. Anything. Nothing. "And I guess we'd have to talk about terminating."

"*No.*"

"You wouldn't want me to get an abortion."

"My God, Faith, no. You know how I feel about that."

"Okay, does that mean you'd marry me?" This was just cruel, but he was pissing her off. He sputtered, ducked his head, blinked like a man in a sandstorm. "Right," she continued, "well, I noticed we don't use condoms, so I guess I better be on birth control. Unless you've got a little secret you aren't telling me." She made a snipping motion with her fingers.

"Uh, no."

"Interesting. Okay, so what about you and Maggie? What do yall do?"

"Come on, Faith, that's my marriage. That's between her and me."

"I'd say at this point *I'm* what's between you and her. You guys must do something, right? You had four kids in a row, boom boom boom. Then finito."

"I'm really not comfortable talking about this."

"Oh my, so sensitive! And you work at the White House? Making policy on this for 320 million Americans?"

"Stop it."

"Are we not adults? Adult people who presumably take responsibility for our choices?"

His voice shaky, like a man on the verge of passing out. "We do rhythm. I guess."

"You *guess*? Harvey, you're killing me, man. You don't know? I mean, can't you *tell*?"

He swallowed. It went down hard.

"You know what I think? I think Maggie's on the pill."

"No. She feels the same way I do about that."

"IUD?"

He recoiled. "No!"

"You user. You really don't know, do you."

He turned blank-eyed vague, like a little boy caught with firecrackers in his pocket.

"I'm on the pill, just FYI. So you just let me know if that's a deal-breaker."

It was not a dealbreaker. For you either, she reminds herself; for all his wussy Catholic anguish and hypocrisy, she kept taking him into her bed. And will again, she supposes, if she gets the chance. She finishes her latte and checks her watch against the dashboard clock. Time's up. She reaches under her dress and pinches the inside of her thigh really hard, and decides to give him five more minutes.

22

It's a warm sunny day in the countryside, with chiming birdsong all around like candy for the ears. Lush green grass, rolling hills, a picturesque patch of woods in the middle distance. The path leads that way in easy, lazy curves, through acres of flowers and humming bumblebees. The air gentle as bathwater, enough butterflies around for a ticker tape parade. Clarence has a staff in his hand, but the walking is smooth. The path is a kind of dense-packed sphagnum that gives and springs with every step, a return of energy that serves as splendid therapy for his muscles. He hasn't felt this good since—he can't remember. Lighter than air, no aches, no pains, and a bracing clarity in all his systems. The man beside him seems to know this, he's watching Clarence and nodding and smiling. He, too, has a staff, and keeps easy pace with Clarence, a big-boned white fella with a generous gut, could stand to shed a few. Long shaggy hair going gray, graying beard and mustache, and he wears the kind of blocky steel-frame glasses that were the style during the eighties. His face kindly, relaxed. Faintly mischievous. An old hippie who's aged gracefully into the bourgeoisie, but with the glint of subversion still in his eyes. His voice thrums with the musical resonance of an old beer barrel:

"It's cool."

Clarence nods. He's aware of certain gaps, but a passing swirl of lemon-colored butterflies briefly distracts him.

"I think I might be a little confused."

"Totally normal! Take your time, hoss. We're in no rush."

Clarence does a quick physical inventory, spine, lungs, liver, gut, everything running like a well-oiled sausage machine. He tries to remember how he got here but comes up blank. The lapse of continuity, of causal sequence, brings on a queasy feeling, and this, at least, seems familiar.

"I guess I'm dreaming."

"Totally normal you would think that! But you're not. So try not to flake on me."

Clarence doesn't know what to say, so he says nothing. The path is tracking on a gentle uphill grade. The woods are close enough now that he can feel cool air breathing out of the shadows. He side-eyes his companion, who returns his regard with a certain fondness. The man does look familiar.

"Do I know you?"

The man laughs and holds out his hand. "Terry."

They shake.

"Clarence."

"I know who you are."

"Terry," Clarence says, and stalls out. Then he has it. "You're the guy who wrote *Dr. Strangelove.*"

Terry beams.

"I heard you speak at the Dallas Art Museum years ago! I brought my students, I signed us up when I saw you were coming. We watched *Dr. Strangelove* and *Easy Rider* in class the week before you came."

"I remember those kids! Really sweet, bright kids. They asked great questions."

"Those were mine. But aren't you . . ." Suddenly it seems impolite to say it. "Dead?"

This gets a big laugh. "I have passed on from the earthly realm, yes I have, Clarence. Terry Southern is dead as a doornail, if you want to get technical about it. But no worries, C.T. You're not."

For the first time Clarence is frightened. He wants to stop but his legs keep going, carrying him closer to the woods.

"Would you like me to explain?"

"Please," Clarence answers, queasily. And hurry it up, he wants to add, before we get to those woods.

"There's a lot about this you can't understand, but just to put it in layman's terms, you're in the in-between. You took a bad knock on your head, remember? In the parking lot?"

Clarence nods. Actually he does, now that Terry mentions it. He's known all along, it's just that he forgot to remember.

"So while you're in the neighborhood, so to speak, some of the chiefs thought it would be a good idea to bring you in for a chat. Fill you in on a few items of concern."

"The chiefs."

"The brass, the elders. Senior level. The ones who walked through fire and back."

"Are they up there?" Clarence nods at the woods.

"Nah, it's just me today. I'm your designated point person, guide, whatever you want to call it. To my great pleasure and honor, I might add."

Clarence nods. *Why couldn't it be Baldwin?* he thinks, or does he say it out loud? Terry laughs.

"Jimmy's got the week off. Sorry, you're stuck with me."

"No, I didn't mean—"

"Clarence, it's cool, brother. Jimmy's a stone genius, right? Who wouldn't want to hang with James Baldwin if they got the chance? But you and I are both North Texas guys. We're—well, let me just say we are connected in all kinds of strange and wonderful ways. So. How you feeling?"

"Shaky."

"Steady on, daddio, I got you. There's a nice little spot up here where we can sit and talk."

Now Clarence is thinking of Gayle, wondering if he has the guts to ask about her. His sweet baby, gone far too soon, too young; *he's* the one who was supposed to go first. If she's here, if he could see her—he knows it would break his heart all over again, and he would do it. Do every station of that pain just to have a glimpse of her.

Whispery high grasses front the tree line like ornamental fringe. The temperature drops a few degrees as soon as they pass into the shade. The trees are ancient, enormous: Oaks, elms, beeches, their billowing canopies sculpt blimp-sized vaults of space. It's cathedral acoustics here, the birdsong as sweet and belling as a children's choir. Furry woodland critters frisk and scamper about; the sight of humans sends them into ecstasies of alarm. As they move deeper into the woods, vocabulary from British Romantic poetry gets going in Clarence's head. Glade. Copse. Swale. Leaf-laden boughs. And the air so fresh and pure, like getting a micro-vitamin bump with every breath.

At first he refuses to credit what he's seeing along the path. The thing is just too weird for his rational mind to grasp. Most of the people he doesn't recognize, ordinary-seeming people at first, in long-ago clothes and vintage hairstyles. Women in housedresses and aprons. Dust Bowl farmers, Depression-era workingmen. But soon it's GIs in battle fatigues, then Frenchies smoking and drinking at an outdoor café, then greasy-haired beatniks in black turtlenecks. Next, smiling baton twirlers in spangly uniforms with "Ole Miss" blazoned across their womanly chests. Each scene materializes as a see-through hologram, a live-action tableau projected onto some sort of transparent screen or panel. Now they come upon Richard Nixon, of all people. The former president is hunched behind a gargantuan desk in a dark suit and tie, breathlessly muttering into a Dictaphone mic.

"I, uh," Clarence begins, and gives up.

Terry laughs. "Crazy, right?"

"What . . ." He can't even form the proper question.

"These are my pods. The stuff of life, or as you're seeing along here, my particular life. Everybody has them."

They come upon a tableau featuring the old *Lawrence Welk Show*, with the venerable maestro of schmaltz himself conducting his orchestra while Bobby and Sissy do wholesome turns about the dance floor. The perspective bends around to the back of the iconic bubble machine, where a man stripped to the waist, sweaty and grimy as a stoker, pumps the apparatus as if working a giant bellows. It looks like awful work, medieval work, literally backbreaking; so much suffering to produce silly clouds of bubbles. The man stands upright to wipe the sweat from his face, and Clarence recognizes the late actor Dennis Hopper. This miserable creature looks their way, and his eyes go wide.

"Terry!" he cries. "Hey Terry! I'm still here, man!"

Terry answers mildly, and rather sadly, it seems to Clarence.

"I can see that, Den."

"Man, this sucks so bad! I'm dying here, Terry, I can't take any more of this squaresville shit. Wouldja please put in a good word for me?"

"I do, Dennis. Every chance I get."

"How much longer? Terry, baby, they're killing me here! That old man," Hopper lowers his voice, sneaks a glance at the ever-smiling Mr. Welk, "he's a slave driver. Everybody thinks he's so sweet, he's a fucking monster. I haven't had a break since I got here."

"I'm truly sorry, Den. I'll see what I can do."

"Hey listen, you got any dope on you? I could *really* use some decent dope right now. Or something harder if you got it, anything. I'm dying here."

"Den, baby, you know we don't do that here. Look, I'm sorry but I've gotta go. Hang in there, daddio. I'll see what I can do for you."

"Terry! Terry! Wait! Oh man, *please* don't leave me here!"

They move on. Terry turns silent, thoughtful, his lower lip drooping like a melancholy child's. Presently Clarence speaks.

"What was that about?"

"Oh, yeah. He and Fonda sorta did me over on the royalties for *Easy Rider*. I basically gave them the script for free, because it was all between buddies, right? No contract, I think they got me a couple of thousand from the producers for it. Then the movie hits and they clear something like nine, ten million apiece on the royalties. And never threw me a dime, and I was hurting, pretty much broke those last years. I was begging 'em, dig? My old party pals. But they didn't want to know me anymore."

"What happened to Fonda?"

"He's a roadie for Zamfir. Not as bad as *that*." Terry jerks a thumb over his shoulder. "Den gets it worse 'cause he went around saying he wrote the script. Still, you know, I hate seeing my old chums that way. If it was up to me I'd turn 'em loose this minute."

"But it's not up to you."

"'Fraid not."

They pass more pods. A little boy with a Mowgli-ish mop of hair playing in the snow. George Harrison and John Lennon sitting knee to knee, jamming quietly on their guitars. Henry Kissinger digging holes in a barren field, a mountain of bones towering at his back. Eventually the pods fade away, and they come to a majestic high-roofed forest shelter made of stone and rough-hewn logs. A massive stone fireplace walls off one end of the shelter, the other three sides open to the weather. Canvas camp chairs are arranged about the dormant fireplace, and hundreds of books rise in waist-high stacks from the floor. A few old couches are scattered around, random chairs, small tables. Terry ushers Clarence into the shelter.

"Still think you're dreaming?"

"I think I've decided just to let it happen."

Terry laughs. "Good man. You're doing great."

They each take a camp chair. Clarence stretches out his legs, casts his eyes over the books. All hardbacks, their cloth covers faded and worn. Butterflies etch scribble-scrabble patterns through shelter airspace, which smells of woodsmoke and orange marmalade.

"Terry?"

"Clarence."

"Am I going back?" He's thinking of Gayle now; has not for a moment, in fact, not been thinking about her.

"That's the deal." Terry studies him. "Do you want to go back?"

"It's awfully nice here." He hesitates. "But I've got people back there. I really don't think I'm ready to leave them yet."

Terry nods. “That’s always the hardest part. But you don’t have to worry about that today. You’re going back.”

It sounds like a marching order. Clarence envisions elaborate chains of command backing it up. “All right. I’m okay with that.”

“Good. Because we want you to keep an eye on those guys.”

“What guys?”

“The guys you’ve been watching. Those are really bad people, a lot of them. Most of them are just normally bad, which is bad enough, but the system’s built to handle cats like that. But some of them—look, we aren’t sure. But we’re getting indications they might have some seriously wicked juju going for them. Heart of darkness–type stuff, except a thousand times worse. Something may have gotten loose that really shouldn’t have.”

“What?”

“I’m not at liberty to say. You wouldn’t understand anyway, no offense. But I can tell you this, it affects us too. Those of us you might regard as the technically dead. We aren’t out of it. We’re still connected to all of you. Even the quote unquote dead aren’t safe, and we’re counting on you to get it right. There’s a certain kind of darkness we could *all* disappear into, if this shit keeps on. If it’s what we think it might be.” He studies Clarence for a moment. “You with me, brother?”

“I’m with you. But keeping an eye on them—I’m not sure what I’m supposed to do.”

“Witness. Report. Get the word out. That’s what you do, right?”

“That’s what I do,” Clarence concedes. “Just one more thing.”

“Yeah?”

“I assume I’m going to remember all this?”

“Yes you will, as long as you don’t flake.”

So Clarence thinks: I better not flake. Gayle, he reminds himself, ask him about Gayle. He needs to do it soon because Terry is looking at his watch, which, Clarence now sees, is its own tiny 3D planetarium, stars, comets, planets, and moons whirring around a nutshell of outer space.

“Clarence, sorry to leave you, daddy, but I gotta go. I’m due for lunch with Lafayette and Big Mama Thornton.”

"Wait. Lafayette?"

"The one and only. He's a great guy, and Big Mama—let's just say we have a vibe. There is most definitely a vibe. We've got a regular thing going, lunch every lunar node. We always laugh a lot."

"So that's how it is here?"

"Oh yeah, a lot of hanging out. I'm going to a party tonight at August Wilson's. Jimmy'll be there, I'll say hello for you."

"Uh, yes. Please do." Clarence realizes this is a rare opportunity, perhaps unique in the annals of human experience. "What else goes on around here?"

"Oh, we hang out a lot, like I said. Go for walks in the woods, eat and sleep whenever we want. There's a curriculum, but that's sort of hard to explain. Just think of it as the coolest college you could ever go to. And we get to read as much as we want, whatever we want." Terry nods toward the stacks of books. "Borges was right, it really *is* kind of a library. Anyway." He has another look at his watch, and rises. Clarence gathers himself to stand, but Terry shoos him back.

"You just sit tight, bro, you're good. Relax. Take a nap, read a book if you want. You'll be heading back soon."

Clarence looks up at Terry, who's smiling down at him. If God were to manifest in the form of a white man of comfortable age, as so many insist is the case, you could do worse than a face like that.

"Do I need to do anything?"

"Negative. Everything's arranged."

He digs deep and manages to get it out, the question that's been pressing him from the start. "I don't mean to talk out of turn, but, uhm—do you know anything about my wife?"

Terry smiles and answers briskly, "She's doing great. That was passed on to me to tell you, if you asked."

Clarence coughs to camouflage the sudden catch in his throat. "Where, ah, is she? Here?"

"She's spending time with her people right now."

"Her people."

"Her family. The line. We all do when we first get here. She's doing great, Clarence. You don't have to worry about her."

"Well, she was always pretty good at taking care of herself."

"As she continues to be."

Clarence weeps. It's not that he's unhappy, strictly speaking. He feels the loss as keenly as ever, but it's more that he's overwhelmed by the beautiful logic of this place. It just makes so much sense, all of it.

"That's all right, man," Terry says, "just let it all out. I've cried more times than I can count since getting here. Cry till you're dry, that's what we say around here."

"I'm not usually like this," Clarence manages.

"Hey, you're allowed. We hit you with a lot! All right, Clarence. Clarence, my man. Clarence Thomas Jr." Terry holds out his hand, and they shake. "It's been a pleasure and an honor. Catch you on the flip-flop, brother."

Terry is here and then he isn't; it's as if Clarence dozed off for a moment. He's slumped in the chair with his hands folded on his stomach, feeling supremely relaxed. There's a small pillow behind his neck—when did that happen?—and now he sleepily lolls his head to the side and looks over the stacks of books. He'd really like to check them out, but it feels so good, just this. Sitting here. Floating, it seems like. He can feel himself nodding out, and his last awareness is of tears leaking out the sides of his eyes, skittering down his cheeks in tiny baby steps.

23

Earliest early morning, still dark outside, she swings by the kitchen for coffee and there's Bitsy at the counter with his laptop, scrolling the news. She pours herself a cup, then leans across the counter to top him off. For the moment they're alone.

"I thank you."

"De nada."

"Miss Faith."

"Sir."

This is how they do sometimes.

"How come mass shooters almost never black?"

Oh shit. She comes around the counter for a look. Massacre in LA late last night, at a nightclub complex near downtown.

"Bitsy, you got me."

"We killing ourselves."

"Sure seems like it."

"Never did care for guns," he says in a musing voice. "My daddy had a Sears shotgun, pass down from his daddy. My brothers'd go out and shoot, shoot for dove. I didn't care nothing for it."

"It's not really my thing either. What's the latest?"

Bitty scrolls down. "Thirty-six dead, seventy hurt. They still finding the bodies."

"Jesus, did he drive a tank in there?"

A statement will be wanting. She hustles to her cube in the comms room and writes the words. Before the statement is released Rasputin will add his own touch: "We must love one another, and raise our children." But this latest in the steady drumbeat of massacres stays on her mind throughout the morning, and eventually links to a thought. Is this the civil war everybody's talking about? Raids, sorties, ambushes, self-regulating militias of one. Mass bloodshed as prerogative, as policy. Guns guns guns and so many shots already fired, so many fallen. The alleged killer went down shooting it out with the cops, white male, forty-two years old, IT guy, divorced. On SonicX ██████ surmises a White Guard connection and follows up with posts comingling the White Guard with Marxists, Black Lives Matter, transgender illegals, Venezuela.

"Did you know," Belinda asks Faith this same morning, "that Charlie went to jail?"

"I did not, Belinda."

"When he was in his thirties. He did two years."

"For?"

"Securities fraud."

"Well. I'm sure he came out fully rehabilitated."

They hold it in for a second, then burst out laughing. Belinda says nothing about the First Lady situation, and Faith doesn't ask. Maybe it was all a bad dream. Harvey never called back, a fact that sits in her brain like a radioactive implant. None of her old White House crew ever calls, nobody from comms, the show, safe to assume she's dead to them. Even if she returns in triumph someday, it won't be the same. *She* won't be the same. Living the lie is having a nebulizing effect on her personality, might be only a matter of time before she dissolves into air.

They monitor the unfolding LA situation. The White House announces a tripartite rare earth minerals deal with Ukraine and Russia.

"The earths," █████ calls these essential resources. Strip away the window dressing, and it's plain the US and Russia are carving up Ukraine like it's Congo in the 1880s. This is also the morning that Vice President Greene calls and demands to speak to Rasputin personally, and the Wisconsin Department of Health Services declares the entire water supply of Milwaukee unsafe for human consumption, and the Freedom Caucus forces an intraparty budget standoff, jeopardizing the months-in-the-making omnibus spending bill. Faith crafts a statement on the budget impasse and sends it up for review, and shortly she's summoned to Twiss's office. They've marked it up, and the Candidate himself adds a riff from Isaiah 1:18: "Come now, and let us reason together." She's leaving with the markup when he calls her back.

"Faith, have you seen Fake News?"

"Excuse me?"

"Our friend Clarence Thomas. We have not seen him for several days."

She realizes this is true. "I don't know. I can ask around."

"Please do. And would you call him for me, please? Tell him his friend Grishka misses his smiling face."

Has ever a presidential candidate talked about a reporter this way? Man's a unicorn, for sure. She calls Clarence's cell and leaves a message. An hour later with no word, she calls up *The Dallas Daily* and gets the chief. Oh. Omigod. That's awful. When did this happen? Omigod. She jots it all down and goes in search of the Candidate, but first she comes across Bitsy in the kitchen.

"Hey, Clarence Thomas is in the hospital."

"Which one?"

"*Dallas Daily* Clarence Thomas. He had some sort of accident, head injury. They've got him at Baylor in an induced coma while his brain swelling goes down."

"What happened?"

"Nobody knows. Somebody found him in the parking lot next to the paper's office, they think he tripped and hit his head. He was out cold."

She conveys all the details available to her. Condition critical but stable. Prognosis cautiously good. Timing, all depends. She and Bitsy decide that the campaign will send flowers and, assuming he's willing, a personal note from the Candidate.

"Maybe I'll go see him," Bitsy says all solemn and churchy. Faith is surprised; she didn't know they were close. Or maybe it's a black thing, some unspoken bond or code. Unspoken to honkies, anyway. It's on the afternoon of the day of this same morning that she will have one of the gravest shocks of her life. Later she'll go back and look at the Candidate's calendar, and there it will be in plain English, plain as the nose on her face, all very anodyne and innocent in the two o'clock slot:

2–3:15 GR, PT, RN, CC, BH meet w/ American Eagle PAC principals and CEO

But how was she to know who or what American Eagle is? So many billionaires and their PACs, so little time. Midafternoon, she's traversing the long rear-of-house hallway on her way to the rec/war room and there's a man coming the other way, backlit by the big picture window at the end of the hall. The light is always sketchy back here. Can fixtures throw mingy little silo beams, and that glare from the picture window fills the hallway like fog, but she has a snap impression of an older man in pressed jeans and a white dress shirt, rangy, slightly stooped, moving with a tentative, quizzical air. A visitor. A visitor looking for the bathroom. Gucci loafers, a friable thatch of tinted black hair. Faith, ever helpful, smiles and turns to point the way, is about to cry "Almost there!" or some such mindless chirple when she realizes he's goggling at her in abject terror. The next second all the air goes out of her. She, too, is terrified; it's as if she's stumbled on a ghost from her ancestral line, a creature she's never seen and knows at once. He averts his eyes and picks up speed as they pass. She wheels around; her heart's combusting like a gas explosion. "Hey!" she cries, but he keeps going. "Wait!" She wants to tell him it's okay, she doesn't mean him any harm, but he practically leaps for the bathroom and slams the door. The next moment she hears the crisp spin-snap of the deadbolt.

Well, hell. Fuck. What the fucking hell. It's several moments before she can catch her breath, and now the contrail of his cologne is wafting by, a scoundrelly tart-persimmon smell that nearly decks her. Of course he would be the kind of older guy who wears too much. Her father. Bio-dad. In the flesh. Here in the long empty hallway she turns this way and that, not quite bouncing off the walls. She thinks maybe she should just leave him alone, but dammit! She's his daughter. He should have to say hello; common courtesy demands that much. With her poor heart flipping and flopping like a hooked fish she backtracks to the bathroom and stands by the door. All quiet in there, not a tinkle or peep. She can feel him on the other side, listening.

Perhaps a minute passes this way.

"You're going to have to come out sometime," she says finally.

He clears his throat, slightly echoey in the bathroom acoustics, and when he speaks his voice is surprisingly matter-of-fact.

"I don't have to do anything."

The first words he's ever spoken to her.

"I'm just going to stand here until you come out."

Long pause. "Why." Again that bland matter-of-factness. They could be discussing a swatch of industrial carpeting.

"You have to look me in the face. You have to say hello to me." She pauses. "Your own daughter deserves that much, don't you think?"

Long silence. It makes her want to kick the door.

"Come on, that too much for you? What are you so scared of, *old man*."

Now he speaks: "I resent that."

Is her heart breaking? It would if she let it. "I don't want anything from you. I'm just asking you to come out here and look me in the face. And say hello. Just like you would any other person."

Nothing. She hears the scrape of Gucci soles on tile, a faint rustle. Then murmurs; he's on his phone. Within the minute a very large Samoan-looking guy in a black suit is plodding down the hall toward her. Bio-dad's body man; he's even taller than Rasputin and twice as wide, and there's real skill, a kind of lumbering wizardry, in the way he hazes Faith away without touching her. His lack of affect is part of it, that stony face, the way he stares over her head as the force field of his mass drives her back. The bathroom door flies opens and Clyde Quickly scampers down the hall. For a second she thinks she'll stomp the Samoan's foot with her stilettos and pursue, but what would be the point. She holds up her hands.

"All right," she says to the Samoan, "okay, I give up. You can go on back to your boy now."

Savant of esoteric financial instruments, currency wizard, arbitrage ace, founder and majority shareholder of his own commercial bank, Clyde Quickly became a billionaire in his thirties, back when having a billion dollars was something special. He charted new ground as one of the first celebrity billionaires, playing megastakes poker in TV tournaments from Vegas to Monaco, dabbling in Formula 1, setting meaningless speed records in his souped-up Bell helicopter. He continues to wheel and deal in finance—crypto and AI are his current jams—but his latest ego project is the massive casino and entertainment complex he's pitching for downtown Dallas. Damn irritating, then, that the Texas legislature has yet to legalize casino gambling, but the smart money says it's only a matter of time.

He was forty-four when Faith was conceived—she did the numbers when she was twelve—and married to his second wife. Eventually he left her and went back to wife number one. Now he's on number four—five, if you count number one twice—and seems well settled in a low-drama phase of life. Walking the line he is, straight and narrow; it wouldn't do for the aspiring casino king of Dallas to have a fresh scandal on his hands, not with all the Baptists in the legislature ready to pounce.

She supposes this is why, for all his billions, his bank, his fleet of helicopters, his fancy houses and ranches and boats, he can't afford to give her a simple hello. She's deep in thought, or shock, when Rasputin finds her at her desk. "Come," he says, plucking her coat off the seat back and holding it open. "We are going for a walk."

They exit out the back, cross the pool deck, and proceed along the perimeter of the Super Bowl turf. Faith stuffs her hands in her pockets and turtles deep into her coat. It's forty degrees and blowing hard from the north, gusts booming through the tree line like a cannonade. Dark, chunky clouds sail overhead, as elaborate and brooding as Spanish galleons. She wants to ask isn't he cold—he's in shirtsleeves—but she's so glum and numb that she doubts her mouth works. Like she's had a root canal or some similar oral misery and the whole lower half of her face is dead.

"You saw him," Rasputin intones.

She has to blink back a flash-burn of tears.

"I am sorry."

She shrugs. Out comes a sigh like it's her very last breath.

"Did you speak?"

She swivels her jaw, runs her tongue around the racetrack of her teeth. "Hardly." Okay, so the apparatus works. "Did he say anything to you?"

"Faith, he did not."

"But you knew."

"I saw his face, and I knew."

With his Rasputin x-ray vision, of course.

"It's nice to know I made an impression."

"Oh my dear, very much. His natural daughter, of course you would."

"He *knew* me, that's the thing," she blurts. "He knew me right away, it's so weird." The plastic grass crunches faintly under their feet. "Did he even know I'm working for you?"

"I think not."

"I think you're right. I seemed to be quite the shock." So at least there's that, the satisfaction of freaking him out. The downside being she's no less traumatized than he.

"I wish you would've warned me," she finds herself saying, and tries to purge the whininess from her voice. "I'd have been happy to make myself scarce—I don't want to cause problems. And to tell you the truth, I really didn't need that. I've done just fine all these years without seeing him face-to-face."

They reach the far corner of the artificial field and turn left, tracking the back of the end zone. Off to their right is a creek bed lined with cottonwood and hackberry trees, a feral hedge of brambles and woodland crud. Coyotes live down there in the cut, so sly and secretive you wouldn't know if not for the sirens. Let any kind of first responder vehicle sound the alarm, and the clever coyotes can't help themselves, they tune up and howl like a canine Tabernacle Choir.

"God has a plan, Faith."

And who is she to disagree.

"Better for you to act normally, freely. If God intends for Faith Spack to meet her natural father, it is not for Rasputin to interfere with His plan."

"Right. Well, His plan made me feel pretty shitty." She glances skyward. "No disrespect."

"However low the encounter made you feel, I think your father is feeling very much the worst."

"I doubt that."

"No! He is! He is completely tortured with guilt!" Rasputin's vehemence snaps her spine up straight. "We are talking about a man who has chosen to emasculate himself with regard to his natural duty. His duty to you. His magnificent daughter."

Her eyes brim over with another burn of tears. "Well," she has to pause and inhale the slurry slipping from her nose, "I just hope I didn't blow your meeting."

"Oh my dear Faith, not at all." He chuckles and takes her arm in his, and abruptly she's all New Year's and July Fourth inside, happy fireworks shooting off everywhere. "Clyde Quickly and his group are super on board with us."

Her arm in his makes her giggle without meaning to. She tries to walk normally even though she's floating several feet off the ground. "What's he like?"

Rasputin tucks her arm a bit closer. "Smart. Cordial. Money is his daily bread. He performs very well in the role of gentleman."

"Performs?"

"Performs."

"Not the real thing?"

"He is a rogue."

She laughs. "What makes you say that?"

Rasputin just smiles.

"So he's on board?"

"He has accepted to be my honorary Texas co-chair."

"Oh. Wow. ██████'s not gonna like that at all."

Another stab in the heart for the president, and she doesn't even care. Later she'll get around to caring, but for now this is all she could ever want, walking arm in arm with this dazzling man through blustery *Wuthering Heights* weather. Hopefully without being too obvious about it, she slows the pace, trying to make it last, but eventually the palace with all its add-ons and amenities looms before them.

"Faith," says Rasputin, and he pauses. Here comes an important announcement. "You need not ever be frightened of your father."

She winces. Cut her to the quick, that.

"Never, Faith. You are exemplary. In this situation you are totally without fault."

"I know. I mean I know it mentally, rationally. But when it comes to him I just feel . . . inadequate?" A weak laugh stutters out of her. "Like I won't ever measure up. I'll always be his little bastard. His mistake." Then it hits her in a way that she's able to speak. "I guess what I'm saying is, he makes me feel dirty. Shabby. It all just makes me so ashamed."

Rasputin turns and takes her shoulders in his hands, which are like welding mitts. He stoops so that they're eye to eye. "Faith, no. You are strong. You are good. You are brilliant and beautiful. He is a fool for denying you, and the entire shame is his."

She is, frankly, swooning. It takes all her strength to keep her eyes from rolling back in her head.

"The entire shame is his. Do you hear me, child?"

"Yes," she whispers.

"Do you believe me?"

"Yes," she whispers again. "I do."

"Good girl. Good girl. Set your heart and mind to this. You can do anything, Faith. You are strong and good and God loves you very much."

He kisses her forehead, and the touch of his lips is a revelation. For all her life, despite all the churchgoing and preaching and vacation Bible school that Christie put her through, Faith didn't have a clue, but now she knows: A blessing is an actual thing in the world. A physical thing, a fire within, a unity. An everything orgasm. No wonder all the saints and martyrs were mad for it. With effort she opens her eyes—when did they close?—and it's as if she's come from a long way off. Rasputin is smiling, and his eyes, dear God, they are portals to everlasting glory.

"Faith, I am here for you. Grishka will always be your true friend."

He squeezes her shoulders and wraps her in a tender embrace, and she goes off again, blessings in multiples. She thinks she might faint. He pulls back and brushes the tears from her cheeks, and he's smiling, laughing, and so is she.

"My dear girl," he says.

So this is how he does it, she decides over the next several days, working it out in her mind even as she's losing her mind. Her very own theory, the highly refined Spack Hypothesis, based on tense observation of her borderline demented state. The animal secretions, the tingling nerves like pincers under her skin, the outrageous sensual pitch whereby peeling an orange, brushing her hair, slipping into her Jimmy Choos triggers a head-spinning glandular rush. "Tantalize" is the word she lands on. After Tantalus; to excite; to tempt and withhold. Rasputin entices and teases the female to the point of derangement. The goal is not so much submission as delirium, you are required to come to his bed in a state of erotic abandon.

She understands, or at least thinks she does, but understanding doesn't make resisting any easier. Or maybe resistance is also required; the awful torture, self-inflicted, of holding out and holding on. *Tantalize.* Resisting involves cold showers twice a day, night masturbations, breaking from work to dash over to the gym and pound the crap out of the heavy bag. Praying. Pinching her thigh really hard. Until late one wild, desperate night she can't take it anymore. As if in a dream, a kind of preprogrammed hypnotic trance, she leaves her room on the second floor and pads barefoot to the grand central staircase. She's wearing sweats, nothing underneath except a triple spritz of Dolce & Gabbana Blue. She silently ascends to the third floor, where she's never been. At the top of the stairs, a Secret Service agent is slouched in a chair playing video games on his phone.

"I have an urgent message for him," she murmurs. The agent looks her over, then tips his head toward the double doors across the mezzanine. Apparently they're used to women showing up in the middle of the night. Faith makes her way across the mezzanine feeling fluttery, virginal. Weak in the knees. She eases open the heavy doors and slips past, finds herself in a large formal sitting room. Ornate furniture materializes out of the shadows—Chesterfield chairs, an elegant game table set with chess pieces, a couch not quite as long as a semitrailer. She stands there trembling, looking around as if casing the place. What's this about, you planning to steal something? She directs herself down a dim hallway. Half-open doors to the left and right reveal a bathroom, a small study, a home theater furnished with floor pillows and a low-slung sectional. She seems to be dangling in zero gravity, groping for something to hang on to. She passes a darkened workout room, then a prayer alcove with an altar and banks of devotional candles, a handful of them still burning. A spicy, mossy, mushroom smell pervades this end of the suite. His smell. She knows from their workouts. Behind the closed door at the end of the hall she hears his voice, but a more guttural, urgent version than she's used to.

Wicked! Wicked! Wicked!

A woman's long, deep moan overlaps his voice, a rapturous female purr of bliss. Faith's nethers are instantly slick.

You are wicked!

I am, I am, I am so fucking bad.

Wicked! Wicked! Wicked!

"Me too," coos a pouty third voice.

"And you must suffer," Rasputin answers, and there's a sharp, light slap, followed by girlish shrieks and giggles. Faith puts a hand on the wall to steady herself. For the next minute this is just about the hottest stuff she's ever heard. She knows those voices, Tiffany, Renata, and there might be a third woman in there, with all the tussling and dirty cross talk it's hard to tell. Faith grows lightheaded, short of breath. None of it seems real. Some sort of primal spell or suction seems to be pulling her in. She's got her hand on the doorknob, determined to see it through, and the next moment she's staggering backward with her hands over her face, silently weeping. Who *are* these people? What is she doing here? She has never felt so lost, so bereft. So unreal to herself. What she wants—oh please dear God not that, but she can't help it. Right now, more than anything, she wants her mother.

24

He nearly missed Christmas. He was home by then, but the headaches and sensitivity to noise and light made him more or less a recluse. People dropped by the house in ones and twos, sisters, brothers-in-law, nieces and nephews, Renfro. Nelson came every day, sometimes with Emerald, who happened to be the only person in his hospital room when he finally peered out of his coma fog.

"Emerald," he said, or croaked, his throat raw from the ventilator, and the moment would go down in family lore, that he knew her, this total stranger, even said her name. How did he know? Well, just by process of elimination. Who else could it be, this good-looking blonde in the leather jacket sitting by his bed? Plus he vaguely recalled her face from the palace.

"Are you in pain?" she asked, then added, "Nelson's outside. He had to take a call."

Clarence was tubed and wired up like a mainframe computer, mouth dry as crackers, throat blowtorched to a charcoal crisp. It took him a while to realize that this other thing in the room was his headache. Later he would learn that he'd been out for four days and semi-out for a fifth, slowly surfacing as they dialed down the coma drugs. Like the worst hangover ever, comparable to the aftermath of a weeklong bender in NOLA. He didn't remember much at first, and then he did. Delivering the samovar, he remembered. The parking lot, check, and the man messing under his car, and the second man coming at him from the side. No, nobody touched him; he managed the klutz flop on his own. He told Nelson, Bitsy, Renfro, only those with a need to know, and sure as hell saw no gain in getting the cops involved. Nelson combed over the car and found nothing, naturally. Whatever the spooks had been doing they'd quickly undone, GPS tracker probably, complete overkill. He wasn't hard to find, but those guys had groovy skills they were determined to use, an expense account to pad. After two more days at Baylor, he was transferred to a rehab center where he couldn't get out of bed without setting off alarms. There they coached his body back to remembering how to do. Walking, talking, tying his shoelaces. On the afternoon of the cold and rainy winter solstice he was released, and sisters Dolly and Carrie drove him home.

He feels worse than he says he does. Dizziness, nausea, the damn headaches. Brain fuzz like a burlap sack over his head. He can't read or look at screens for more than a few minutes at a time, so he mostly lays up in the recliner with his eyes closed and listens to the TV news, flips to music whenever he's had enough. FOMO, that's what they call it these days? Fear of missing out, hell, nothing new about that. He's down for the count, feels like. Out and definitely not about. Renfro comes by with a gag gift fruitcake, and, as Clarence requested, all the Terry Southern books he can lay his hands on. He tells Clarence that Duncan, the deputy editor, is going to cover Rasputin's January 2 launch, along with Renfro himself.

"See what a stud you are? It takes two of us to do your job."

Sickbed flattery is nice. Clarence makes noises about maybe being well enough to work by then, and Renfro smiles. "We'll play it by ear." Humoring him, and they both know it. The crowd roar alone would probably finish him off, though by the twenty-fifth he's feeling just steady enough to agree to Christmas dinner at Dolly's with all the family. That morning President █████ posts his Christmas greeting to the nation on SonicX—

Merry Christmas to everyone, not including the crooked and corrupt hacks in the Republican Party who are trying to deny me this historic third nomination, and all the globalist billionaires and my former so-called friends supporting the Marxist and communists agenda that would love nothing more than to take away our freedoms, and all the people I totally and completely despise because they want to destroy America and make us slaves.

—while Rasputin also posts holiday greetings:

I join with all Christians in celebrating with joy the birth of Our Blessed Redeemer. To all of our brothers and sisters of different faiths, we extend our most sincere wishes to you for peace, health, dignity, and strength during this Holy Christmas season and in the New Year to come.

Clarence sits in his bathrobe and slippers at the dining room table, eating Frosted Mini-Wheats and studying the posts for clues. Normally bad versus heart of darkness bad, how is he supposed to know one from the other? That he's applying the Terry Southern standard seems as natural as spooning in cereal and milk. He won't belabor whether his time in the in-between was quote unquote real, a genuine spirit sojourn as opposed to some amazingly coherent detritus his coma mind tossed up. It's as real to him as the memory of his mother's face, and the feeling—the settledness, the sense of peace—is much the same. In a way the total randomness seems a kind of proof. Terry Southern hadn't crossed his mind in years, then *that's* the guy waiting for him on the other side, this long-gone white man bodying forth in living color. Once he was home, Clarence went online and researched *Easy Rider*, and the tale of the royalties checked out. Fonda and Hopper kept all the millions for themselves; even years later, when they were rich and riding high and Southern was old and sick and broke, they were still blowing him off. All of this is news to Clarence, this obscure Hollywood intrigue from decades ago, as far outside his knowledge base as advanced string theory.

So there's your proof, for anyone who needs it. The in-between happened, on some level. It lives in his head, and as an organizing principle it seems strikingly apt to the situation, so on this sunny Christmas morning with the *Messiah* playing on his stereo, Clarence considers the quality and substance of two truly unique Americans, ████████ ████████ and Grigory Yefimovich Rasputin. For many years he's been satisfied that ████████ is bad news, but just how bad is the present question, eschatologically bad or merely world-historical bad? And as for that one who came into the world as Patrick Walsh Strickland . . . his phone buzzes. He has a look and flinches hard enough to activate a fresh headache. Speak of the devil. He hesitates to open the text, but must.

> Happy Christmas Fake News! Blessings to you and your family on this joyful Holy Day. I hope and pray you are healing, my friend. Come see me as soon as you can. Much is happening! Peace and blessings on you, Grishka

Well. He's sitting here wondering how to respond when Nelson's BMW pulls into the driveway, and a moment later Nelson and Emerald are crossing the yard bearing parcels. He's still in his robe and pj's, unshowered, scruffy-cheeked—what the hell, it's Christmas. He opens the door and they bring in all of outdoors with them, sunlight and earth energy and fresh cold air like the tangiest peppermint you ever tasted. Smiles, hugs, shuffling of parcels, it's a happy ruckus here in the foyer. "We're not gonna stay but a minute!" Nelson announces, but they've brought coffee from Trader Joe's and a fancy Christmas brioche, so of course he makes them stay. It's Christmas! Merry Christmas!

For unto us,
A child is born,
Unto us,
A son is giiiivennn

Bursting with vigor, these two, the high fine color in their cheeks and their bodies practically crackling with good health. It's obvious to Clarence that they made love this morning, and what better start could you wish for your Christmas Day, you and your baby waking up in that special way. They settle in the dining room, best sunlight in the house, and everybody helps with the plates and cups. Clarence can't quite believe how beautiful Emerald is. Gold-flecked hazel eyes, blond hair fluffed and gleaming, she could be on TV. He catches himself—she *is* on TV. And so lively this morning, giggling, giddy. Nelson clearly makes her happy.

"Ah, your tree!" she cries. "It's here!"

The tree came to him in the hospital, a get-well gift from Rasputin. An actual *tree*, of suitable size for indoors, but still. It's a dwarf lemon with cutting-edge grafts (the pun can't be helped) from a tangerine tree, so you get two kinds of citrus for the price of one. A modern marvel, and a real pain in the ass to get it home. Now it's parked in the sunniest spot in his living room.

"I've got a friend with a pickup truck," Clarence says. "He hauled it for me."

"It looks very happy there," Emerald remarks, and for a moment they all admire the tree.

"You'll want a grow light for it come summer," Nelson advises. "All the shade you get around here."

The kids have a full day ahead of them. Christmas brunch with Nelson's friends, a big afternoon celebration at the Rasputin estate, then family dinner tonight at Dolly's. No mention of Emerald's family, Clarence notes. He watches her with more than sociable attention. Nelson sees him watching, and smart Nelson knows what that's about. It doesn't take much these days to activate his uncle's paranoia. A samovar, a beer can through the window, a drop-dead gorgeous woman hanging around. Baldwin had some choice thoughts about black paranoia and the spin-up it could do on your mind. How after a while you might give up trying to tell the real threats from the imaginary.

Let it go, man. For one day at least. If Nelson is sleeping with the enemy, sooner or later they'll figure it out. "What's that music?" Emerald asks.

"Handel's *Messiah*," Clarence answers.

"Handel's *Messiah*," she repeats. "It's wonderful. Like angels singing." She listens for a moment. "I guess it's old?"

"Pretty old," Clarence answers easily. He can see Nelson is embarrassed for her. Don't be, he wants to say. Not on my account.

"Uncle Key knows a lot about a lot of things. Movies, history, art, you can ask him anything about jazz, classical music. He is a true Renaissance man."

Emerald's smile turns a little glassy; she doesn't know what a Renaissance man is. And why would she? Raised in a meth-head trailer park outside Amarillo, and that was the easy part, according to what Nelson has told him. Thanks to grit and hustle and lucky good looks she survived, she's making her way. Everybody says she was a soldier when Clarence was in the hospital, visiting daily to spell whoever was on watch.

She asks how he's feeling. He lies. She jumps up to pour more coffee for everyone, enthuses over the house and decor. A naturally caffeinated girl, this one, rocking a couple of extra turbo boosts this morning. Presently she asks to use the bathroom, and Clarence points the way. He wearily supposes he won't be able to stop himself from searching for spyware later. He and Nelson both take a reset breath once she's gone.

"How old you say she is?"

"She'll be twenty-three next month."

Clarence raises his brow, looks to the side.

"Key. Come on."

"Did I say anything?"

"She's young. I know."

"Nothing wrong with young. Old either, for that matter. You guys seem good."

"We are. Real good."

"You feeling serious about this girl?"

"Might. Maybe she's a little rough around the edges . . ."

"Who isn't. You got any clarity on the deal out there?"

"Not really. To tell you the truth, I don't even think about it much. Whatever it is, it's got nothing on us."

"She's into you."

"Feels like it."

"*Looks* like it, from where I'm sitting."

"She's talking about not being a Maiden anymore. Which, you know. That's fine by me."

"You're a good man. She sees that."

He laughs. "She says I'm *old*."

"Well you are, compared to twenty-two. She coming tonight?"

"She'll be working. Holiday shift, she gets overtime. She's all about that." Bootsteps in the hall mark her return, and he calls over his shoulder, "We aren't talking about you."

"Fine with me if you are," she says breezily. "Anybody need anything?"

Nobody needs anything. She sits and tears off a bite of brioche. Clarence decides to probe, but it's got nothing to do with politics. This is family, and as an elder he feels a certain amount of nosiness is his prerogative.

"Emerald, what's going on with your family today?"

She adjusts smoothly, with only the slightest, briefest pinch of her features. "I'll call my mom at some point, no rush on that. She likes to sleep in. And my brother, I'm not sure what he's up to today."

"How about your father?"

"He's not really in the picture."

"Your mother and brother, they live around here?"

"Mom's in Amarillo. My brother lives in Midland. He works on rigs."

"Then he's a hardworking man."

"He'd like something better." She shrugs, drops her eyes to her lap. Something hard in that shrug, a willful turning away. "I don't really know. I haven't talked to him in a while."

"And your mom, what does she do?"

"She's on disability."

He stops there, before the interrogation begins to seem less than polite. Someday she'll have to work on that thing inside the shrug, the fade in her eyes when she's not on full alert. Right now youth and adrenaline are carrying her along, but sooner or later she'll hit the wall, and Clarence worries for her, the worry ingrained from all his years of teaching. They have so much to get through, the kids. It's a miracle anybody makes it to thirty.

From the time Nelson says they're leaving to when they actually leave is at least twenty minutes. Long goodbyes are a family tradition. Clarence sees them to the door and receives a hug from each one. Emerald's clench is surprisingly fierce, emphatic. Then off they go into the day, into sunshine, life, and for a little while afterward his heart aches. He wanted to go with them.

What he'd like to know is why's he so damn tired all the time. He gets the whole TBI spectrum of symptoms thing, but this dog-days torpor seems excessive. The headache is his constant, codependent friend. He left it home for Christmas dinner and it was waiting up for him when he returned, poleaxed him with a rolling pin when he walked through the door. Ever since he's been a human tree sloth in the recliner, manages to stir about every three hours. His own warped headspace aside, it's strange days on the TV news. Mount St. Helens is blowing flying saucer–shaped smoke rings into the atmosphere. North Jersey emits a 5.2 earthquake that sets the Manhattan skyline swaying. Thousands of sheep die overnight in Montana for no discernible reason. Vice President Greene and the evangelical chorus proclaim these are warnings from God to repent of our unholy LGBTQ ways. Back-channel holiday maneuvering on the budget impasse makes it worse, and from Mar-a-Lago President █████ lashes out at his erstwhile allies in the Freedom Caucus. His shock troops, the true believers; the very people he endorsed and campaigned for in election after election. In a never-ending loop the TV commentators ask one another: Has the president lost control of his party?

In print, the more sardonically inclined scribes have taken to calling a certain candidate "the Rasputin," as if "the █████" didn't go stale about twenty years ago. In the same rambling press conference where he blisters the Freedom Caucus, █████ gets off a free-associative rant about monasteries and sexual deviancy, the kinky things monks get up to behind those walls. "We all know the stories, right, folks? And that guy, Fake Russian, how many years did he spend with the monks? Some of the things we're hearing coming out of that house in Texas, the sex house, that's what some people are calling it. I'm starting to think all the people at that house belong in the zoo."

It never ends, Clarence thinks, the noise, the spectacle, at some point our national life dropped acid and took up residence in a carnival mad house. None of which helps his headache. It's damn depressing, actually, hurting all the time, wondering if this is how it's going to be the rest of the way. Three days after Christmas he's scrounging around the kitchen for lunch when his phone buzzes, and BITSY BOWMAN pops up on the screen. He clicks in.

"Yo."

"Fake News," says a voice like a gong. Not Bitsy. Clarence's pulse about doubles, sets off a speed-bag drubbing in his head.

"Russkie."

"Where are you?"

"Home."

"Why are you not here with the other reporters?"

"Well. 'Cause I'm at home fixing lunch."

Long pause. Clarence pictures a tortoise confronting a stump.

"You are still injured."

"Afraid so."

"This saddens me."

"Thanks. Thank you. Me too."

"Your pain, it is significant."

"I'm pretty uncomfortable, a lot of the time. It comes and goes."

"Yes. As we are talking I can feel it."

Clarence lets that pass.

"My friend, we are going to need you in Iowa."

"*We?*"

"The country, of course!"

"Well, I appreciate that. I guess I'm gradually getting better. But it's slow."

"Come see me tomorrow."

"I'd like to. But I'm really not up to driving these days."

"We will send a car for you," Rasputin says. "Two p.m." He clicks off.

Nobody follows up to ask for his address, yet an Escalade arrives for him promptly at two, a gleaming cream-colored eco-havoc machine that swallows him up like a cloud. He brings an airline puke bag just in case, but the enormous vehicle floats him ever so softly the thirty miles to the palace. Faith Spack meets him in the marble foyer and asks for his phone.

"Because," she says preemptively, "we're off the record today. Really sorry about your accident, man."

"Thanks."

"So what happened? We heard you tripped in a parking lot and hit your head."

"Yes. I tripped in a parking lot and hit my head."

"And you were in the hospital. In a coma!"

"That's what they tell me."

"Coma, wow, that's scary stuff." She seems more hyper than usual, her eyes flitting all over the place. Does it still hurt? she asks. Did you get the lemon tree? She deposits him in the *Game of Thrones* dining room. Party of one, table for . . . he counts thirty-two chairs. One of the nice cooks brings him a bottle of water and a plate of cookies and grapes. Staffers pass through and pay him about as much mind as a fly. He's nervous. He just now realizes this. What the in-between did, it sharpened his sense of the stakes: Not just earth but heaven above might be in play. And according to the scenario described by the spirit of Terry Southern, he might be this very moment sitting in the belly of the beast.

A young staffer passes through with a dustbuster, idly switching it on and off. Then Charlie Cupps, who scowls at Clarence without seeming to recognize him, followed by Belinda with her laptop lodged in the crook of her arm. She spots Clarence and makes a beeline his way.

"How's your head?"

"Sore."

"You got knocked out, I heard."

"I did."

"What's it like?"

"What's it *like*?"

"You know, being out. Unconscious. I've always wondered."

He pretends to consider. "Black."

"Black? That's all?"

"You seem disappointed."

"I was just hoping it would be more interesting than that."

"Sorry. Not everything is interesting."

"People say I'm easily bored. They've been saying that since I was two."

"Have they now." She's standing so close that he's aware of her body heat. A pretty girl, and young, can't be more than twenty, twenty-one. Big liquid brown eyes, faint dustings of mauve and violet makeup. All of a sudden Clarence is pretty sure where the audio files are coming from.

"What'd you say your name is?"

"Belinda."

"Right, Belinda. Easily bored Belinda." This feels creepy, like he's making a move on her, but he's not. "I'm Clarence."

"Sir, I know who you are. You're Grishka's favorite reporter."

"Am I now. And why is that."

"I don't know, maybe because you're black? His whole Pushkin thing—"

"Uh, hello?" Charlie Cupps pokes his gnarly head past the doorframe. "Far be it from me to intrude on your social hour—"

"Coming!" Belinda yelps. She gives Clarence a keen look and scampers off. Clarence takes a sip of water. He needs to think about Belinda and the audio files, but the local sights keep distracting him. The staffer with the dustbuster troops through again, then Faith escorting a hipster photographer and two gear-laden assistants. Then a guy with a ladder, one of the maintenance staff. Next, a threesome of giggling, whispering Maidens in elf costumes, complete with pointy hats and curlicue-toe shoes. Like watching a Fellini movie, sitting here. Presently Bitsy appears.

"There you are."

"Here I am."

"Why they put you in here?"

"It's fine. I'm not easily bored."

Bitsy sits, props his crutches against the table.

"How you keeping?"

"Getting on. You?"

"Fair enough. Launch got everybody so stirred up, can't hear myself think. Grishka says your head still bothering you."

"Yep."

"Sorry to hear that." He leans close and lowers his voice. "They still around?"

"I don't think so. I think I scared them off, falling out like that."

Bitsy nods. "You never tell the cops?"

"No point to it. I'm a brother who had a concussion and thinks he saw somebody messing under his car. They aren't about to waste their time."

"I hear that. Grishka ask me what I think happen, I tell him I don't know, wutten there. But he feel something not right about it."

"Huh. But how would he know."

"Man got his nose to the breeze, like, he *know*. Know stuff he got no way of knowing."

"Well, all I know is I saw what I saw, and I tripped. And my head's hurt like hell ever since."

"Grishka might have some strategy that way. If you inclined."

Clarence is pretty sure he follows, but maybe not.

"You know he got a gift," Bitsy adds.

"Right. You're saying he would . . ."

"He willing to try. But only if you want him to."

Clarence ponders. He's just about desperate enough. And he'd be peeling back another layer of the Rasputin enigma.

"Is that why he invited me?"

"Grishka only wanna help people. Just his way."

What the hell. "Sure," he says with a chuckle, embarrassed that he's actually agreeing to this. Bitsy pulls out his phone and sends a text, and within seconds a text comes back.

"All right now," he says, gathering his crutches. "You ready?"

Clarence tells himself he's pulling off something of a journalistic coup. The ultimate up close encounter with the Candidate, even if it has to be off the record. He follows Bitsy back to the rec/war room. Rasputin is seated at the semicircular command center, and rises at once to greet them. At least forty people working in here, Clarence notes, junior aides, senior aides, everyone busy-busy-busy on their phones and computers. Many are wearing "Spiritual Gangsta" hoodies, the latest in Rasputinhead merch. The wrestler takes both of Clarence's hands in his.

"My brother," he says. "I am very glad to see you."

"It's good to see you too," Clarence answers, trying to keep it casual. But Rasputin's eyes home in on him like they're about to spit bullets.

"You are in pain."

Clarence finds he can only nod. Rasputin places his hands atop Clarence's head and starts feeling around. When his hands reach the back, he—Rasputin—gives a surprised huff. Now people are watching. Clarence feels a strange coursing in his spine like millions of iron filings streaking upward. Rasputin mumbles some words, possibly Russian, then faster than snapping fingers he's got the reporter's head in an elbow lock and both hands clamped around his skull. Clarence gasps. He tries to pull free, but those hands have the implacable grip of molded steel, and now they're squeezing, his skull is about to explode like a chocolate Easter egg. Rasputin makes a high-pitched whinnying sound, and a blast of sheet lightning obliterates Clarence's brain. The next thing he knows, Rasputin is roughly brushing him down with his big hands, flinging outward as if dashing off bugs or dirt. The wrestler is grunting, huffing, breathing heavy. He works all the way down to Clarence's ankles, then back up to his head.

"Deep breath," he commands.

Clarence opens his eyes. Everyone in the room is staring, and Faith Spack's close by, she's staring too. They could be singers holding a high note, all those wide-open mouths.

"Deep breath," Rasputin reminds him, and that breath, it's like his very first ever. He tries a few more. Oh, yes. He blinks and smiles, and couldn't care less that all these people are witnessing this most intimate moment.

"Okay?" Rasputin asks. He has his hands on Clarence's shoulders and is stooping, peering at him with tender concern.

"I'm good." It's the truth. Not an ache or stitch or throb anywhere. "This is amazing."

"Good!" Rasputin cries. "All praise and glory to our merciful God!" He turns to the room with a flourish, presenting Clarence like a rabbit he's pulled out of his hat, and everyone cheers.

Later he'll decide he was in shock. His vision spotty, sound filtered through a band of radio static. Rasputin told him to go home and rest. No exertion for several days, let your body heal. You will know when you are well, then we will see you in Iowa.

He barely remembers Faith and Bitsy walking him outside. They helped him into the Escalade's back seat and buckled him in.

"Remember," Faith said, just before shutting the door. "Everything off the record."

25

Iowa, what the hell? All this peaceful rolling prairie covered in pristine snow, mile after mile of hospital white dotted with farms, grain silos, determinedly modest towns, there seems no healthier, more sanitary place on earth, then you step off the bus and whammo, it hits you in the face like a steaming cow patty. Iowa, lovely Iowa, wholesome Iowa . . . stinks! Forget Cedar Rapids with its Archer-Daniels-Midland complex belching smoke like the pits of Mordor, Cedar Rapids can't help smelling like a suet factory, but out here? Surely not the wide-open yonders of America's heartland with all that brisk, bleached air sweeping down from Canada and fields of antiseptic snow stretching as far as the eye can see.

And yet the barnyard funk pervades. Faith hates to think ill of Iowa on her first trip ever, but the nose knows and stink don't lie. The *Chicago Trib* guy tells her that lead levels in Iowa children exceed those of Flint, and hunters carry water into the field for their dogs, lest they die of drinking from the nitrate-rich ponds and streams. Faith resolves to drink only bottled water, but the air, well, what can you do. Meanwhile the little towns and hamlets scroll by in a sleep-deprivation blur. Honecker. Neary. Stoops. Umholtz. The good people of Iowa gather for Rasputin in their school gyms and cafeterias and their VFW halls, honest if haggard farm folk with seasonal affective disorder written all over their faces. The men tend toward bedhead hair and stubble, and bashful, shifty eyes: entire towns' worths of Boo Radleys. For the hell of it, just to see what will happen, Faith sometimes flashes one of the guys a dazzler of a big-city blonde smile, and such alarm this provokes! Panic, confusion, wonder—she's smiling at *me*? Sad to think they will ponder this moment for the rest of their lives.

The women interest her more. Edgier they are, more alert and correspondingly more guarded; they eye Faith with fierce curiosity, and if she catches them watching they abruptly turn away, reach for the nearest kid. Not a wisp of makeup, scant hair care, their clothes resolutely workaday. The older press hands have never seen so many women turn out for a candidate here, and it's mostly women, mostly middle-aged, who fall prey to the Weeps. Built into the schedule are ten-minute segments at every stop for Rasputin to manage the weepers. Faith thinks she gets it, passing mile after mile of hollow-looking farmhouses with their bleak windbreaks of trees, the neighbor homes standing off on the gray horizon like distant ships at sea. The inner life that surely ferments in such drudgy isolation, the simmer of homicidal and sexual angst. They come out, they weep, they get touched by Rasputin, meltdown and catharsis in one compact package. Faith gets it. She knows all the feelings. Standing at the back, she sometimes closes her eyes and concentrates on his voice, the hum of it, the deep, rich, vibratory buzz that goes straight for your center, it is the subtlest pussy grab of all time.

But all psychosexual voodoo aside, he's a phenom at retail politics. Give him five minutes with the bedheads and Boo Radleys, he has them grinning like orphans on a Ferris wheel. He dresses out every morning in jeans, ropers, and sheeny tracksuit pullovers, and working the crowds, time seems to slow down for him, he has a touch and a selfie smile for everyone. The old campaign pros are wowed; not since the Bill Man have they seen raw talent like this. Obama came close, Obama was rare, but for sheer animal magnetism you have to go back to Clinton or one of the Kennedys for worthy comparisons to the Wrath of God. Even the crusty local pols are falling under his spell. Every day the bus takes on a rotating cast of state senators and reps, county commissioners, judges, landed feudal lords and the like. No endorsement required, we just want you to ride along and see for yourself what the New Awakening is about. So Senator Locklips and Representative Grimglower climb aboard for their scheduled two or three stops, they sit up front and chat with the Candidate and maybe they even introduce him to the folks as a courtesy, no endorsement implied. But pretty quick they feel the magic. The way he connects with the little people and brings the love, and they love him back, oh how they swoon! And they might even have a little love left over for a tired old legislator or judge. Hm, well now, mind if we ride a little longer? And in the meantime Representative Roozles and Judge Legbail come aboard, and Senator Soursop, and Commissioners Dogflaws and Waterwolf, and by the end of the day the New Awakening Express is a rollicking circus of local color, it's standing room only and everybody's having a helluva grand time and here come the endorsements, they practically trample one another to get to the mic, herd spontaneity from people who haven't made an impulse move since they went all the way the night of their senior prom.

It's a hoot, watching these crafty old pols lose their heads. Throwing ████ in the ditch and calculation to the wind; maybe tomorrow they'll be having morning-after regrets, but then they'll remember the love, that good warm glow they felt inside, and they'll decide they were part of something special.

"Is it always this easy?" Faith asks Roy Nadler on the bus one day, halfway between nowhere and not much else.

"*Never*," he declares, veteran of a hundred campaigns. Everything's going their way, polls, messaging, money, crowds, not to mention millions of dollars' worth of unpaid media. Two press buses trail the New Awakening Express, along with a brightly colored kite tail of TV news vans and miscellaneous rentals, and the White Guard in their pickups and military-grade SUVs. Snailing their way across the snows and blows of Iowa, they are their own portable traffic jam, a blood clot baffling the asphalt arteries of the Hawkeye State.

████ flies, Rasputin goes ground; it's a useful contrast. Faith rarely sticks around for the Candidate's speech. She's usually in the lobby or down a hallway working her phones, these days she's packing, God help her, three. Concomitant with the January 2 rally, the campaign released a point-by-point platform, and she's fielding endless follow-up on that, in addition to administering to the nonstop needs and bitchery of the traveling press. For the most part, the platform reads standard hard-right conservative, but here's the surprise that's not really a surprise, it carves out politic nuance on abortion and LGBTQ rights. They're taking cannon fire from left and center, sniping from the right, fine, she can handle it. Red lightning in all her phones, that too she can handle, same for the secret agent jitters, lying to her mother, getting by on three or four hours of sleep a night. No, the only thing that's really beyond her coping skills is the fact that the world is treating this *like a normal campaign*. As if Rasputin is a candidate like any other, as standard issue as your average octogenarian senator or feisty, overachieving, up-from-the-ranks political mom. She's waiting for someone to call them on it, the bad joke, the blatant con of it all. That Rasputin belongs to the cosplaying cartoon world of pro wrestling, not the real-world world of nuclear threat and class warfare and global warming.

People, hello! Anybody home? For sure the algorithms love him, which means the media can't get enough, meanwhile poor Faith is flailing around in analog world, where a tequila-shots meltiness suffuses everything. The one part of her life that seems firmly tethered to reality is the very thing she currently hates most about herself. The spy stuff, the covert call-ins to her handlers. She relays grab bags of intel and campaign gossip, along with her humble advice from the field: Would the president please start pounding the fact that RASPUTIN IS NOT REAL. He is a creation, a persona, a collaborative and collective fiction, a soufflé of branding even airier than the "█████" that *The Apprentice* piped into the homes and hearts of millions of Americans. But even as she insists on the irreality of Rasputin, she's thinking he might be realer than anything. Healing the weepers, that's real. Curing Clarence Thomas, real. The crowds, the poll numbers, the lights-out fundraising, real. The quaking lust he inspires in every woman in sight, definitely real. For this Faith offers herself as proof, though why she backed away at the critical moment, she still hasn't figured that out. Perhaps a basic failure of nerve. Whatever they had going on in there, ménage à trois, quatre, cinq, advanced bedroom stuff, and her sensing she's not cut out for the sexual big leagues? Other times she's convinced it was her survival instinct kicking in. Her grasp of self and reality shaky enough as it is, had she joined his bed that night she might have disappeared with a puff, never to be seen again, into the voluptuous realms of Rasputin World.

She supposes he knows about her midnight trek up to his suite. Why not, since he seems to know everything about everyone, but he's as sweet and respectful toward her as ever. They've had several heart-to-hearts about bio-dad. Rasputin gently probes and consoles, but she's fine, really. In a way it seems inevitable that she'll end up in his bed. Sooner or later, just as a natural extension of the relationship. Sometimes she's about *this close* to jumping his bones. They're always on the same floor at whatever hotel they're staying, but by two or three in the morning or whenever the day ends, sex seems about as appealing as a ruptured spleen.

"Watch out," Belinda warned the last time she was in Iowa. She and Charlie swan in for the occasional check-in, and promptly swan back out. "It's coming."

"What."

"The big one."

"The big one. Is that a new Whataburger thing?"

Belinda answered with her Manson-girl murderess stare. The big one, no laughing matter. Faith considers herself warned.

Saturday, ten a.m., they're in tiny Clark, Iowa, population 1,045. A grain silo town, the twin barrels of the eight-story cylinders are the tallest facts for miles around, a sprinkling of church steeples offering feeble competition. The New Awakening Express idles outside the beige brick Clark Middle School. Faith stands on the sunny side of the bus texting with *People*, *Vogue*, *Vanity Fair*; Bardem Hayes has dumped the magazines in her brief and they want features on the hottest candidate in the land,

Rasputin as you've never seen him. And they all want exclusives, hah. Her leather gloves stop just short of her fingertips, revealing blue surgical latex underneath. People mill around the school, reporters, campaign staff, civilians, everyone's bundled up like polar explorers. Even in the bright sunshine it's unbelievably cold. Faith is pondering the travesty of this when a rare black face comes into view.

"Hey!" she cries. "Clarence!"

He turns and walks her way.

"When'd you get in?"

"Flew to Des Moines yesterday. Drove up this morning."

"Welcome aboard, man. How you doing?"

"Pretty good," he says lightly. He's wearing jeans, boots, a black puffy jacket, and an astrakhan hat like the kind Malcolm X used to wear. "I see you brought the junior Klan today." He nods at the White Guard stationed at presumably strategic points around the school. Camouflage, body armor, headsets, Oakley shades, they are maximally accessorized with all the latest. Then there are the guns. Why not join the army if you're so badass?

"Oh God, ignore them, please. They've got nothing to do with us."

"Really now."

"I know, I know, it's a terrible look." But he's barely listening, she sees. He obviously considers her a frivolous person. "They just show up, it's not like we can make them stop."

"Has he asked them to stop?"

"Uhm, I'm not sure in so many words. But as you know he condemns violence of all kinds. Listen, it's great to see you. We were all really worried about you."

This brings him up short. "Well, I appreciate that. I was a little worried myself."

"Is your head okay?"

He actually cracks a bit of a smile. "Yes, I think my head's okay."

"I've been thinking about that. What Grishka did, at the house. I was there."

"I know you were. You walked me out to the car. You and Bitsy."

"I wasn't sure you remembered."

"I don't know why you'd think that." He looks toward the school. "What time does it start?"

"Now. Any minute."

"I better get in there. Check you later."

Okay, so he doesn't want to talk about it, the apparent healing feat that she suddenly wants to talk about more than anything. As in: Was it real? Medical? Factual? As real as those grain silos, real as the bald eagle cruising the blue-rinse sky above? Eventually she makes her way inside to the school cafeteria, where it's a packed house and the temperature's pushing a stuffy eighty degrees. Faith feels her nose clogging up as Rasputin speaks of Christian values, law and order, grain export policy, and China's ramped-up saber-rattling toward Taiwan. The budget impasse and the "abstract" people in Washington. He's describing his proposed US–Russia Christian superpower alliance when a woman near the front falls out weeping, and within seconds they've got an entire cluster on their hands. Chuck and Cecil, the campaign's designated bouncers, quickly wrangle them to the front and Rasputin does his thing. The crowd is rapt, and for as long as it lasts no one seems to breathe. "My friends," Rasputin intones as the last weeper is led back to her seat, "you have just witnessed the healing power of God's love," and for this Clark awards him—Him?—a leap-to-the-feet standing ovation.

A great icebreaker, these miracle cures, real bonding between crowd and Candidate, with some of the flavor of the old-time tent revival. Come down, come on down, come down and be saved! Next stop, Hintz, then on to Landry, Meyercough, Temple, packed houses all the way. Near Stanley they stop at a prosperous, camera-friendly family farm where Rasputin tosses hay bales around like footballs, takes a pair of Angus calves under his arms and lifts them off the ground, and chops wood with lumberjack ease. Then he gives a little speech about the ageless wisdom of farm folk, "the eternal ones" who live close to the land. Seasons, weather, beasts of the field, sowing and reaping. "You are the true stewards of God's creation." Faith stands to the side thinking of Marx's line about the idiocy of rural life, which seems harsh, but out here you sort of see his point. The empty miles, the dead horizon, all that high squeening sky overhead, there's something brain-draining about it. She swears she can feel her IQ dropping.

Me and Marx, she laughs to herself, couple of city snobs. No wonder the heartland hates the coastal elites. Late afternoon they do the high school gym in Harlowe, same wall-to-wall crowd as everywhere; the Wrath of God advance team never fails. By this point Faith's nose is a prize yam, and some sort of mucoid clabber is colonizing her chest. Can we go home now, please? Home tonight being the Marriott Hotel in Ames. During audience Q and A, a smiling citizen asks the Candidate who's the toughest opponent he ever faced.

"Besides Satan?" Rasputin deadpans, and everyone laughs. Someone asks if it's true that he wrestled with a broken leg at SummerSlam two years ago, and does he have any comment on the rumor that his old nemesis the Tuckahoe Terror is coming out of retirement. Next, how does it feel to have President ██████ call you "absolute evil." Again the deadpan: "I think this president sometimes speaks without thinking." More laughs. "But in all seriousness, it makes me sad. Even for all of my human flaws and imperfections, I am still God's creature. And the same is true for the president."

Then it gets weird. A nicely dressed older woman, petite, well-spoken, stands to say that her grandmother, born and raised in Ukraine, was a girl of eleven when Rasputin passed through her village in the year 1913. "The entire town was ordered to line up on the street in his honor," she says. "It was a warm day and the top of his car was down, and when he went by he looked directly at my grandmother, and he gave her the evil eye."

The crowd gasps. The woman falters, gathers her nerve, forges on.

"She said she felt it right away, like a blade or an arrow piercing her heart. For her whole life she claimed our family is cursed, and when you look at all the things we've been through—well, I won't bore everyone with my family history! But I'd like to ask you, sir, today, if you're able, if you would please undo whatever Rasputin did to my grandmother in 1913."

Silence. Silence as profound as the deaf know it.

"Madame," Rasputin says in a quiet voice. "What is your name, please."

"Valerie. Valerie Brewer. Mrs. John D. Brewer."

"Mrs. Brewer. Please come forward."

Something volatile suddenly infuses the air, some tasteless, odorless substance that might explode at the first false move. Chuck and Cecil meet Mrs. Brewer at the bottom of the bleachers and escort her to the temporary stage. She's trembling all over, Faith sees. Terrified, yet determined; a brave woman carrying the burden of generations on her delicate shoulders. Rasputin greets her with a smile and a few private words, and clasps her hands in his and draws her to him. Her head tops out somewhere around the middle of his rib cage. His eyes close, his lips move silently. Is it a prayer? A spell? In short order Mrs. Brewer shudders, a kind of mini-convulsion or spasm rattles her frame. Rasputin lifts his right hand and makes the sign of the cross over her head, two fingers in the Old Believer style. He embraces her as if to seal the deal—it's like she's walked into a closet, so thoroughly does she disappear—then he steps back and stoops low to meet her eye.

Valerie Brewer, Mrs. John D., sucks in a breath and blinks rapidly for several seconds. And like trumpets blaring forth at Easter sunrise, she turns a brilliant smile to the crowd and cries, "I feel better already!"

Just another day's work on the New Awakening Express. Faith slips out to the lobby and finds a quiet spot to work her phones. She's texting the pushies at *People* when Ricardo Levy booms through the door and heads for her. Iowans milling about the lobby stop in their tracks, whisper and point. Ricardo is as famous as his wrestlers and many times richer, but for all his celebrity, his wealth, his carefully curated muscles, there's an ungainliness about him, a galootish sort of chin-first swagger that seems destined for calamity.

"Isn't he *great*!" he cries, sloshing into Faith's personal space. "Have you ever seen anything like it? That guy makes history every time he gets off the bus. Don't you want some of that?"

"Some of what?"

"*That!* Heat, magic." He seems not to notice the crowd gathering around. They keep their distance but are quick with their phones, snapping pictures and texting.

"I think I've got some already. I'm senior staff on his campaign, remember?"

"*Noooo*, I'm talking about wrestling! Slice off a piece of that pie for yourself, honey. Have you thought any more about it?"

"Not at all."

"Faith! I'm offering you the opportunity of a lifetime here! Little Faith Spack of *Nashville Next Gen* all grown up and ready to rumble, now she's taking on AWW. You would kill."

"Ricardo, that Faith went away a long time ago."

The crowd's pushing in closer. They glance left, right, behind—they're looking for the video cameras, Faith realizes. They think they've wandered into a Ricardo Levy promotional stunt.

"Then let's bring her back! That sassy little hell on wheels, that's what everybody loved you for. You spoke your mind. You put it right out there."

"That wasn't me. That was some other girl."

"Of course it was *you*, that Faith was you, part of you, still you. I mean, who *is* anybody, really? We're more of a blur than any fixed thing, we're this way in one situation, that way in another, we're just basically making it up as we go along. You tap into a specific part of yourself, that's where the character lives, it's you but a very selective version of you. You push this part forward, pull this part back, and we're *real good* at blurring the lines. You've done it before, Faith, and you, were, beautiful. I've been watching your old shows. I can help you do it again, and for a helluva lot more money this time. Let's do this, Faith. Trust me. I can make you a very wealthy woman."

She takes in his big face, the spitballs pooling at the corners of his mouth, his pleading con-man eyes, and there's no help for it, she bursts out laughing.

"You're deranged."

Now he's laughing too, whuffing like a horse gulping water. At last he seems to notice they've drawn a crowd, and throws out a perfunctory wave to the little people. "Maybe," he says, lowering his voice, "but think about it—one of my guys could be the next president of the United States." He glances over his shoulder, drops his voice to a murmur. "Actually, Faith, I sort of run this country. Oh, you think I'm joking? No no no no, sweetie, don't make that mistake. I'm the guy who knows what America wants, what it *needs*—nobody knows the soul of this country like me. Everything that's happening with Grishka proves it."

"I'm sorry. I just can't do this right now."

"Come on girl, work with me. Let me make you rich and famous." Abruptly he turns to the crowd. "Hey everybody! This is Faith Spack from *Nashville Next Gen*, remember her?"

There's a smattering of cheers, scattered applause. Ricardo raises his voice, his arms, swells into emcee mode. "Don't you think she'd be huge on AWW?"

Big cheers now, clapping, wolf whistles. Ricardo windmills his arms, whipping up the noise, but when he turns back to Faith he's eerily matter-of-fact. "See what I mean? You'd be huge."

Hours later the New Awakening Express is rolling up to the Ames Marriott. Twiss calls a staff meeting for 10:30 p.m., which, he notes after glancing at his watch, gives everybody ninety minutes to do whatever they need to do. Faith checks into her room, enjoys a non–public restroom pee, does a quick cleanup, and changes into jeans. She stashes the spy phone in the safe and heads downstairs for nourishment, where the potential dinner company looks grim. Eating alone, she's okay with that tonight. She buttons up her coat, wraps her scarf mummy-style around her head, and hoofs a quarter-mile of frozen parking lot to the T.J. McDuff's across the way. McDuff's is a chain, a kind of Midwestern-hip Applebee's for the Instagram set, with a grossly overdetermined food and drink menu for which Faith holds AI responsible. Inside, no tables available; would she like to try the bar? Where there's a single open seat, to the left of which sits one Clarence Thomas Jr. Well, any port in a storm.

"Mind if I . . ."

His eyes slide her way, followed by his face. "Be my guest." Neither hot nor cold, but cool personified. She rustles about getting settled, filling the silence until the bartender comes over. White, hunky, mustached, he's AI too. She orders hot tea and a glass of water, and, impulsively, a margarita on the rocks. "For the citrus," she adds as a joke, but neither man laughs. The bartender serves her water right away, and she digs a tube of Airborne out of her purse and drops in a tablet. The water fizzes up like party time. She turns to Clarence.

"So how was your day?"

He hesitates a half beat, as if confused. "About the same as yours, I expect."

"No, yeah, it's all the same thing, I guess. Except you're on the other side of the mirror, so to speak."

He cocks his head and gives her a slightly less aloof look. Like maybe she's not a complete nitwit. He's eating clam chowder and crackers, and arrayed about his bowl are a phone, a Moleskine notebook, and an open paperback.

"Well, from my side of the mirror it was a pretty interesting day. Plenty to see out there. Plenty to think about."

"And what are you thinking?"

"About?"

"Come on, man, my guy! The campaign. How we're doing."

"Your guy. Well, he's good. He's the first to really put █████ back on his heels, and that," he pauses, "I'm sure that's very satisfying to a lot of people." He shreds a packet of crackers into his chowder. "The campaign," he continues, stirring in the crackers, "anybody can see you're on a roll. You've got money, momentum, organization, it's all going your way." *But,* Faith thinks a split second before he says it. "But you haven't been tested. So we'll have to see what happens then."

"But we're tested every day. We're out there busting our buns."

"Sure, I get that. But you haven't had your crisis yet."

"Who says we will?"

"Oh, you will. Everybody's got something in their past, their present.

I don't know why a professional wrestler would be any different, even if he is the most Christian cat since Aquinas. Anyway," Clarence intakes a spoonful of chowder, "it's coming."

It's coming, unnerving echoes of Belinda. *The big one.* One really big one instantly comes to mind, and in her paranoia Faith wonders how much he knows.

"So what do you think it's going to be?"

He laughs. "What it always is. Sex. Money. Both."

She takes a sip of water. "I read up on the *Khlysty*."

He gives her an appraising look. "Did you now."

"Well, the Wiki version. Plus a few other places. I really don't think that's him."

Clarence nods. Go on.

"I mean, he's different, yeah. But not like that."

"He sure has a lot of women around."

"He does, yes," she carefully agrees, only now detecting some confusion in herself. Is she working for ██████ or Rasputin? "But it's not a *Khlysty* thing."

"Are we on the record?"

"Background."

He gives her a tetchy look, vaguely admonishing. "Okay, so if it's not a *Khlysty* thing, is it a First Lady thing?"

"Whoa ho, no sir, no indeed. I hear the rumors like everybody else, but no. Not her. Case closed."

Perhaps for an instant her eye contact is too direct, and maybe he sees all is not as she claims it to be. *Sloppy*, she berates herself, or maybe not? Again the confusion, ██████ or Rasputin, and which way does the sloppiness cut? Her tea comes, the margarita close behind. She pulls out another Airborne and drops it in the drink; Clarence watches with a faintly critical air. "Same as him," she says when the bartender asks if she wants to order food. It's only after he leaves that she turns to Clarence.

"I assume the chowder's okay?"

"Okay," he says with no great enthusiasm. She finishes off her water, has a couple of sips of tea, then tries the drink. Too sweet, as she knew it would be. The bartender returns to clear away the remains of Clarence's meal. He pours the reporter a fresh club soda and drops in a lime, and Faith assuming all this time he was drinking gin and tonic. She resolves to be more attentive.

"May I ask you something?"

He raises his brow, inclines his head a few degrees.

"What was that about last week, at Southlake. Wait, was it last week? My God, seems like about a year ago. But last week when you came to the house and he, you know—"

"I know what you're talking about."

"Right. So when he—"

"You were there. You saw it."

"Yeah, no, I did. But I—okay. Okay. This is kind of awkward. I mean, he's my guy, my candidate, like I'm already supposed to know everything about him, right?" She squeaks out an apologetic laugh. "But I guess I'm trying to get my head around what happened. To you. Like, did it work."

"You want to know if he did some sort of cure on me."

"Well. Yes."

Clarence turns and faces forward, presents his profile to her. After a moment he nods.

"I don't know what you'd call it. But it was something. Something happened."

"You felt it."

"I most definitely felt something."

"And it, uhm, helped. It worked. You're feeling okay."

"All true."

Her chowder comes, and a refill of water, and a straw basket heaped with an assortment of cellophane-wrapped crackers. She goes for the crackers first.

"What does your doctor say about it?"

"I haven't been to the doctor." Now he smiles, mostly to himself. "So here I am sitting with the Candidate's deputy press secretary, and I'm the one being interviewed."

"Oh, sorry. But I'm just, you know. Trying to get some clarity on some things."

"You're trying to figure out if he's the real deal."

"Well, I believe in him and everything, as a candidate, a person, I think he'd make a great president. But some of this other stuff, I really don't know what to make of it."

"Well, I'd say the people who think they do aren't really thinking."

"Well okay! That makes me feel better."

"Hey, Faith."

"What?"

"Your soup's getting cold."

Right, that. Food. Sustenance. Most of the staff are gaining weight and she's shed four pounds already, her mother is going to be so proud. Clarence orders a brandy, which in purely social terms she interprets as a victory: He's in no hurry to be rid of her. What is he reading? He shows her the cover: Orwell, *Homage to Catalonia*.

"I read it in college," she says. "The only part I remember is him getting shot."

Clarence nods. "Famous passage."

"And how in the republic everybody called each other comrade, no more mister or missus. And how the Russians basically fucked them over. All those assholes with their lists and their machine pistols."

"There you go. Sounds like you remember a lot."

The chowder disappears in about a minute, she's not sure how. She munches crackers and checks her phone, 10:05, and orders a small dinner salad on condition that the bartender can get it to her in the next two minutes.

"Someplace you've gotta be?"

"Staff meeting at ten thirty."

"Rough."

"Actually I think this is going to be a fairly early night. Hey, you want me to get you a place on the bus? Save you from driving all those miles by yourself."

"I'm fine. But thanks."

"You don't want to be tied down."

"Maybe something like that."

"How long are you here for?"

"Not sure. Just playing it by ear."

"I get it. You're hanging around for when we have our crisis."

He laughs, doesn't deny it. Reporters, Christ, even the nice ones are jackals, and by the way where's her salad, dammit. To keep from chewing ice she checks her primary phone, where texts and emails are piling up like a week's worth of dirty dishes. From the corner of her eye she sees Clarence is checking his phone as well. She's about to tap into a text from Nadler when her screen throws a fit, red lightning zapping and hairballing everywhere. Oh shit, not here. Please not in front of the press. Then she's aware of a sudden thickening, a palpable drag or heaviness in the air, and sound turns briefly smeary before ceasing with a rubbery vacuum pop. She looks up. Nothing and no one is moving. The bartender, customers, the TVs over the bar, the entire world is frozen in place. Her mind stutters, blanks out. It doesn't process. There's the fact of what she's seeing, and the fact that her mind has no place for it. Then there's movement to her left, Clarence. He turns to look at her.

"You seeing this?" he murmurs, but she can't talk. He puts his hand over hers, and she looks down at their hands. She feels weak all over, clammy, woozy, and thinks she might be sick.

"This is a dream," she announces, taking care to speak very slowly and clearly. "I'm dreaming. In a second I'm going to wake up." From earliest childhood the trick has always bailed her out of nightmares, but not this time. Clarence tightens his grip on her hand.

"I thought so too, my first time. Or I was losing my mind."

She stares at him a moment, then shuts her eyes and shakes her head so hard that she can feel her brain sloshing around her brain pan. She opens her eyes. Same. If she had a fork she'd stab herself, but there's only the spoon.

"What is this?" she whispers.

"I don't know. Some sort of tear in the space-time fabric, maybe."

"I," she attempts, and gives up. Then tries again, in the same husky whisper: "Are we crazy?"

"I don't think so. I'm seeing what you're seeing. I don't think crazy works that way."

She decides to stare at her soup bowl until it's over. Normality returns first as sound, a long theremin smear emerging from the void, then there's a pop, some sort of pressure release, and the material world resumes its flow. Faith looks up, and the first thing she sees is the bartender smirking at her and Clarence's joined hands.

"You okay?" Clarence murmurs. "It's over. You're good. You want to go?"

Later, thinking back on it, she'll have no memory of paying her tab, so either Clarence paid or she was operating on automatic. It takes the bitter cold of the parking lot to snap her out of it, same as a couple of hard slaps like they do in the movies. Clarence has his arm around her shoulders and that's fine, she's none too steady on her feet. The Marriott looms across the way like a beached container ship.

"What was that." Her voice all shivery, and not from the cold.

"I wish I could tell you."

"It's happened to you before."

"Several times. I think it has something to do with phones. It never happens unless I'm on my phone—the screen freezes up, then everything freezes. The whole world just stops."

She thinks about this. And whether talking about it makes it more real, and is that good or bad.

"My phone's been acting up too," she says finally.

"Really." Their footsteps snap on the cold asphalt like pistol shots.

"Red lightning," she says. "All up in my screen, storms of it. I never know when it's going to happen. I switch out phones, it keeps happening. Wait."

"What?"

"Is this going to keep happening to me now?"

"I don't know. I don't know what to tell you. But that's the first time it happened to me with someone else."

Oh, God. Why me. Approaching the hotel's porte cochere they separate. Now they're just two people who happen to be walking in the same direction.

"You okay?"

"I don't know. I still think I might be dreaming."

"Ain't no dream, sister. Sorry to break it to you."

26

Lately he's thinking about something Orwell wrote, but it's not in *Catalonia*. So *Burmese Days*, maybe, or *Down and Out*, a line to the effect that there's a time in every person's life when their character is set forever. Fair enough, but Orwell died at forty-seven. Give him another fifteen or twenty years, he might have faced the kind of overhaul that Clarence finds himself confronting. *His* character, formed in the racial seethe of post–Jim Crow Texas circa 1977, with further annealing in the lies, blood politics, and nouveau-colonial loot grab of Reagan's Central American wars, has been spun upside down and inside out. All his assumptions, pretty much everything he thought he knew about the world and how it works—blown. He might as well be sixteen again, with all those ass-from-elbow existential problems pressing in on him. Context. Proportion. Cause and effect. What he was doing back then without knowing it was trying to construct a personality, a self coherent and elastic and agile enough to get him to his twenties.

You would think it worked out all right, this self. It's still here, walking and talking, trying to do the work, but basic principles of discernment have turned to mush. All bets off, once you allow for the possibility of miracles in your life. He observes Rasputin with the weepers and now the coma kids, the healing touch he lays on them, and thinks that maybe he, Clarence, doesn't know anything. His body was profoundly, perhaps permanently damaged, and now it isn't. Call it what you want, miracle, mystery, X-file anomaly, it is what it is, and once you open the door to the reality of such a thing the whole house feels like it's coming apart. Prophecy and resurrection, redeemers and devils, time warps and miracle cures, you could spin yourself up so high with signs and wonders that you might never come down.

He feels like he has a better understanding of his fellow Americans now. We are living in the era of the great spin-up, the mass unmooring of the American mind; God knows the culture offers precious little to hang onto. His own unmooring plays on a more or less continuous memory loop. The humiliation of Rasputin seizing his head in front of all those people, then the panic, the primal alarm as he began to squeeze. The quick buildup to the moment of maximum pressure, then the flash, the blue-white arc blinding him from the inside. What followed once the shock wore off were several days of stupefying peacefulness. A high most mellow and serene, and even the brain fog felt right, like a swaddle of softest gauze guarding his head while it healed. Soon he was fine. Is fine. And hell no he hasn't gone to the doctor. He doesn't want any doctor dumping on it.

Curing weepers and coma kids is one thing—power of suggestion, action-hero doses of placebo effect—but healing a documented TBI is altogether next level. Clarence keeps it to himself, ponders, listens to Big Mama Thornton in his downtime. *Keep an eye on those people.* █████? Rasputin? Both? He can't be everywhere at once, but at least he's here. Day two of his Iowa odyssey, he's up at five to study the news. █████'s violence advocacy is going into hyperdrive and the casualties mount accordingly. Overnight clashes in St. Louis, Memphis, Greensboro, Los Angeles, and elsewhere yield nine dead, scores wounded, hundreds of arrests. "This is not who we are," the editorial board of *The Wall Street Journal* boldly whines. Rapid Support Forces are dispatched to the Territorial Control Center in El Paso to quell rioting after a five-year-old girl dies of hypothermia, and Vice President Greene suspends her rally in Davenport, Iowa, when the Weeps run amok. Between the

Weeps and heavy harassment by militias, the Democratic candidates have all but quit holding in-person events. And in a SonicX post at 5:34 this morning, ██████ proposes holding this summer's Republican convention on a luxury cruise ship in Biscayne Bay to avoid infiltration by "the evil ones."

Clarence takes a break to shower and shave, and when he returns news is breaking of a video purporting to show Rasputin in flagrante with three women. The reporter holds his nose, and along with the rest of the country has his obligatory leer. It certainly *looks* like Rasputin, not that that means anything; the Rodney King, seeing-is-believing days are long gone. The campaign issues a statement declaring the video "a scandalous fake," and at the day's first rally, a packed house at the old Grange Hall in Chilton, the Candidate shrugs it off.

"That is my face in the video, yes," he tells the crowd with a droll smile. "But that is not the rest of me, I assure you."

The men smirk and chuckle, the women do small fluttery things with their hands. Clarence counts zero blacks in the audience, seven Hispanics; and waiting outside, all those thousands of miles of lily-white snow. Note to self: The blackest I ever felt was a January in Iowa. During Q and A, Rasputin is asked if the obscene fake video is the work of the devil.

"Well," the Candidate muses, "we may consider it this way. There are enemies who are demons, and there are enemies who are humans, and they help one another."

The crowd is thrilled. Hot murmurs, shivers, ecstatically avid eyes, Chilton is ready to follow Rasputin to the gates of hell. As the Q and A is winding down Clarence gets a text from Faith inviting him to ride the New Awakening Express to Mallard, their next stop. Grishka wants to see you she adds.

Clarence: I want to see him too. But what about my car.
Faith: Staff will drive it to Mallard.

Twenty minutes later he's boarding the bus, an enormous luxury land-ship with a snappy blue-and-gray exterior, "New Awakening Express" blazing down the sides in four-foot script. Inside, Clarence is enveloped by the heavy gastrointestinal thrum of an idling diesel engine. Rows of four-across leather seats fill out the front, followed by banquette tables and a lounge area and more seats, then the door to the rearward private quarters, a refuge for the weary rock star or well-funded candidate. Faith deposits Clarence on the front row and drops her satchel in the adjacent seat. "Back in a sec," she says, and angles her way down the aisle. Staffers climb aboard yakking and laughing, cocky as a team with no defeats, then their eyes fall on Clarence and they go silent. What's *he* doing here? Outside, Chiltonians gather to see the bus off. They laugh, bounce on their toes, wave at the blackout windows, giddy from their hour with the Wrath of God. Dave Buffilini, assistant deputy director of field operations, or some such, is the last to board. "Wheels up," he tells the driver, and the door closes with a heaving cetacean sigh, and they're off. Faith comes careering up the aisle and drops into her seat.

"I'll take you back in a bit. He's praying right now."

Clarence glances over to see if she's joking. Apparently not. Her respiratory distress is worse today. Hacking, snorting, sniffling, and her voice is funny, as if her hard palate has dissolved into the bog of her sinus cavities. She does a quick check of each of her phones. He notes the surgical gloves. Presently she stows the phones in her satchel, peels off the gloves, and leans in close enough that their shoulders touch.

"I'm still freaking," she murmurs, so low that he can barely hear her over the bus hum.

He nods.

"You aren't?"

"I might be getting used to it."

"No way. It's just too . . ." Her mouth crimps sideways, and she gnaws the inside of her cheek for a moment. "Why us?"

"Maybe it's not just us. Maybe it's a lot of people. They just don't talk about it."

"No shit. Last night I was like, I ought to call my old shrink and get some pills or something, but he'd probably call my mom and have me committed." She hesitates. "Is it a sign, do you think?"

"Of what."

"Well," she begins, and hesitates. "The end times." She watches his face. "Oh God, you think I'm crazy."

He answers firmly: "I do not think you're crazy."

Her head flops back against the seat, and she rolls her face toward his. It's a strikingly pretty face, with a tidy WASP blade of a nose, big blue eyes, fresh cup-of-cream complexion. Plump with tears, those eyes, seemingly dazed, yearning. Clarence's throat seizes up, and his heart performs an entirely inappropriate thump. No. Stop that. His reptile brain has badly misread the situation. A woman presenting her face this way, the subcortex crudely signals she wants to be kissed, and he knows better than that.

"Faith, you're okay." He keeps his voice very low. "You aren't crazy, and neither am I. Whatever's happening, we've just gotta roll with it."

She puts the back of her hand to her nose as if stifling a sneeze. Some sort of complicated suction and clearing action happens, all very discreet behind her hand. Newly composed, she turns back to him, and he has a slightly softer version of the clutch response. That the feeling lingers will trouble him a great deal.

"Bitsy told me about when you were a prisoner. In," she flounders, but he says nothing. "He said you almost died."

"Well. It seemed possible at the time."

"He said they kept you in a cell. They beat you every day."

Clarence nods.

"So I guess you rolled with it."

Ah, nice setup. She's clever. "I guess I did. As much as possible."

"So what about the parts you couldn't roll with. You just had to take it?"

"I guess so. I guess that's one way to put it."

"All right, so what happens when a person's had all they can take?"

"I don't know. Maybe we don't know till the very end."

"Maybe that's how it ends."

"May be. That could be one definition."

"Which is worse?"

"Say again?"

"Now or then, which is worse. I mean, I think I *know* which is worse, for you. Being in that cell. Getting beat on. But that was just you. It's not like the whole world was at stake."

"You think the whole world is at stake."

"Don't you? Whatever that was last night, man, come on, something's really seriously wrong out there. I mean the world, reality, basic laws of physics. Space and time." She gives him the big eyes and there it is again, the clutch-thump, the cardiac rush. Man his age, get a grip. "Anyway," she says, "I really don't know how I'm supposed to roll with that."

"Except what else can you do."

She thinks about that. "When did it start. For you."

"Last summer."

"*Jesus!*" she hisses. "And all this time . . . You haven't told anyone?"

"Nope."

"Dude." She gives him a look, wary, admiring. Word comes forward: Rasputin will see the reporter now. They take a moment to reset, then stand, their conspiracy of two venturing into the so-called normal world. Rasputin is seated at the rearmost banquette table with three well-fed Iowa politicos in sport coats, open collars, class rings on their chunky fingers. The Iowans sport lapel pins in the shape of tiny shovels, signifying the hardcore fiscal stance: Stop digging America deeper into debt. Ruddy pink and salmon skin tones predominate, and their faces sour theatrically at the sight of Clarence, the media, the enemy of all that is good and true. That he's black obliges them to be a little less overtly rude, and so they loathe him even more.

"Fake News!" Rasputin cries.

"Russkie."

The pols rear back. "Now wait a second, fella," one of the no-neck gentlemen rowls.

"No, no, no," Rasputin laughs, "we are just spoofing each other," his slangy "spoofing" deployed in the determinedly casual way of a non-native speaker, and Clarence thinks, this guy's so good you could almost forget he's as American as Obama. "Fake News is my man,"

Rasputin explains to the pols. "He found me in Southlake before anybody, ██████, the medias, our faith leaders, he was the very first. He is my scribe, my Pushkin. Come, come, Clarence, sit."

It's painful to watch the pols trying to locate Pushkin in their mental contact lists. Faith shoos them over to make room for Clarence and lays down the ground rules: This is mainly a social visit, everything's off the record except for those limited instances where Clarence specifically requests otherwise. So we're good?

"All good," Clarence says. Rasputin is beaming at him.

"Clarence, my friend. I am very happy to see you."

"Thanks. I'm happy to see you too."

For several seconds the Candidate drills him with the mystic, all-seeing Rasputin stare. The pols watch. At the long table across the aisle, Twiss, Nadler, and senior staff look up from their phones, they're watching too. And Faith, who's standing in the aisle with her rump propped against a nearby setback. Iowa flows past the windows like a tight-lipped Scandinavian movie, palette of sober Lutheran grays and ghostly whites.

"You are well," Rasputin announces.

"I am," Clarence confirms.

"Yes, I feel it. Clarence was seriously injured several weeks ago," he tells the pols. "Head injury, concussion, coma, very serious. But by the power of the merciful Almighty, he is well."

"Praise God," says one pol.

"Amen," says another.

"Glory to Him," says the third.

Faith's eyes are steady on Clarence, tense with fear and portent, and he becomes aware of a performance imperative. Soooooo . . . how's Iowa? Fantastic, super, great, the crowds are warm and welcoming everywhere we go. "Americans are good," Rasputin declares, and the pols solemnly agree. He'll do two more days in Iowa, then fly to Dallas for an evening fundraiser, then overnight to New Hampshire for a day there, then back to Iowa for the final run-up to the caucuses. The pols think he might break sixty percent on caucus night, a strong showing by any measure, but to break sixty against a sitting president would be "nuclear." Even sixty-five's not out of the question; they've never seen Iowans respond to a candidate as they have to this man.

"Why do you think that is?" Clarence asks.

"He's a true Christian," says one of the pols. "An agent of holy governance against the armies of Lucifer."

"Woke's just about to kill this country," says a second. "You know Ephesians? Principalities and powers? The same thing's happening here."

"It all goes back to secular humanism," says the third. "Tell him," he urges Rasputin, "tell him what you were telling us just now."

"Yes," the Candidate picks up smoothly, "we were discussing the fall of Byzantium to the Ottoman armies in 1453, and the loss of our precious Constantinople to Islam. It was a military defeat, true, but Byzantium's resolve was already weakened by the moral relativism of Europe."

"And it's happening all over again!" cries the first pol. "We've gone soft, weak. Flabby."

"We've got to get back to strong Christian values," says the second. "Doing the will of heaven on earth."

"Like the Russian Orthodox Church," says the third.

"Really," says a somewhat flabbergasted Clarence. "What do you know about the Russian Orthodox Church?"

A lot! they cry. The Russian church is holding the line! "Russia is a highly Christian nation because of their church," the first pol says. "They have strong leaders, that's why they're winning," says the second. "We need someone like Putin to be our president," offers the third. Clarence looks to Rasputin, who smiles like the cat that ate the eagle. The reporter turns back to the pols. "All right, what about the sex video that dropped today. Do you think that's going to change how Iowans feel about this candidate?"

Everyone recoils like he's thrown acid in their face. The pols snarl, which is satisfying. Senior staff come halfway out of their seats.

"Clarence," Faith warns, and she looks to Twiss, who looks from her to Rasputin to Clarence.

"Off limits," he says.

But Rasputin is bemused. "We can talk about that silly little thing if you want," he says, so Clarence pulls up a clip of ████ on the stump in Ball (was this planned?), Iowa, this morning. "That video," the president says to the crowd,

> is it fake, is it real, we're hearing all kinds of things about that video, I guess nobody really knows. Or maybe they do, some of the people we're hearing from, and these are experts, expert people, they're saying it looks pretty real to them! And there's gonna be more, that's what we're hearing, people are saying that. Yeah, more videos, wooo boy, okay? I'm told at least one is going to be released fairly soon—

and so on and so forth, a long rap of the president's trademark weaselly wigwag of slander once removed. *I'm* not saying, *they're* saying. Nobody *really* knows, but what we're *hearing*, and *some* people, and *fairly soon*, and *all kinds of things*, fourth-rate rhetorical tricks so far beneath the office of the presidency that all Americans within the sound of ████'s voice should cover their ears in shame.

"I am sure—okay, this is for you, Fake News. On the record." Rasputin raises his hand, forestalling objections from staff, and Clarence activates the record function on his phone. "I suspect," Rasputin resumes, directing his words at the phone, "that what the president says is correct, we can expect more charming videos of this nature. I am sure there is an endless supply of such things, thanks to the miracle of AI. And so I ask my fellow Americans please to exercise your judgment when assessing these creations. Yes, I am a man. I am a man who is naturally attracted to women, as God intends according to nature and my Christian faith. But these video creatures—no. My fellow Americans, please do not think for one second that is me."

"We're done with the video," Twiss announces, and the pols chirp and caw in support, and senior staff look ready to throw Clarence off the bus, or under it. Touchy crowd. He switches his phone out of record and looks across the table at Rasputin.

"You do know what's coming, don't you."

The Candidate is relaxed, alert. "What is coming."

"The women, man! All the women you've got hanging around. So far you've gotten a pass on your lifestyle, but that's not going to last much longer. They're going to hit you hard on the women, and they're going to keep on hitting."

Rasputin nods. Takes his time. He looks to Twiss, staff, the pols, measuring the quality of their concern, and Clarence realizes they're mortified, as in: embarrassed. We don't talk about the women, we don't hear them, see them, smell them, they simply aren't there. So what the fuck kind of presidential campaign is this, staff's too prissy to come up with a woman strategy?

"Turn it on," Rasputin says, nodding at Clarence's phone.

"On the record?"

"On the record." He ignores all the groaning and squirming from staff and waits until Clarence is set. "Okay, Fake News, you just asked me about 'the women,' as you put it. My 'lifestyle.' I assume you are referencing to the Maidens?"

"We can start with them."

"Okay then. I will tell you frankly, sir, we are family at my house. Maidens, cooks, coaches, trainers, housekeeping, we are all brothers and sisters and this is our holy community. We take care of each other. We love and cherish each other. Each one does our work and everyone contributes, and let me tell you, this is a beautiful thing. And as for the Maidens, they are a huge part of the fantastic success of the Wrath of God brand. Are they extremely attractive women? Absolutely! Beauty is a gift and a good from God, and I take heart in their beauty. If not for the Maidens, I would not be the man I am today." He pauses. "I have more to say."

"Go ahead," Clarence replies.

Rasputin draws himself up, becomes even more massive just sitting there. "Therefore," he resumes, his voice rising, "my *lifestyle*, as you call it, this beautiful holy community we have made in Southlake, it is an expression of God's love. It has never been secret, never some shameful cover-up thing. No, totally opposite, it is a glorious thing—I fervently wish for more holy communities such as ours across the land. And as for the people of low mind spreading gossip and lies, may Almighty God have mercy on their souls. Their behavior says more about the state of their souls than anything they can say about me."

"Hear, hear!" cry the pols, and they clap and thump the table in the best beer-hall style. Twiss and staff cheer from the sidelines, score one for the team. You're welcome, Clarence feels like telling them. Fake News just handed you your woman strategy. "Now you know why I like this guy," Rasputin says to the pols. "He is tough. Tough but fair. He challenges me."

Faith consults briefly with Twiss and heads to the front. Rasputin retires to his private quarters to refresh for the next event and leaves Clarence with the pols, who pass the final miles ragging on him about the liberal bias of the press. They keep at it until the bus pulls up to the Mallard Senior High School gym, home of the Fighting Ducks. Nice, an entire town with a sense of humor. Faith is waiting for him when he steps off the bus.

"Your keys are coming," she says gruffly, face down to her phone. She taps out a few words. "You call that a social visit?"

"He's running for president. This doesn't seem like the time for small talk. You know, considering the entire world's at stake. Remember?" She keeps her face to her phone. "I do believe you are upset with me, Faith."

"*No.* Yes. No, Jesus, I don't know, I don't know anything anymore. Here look, here comes Nathan with your keys."

"He drove?"

Nathan looks about fourteen.

"Nathan, give him the keys."

"My name's Nathaniel, ma'am."

"For God's sake *please* don't ma'am me. Give him the keys, whatever your name is. I've gotta go."

The White Guard is setting up its security perimeter. Each little squad glares at Clarence as he walks by, and he pops them the peace sign. In the parking lot his rental car is comfortably warm from the drive. He sits in the passenger seat and makes notes and scrolls the news, waiting for the start of lunch hour at the Lew Sterrett Justice Center in Dallas, a mandate as rigorously honored as the death penalty. At 12:01 he calls his nephew. Nelson clicks in on the first ring.

"Uncle."

"You saw it?"

"Of course I saw it, everybody's seen it. Emerald says it's bullshit."

"Okay."

"She says he really, really loves women, and they love him back. But it's not like that."

"Okay."

"You want to know what it's like."

"Well, it's my job."

"I didn't ask. She didn't say. She just said it's not like that. And she told me to tell you that."

"She did."

"Yep. She's pretty upset. She says all the Maidens are."

"Angry?"

"Angry, frustrated, hurt, all of the above. They're very devoted to him."

"Just to be clear, you're saying she said that's not him in the video."

Nelson coughs. This is awkward for everyone. "In so many words, yeah, basically. I mean, it was implied. Um, Key?"

"Yeah?"

"Why does it even matter who he sleeps with? Politically, I mean. Who cares who the president sleeps with as long as he does the damn job."

"Good question. Only thing I can tell you is, this country has a lot of funny ideas about sex. About what's dirty, immoral, put it that way. Slaughtering black and brown people all over the world, not a problem. Sex, getting it on, having a good time in bed—problem."

"Except █████. All the shit he's gotten away with."

But Clarence is thinking. "Gandhi," he says.

"Gandhi," Nelson echoes. A prompt.

"Last years of his life, I guess he was a widower by then? Every night he slept with two young women in his bed. Everybody naked, no sex. He supposedly did it as a form of discipline, spiritual practice. Maybe that's what this guy is about."

"Maybe."

They're silent for a moment.

"I'm not going to ask Emerald for an interview."

"I didn't think you would. But thanks."

"But if any of the others . . ."

"I'll pass it on."

From Mallard to Kraynak to Smathers to Waterloo, Clarence follows the New Awakening Express through the long gray dusk of afternoon and decides he ought to have another look at *The Scarlet Letter.* His last contact with that book being around, oh, fifty years ago? Eleventh-grade English, Mrs. McGinnis, might as well have been the Middle Ages, but today of all days it rises in his mind. The first big American novel, at least by reputation, and it's about, please note, SEX. Sex and the Puritans. Nitro, meet glycerin. His adult self suspects Hawthorne was onto something, and had old Mrs. McGinnis had the training, the fortitude, the presence of mind to point out that the novel's about *sex*, perhaps a few knuckleheads might have been inspired to hack through all those thickets of *thee*'s and *thou*'s in search of something real.

Grigory Rasputin, the Wrath of God, the world's most famous fake Russian, might be the most sexualized presidential candidate in the nation's history. A candidate brought to you by the primal theater of All World Wrestling with its bulging manly muscles and quivering flesh, he is the pagan king borne forth on the fulsome bosom of his mouthwatering harem. Add to that his exotic strain of Christianism, and you've got a product primed to drive the American mind right off the ragged edge of reason.

Keep an eye on those people, Clarence's fellow North Texan urged him. Trying, my man. Fronting it all the way. From his press colleagues he hears of stirrings in the dead of night, shadowy figures in the hotel parking lots and back stairways. Sometimes they're in monks' habits or dark billows of clerical robes, "like the freaking DaVinci code," says *The Atlanta Journal-Constitution*. The Philly *Inquirer* claims she saw the Winklevoss twins one night, the billionaire crypto bros done up in the habits and hoods of Franciscan friars. Other rumors speak of the First Lady, Snoop, Miriam Adelson, emissaries from Elon Musk.

At this point anything seems possible. In Smathers, population 6,711, two coma kids are wheeled into the gym on gurneys, and it gets downright biblical. "Resignation Syndrome" cropped up contemporaneous with the budget impasse saturating the news, scattered cases of otherwise healthy teenagers lapsing overnight into coma-like states. So far fewer than a hundred cases have been reported, but the dread is nationwide. "It's almost like these kids have given up," *The New York Times* quotes the head of psychiatry at the Mayo Clinic, and various theories are floated. Social media overload. The protracted stress of gaining admission to the college of your choice. Vitamin D deficiency coupled with post-holiday depression. In Smathers the Candidate steps off the stage as soon as the kids are wheeled in, and he does each one in turn. Takes their hand, strokes it, leans in, and murmurs some words. Signs the cross, then gently touches his signing hand to their heads, and don't those kids sit right up like they've got springs in their backs. In short order a thousand videos viralize, "Lazarus was real" being one of the more popular tags, and the sex tape promptly drops off the charts. Clarence is shuffling out of the gym with the rest of the press when Faith texts:

Would someone please tell me what the fuck is going on?

As if he'd know. In Waterloo it's only weepers, no kids. Penned up with the rest of the media, Clarence seems to recall—he's too tired to look it up right now—the young Hawthorne broke off a marriage engagement, thereby "ruining" the girl. Passion. Desire. Schizo customs and mores. After Waterloo it's a long cold drive to Des Moines with the rest of the caravan, three press buses now and a fleet's worth of rentals. Sleet and snow hammer down, sand and salt muck up the headlights, the White Guard is MIA but everybody else blasts along at eighty miles an hour, herd instinct manifesting as a freeway suicide run. It's midnight when he checks into his room, and after two by the time he posts his story. Within a minute his phone buzzes. Has she been watching the website?

Faith: Did it happen to you today?
Clarence: No. You?
Faith: No. But still sort of freaking.
Clarence: Normal. Gotta roll with it.
Faith: Copy that. But its not why I'm freaking.
Clarence: Do tell.
Faith: Feels like something huge is coming.
Clarence: What.
Faith: IDK.
Clarence: A feeling can be information.
Faith: Actually I think I do know. But I can't tell you.
Clarence: Up to you.

Then dot-dot-dot, message pending.

Faith: Where you staying.
Clarence: Hyatt.
Faith: Same.

Dot-dot-dot, pulsing roughly with the rhythm of his heart.

Faith: I can't sleep.

He stares at this for a good fifteen seconds. Feeling the pull, for sure. Feeling it bad. Having forgotten how good feeling it bad can feel. He knows right away how he's going to answer, but for these few moments he dangles, letting the fantasy breathe. Forty years' difference between them, it's alluring, it's absurd. Man, don't be a fool.

Clarence: Try. You got something for that?

Faith: Ambien.

Clarence: Take one. Not two. Call me in the morning.

And out.

27

The schedule wobbles, stutters, doesn't quite jump the rails. Rasputin returns to Texas a day early to deal with "personal business." Editors and producers fret over whether to spend big and send their people to Southlake or spend less to have them doing nothing in Des Moines. "I think he's a pervert, frankly," the president says of his rival at a morning rally in Council Bluffs, and he tells the country to "stay tuned." That afternoon, in faraway Charlotte, North Carolina, one Tim Tomlinson of Gaffney, SC, holds a press conference under the auspices of the ██████ campaign at which he claims to have seen Rasputin entering a hotel room with two young blond females, identical twins, during the weekend of the 2019 Carolinas Crunch-A-Thon.

"I was staying right across the hall from him," asserts Tomlinson, forty-three, an assistant branch manager for Truist Bank. "I saw it as plain as I'm seeing all of you right now. What stuck in my mind was they were twins. Something like that definitely makes an impression."

Weak, Clarence thinks, watching it live in his room at the Des Moines Hyatt, his notebooks and a paperback copy of *The Scarlet Letter* scattered around him on the bed. If they produced the actual twins, now that would be a story. He texts Faith.

Clarence: Statement coming?

Faith: You bet.

Clarence: I'm assuming twins are bogus.

Faith: Correct.

Clarence: You good?

Faith: Good as a gal can be. Sorry to bug you the other night. I was sort of out of my mind.

Clarence: You didn't bug me. It's a lot to process. Can you give me anything about the "personal business."

Faith: No sorry. But off the record its no big deal.

You didn't bug me. Only his mind has been churning ever since. *I can't sleep.* You and me both, little sister. He spends the rest of the afternoon making the rounds of state headquarters, comparing the quality of the merchandise and soaking up vibes. At Rasputin headquarters all hands are staying calm and carrying on. A young, fresh-faced Spiritual Gangsta gifts him a T-shirt and chirps, "We appreciate the media!" At ████ headquarters they're eager to vent. Rasputin is a *terrible* candidate, a *pathetic* candidate. He's brain damaged. He can barely speak English. He's a pervert, a loser, a hypocrite. Then it's on to Vice President Greene's headquarters, where the bare-bones staff of three refuses to talk to him. He walks around admiring the candidate's allegiance to the color red. Red everything, bright red, big bold brilliant red. Scarlet, even. When he pulls out his notebook to make a few notes, they tell him to leave.

Rasputin attends the Dallas fundraiser as planned, arrives in Concord the next morning at six a.m., and does the full day in New Hampshire. Another sex tape drops, neither more nor less credible than the first, and in DC an exotic dancer doing business as Misty DeBry holds a press conference at the ████ Hotel. With slick lawyers covering her flanks and longtime ████ ally Roger Stone lurking in the wings, Ms. DeBry claims to have had "intimate relations" with Rasputin at the

Las Vegas Bellagio four years ago. In a matter of hours her story craters. Credit card records, cell phone records, and tax records all show she was in Phoenix at the time in question, working a club gig that happened to coincide with the annual NRA convention.

Scandal in this country's just not what it used to be, Clarence reflects. If you're gonna stir shit, at least make sure it stinks.

Nobody tells her why the unscheduled day in Texas. Rasputin and ultra-senior staff fly to Dallas; the rest of the staff, Faith included, fly straight to Concord. The next day it's a nonstop blitz around the Granite State and a late flight back to Iowa. She staggers into her room at the Hyatt and, ever dutiful, activates the spy phone. Multiple calls to her contact number ring out. Figures. I'm out here killing myself and they're snug in their Georgetown apartments streaming old *Friends* episodes. In a huff she texts Stephen Miller the code word, Flags. A minute later a text pings the spy phone from an unknown number. Two words. You're fired.

Bardem Hayes sends out an early morning email blast calling a press conference for ten a.m. in the Cheyenne Room of the Hyatt. The Candidate will make brief remarks and take questions, then resume his previously announced schedule with a rally at the Blalock Center in West Des Moines. Clarence checks in with Renfro. Nobody knows anything there. He texts Faith, she doesn't answer. He elevators down to the lobby and engages in reckless speculation with his media peers. Yet another "bimbo eruption" is the consensus. X-rated video, more strippers, maybe a rogue Maiden or groupie out to make a buck, and Rasputin intends to get ahead of it. Which means it's serious. Mainstream media is licking its chops.

The Cheyenne Room's not bad, not if you like your regal gold color scheme flavored with shades of rancid butter. Gold ceiling, paisley gold-flocked walls, and a faux-marble gold floor that's slightly tacky underfoot, some sort of petroleum-based synthetic in the finish. The past few minutes a late rumor has burned through the room: He's calling it quits. No. Yes. The biggest political happening since *Dobbs v. Jackson* is crashing out, so it must be bad, whatever it is, woman trouble, man trouble, kinky monk in the closet trouble. For days █████ has been peddling slander about unnatural acts, who knows, maybe he had the goods all along.

Seated dead center near the front, Clarence has an excellent view of senior staff entering from a side door, taking up position along the rear of the riser that serves as the stage. Just their expressions set off hot whisperings among the press. Ashen, they are. Gutted. Grieving. Has someone died? Faith is a ghastly, bled-by-vampires white, jaw slack as a torn sail, blue eyes fuddled and blear. Campaign heavyweights Chuck and Cecil enter through the side door, followed by Secret Service agents, and then, finally, Rasputin, and he's leading the First Lady by the hand.

Clarence will remember a sharp, loud *crack* like a steel beam snapping, a glacier falling into the sea, and he will remember as well a punch to the stomach coming out of nowhere, recalling the whack to the solar plexus at that long-ago rally in Columbia. Then the shrieking of the crowd like a bunch of howler monkeys, and right away there are weepers to deal with, their merely human nervous systems buckling under the strain. The First Lady remains at Rasputin's side as the weepers are brought forward, and to each one she offers quiet words of her own, a comforting pat on the shoulder or arm. Camera flashes make for a strobing firestorm. White noise fills the room like crashing chandeliers. Sensory overload renders Clarence somewhat breathless. It's just sound, he tells himself, sound and light, though his stomach aches from that invisible punch. For several minutes Chuck and Cecil have their hands full with the weepers, but Rasputin doing his thing has a settling effect on the room. The tender way he pulls each person to his chest. The enveloping embrace, then the eye-to-eye close-up, the smile and gentle words of blessing. By the time he and █████ mount the riser, the room is merely loud as opposed to hysterical. Front center stage there is a single mic on a naked microphone stand, no podium rampart to hide behind. Rasputin walks up to the mic, and the room goes silent. ████████ stands to his side and slightly behind, within easy arm's reach.

"Ladies and gentlemen of the media," he intones, and his voice is deep and strong. "My fellow Americans. Brothers and sisters. ████████ and I come before you today to tell you the truth that is in our hearts. And so I will speak plainly, no beating around the bush. In the course of coming to know this remarkable woman, I," here his voice briefly catches, snagging on the sharp teeth of passion, "I fell in love with her. I make no excuse for myself. I tell you in total honesty, this was never my intention. But sometimes these things happen, yes? What has formed between us is a human thing, a very powerful thing, and I am sure all who have experienced it know that which of I speak. Again, I make no excuse. I ask no pardon of myself. And I vouchsafe to you, as a man of faith, we have not known each other in that most intimate way of man and woman. That is for marriage only, and God's blessing—"

ARE YOU GOING TO MARRY HER? a dozen journalists yell in a dozen different ways.

"Yes," Rasputin answers, calmly, firmly. "We will marry. That is our plan, if it be God's will to grant us this blessing. No," he seamlessly volleys the predictable follow-up, "we do not have a date. That would be quite premature." More shouts, a Babel of shouting. "Oh, do I consider myself a sinner, you ask. My brothers and sisters, I am indeed a sinner. I am as sorely needful of redemption as any man who ever walked God's earth. And I am also," he glances back at ████████, a sweetly vulnerable reflex, "as deeply in love as I believe any man has ever been. Truly, I have never felt like this in my life."

His voice lulling, hypnotic, the ultimate bedroom voice; half the women in sight have tears streaming down their cheeks. Faith too, Clarence notes. Maybe she's in love with him. More than maybe; it would explain why she's so completely wrecked, hiccuping sobs like a toddler who's skinned her knees. Presently the Candidate yields to ████████, and she steps up to the mic with her hands demurely clasped in front, her frame ruler-straight and statuesque. A babe bomb. Not for nothing was she a top model from her teens.

"Many months ago," she begins in her trademark silky monotone, "Grishka and I began a spiritual journey together. Thanks to him I began to open my heart to the wonder of God's love, and on this journey, without expecting it, I found myself falling in love with this amazing man. Let me be frank: I did not intend for this to happen. But in truth I felt a terrible emptiness in my life. Spiritual emptiness, emotional emptiness. And I was deeply unhappy in my marriage, for many reasons, which perhaps can best be expressed this way: I woke up one morning and realized I was terribly alone. I know many women who are listening will understand what I mean. For so long I have tried to present the image of a happy marriage, but I cannot live that lie any longer. No more lies, please, ever. Grishka and I are here before you today because we wish to live in total honesty. Honesty in ourselves, with each other, with all of you. We are in love and this is a beautiful thing, but it is complicated, for obvious reasons. But even that we will not hide from, but face directly. Now, if you have questions—"

DOES THE PRESIDENT KNOW?

"Yes, he knows."

WHEN DID YOU TELL HIM WHEN WHEN OVER THE PHONE IN PERSON HOW WHAT DID HE SAY?????

"We have spoken. The rest is private between ██████ and me."

DOES ██████ KNOW?

"Yes, our son knows."

IS HE ANGRY SAD OKAY UPSET WHEN DID HE KNOW?????

"As I am sure you will understand, this is a very difficult time for me and my family. I ask you to please respect our privacy. Our son's especially."

WHAT ABOUT THE DIVORCE WHEN WHO WHERE DO YOU HAVE AN ATTORNEY????

"My attorneys will be filing the papers shortly."

TODAY TOMORROW THIS WEEK THIS MONTH WHEN WHEN WHEN????

"Today."

The room erupts for no reason except as journalistic venting, it's simply too much stimulus for the media mind to bear. Or maybe it's the old Puritan bugaboo about divorce, Clarence thinks, a visitation of angry spirits. Rasputin smoothly switches out for ██████████ at the mic and raises his arm, sweeping it over the crowd as if calming the waters. And it works, by God. Another miracle. Clarence supposes Jesus of Nazareth had this same command presence.

"Friends," he amiably booms into the mic. "Countrymen. Brothers and sisters. Is there something you are forgetting?"

ARE YOU STILL RUNNING FOR PRESIDENT?

The big man smiles and offers a little bow in that direction. "Ah, excellent question. And the answer is . . . yes! I am still very much a candidate for the presidency of the United States. What has happened here today"—he lifts both arms and widens his eyes in a show of candor—"it is real, it is human. ██████████ and I come before you in all our humanity, with all our strengths, our flaws and weaknesses, and most of all with that essential part of ourselves that is always striving to be better. America is a great democracy, my friends. And the foundation of our democracy is this: We each bring the experiences of our lives into the civic realm. All we have endured, all we have done and learned accompanies us into the civic, and *that*, my brothers and sisters, is the essence of democracy. And I tell you, it is a beautiful thing. Whether I am to be president of this beautiful democracy, I leave it to the American people to decide.

"And now," he glances at his watch, "I have to go! I will see all of you shortly in West Des Moines."

Pearl Harbor, the Kennedys, MLK, 9/11, where were you when . . . I was there, Clarence says to that future discussant. I saw it live, up close, in person, and just when we thought it couldn't get any nuttier. A candidate for president snaking the wife of the sitting president, gonna be hell to pay and God save the republic. He goes up to his room and splashes water on his face, then sits on the edge of the bed with the remote and surfs the news. No great fund of insight there. He puts in phone and text messages to Faith, and calls Bitsy, who picks up promptly.

"Clarence."

"Bitsy."

For several moments neither man speaks.

"You okay?"

"Debatin' with myself around that. Worried for him, mainly. And her. That thing ate 'em up before they know it was hungry. We off the record, right?"

"Completely. I'm just calling to see how you're doing."

"Well, I appreciate that. I reckon I'm all right."

"And him?"

"Hunh. I'll tell you straight-out, I never seen him like this over a woman. She have made him a very happy man."

"How about her?"

"She seem okay. She got the worry about her, but I think Grishka make her happy. Way better than old Trunk. You in Iowa?"

"I am."

"So you saw all that."

"I did."

Bitsy hesitates. "He not gonna be president, is he."

"Normally I'd say no. But I don't know."

"Normal don't apply."

"Not these days."

"You wonder if it ever coming back. Hang on." He speaks to someone off phone, returns. "Sorry, but I gotta see about this. All the people out there gone crazy, they trying to come over the wall."

"Wait. They're storming the wall?"

"That's what they tellin' me."

"Wow. Well. Be careful out there."

"Amen."

They click off. He calls Renfro.

"Damnedest thing I ever saw," his editor greets him.

"Pretty much."

"Blowing up there?"

"Full on. Listen, I just talked to Bitsy Bowman. He said they're storming the wall at Southlake."

"Literally?"

"What he said. You might wanna send somebody out there." Clarence hangs fire while his editor taps out a text on another phone. "So I guess we are witnessing history, Ren."

"And a damn piss-poor version of it too. When the hell did American politics turn into a soap opera?"

"I'll get back to you on that. So. I've been thinking about that audio file."

"Uh-huh."

"He claims they aren't having sex. Well, intercourse." Clarence references his notes. "'That most intimate way of man and woman,' or whatever."

"Might be true, technically. Lots of ways to please your lady."

Clarence ponders for a moment. "We could analyze that file from here to Sunday, we still can't use it."

"Nope. We are a reputable news organization. And we've got you. If you can get a one-on-one with him, or even better her, the two of them together. He loves you."

"I don't know if he loves me that much."

"Let's find out. He could probably stand to see a friendly face right now."

"I'll work on it. But in the meantime, what's the story?"

"The story. The story is, is she a deal killer."

"Okay." Clarence finds a pen and starts making notes.

"Has trust been broken. Will voters turn on him, turn back to █████. And is there any sort of sympathy factor for █████. Or just the opposite, has he been shown to be a shell of a man unfit for the presidency. A guy like him, forget about politics for a minute. His wife running off with a young stud, that's the ultimate humiliation."

"And it couldn't happen to a nicer guy."

"There you go, the schadenfreude factor. Let's keep an eye on the flash polls. And—whoa. The Dow's down a thousand points in the last five minutes."

"And away we go."

"And away we go. If you'd told me six months ago . . ."

"Right."

28

She is alone. Profoundly, utterly, woefully alone, not a person on this earth she can bare her soul to, or certainly no one who could make it better. Staff is told about a minute before the presser, then they're marched out there to look cool and collected while the heavens fall and the earth cracks open beneath their feet. The sight of Rasputin and the First Lady holding hands sends Faith right out of her head. Something essential seems to detach from her corporeal self, ego, consciousness, anima, whatever you call core Faithness, and like a balloon slipping the leash she floats up and away, a sentient blob hovering over the political scandal of the century.

Quite mystical, it all is. Not sleeping for thirty hours might have something to do with it. Middle of the night last night she texted Harvey, Why? Then Don't do this to me. Then Call me you guys owe me that at least. And as soon as she gets a moment to herself after the presser, I didn't know. A smoky blue-gray film, a fuggy haze like Houston humidity, makes reality seem very fragile at the moment. So what's she supposed to do now, quit? Confess? Plead menstrual cramps and crawl off to her room? Inertia carries her forward. Nadler and Bardem appointed her campaign liaison to the talk shows, which are already calling. *Dr. Phil. The View.* Oprah's people dangle the prospect of a special edition.

Everybody wants ██████████. Rasputin would be fine, great, sure, the two of them together, but mainly they want a heart-to-heart with the newly estranged FLOTUS. Worth noting that there's never been a divorce in the White House. History beckons. Will our generation rise to the challenge?

Social media is trending 60–40 favorable for Rasputin. The Dow drops 1,500, catches its breath, and streaks into positive territory. "██████████ Magdalene!!!" screams the *New York Post* website, going hard at the holy man's whore angle. On CNN a family law expert enumerates the causes of action available to the president, with alienation of affection being the biggie. Christie calls five times in seven minutes. Against her better judgment, Faith answers on the sixth.

"Mom."

"Oh my God, *what* is going on there?"

"Just a little bit crazy right now."

"Did you *know*?"

She can't go there. "No."

"You didn't?" Christie is ready to be angry if she did.

"Of course not, nobody did. Well, at my level. I guess a few of the highers did. And security, they would have to know."

"How long has this been going on?"

"All I know is he started coming to the White House last summer. They did seem to spend a fair amount of time together. For, uh, spiritual counseling."

"Well, it's all quite . . ." For once, words fail Christie Spack. "When he walked out in front of the cameras with her, I literally *screamed*. Literally. Screamed."

"It was pretty intense."

"I have to say, you seemed quite upset out there."

"I did?"

"You were crying."

"No. Really?" She has no recollection of this. "Well, they didn't tell us till just before we went out there. I guess they didn't want anybody leaking it."

"Listen, I want you to tell him we're with him. Whatever sins he's committed, they're just venial, not mortal sins, and anyway if he says they haven't slept together, I believe him. And as for falling in love, who can help that? When it happens it happens. Our hearts are not robots, Faith."

"No."

"You tell him! Tell him we love him and we love her too, the American people are on their side. And they look so good together! It really is a beautiful story when you think about it. Somebody's going to make a movie about them someday."

Someday, like next week? She suspects the phones are already burning up in Tinkle Town, meanwhile political violence is flaring all over the country, White Guard and ers throwing down in the streets. Louisville, Cleveland, Richmond, multiple hot spots in Chicago, a pitched battle in Tallahassee at Rasputin headquarters. And from the White House, not a peep. What *that* scene is like Faith can pretty much imagine, raging around the West Wing like the cocaine bear. *You're fired*, was that the president coming to her personally? A momentarily soothing throwback to his *Apprentice* glory days? She wonders if it's because they think she underperformed, or do they think she flipped. And she tried *so hard*. Loyal to the end despite all the tribulations and temptations, and now she's dead to them. It makes her want to weep, or take to bed and sleep for a month. Amid the heaviest security yet, they pile onto the New Awakening Express and head for the L. H. "Chumper" Blalock Recreation Center in West Des Moines. It's staff only on the bus, the Candidate traveling separately. With *her*? everybody wonders, but nobody asks.

On the ride over, Twiss, Nadler, and Bardem trudge up the aisle to Faith's row. "What's he going to do?" Twiss asks her, meaning . The president's silence is grinding on everyone's nerves. Faith reflects on her three years among the Steve Bannons and Stephen Millers and other exemplary humanitarians of the White House.

"He's going to do what he always does. Flood the zone with shit."

The Blalock Center is mobbed. Thousands without, thousands

within, and as soon as Rasputin takes the stage a thunderous chant booms forth—

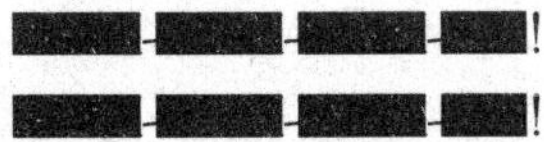

And this is the heartland, the Midwestern suspenders version of the South's Bible Belt. If Rasputin can sell it here, he can sell it anywhere. His smile beams out to every nook and cranny of this cavernous multi-court basketball complex. He seems happier and more beatific than ever, loosed, unburdened, and watching him on a monitor backstage, Faith and her colleagues are moved to see the Candidate so much at peace. What seemed this morning to mark the campaign's demise might be their speed rail to the presidency.

When at last West Des Moines lets him speak, he thanks them for the love. "And █████ thanks you too! She has been through a lot lately, so she is taking a little break. But you will all be seeing more of her soon."

Big cheers for that. Faith watches for a while, then drags a folding chair off to the side and goes back to the phones. She feels woozy, punchy. Time keeps sliding and skidding in classic sleep-deprivation mode, and her poor body aches like she's been breaking rocks. Mood swings like a motherfucker, those too, and her nose feels like a travel-size version of the London fatberg. She fires off an impulse text to Harvey on her personal phone, Fuck you I did everything you people asked me to. In about a minute the phone buzzes. She checks the screen, then pushes through the nearest door and hotfoots it down a mostly deserted hall before clicking on.

"My goodness. To what do I owe this great honor."

"Faith." *Faith.* At the sound of his voice something starts pulling her down, some sort of interior undertow. She fights it.

"Yes, that's me. Hope and Charity are on the other line."

"I didn't have anything to do with it. I only found out after."

"Yeah, well, whosever idea it was, did it occur to them it might not be the greatest idea to cut me loose? Like in addition to losing a damn good soldier, you might really piss me off?"

"I know, I know. Who knows what those people think."

"Which people."

"You know. The usual."

"Him?"

"Well, he's sort of lashing out at everybody right now. Look, we really can't be talking, but I want you to know I wouldn't have done it. You've been stellar. In every way. It's just this one thing you let us down on, and it just happens to be a very big thing."

"I was in touch with Miller. I kept him apprised on everything."

"I know."

"But nobody saw *this* coming. I sure didn't."

"I believe you. But you know how it is. Something has to give."

"In this case, me."

He falls silent. All her body fluids seem to have drained into her feet. "I miss you," he murmurs.

Her chest hurts. She can't speak.

"I miss you so much. I think about you all the time."

She leans her shoulder against the wall and lets the sheetrock hold her up.

"Faith? You there?"

"I'm here," she whispers.

A grassy rustling hisses through the line. "Are you in love with him?"

She comes off the wall like a ricochet. "*What?* In love with *who*?"

"Him. Rasputin."

"Harvey," she groans. "For Christ sake."

"Well, the way you were crying at the press conference. It's like your heart was broken."

"Listen, I'm sick as a dog, I've had about five hours' sleep in the past two weeks, and I got fired last night by a bunch of people I've been killing myself for. Then it's a total shitstorm today, forgive me if I lost it for a minute out there." She pauses. He seems to be waiting on her. Right, he asked her a question. At the moment she's not feeling much mercy for him. "Am I in love with him. I tell you what, I'm about as much in love with him as every other woman around here."

"Wow. Okay."

"I called you, Harvey. Remember? Christmas? I needed you and called and you didn't call me back."

"Faith. You know I couldn't."

"Yes you could. You just did."

"Well, there's a good reason for that. A bunch of us are wondering where exactly you stand."

"Excuse me?"

"Where you stand. Are you with the president or not?"

For all the absurdity of the question, she knows she should stall. Something crucial seems to hang in the balance, but she's too angry and addled to patiently think it through.

"How the hell am I supposed to answer that? You guys *fired* me, Harvey, I'm fucking *fired*. I would think that makes me irrelevant."

He sighs. "You know I don't like it when you use language like that."

"What," she sputters, "what do you even *want*, man? I've done everything you guys asked me to, what else do you want?"

"You know what? You just told me you're in love with the man who's trying to unseat the president. I guess that's all I really need to know."

"Harvey, if you only knew half of what you need to know . . . Christ, whatever, forget it. I can't talk to you right now."

She clicks off and retreats to an opportune women's room. She's not sure what just happened, but she thinks she probably handled it badly, whatever it was. She's shaking, that's a sign. She feels like crying and throwing up. All these years she's gone around thinking she's so tough, in reality she's a squab, a spat, a dandelion puff. Sitting on the pot she wonders if she should just fold, now. Tell Bardem she's had enough and head for the airport, but merely the thought of walking away from Grishka doubles her over. No. Nope. He's the drug, she's the addict. When she returns backstage the heavy-metal *Swan Lake* theme is playing, the soundtrack for the selfie and autograph segment of the proceedings. Bardem rips her for disappearing and not calling *People* back, and Nadler rips her for not closing with

Oprah's people yet, and she has about seventy new texts and a dozen voicemails, and again she cycles through the thought process of why she's still here. Then Clarence Thomas saunters backstage, basically the equivalent of a South Korean strolling over to the North. He heads for her.

"How did you get back here?"

"You'd be surprised where a name like mine can get you."

Lord. Bunch of dolts running security.

"All right, what do you want?"

He shies, recovers. "I just wanted to check on you."

Huh?

He chuckles. "Faith. Is that so strange?"

This one small dose of mercy cracks her open, but she can't be seen crying, not here, not with him. As her face melts she ducks into the same hallway as before and fetches up at a water fountain. "I'm sorry," she says over her shoulder to Clarence, who, politely or nosily, has followed. "I don't usually lose my composure."

"Quite all right if you do."

He stands easy as she leans over the water fountain and snorts and blubbers, dipping down for a drink whenever someone walks by. It doesn't last long, then she's digging around her satchel for tissues. He offers his handkerchief, which is not only clean but neatly ironed as well.

"Oh God, no. I'm not going to snot all over your nice clean handkerchief."

"That's all right. Keep it."

She takes the handkerchief and downloads a couple of juicy blows.

"I'm sort of a mess."

"Politics will do that to you."

"I don't know anything anymore. I mean," she pauses to look up and down the hall, "I'm working for a guy who thinks he's Rasputin who's running for president, and now he's got some sort of affair going with the president's *wife*? Like, how did I get here? What am I doing?"

"That's life, you know, one damn thing after another. I have to say, you look awfully tired."

"I haven't slept since, uh, New Hampshire? I don't even know when that was." She surrenders momentarily to another crying fit.

"I think that's ninety percent of your problem right there. You're exhausted."

"No, I really don't think so. I think my problem is my life is completely fucked up."

"That's extreme."

"I just," she begins, and quits.

"Go on," he coaxes.

"I wish . . ." She stalls out again.

"I'm listening."

"I don't even know. What I want. Who I am. What I'm doing."

"Yeah, sounds like you're having a full-blown existential crisis. And those are all valid questions, by the way. But don't even think about trying to figure it out right now. Just focus on getting through the day, and go to bed as early as you can. You look about as done in as anybody I've ever seen, if you'll excuse my saying."

She nods, and delivers another honking discharge into his handkerchief.

"Why are you being so nice to me?"

"Faith, come on. Why wouldn't I be?"

"Because most people are total shits."

He ponders for a moment. "You know? More and more I think I might agree with you."

He sees her to the bus. Two more rallies are scheduled for this afternoon in the greater Des Moines area. The love pours forth at Prairie Meadows Casino Hotel in Altoona, marred only by a nonlethal clash two blocks away between Rapid Support Forces and the White Guard. The campaign is en route to Ankeny Centennial High School when the ██████ bomb finally drops:

THE COMMITTEE TO RE-ELECT THE PRESIDENT

This is the official statement of the Committee to Re-Elect the President in response to recent events. We hereby declare to the American people the followng:

—The MAGA movement is first and foremost a moral movement. It stands for sanctity of the family, Judeao-Christian ethics, and the belief that ours is a nation especially blessed and favored by God. MAGA is guided at all times by the Holy Bible and the traditonal moral values that have made America the greatest nation on earth!

—President ██████'s personal attorneys will soon be filing multple counterclaims in the divorce proceedings initiated today by ████████████████████, including for adultry, physical and emotional distress, loss of consortium, breech of contract, and forfeiture of all monetary claims asserted by █████████████ under any heretofore executed prenuptial agreements.

—Also in consultation with his personal attorneys, President ██████ is actively considering filing one or more civil actions against one Grigory Yefimovich Rasputin, better known as "Fake Russian," also formerly known as Patrick Walsh Strickland, for multiple cases of action, including for alienation of affection, tortitious interference with contract, misappropriation of funds, RICO violations, defammation of character, and corprate espionage.

—In light of widespread violence being instigated by Fake Russian's supporters in the so-called White Guard and other pro-Rasputin gangs, President ██████ has called an emergency Homeland Security Council meeting to discuss enhanced domestic security measures, strongly including the possibility of President ██████ activating the Insurrection Act.

—Numrous individuals will soon step forward to attest to Fake Russian's disgusting moral character, including former aides, business associates, sexual partners, and at least one former so-called "Maiden."

—The Secretary of the Army is reviewing, and will soon release, sealed documents pertaining to the 2006–2007 war crimes investigation into then-Staff Sergeant Patrick Walsh Strickland's role in the death of a detainee in the Afghan theater of war in 2006. Prosecutors in the Army Judge Advocate General's office recommended court martial and prison for Sergeant "Fake Russian" Strickland in that case. The investigation ultimately led to Fake Russian receiving an official reprimand on his Army Service record.

—As further evidence of Fake Russian's dishonesty, hypocrisy, sexual pervertedness, con artist character, and all around reprobate behavior, President ████ directs the American People's attention to the disgustingly low morals of many of his closest associates, such as:

—Charles A. Cupps, Fake Russian's longtime business manager, who in 1996 was convicted of securities fraud and served two years in Federal prison.

—Belinda Maria Chapa, his assistant business manager, currently on probation for assault with a deadly weapon.

—Clyde Quickly, Dallas-based financier and the recently named co-chair of Fake Russia's Texas campaign, has fathered at least one illigetimate child with Faith & Fitness "entrepreneur" Christie Spack. This child, former *Nashville Next Gen* reality-TV "star" Faith Spack, aged 26, currently works for the Fake Russian campaign as deputy communications director.

—numarous close friends and associates of Fake Russian's were criminally convicted in Japan in 2014 and 2015 for running a drug trafficking ring specializing on steroids and other performance-enhancing drugs. People familiar with these cases still question why "Rasputin" himself was never prosecuted.

Rasputin is a fraud, a fake, a con man, a potential foreign

spy, a home wrecker and sexual predator, and in the coming days we will amply prove to the American people that this man is an utter disgrace to humanity. STAY TUNED!!!!!! If the Fake Russian is elected president, our great nation is DOOMED.

Faith registers the gasps, yips, and yelps of her colleagues as they reach the section setting forth her paternity. She lingers over it only briefly, and reads on to the end. Flood the zone with shit, so she called that right, and she's just one more turd in the sea of sludge. She thinks of Harvey and asks herself, Am I surprised? Not really. Not even angry, all that much. Just really, really sad. Defeated. Defeated by love and politics.

Abby Lipscomb, one of the comms minions, is in the seat beside her. She speaks softly, gingerly, as if to a mental patient.

"Faith. I had no idea."

Faith shrugs. Like a soldier taking a bullet in the heat of battle, she hardly feels anything.

"Did you know?"

This makes her laugh. "Of course I knew. I've always known."

Abby ponders. Faith can practically hear the wheels spinning. "Do you . . . does he . . . do you guys have a relationship?"

"I've had one conversation with that man in my entire life."

"Ow. Harsh."

She starts to text Christie, but now a bunch of men are crowding the aisle next to her. Twiss, Nadler, Bardem, Buffilini. They look as grim as church elders at a book burning.

"Is it true?" Nadler asks.

Faith nods.

"You should have told us."

"Ah, no, I don't think so, I'm not obliged to tell you any such thing. That's my personal life. And anyway, Grishka's known for months. Maybe *he* should have told you."

This rocks them back. Twiss is the first to recover. "The fact remains,

Faith, you should have warned us. This campaign doesn't need any more complications right now."

"I'm sorry. Would it help if I kill myself?"

Abby bursts out laughing, which doesn't improve Faith's standing with the boss. "The media's going to be all over her," Bardem says, as if she's not sitting right here. "As soon as she shows her face it'll be a feeding frenzy."

"Right," Nadler says, and turns to Faith. "So you're going to stay on the bus. Stay out of sight until we figure out what to do with you."

"What to *do* with me? You don't have to *do* anything, just let me do my job."

"You're not doing squat until we get this figured out. Bardem will deal with the shows. You are not to talk to anybody in the media, or anybody else for that matter. Not one word."

When they arrive in Ankeny she sits tight while the rest of the staff de-bus. She gets a pat or two on the shoulder, some glancing looks of concern, but mainly it's like she's turned blue or sprouted a second head, damaged goods until her status is clarified. Once everyone's gone she sits quietly for several minutes. She could leave, get off the bus and walk away from the whole deal, but she can't think of a good reason why. The muffled rumble of the bus is soothing, womb-like. It's warm in here. She's all right. What a relief to no longer be someone's darkest secret, and as for the macro situation, the infinite web of sociopolitical ramifications, it's so much more massive than puny little Faith Spack that she feels quite Zen about it all. So stay on the bus, she tells herself, finding no compelling case for getting off. Perhaps she's an essentially passive person, a child of inertia, but now, while she's feeling calm and centered, seems like a good time to face her mother. She scrolls up the number and hits Call, and for once it rolls over to voicemail. This is troubling. She's wondering what to do when a call pops up. Clarence. She clicks in.

"I just tried to call my mother and she didn't pick up."

"Is this unusual?"

"Very."

"Well, give it a minute. You never know. Maybe she's in the shower."

"I'm not supposed to talk to you, by the way. Or anybody. I'm embargoed."

"Do tell."

"They're trying to figure out what to do with me. And in the meantime," she has a look at her surroundings, "I guess you could say I'm in a secure location."

"You all right with that?"

"All right enough." She takes stock. "A lot better than I was earlier, which seems weird, right? Now that the whole world knows I'm Clyde Quickly's little bastard bitch."

"Faith, don't talk that way. There's a heckuva lot more to you than that. Look, now the spotlight's going to be on you, at least for a little while. They're gonna be coming at you hard, that's just the way it is. So if you find yourself needing a bolt-hole at any point, I'm in room 726 at the Hyatt. Just FYI."

"Uh, okay." Now she's scared.

"On the up and up," he adds. "Just in case." He's embarrassed, she realizes. Now she's embarrassed too.

"Thanks. Thank you. But I really don't think they're going to kill me." That he says nothing scares her all over again. "I'm kidding."

"I know you are."

"I mean, this isn't, um, El Salvador."

"I don't care where in the world you are, power is power and some people will do anything to get it."

"Dude, you're talking to a girl who worked in the White House for three years."

"There you go. You know it better than me. But be careful. You're in it in a different way now."

"I am a very minor detail." Her phone buzzes. "Mom's calling," she says, and Clarence says "Go," and she clicks over.

"Mom."

"Faith. My sweet girl."

Christie sounds far too calm.

"Mom, did you, ahm, have you heard?"

"I certainly have!"

"I'm so sorry."

Christie laughs. "For what? It's out, finally. After all these years. He's been such a hero in this town for so long, it's high time people know the other side of that man. And now you'll start getting some of the respect you deserve as his daughter."

"I don't know about that. I just hope you're okay."

"I'm perfectly lovely! The truth is never a disgrace to the righteous of heart. If people want to think I'm a tramp for having an affair with him when I was all of twenty, fine, they're welcome to. That's a small price to pay for the truth."

To say her mother sounds chill would be pushing it, but she is drastically not how Faith expected her to be. Not on a tear. No cackling madwoman laughter or life-regret sobs, no PTSD rage spree, nor is she curled into a fetal ball in the closet. It seems that Christie Spack has experienced a psychotic break into serenity.

"Mother. This is so impressive of you."

"Honey, you and I have been waiting for this day for a long time." Well, *you* have, Faith thinks. "And now it's out. And you and I didn't have a thing to do with it."

"Right." Now she plays a juvenile trick on herself and pretends not to know what she knows. "How do you think they found out?"

"█████ is the president, dear. If there's something he wants to know I'm sure there are all kinds of ways he can find out. There's the FBI, and the CIA, and the Pentagon, and spy satellites, and who knows what else."

"Good point."

"We have honored the NDA to the letter."

"Mmm hm." Might be a bit of a technical problem there.

"Our conscience is clear."

"That's true."

"And you'll continue to have the benefit of your trust fund. Which is as it should be."

"I guess so." Perhaps now is the time to say fuck you to the trust fund, which would be noble and brave and probably also really dumb. When they click off she finds a new text waiting for her.

> Ricardo Levy: WOW!!!! AMAZING!!!! GREAT for your BRAND!!!!
> Lets make you a HUGE $TAR!!!!!

Faith taps Delete, thinking: I would rather die.

In due course staff is piling back on the bus. It was a so-so rally with some hecklers and derogatory signage, a downer ending to a tumultuous day. Another sex tape drops while they're en route to the hotel. So this is how it's going to be? Flooding the zone 24–7 and why not, so far the American people have demonstrated an endless appetite for shit. In her room Faith kicks off her heels and falls across the bed, she'll be up and back at it after this short commercial break. She has to eat, and there's a staff meeting at ten where "what to do" with her is presumably on the agenda. Next thing she knows it sounds like a SWAT squad is breaking down her door, and her bedside clock reads 12:53 a.m. Oh hell. She stumbles to the door and puts her eye to the peephole. Chuck looms in the fisheye bubble, Cecil at his shoulder. She opens up.

"Hey guys, I—"

They push past her into the room, followed by Nadler and Buffilini. "You"—Nadler points at her—"sit," and when she doesn't comply right away Cecil takes her by the shoulders and backs her into a chair.

"Guys, I'm fine, I just fell asleep. What are you doing?"

Chuck and Cecil are scooping everything out of the chest of drawers and dumping it on the bed, and Nadler is pawing through the piles. Buffilini is making big racket in the bathroom.

"Roy, what the hell?"

He turns to her with a this-too-I-have-to-deal-with? roll of the eyes. "You're fired," he says. "You are leaving, now. This isn't your room anymore."

"Wait, what. I'm *fired*? Just because I fell asleep?"

"You're fired because you're a fucking whore spy."

"I—wait. Stop. Stop for a minute. Would you guys please just stop for a minute?"

They don't stop. Chuck is going around the room collecting her electronics and dumping them in a canvas bag. Cecil has her suitcase open on the bed and is poking through the pockets and flaps.

"Let me explain," she says, but they don't stop what they're doing. "Does Grishka know?"

"He knows," Nadler snaps.

"Can I talk to him?"

"You cannot. You are not to contact him in any way, shape, or form. And if you know what's good for you, you'll keep your damn mouth shut, and I mean *shut*. Forever. You are done."

"Go to hell," she tells him.

In one smooth motion Cecil pivots from the bed and grabs her left breast and twists her nipple so hard she nearly passes out. Chuck is in her closet now.

"The safe," he says to Nadler.

"What's in the safe?" Nadler asks her.

"Fuck you," she manages. The spy phone is in the safe.

"Open it."

"Fuck you."

"Fine, we'll have the hotel drill into it. Which you will pay for."

In the bathroom Buffilini is breaking things. Nadler empties her satchel onto the bed and picks through the contents. Cecil feels up the satchel for bulges and secret pockets, then he and Chuck make Faith stand and give her a leisurely, mocking patdown. Their groping is beyond gratuitous, it is a parody of offensive cupping and kneading and they take great care to include all her tenderest spots. About halfway through it she starts shaking and can't stop. When they're done Cecil holds her by the upper arm while Nadler and Chuck jam all her belongings in the suitcase. Out the window it's snowing, hard. A blizzard.

"Roy," she says, hating the way her voice trembles. "It's the middle of the night."

"That's right. So you will want to be extremely careful out there." He stops what he's doing and gives her a searingly blank look. "Extremely careful."

To this she says nothing. It seems they have achieved an understanding, yes. She is in it in a different way now. She looks around for her heels but Cecil is already frog-marching her out the door with her suitcase thumping and tumbling behind her, she can't get it centered on the wheels. He hustles her down the hall to the elevator and shoves her in, hits the lobby button, and steps out. He stands there staring at her until the doors close. As the elevator descends her chest burns with bottled-up sobs, but she refuses to cry. She's still trembling and doesn't know how to stop. Her breast hurts so badly she thinks real damage might have been done.

When the doors open she steps into the lobby and walks toward the nearest sitting area. She has a pair of Reeboks in her suitcase; she'll put those on and go about finding a hotel, but her gaze falls on two men in dark suits standing on the far side of the lobby, just inside the main entrance. She knows their faces. They're part of the campaign's private security team. One of the men sees her and speaks to the other, and they start her way. She doesn't think, she simply turns and steps back on the elevator and hits the button for the seventh floor, and now, thinking, hits six and eight and nine and ten and eleven and twelve. The men break into a run. She can only stand here and watch them come, and for as long as it lasts the entire rest of her life seems contained in these moments.

The men are three strides away when the doors close. She gets out on the seventh floor, finds 726, and knocks. After a minute he opens the door in a T-shirt and boxers, and she lurches, half stumbles across the threshold. Now she can cry.

29

The preliminary tally is seventeen dead, over two hundred injured in the twenty-four hours following the love declaration. State and local Rasputin offices are hit hard as National Security Brigades and Rapid Support Forces strike the most visible strongholds of the Wrath of God's support. President █████ puts all branches of the military on high alert and threatens full-scale mobilization, asserting in a 5:17 a.m. SonicX post that pro-Rasputin gangs "are burning our cities, raping our women, and tearing the country apart. THEY MUST BE STOPPED BY ANY MEANS NECESSARY." Black helicopters appear in the early morning skies over a dozen state capitals, including Des Moines, where one spins over the Hyatt Hotel for several minutes, rattling windows and nerves and waking even the soundest sleepers.

Clarence is already up. He goes to the window and fingers back the curtain, peers into the predawn murk. He can't see the helicopter but he can sure feel it, his frame vibrating like a stand-up bass. He returns to the desk and sits down at his laptop, where he's got a new story cooking.

> For the ultimate in bogus wars we need only look to two of the founding documents of Western civilization. "The Iliad"

and the "The Odyssey," composed some 3000 years ago, tell the story of the decade-long war between the Trojans and the Greeks, thanks to which we have the Trojan Horse, Achilles' heel, and a pretty bad movie starring Brad Pitt. And what triggered this cruel and bloody war? Helen, beauteous Helen, the Kim Kardashian of her day, ran off with handsome Paris to his hometown of Ilium. When Helen's husband Menelaus found out, he went to his brother King Agamemnon and persuaded him that the entire Pan-Hellenic coalition had to attack and conquer Troy, all so Menelaus could get his wife back.

Reader, can you imagine a lamer excuse for a war? Man can't keep his wife happy, that's his problem. Don't go dragging the country into war just because your woman ran off with another man and left you crying in your Wheaties . . .

She slept in the bed, and he made a pallet and slept on the floor. Rose early to write, and saw the email blast from the campaign calling a press conference for nine a.m., once again in the Cheyenne Room. He'll have to miss it. He's already checked the flights. Presently he sends the story to Renfro and makes a second mini-pot of coffee, then kneels by the bed and gently nudges her awake.

"There's a flight to Dallas at ten-fifty," he murmurs. "How about we get you on that and home to your mom."

"In two days," Rasputin tells the assembled media, "this Saturday, the nineteenth of January, the faithful of the Orthodox Church will celebrate Holy Epiphany, in commemoration of the baptism of our Lord Jesus Christ in the River Jordan. On this day the faithful gather by the living waters of a river, a lake, or the sea, and our priests bless the water, and we ask God to crush all evil things in the water, and to bless and sanctify it with His presence. And then we, the hardiest among us, we immerse ourselves in the water, which you can imagine is really cold in Russia this time of year!"

The media dutifully laugh. Yes, really cold! We can imagine!

"This we do to symbolize the baptism of our Lord Jesus, and to cleanse and purify our souls for the new year. For none among us is without sin, my brothers and sisters. And certainly I, Rasputin, that man, is a sinner, this I freely acknowledge. I am at fault in many aspects of my character and life, and in the matter of the estrangement of the president and First Lady, I certainly bear my measure of fault. Therefore, I pledge that on the day of the Holy Epiphany I will do penance in the living waters of the Potomac River. A special penance; a mortification, if you will. I will enter the river at the southern shore of Theodore Roosevelt Island, and from there I will swim past the Lincoln Memorial, the Jefferson Memorial, and downriver to Mount Vernon, the famous home of George Washington, the father of our country. Thus my swim of mortification will pay tribute to the four great presidents whose faces decorate Mount Rushmore.

"And so I invite you, my brothers and sisters, to commemorate Holy Epiphany with me in Washington, and there we will renew our faith in God and our great country."

Faith and Clarence hear the news on the way to the airport. NPR surrounds clips from Rasputin's remarks with its ever-sober, always reasonable commentary, the perfect straight man for the country's hijinks. Clarence offers to switch it off, but Faith shakes her head.

"It doesn't bother me. I'm done with those people."

She gazes out the window at all the normal everyday Americans going about their normal everyday lives. The sky is crisp cornflower blue, the sun painfully bright; the fresh snow would seem to signal new beginnings, if she'd let it. All she knows is she wants a small life like theirs, obscure, ordinary, of importance only to herself and a few others. A life far removed from politics, though necessarily haunted by the knowledge that America is being run by a bunch of thieves and psychopaths. This morning, as they were preparing to leave, she watched Clarence take a dark, dildo-ish object from the bedside table and put it in his coat pocket. When she asked what it was, he hesitated, then seemed almost to smile.

"This," he said, pulling the thing from his pocket, "is a blackjack."

"Oh. I guess I've never seen one before."

He handed it to her. It was heavier than she expected, its dense weight wrapped in a sheath of slick dark-brown leather. An altogether serious object.

"Do you always have it with you?"

He seemed to consider for a moment. "No." It occurred to her that he processed events through an entirely different frame of reference from hers, one by which he considered her present situation to be more serious than even she herself thought it to be. She'd told him most of it. The scene in the room, where they were rough with her. The two security creeps in the lobby. The theft of her phones and laptop. They'd justified everything by accusing her of spying for the █████ campaign.

"Clarence, those are not good people," she says now. On NPR they have determined that the distance from Roosevelt Island to Mount Vernon is seventeen miles. "This would be a challenging swim even for a seasoned long-distance swimmer in peak condition," opines a guest expert. "And in open water, with January temperatures, I have a hard time seeing him getting very far with this."

Clarence turns down the volume. "I never thought they were."

"I don't know about Grishka. But those people around him—maybe he doesn't really know. Maybe he's naive."

Clarence's head saws side to side.

"You don't think so?"

"No."

"You think he's bad."

Clarence shrugs. "I just don't think he's naive." He pauses, then adds, "Sometimes I think he might be the worst one of all."

"Yeah. Or the best, maybe. You know what's funny about all this? I'm not even all that into politics. I mean it's my job, I've spent my whole career doing it, and I really couldn't care less about most of it."

"Well, you're lucky. That's a luxury a lot of people can't afford."

"What?"

"Not caring."

This feels vaguely like a burn. "I," she begins, meaning to argue with him, but a whiff of a laugh pops out of her chest, light as a bubble bursting. She's shocked, or maybe embarrassed? That it's really so obvious? Because it seems he just handed her the key to everything.

He never asks if it's true, that she was spying for ██████. So at least she's spared that.

The last-minute fare is exorbitant. "You can handle it?" he murmurs, reaching for his wallet, but she smirks as she lays down her credit card, then leans into him and whispers, "I have a trust fund from Clyde." While she buys her ticket he keeps his head on a swivel, and notes that of the twelve American Airlines kiosks in the vicinity, only two are working. Might as well be Salvador forty years ago, swivel-head and all. Walking her to TSA he can't help offering final instructions.

"If anybody messes with you, you go to the oldest, baddest, toughest-looking female gate agent or flight attendant you can find, and you tell her those people are harassing you. And if they try to take you away, give her this." He hands her his business card. "Tell her to call me. But tell her to call security first."

Faith nods. "I'll be okay."

"Yes, probably. But now you know what to do."

"Now I know what to do."

"And you'll keep me posted."

"I'll keep you posted."

Approaching the TSA chute they slow, stop. "Your mom's going to meet you," he says, just to confirm for the tenth time this part of the plan.

"She'll be there."

"She's a pretty tough lady, your mom?"

"She is, actually." Faith meets his eye and blinks, and her throat does a hard clench. "Well, thank you."

"You're welcome."

"No, really, I mean it. Thank you. You sort of saved me."

"Well, like you said. Those are not good people." Now his own throat suddenly jams, a root ball of emotion stuck down there. And him thinking he was beyond such things. "Okay, so let me know when you get there."

"I will." She glances toward security, then turns back to him. "What are you going to do now?"

"Drive back into town," he answers briskly. "Get back to work. Then," he hesitates, as if just now realizing, "I guess I'll be going to Washington."

30

Seventeen miles. Seventeen point three, to be exact, this is the distance from the southern shore of Theodore Roosevelt Island to the Mount Vernon wharf. Seventeen miles with water temperatures in the low forties, and in the forecast, snow flurries, a high for the day that *might* graze thirty degrees, and northeast winds of twelve to fifteen knots. Can't be done, the experts say. Not without training, experience, long and diligent preparation. So he claims he swam a mile every day in the Tura River during his monastery years (except when it froze), that was a long time ago and he's out of practice. Swimming shape isn't the same as wrestling shape, and when you factor in the cold, the wind, the push-pull of the tides and the treacherous currents, odds are he'll crash out long before Mount Vernon.

"He's not gonna finish that swim," █████ tells reporters as he leaves an afternoon rally in Ames.

What makes you say that?

"Trust me," the president says. "I know. He's not gonna finish."

The fix is in? And yet the Metropolitan Police Department's Harbor Patrol promptly issues a permit for the swim. Rasputin goes into strict seclusion in the Presidential Suite of the Watergate, praying, meditating, conferring with trainers and swim gurus. Clarence takes a room at the Hampton Inn in Old Town Alexandria, with nephews Nelson and Kenneth in the room next to his. Nelson insisted on coming, saying something about keeping his radical uncle out of trouble, and insisted on bringing Kenneth as well, six-four, 240 pounds, a starting outside linebacker at Texas Tech. "Key, we might need his muscle," Nelson explained. Like they're going to punch their way out of a civil war? On arrival at Reagan National, Nelson tasks Kenneth with fetching the rental car, and his young cousin pulls around to the terminal in a tomato-red Camaro.

"I was thinking," Nelson says in a forbearing voice, "something a little more discreet would be best?"

"This was all they had," Kenneth says. He's the baby of the family, the youngest child of Clarence's youngest sister, tends to seriousness and solemnity like all the Thomas men. Dark, clean-shaven, hair buzzed close and kempt; a small diamond decorates his left earlobe. It's a dour midwinter day in the nation's capital, but since this is Kenneth's first trip to DC, they spend what's left of the afternoon driving around seeing the sights. Traffic is mean, meaner than Dallas. The White House, the Capitol, the Jefferson and Lincoln Memorials all give off the spooky white glow of irradiated bones. The Washington Monument thrusts skyward like the world's largest letter opener, waiting for the momentous piece of mail that will finally warrant its use.

Nelson, driving, glances around to the back seat. "Kenny, whatcha think?"

Kenneth takes his time. In this he reminds Clarence so much of his own father, deliberation ingrained deep in the family DNA.

"I think they like their history here."

Clarence feels tinglings of claustrophobia, a kind of doomy, *All the President's Men* asphyxiating vibe, as if the sheer volume of state infrastructure exerts its own peculiar pressure. Via the radio and his phone he tracks news updates on the swim, and the media's schizy undercurrents of glee and scorn. Is the swim a cheap gimmick, a stunt? Or a quest worthy of our most profound consideration? █████ federalizes the National Guards of Virginia, Maryland, and North Carolina, citing "heightened security threats," and expands the DC-area Flight-Restricted Zone to thirty nautical miles. NPR interviews a river guide about the lower Potomac's tides and currents, then discusses the hazards of cold-water distance swimming with Dr. Peter Kovacs, longtime medical adviser for the Marathon Swimming Association and himself an accomplished distance swimmer. On his phone Clarence tees up a video posted by the Rasputin campaign in which the Candidate thanks all his "fans and supporters" for their prayers and reminds everyone that he is swimming tomorrow in commemoration of the Epiphany. "So let us keep uppermost in our minds the life of our Lord Savior Jesus Christ, and the supreme sacrifice he made for all of us."

Fox News runs a story on fecal coliform contamination in the Potomac. Then an update: On orders of the president, Black Hawk and Apache helicopters from the 449th Combat Aviation Brigade of the North Carolina National Guard are at this moment en route to Joint Base Andrews.

"I don't like it," Nelson says. "All that firepower on the street, and everybody jumpy as hell. How about we just stay in and watch it on TV."

"Maybe," Clarence says, but he knows he won't. Whatever happens tomorrow, he means to be there. That night they eat Chinese takeout in the nephews' room, which seems a shame. Shouldn't they be out on the town? But air travel and northern weather have flattened their ambition. They watch the news while they eat, and see Paul Twiss declaring on *Hannity* that tomorrow's swim has nothing to do with politics. "He's doing this as an expression of his deep Christian faith," says the campaign chief, speaking in the determinedly saccharine tones of a Sunday school teacher with a sadistic streak. "No surprise the mainstream media doesn't get it, but the American people do. They get the value of putting aside politics to contemplate a higher power." On *All In with Chris Hayes* they watch Bardem Hayes (surely no relation?) parry and thrust with his liberal host. If Rasputin can't complete the swim—if he quits, to put it bluntly—how badly will that hurt his candidacy? "Now that's just stupid," Bardem rowls. "Unless you can name me another candidate who has the guts to get in the water tomorrow."

Clarence has his phone on his thigh, waiting to hear if he has a spot on one of the boats the campaign has chartered for the press. If not, he'll have to report from shore; this section of the river will be closed to boat traffic. "Large crowds," says Anderson Cooper on CNN, "a volatile mix of both Rasputin and █████ supporters, are expected to line the swim route tomorrow."

"And how many you think'll be packing?" Nelson chirps at Anderson.

It's after ten when Clarence gets the email blast. He's not on the list, thus the land plan goes into effect. He'll cover the swim from the hike-and-bike Mount Vernon Trail that tracks the river; the nephews will take turns walking with their uncle and leapfrogging ahead with the car. On Nelson's laptop they game out the route and rendezvous points, and contingency plans if stuff hits the fan. Back in his room, Clarence surfs the news channels while organizing for bed. Media world is having a blast with the Clyde Quickly story, taunting, teasing, razzing, it's ripe for endless yuks and mob-mentality snark. Quickly's statement emphatically denying paternity is run alongside old clips of Faith from *Nashville Next Gen*, and split-screen photos of the billionaire and his younger, spitting-image female version, who has mysteriously disappeared as of two days ago.

The last text Clarence got from Faith, Christie was getting her out of town to a friend's luxury hideaway in Mexico. He's turning down the bedsheets when a text arrives from Bardem Hayes, to him only, not the usual mass blast.

Bardem: Grishka wants you on his escort boat tomorrow. You in?

Clarence: In. Just tell me where and when.

Bardem: Slip X06 at the Wharf Marina. Be there by seven.

31

And so it happens that on the morning of Holy Epiphany, Clarence is standing on the deck of a twenty-four-foot Bennington pontoon boat named *Waterboy* with an unmediated, unobstructed, up close and personal view of the ritual blessing of the waters. The day is dark, cold, somber; Russian. The air has the sharp mineral bite of imminent snow. The venerable Metropolitan Vasily (Kritsky), First Hierarch of the Russian Orthodox Church Outside of Russia, assisted by two slightly less elderly priests, kneels on a pallet at the muddy southern tip of Theodore Roosevelt Island and three times plunges a wooden cross into the Potomac River. *Eye of the storm*, Clarence writes in his notebook; the three priests form their own little bubble of calm amid the darting, buzzing swirl of illegal drones, the dragon fwapping of helicopters, the engine burblings of the flotilla that will accompany the Candidate downriver. *Way back old*, Clarence writes, everything about the ritual seems rooted in deep time, its choreography adhering to a physical logic that slots the body into sync with the natural world. A junior priest stoops to fill a bowl with water from the spot just blessed, and Clarence feels something loosening inside him, a resistance or tension he didn't know he had. The Metropolitan—a dead ringer for Jerry Garcia—takes the bowl, and using a sheaf of fresh basil as his flinger he goes around spattering water on the small group gathered here. Altar boys, acolytes, deacons, the Secret Service, they all bow their heads as the droplets hit them. The Metropolitan works his way around to Rasputin and the First Lady and comes to a stop.

It's a solemn moment. The two junior priests take up position on either side of the Metropolitan, who raises his face to the sky and offers up an incantatory prayer. Rasputin and ████████ stand before him with arms linked, heads bowed. It could be a pagan royal wedding, Clarence thinks, so much in nature with the river running inches from their feet and the misty woods at their back, prayers echoing through the trees with churchly resonance. In her black sable cap, PETA be damned, and matching full-length sable coat, ████████ is not simply gorgeous but desperately, mythically gorgeous, she embodies all the beauty and pathos of tragedy. A "fallen" woman, according to the tabloids, and an immigrant besides, yet here she is standing tall and proud by her man, who in his sleek, black, formfitting Neoprene wetsuit could be a medieval knight armored up for battle.

Prayers rise into helicopter realm. Will blessings rain down? In their heavy black cassocks and capes and their Bundt-cake hats with trailing veils, the priests could be warlocks deploying their old-world magic against the most advanced and up-to-date of the new. The Metropolitan concludes with a sweeping sign of the cross, and Rasputin turns resolutely to the water. He straps on his cap, dons goggles and gloves. The high-visibility swatches of orange on his arms and legs lend him a rakish air. He reels in ████████ for a last kiss, imbuing it with all the passionate urgency of a man going off to war. Now he turns once more to the water, looks to the sky and signs the cross, and with three violent strides he's waist-deep in the river and dives into his first stroke.

It begins, 8:37, Clarence writes. A cheer rises from the crowd lining the Potomac's western bank. Air horns toot, cowbells clang, and *Waterboy* swings to starboard and heads downstream. Kayak 1 falls in on Rasputin's left, Kayak 2 trails a yard or two behind on his right. The sporty Sea-Doo command boat angles out toward the center of the channel. Police and Harbor Patrol vessels sweep the river ahead, and two Secret

Service contingents in commando-style Zodiac boats fan out to cover the flanks. The press boats, charters from a river cruise company, bring up the rear. They are long, low-slung vessels with big picture windows along their sides, basically tourist buses on water.

All good? Nelson texts. He's somewhere over there, amid the army of Rasputinheads on the Mount Vernon Trail. Beyond the MVT lies the George Washington Parkway, where Kenneth is presumably killing time in the tomato-mobile.

All good, Clarence responds. He's in. You okay?

The nephews respond thumbs-up. The massive colonnaded cube of the Lincoln Memorial slowly formalizes out of the mist, and dead ahead, the graceful outlines of the Arlington Memorial Bridge. For a minute Clarence feels almost giddy, as if they're embarking on a journey to the source of the Nile, or up an uncharted tributary of the Amazon. The emotion strikes him as unprofessional, not to mention he's way too cold for so early in the trip. He retreats from the bow back to the relative shelter of the console and takes a seat next to Dave.

"Man, it's brisk."

"Just a little," Dave agrees. He steers with one gloved finger hooked around the wheel. He's a tall, long-jawed white man of advanced middle age, bundled up against the cold like everyone else. Drones are dancing and jerking around like puppets on a string.

"I thought drones aren't allowed on this stretch of the river."

Dave thinks for a moment. "They aren't."

"AND WHAT ABOUT THEM?" Clarence shouts as a Black Hawk helicopter drops through the cloud deck and buzzes the flotilla, clatters downriver. "What's their deal?"

For several moments Dave considers the receding helicopter. "Yeah, you don't need to worry about them. They're cocksuckers."

Watching the group assemble at the marina this morning, Clarence decided these are specialists of some kind. Dave, his three crewmates, the guys in the kayaks, the group on the Sea-Doo, all fit white men who went about their preparations with slightly show-off flourishes.

Ex-military, or maybe some category of expertise beyond that; there's a looseness about them, an air of merriment or irony that Clarence associates with the covert. Even "Chief" seems vaguely ironic, what they call the short, barrel-chested older man with the Boston-inflected voice to whom, all joking aside, everyone defers. His silly hat makes him easy to spot, a red-and-white knit cap with a bobble top, something an adoring preschool granddaughter might gift him for Christmas. It was Chief who passed out the earbuds, networking the group into a running conversation from which Clarence is excluded. Several times already he's started to answer one of his shipmates, only to realize they aren't talking to him.

Awkward, and yet they're all nice enough, their courtesy tinged with slightly too much heartiness. At the moment Nick is braced against the fore lounger, scanning the banks with field glasses. Scoot and Terry are aft organizing the remarkable quantities of equipment and supplies. And up ahead, twenty yards off their bow, there's Rasputin cutting water with strong, even strokes.

"He's a specimen," Dave says, nodding at the dashboard computer screen. Half the display is a digital map of their route, the other half comprised of data lines showing the Candidate's vitals. "See his pulse, there, under a hundred. That's insane."

"Well, he is a professional athlete."

"It's still pretty remarkable. I—okay now." He taps his earbud and mutters something about freaks on the bridge, and suddenly everyone gets busy. Directly ahead, two men have unfurled a banner on the Arlington Bridge and draped it over the rail—

THIS IS ULTRA MAGA COUNTRY!

Scoot and Terry hustle forward, and Clarence follows. The kayaks have already snugged up close to Rasputin, and the Sea-Doo cuts in fast from the left. There is drama on the bridge as cops wrestle the men away from the rail and the banner falls free, fluttering and tumbling to the water where it hits with a crêpey plash. And that's it, show's over.

Rasputin never breaks rhythm. The banner slips by to port, inert as a three-day-old corpse, and they pass under the bridge without further adventure. Clarence gets most of it on his phone and sends the video to Renfro.

"So it begins," Dave says when Clarence returns to the console.

"You're expecting more?"

"Oh yeah. If that's the worst we get today, I'll die a happy white man."

Clarence's ears prick up at that "white." "Like what?"

"Anything. Everything. They said you're a reporter."

"That's right."

"So I guess I better watch what I say around you."

"Nah. I'm harmless."

Dave laughs. Photos and videos of the banner are already popping up on Clarence's news feed. At the one-mile mark the flotilla makes a scheduled stop for Rasputin to take nutrition. Kayak 2 ferries a UCAN gel packet and a bottle of electrolyte water from *Waterboy* to the Candidate, who reclines in the frigid water like it's a mound of pillows. The Sea-Doo, the kayaks, *Waterboy* all feather in close, the Zodiacs and press boats idle on the outer rim. Feeling good, Rasputin reports to Chief, who's leaning over the Sea-Doo's gunnel. No chills, no cramps, arms and legs all good, and the river is in an obliging mood. "Fake News!" he cries on seeing Clarence. "I am so glad you are here!"

"Me too!" he calls back, and feels an embarrassing burst of affection for this man. He points toward the Mount Vernon Trail. "You've got a lot of people over there cheering for you."

"Yes! Are they not wonderful!" He rotates that way and waves, inciting a touchdown roar from the bank. "Chief, how is my stroke?"

"Pull your arms in closer to your head, you want to feel your biceps brushing your ears. And keep your head down, that'll raise your hips. You'll be more efficient."

Several illegal drones swoop in stupid close. An Apache helicopter drops out of the clouds and hovers so low that Clarence can make out the pilot's Fu Manchu mustache. Rasputin contemplates the helicopter while finishing his snack. He seems to be formulating thoughts beyond the obvious complaints that it's loud, irritating, bullying, and completely gratuitous. Presently he hands off his trash to the kayak, pulls his goggles over his eyes, gives each of his gloves a good tug, and sets off.

One mile down, sixteen to go. The banks along this section of river are bog-man colors of peat and mulch. Mist shawls the jigsaw sequence of cuts and inlets, and the shaft of the Washington Monument can be seen to the east, its terminal point lost in the clouds. To the west, Rasputin's army keeps pace with the flotilla. They are several thousand strong, a human meat wave moving along the Mount Vernon Trail with banners, signs, all kinds of flags—American, Spiritual Gangsta, Orthodox Cross, An Appeal to Heaven. And cowbells. And air horns.

Clarence: What up your way.
Nelson: Rowdy.
Kenneth: Same. Crazy traffic. Parked at Gravelly Point.
Clarence: When will you switch?
Kenneth: Nelson's call. Cuz?
Nelson: I'm good for now.

Clarence moves aft and rummages among the lockers and bins, making notes, practically forcing Scoot and Terry into an interview. For nutrition and pain management, there are energy bars and gels, Gatorade, electrolyte water, thermoses of hot tea and soup, bananas, Tums, Motrin, Tylenol, Zantac, Advil. Diving gear in case of emergency: scuba rigs, wetsuits, buoys. About eight different types of military-grade flotation device. Thermal blankets, emergency oxygen, an extensive first aid kit. Then Scoot grins and opens a matte-black locker to reveal a matched pair of futuristic-looking long guns.

"In case we see a bear," he says.

Clarence fills two cups of Starbucks-in-a-box and carries them back to the console. He sets one in Dave's cupholder and gets a brisk "Thank you sir" for his trouble. He sits and reflexively hunches to get the full benefit of the windshield, such as it is. There's a small built-in heater by his feet, and a canvas Bimini overhead, but essentially he's committed to a very long day outdoors, on the water, in subfreezing temperatures, with wind chills dipping into the teens.

"I think we're gonna be drinking a lot of coffee today."

Dave nods. "Good thing we brought a lot of coffee."

"This your boat?"

"Negative."

"Chief's?"

"Chief arranged it. He does a lot of these, or used to."

"These . . ."

"Distance swims. He's an eminence. Coaching, organizing. He probably knows as much about it as anybody."

"That how you know him?"

"Some of us, yeah."

"You a swimmer?"

Dave allows a half smile. "I used to swim a little."

"What do you do when you're not doing this?"

"Oh, you know. Sort of retired, sort of consulting. Probably play way too much golf."

"What kind of consulting?"

"Corporate security."

This seems so on the nose that Clarence wonders if he's being played.

"How would you say our man's doing so far?"

Dave stands and watches Rasputin for several moments. "He looks okay. Form is good. A little fast, maybe. He did the first mile in," he consults the dashboard screen, "just under twenty-seven minutes. That seems quick, unless he's a lot more swimmer than we know about."

The Jefferson Memorial slips by to the east, then a stately, soggy, shire's worth of golf course acreage. Rasputin clears the Fourteenth Street bridges without incident and pauses for his scheduled nutrition break. A swirl of pinhead-sized snowflakes materializes, they dance and flume about the boat without ever seeming to fall. On the Mount Vernon Trail the crowd is thicker, louder. Cowbells and air horns blare like calls to battle. Police cruisers and motorcycles with flashing lights are stationed every fifty or sixty yards, and jellybean-colored TV news vans have invaded the green space along the trail. As Rasputin resumes swimming, one of the press boats lunges in too close and almost tumps the kayaks, and so many reporters jam the windows that the glass fogs up.

With the crowds, the media fever, the buzzing helicopters, Clarence flashes on O. J. in the Bronco. A lone man in motion while the world watches. He checks his phone, and here's a text that makes him smile.

Faith: Is that you on the pontoon boat?
Clarence: That would be me.
Faith: Me and mom watching live. ESPN has the best coverage, Michael Phelps doing color commentary. He gonna make it?
Clarence: TBD. Brutal cold.
Faith: Looks it. Mexico is nice.
Clarence: Warm?
Faith: Perfect. You should come and thaw out when you're done. I need someone to talk to besides mom.

I might take you up on that, he types, at first because it's polite, then he thinks he actually could, if everything goes to hell. If norms of age appropriateness and propriety get tossed into the bonfire along with everything else. You doing ok?

Faith: Ok. Healing ha ha I hate that fucking word. When I think about those people I hope there really is a hell.
Clarence: Yeah, you sound ok.
Faith: Watch yourself out there CT. Those are not good people.

Rounding Gravelly Point, the river widens out, and they're hit with a stiff east wind that seems to bring the entire flotilla, Rasputin included, to a stop. A trick of perspective, Clarence realizes, the slant of the chop misaligned with the rounded edge of the shore. Ahead of them looms the concrete city-state known as Reagan National Airport.

"And here she is," Dave croons, pointing to the big white yacht emerging from the Washington Channel.

"Who?" Clarence asks, not sure if Dave is talking to him or network. The yacht features an elegantly raked multistory superstructure and looks to be about forty-three miles long.

"Miss America."

Clarence looks at him, and Dave laughs.

"█████████."

A police boat accompanies the yacht across the river to the flotilla. Rasputin loses his army as the Mount Vernon Trail turns west for the long detour around Reagan National, and the helicopters and most of the drones clear out. With big jets from Reagan screaming low overhead, Rasputin rolls onto his back for the mile three break. *Waterboy* and the kayaks see to the Candidate's nourishment while Chief himself takes the helm of the Sea-Doo and motors around to the stern of the yacht, where Charlie Cupps immediately starts yapping at him. The First Lady, sabled and chic, emerges from the cabin amid an all-male retinue, and with the help of portable stairs and many more gallant hands than she needs, she clambers over the yacht's transom and takes the big step down to the Sea-Doo. Charlie tries to follow but Chief waves him off, and the boat putt-putts at a ladylike pace over to Rasputin, Chief deftly settling it within arm's reach of the Candidate.

█████████ bends over the gunnel, Rasputin bicycles upright, and they briefly clasp hands. Their *my darlings* carry clearly across the water. A swarm of drones appears out of nowhere; the press boats threaten to capsize as all the reporters rush to this side for their snaps and video. Clarence, too, is recording, and when he plays the video back he'll be struck by the woodenness of the couple's talk. How clearly they project; how seemingly canned the delivery. As if they're speaking lines someone wrote for them.

███████: How are you, my love?

RASPUTIN: I am doing this.

██████: Yes you are, and I am so very proud of you. You are so brave. So strong. I know you will succeed.

RASPUTIN: By the grace of God. Do you know how beautiful you look right now?

██████ [giggling]: Stop it!

RASPUTIN: No, it is true! I am dazzled! You are so beautiful I think I might sink to the bottom.

██████: Please don't. [She reaches down and takes his hand.] Stay here where I can see your handsome face.

RASPUTIN: For a minute. Then I must go.

██████: You are not too tired?

RASPUTIN: Not at all. God is with me. Chief!

CHIEF: Sir!

RASPUTIN: How am I doing?

CHIEF: Just keep doing what you're doing and you'll be fine.

RASPUTIN: May God Almighty grant me the strength. [Turns to First Lady.] Are people watching?

██████: My love, the whole world is watching! Everyone is cheering for you!

RASPUTIN: Then I would be rude to keep them waiting. So now it is time.

██████ [releasing his hand]: Swim on, my love. Be strong. I am with you to the end.

Who actually talks like this, zombies? Zombies in love? Clarence sends the video to Renfro with "Too stupid to believe?" as the subject line, then hunkers down behind the console and has a bad couple of minutes wondering where is the real in all this. That creature up there in the water, that is a person, swimming, a human being in water. Beyond that the facts get dodgy pretty quick, starting with the proposition that the swimmer is a product of the famously fake/not-fake world of professional wrestling. This so-called Rasputin. "Rasputin." Who in fact seems neither more nor less authentic than that maestro of mass media manipulation known as "██████." The artifice industrial complex is so vast, so brainy, so richly and obscenely capitalized that its armature envelops the globe, and here Clarence is plinking at it in the moral equivalent of a BB gun taking on a battleship. The yacht comes about as if purposely flashing its ass at him and there's the name on the stern, *Capitol Gains*, and even that seems part of it.

He texts Renfro, See if you can find ownership of FLOTUS yacht CAPITOL sic GAINS. The First Lady remains on the Sea-Doo for now. She sits up front with Chief, and the old man quickly has her smiling and laughing, he is apparently quite the charmer. Dave mumbles something to network, and Kayak 2 moves up to join Kayak 1 on Rasputin's left, giving him a fraction more cover from the wind. Clarence leans over for a look at the dashboard screen. That's Maryland to the east, they've left DC behind. Rippling snowfall over there, fog, gloom, might as well be Siberia. On their right Reagan National seems to go on forever.

"You okay?"

He looks over to see if Dave is talking to him or network.

"I'm fine." It's as if he sensed Clarence's discouragement.

"We've got a long way to go. Whenever you think you've had enough, we can drop you onshore."

Clarence shakes his head. "I'm in for the duration."

"Suit yourself. We've got overalls back there if you want another layer." Dave stands and watches Rasputin for several strokes. "That wind's beating him to pieces. But the tide's starting to run our way. So he has that going for him."

Clarence nods and makes notes. Waves slap the pontoons, thrash the underside of the deck like prisoners desperate to escape.

"Who are you guys?"

Dave turns to him. "Say what?"

"Who are you guys. CIA? Ex-SEALs? Delta Force?"

Dave responds with an easy laugh. "Oh man, we're not nearly as high-powered as that. We're basically just a bunch of old retired farts with too much time on our hands."

"No," Clarence says, "I don't think so. I think you guys are pros."

"Pros! What kind of pros, you think."

"Spooks."

Dave smiles. "You ever met a spook?"

"I have, actually."

"Oh yeah?" He seems genuinely interested. "Where was this?"

"Central America. In the eighties. Salvador and Honduras, mainly."

"Really now." Dave's voice is a shade milder than it was a moment ago. "And what were you doing there?"

"Same as now. Reporting."

"You find any stories?"

"Maybe more than I bargained for."

Dave gives him a neutral look, then turns and scans the river side to side. "My friend, I can't speak to your experience there. But I can tell you this, these are all good people. We signed on to get that man safely in and out of the water, and that's what we're going to do."

"Signed on with who?"

Dave shrugs. "That's Chief's area."

"And you're his boys."

"That's pretty much it. Look, we aren't your story. There's your story." He points to the dashboard screen. "First mile his stroke rate was sixty-five. Then sixty, then fifty-seven, and his times are slipping with it. He keeps trending that way, you'll know he's in trouble."

Non-spook spooks, this seems of a piece with the larger situation. Word gets around that Clarence thinks they're spooks, and for this they give him a certain amount of good-natured razzing. South of Reagan National, the Mount Vernon Trail links up again with the river, and Rasputin's army is waiting for him, their racket booming across the shallows. Chief returns the First Lady to *Capitol Gains*. The Apaches and Black Hawks alternate harassing runs, and Clarence tracks the miles and stroke rates in his notebook. 57. 58. 54. Ownership listed under Hill Group Partners, Ltd., Renfro texts. Who the hell are they? a frayed and testy Clarence texts back, and Renfro responds: Still digging. They're approaching Alexandria when Nelson calls.

"I'm with Kenneth."

"Okay."

"In the car. We're going to lunch."

"Sure."

"We heard shots. *Bap-bap-bap-bap-bap*, semiautomatic. Twenty rounds at least."

"*Where.*"

"Over there, inland. Away from the water."

"I want you," Clarence says, bearing down on every syllable, "to go back to the hotel. Now."

"We're fine. It's not that close. Hear the sirens? Cops are on it."

"They're just as likely to roll you up as anybody. And in that car you might as well hang out a sign."

"Key, we're fine. We're pulling in now. I'll call you when we're done."

"Go back to the hotel, please," Clarence begs, but Nelson has already clicked off. "Shots fired," he tells Dave, and waves his arm toward Alexandria, "that way." Dave relays the news to network, and within moments reports are crowding the news feed, White Guard and [illegible]ers clashing in the Huntington Park vicinity. Up ahead Rasputin churns as relentlessly as a stump grinder. Goddammit, Clarence thinks, we aren't even halfway. He's exhausted and all he's doing is sitting here. Nick spells Dave at the helm and turns a wild grin on Clarence.

"Whaddeya think?"

"I think we're all out of our minds."

"Hell yeah!" Nick cackles. He's in his thirties, sinewy, stubbled, the youngster of the crew. "Ain't no normal out here, we're all fucking nuts! Him most of all!" He lifts his chin at Rasputin. "People die all the time doing this stuff, you know."

"I believe it."

"I've seen 'em do it. But this guy," he looks to Rasputin, "no way he's this good. We're just waiting for the drugs to wear off."

Clarence supposes he has to ask: "I assume you're kidding."

Nick just laughs. Citing the violence in Huntington Park, the White House issues a statement calling on Rasputin to "cease this pointless and ridiculous stunt." Campaigning in Iowa, the president offers his personal take on the developing situation. "If Fake Russian wants to go out there and splash around like shark bait, that's his stupid business. But he's stirring up so much division with this, so much violence and crime we're seeing from his people. If he really cared about the country, he would stop right now."

Faith texts: The news says there's shooting.

Nearby, Clarence responds. Huntington Park, wherever that is.

Nearby, Faith confirms. He should stop. They're not going to let him finish anyway. Who are those people on the boat with you?

Not sure, Clarence answers. For several seconds he watches the pulsing dot-dot-dot.

Faith: You got a plan?

Clarence: Stay on the boat till it's over.

Faith: Get a better plan.

Scoot comes around with Yeti cups of steaming chicken soup for everyone, and Clarence feels saved for the time being. He hunkers down behind the console and follows news reports on the shooting, wondering if this is the day the lid comes off. One of the press boats, *Potomac Princess*, is lagging, and word comes that it's been hit by the Weeps. Dave and the crew have a laugh as it woozily wheels about and limps upriver, looking for all the world like a casualty of war. The rest of the flotilla plods on. Clarence marks miles five, six, and seven, the maddeningly slow pace doing a number on his mind. They pass under the Woodrow Wilson Bridge amid snow flurries, the sprezzatura of low-flying helicopters, a mad chorus of car horns from the interstate. Just south of the Jones Point Lighthouse they pause for Rasputin to take nourishment.

Halfway there, more or less. Rasputin looks gassed. Nobody says it but everybody sees it, his face moon-pale, lips the blanched brown of drowned earthworms. The Sea-Doo, the kayaks, and *Waterboy* have coalesced around the Candidate in a kind of floating doughnut. He drinks water and looks around the doughnut as if searching for a familiar face, sparks up a smile when he sees Clarence.

"Fake News, you are still here."

"Of course I am. I'm going all the way."

"You are not too disheartened with this weather?"

"Grishka, I've got it easy. You're the one down there doing all the work."

"Well," he pauses for a bite of waffle bar, "it is God's work. Joyful work. I swim for Him, and America."

He's resting his arm on the nearest kayak, a first. He asks for a few sips of hot tea, then Tums, this from a man who famously refuses all medications. "Well," he says, surveying the flotilla as he placidly munches his Tums, "I suppose I must be going. Pray for me." He resets his goggles, throws out a wave to his fans onshore, and sets off.

Clarence's watch reads 2:30. They'll be finishing in the dark, assuming they finish. He returns to the console and sits. Dave is back at the helm.

"He doesn't know about the shooting."

Dave tightlines his mouth, shakes his head.

"Don't you think he should know?"

"That's Chief's call. Chief says no."

"I think he'd want to know."

"Well, Chief thinks he's got enough on his mind right now."

Clarence shuts up. Something's not right and he has no idea what it is. Reports on Huntington Park put the tally at two dead, thirteen wounded. He hopes Twiss and company are discussing aborting the swim, and parts of him, the cold, miserable, cowardly, selfish parts, fervently wish they would. "I'm not stopping him," █████ says from Iowa. "This is his deal, all the blood's going to be on his hands. If he really cares about the country he'll stop right now, but he doesn't care. He wants to tear everything down." The nephews text: They've parked the car at the Belle Haven parking lot and are walking back this way. Renfro texts: The majority owner of Hill Group is something called Slumdog Trillionaires LLC, registered in Nevada. Clarence texts back: Obviously a bunch of assholes. Renfro answers: Still digging. On the news feed, Virginia state troopers intercept a van of heavily armed

Jebs a mile from the George Washington Parkway, and Faith texts that her mother is out on the balcony praying. Rasputin's numbers trend better for miles nine and ten, and the spooks are impressed. "Don't know where he's getting it from," Scoot mumbles. Halfway through mile eleven the Candidate stops and asks for two extra-strength Tylenol, complaining of shoulder pain. The boats switch on their running lights, and Kayak 1 attaches a little LED light to Rasputin's cap. With the snow squalls, the clouds the color of gutter sludge, it's going to be dusk the rest of the day. They're creeping past Dyke Marsh when the Sea-Doo sidles up to *Waterboy*, and with a neat hop Chief goes from the Sea-Doo to the pontoon boat and lets himself through the gate.

"Nicko, how about a swim."

"I thought you'd never ask."

"All right, suit up. Don't push it, just keep him steady. Aim for thirty-five-minute miles and let's see how he does."

"Got it, Chief."

"Keep to his left."

"Roger that."

"I'm thinking you'll do a couple of miles, then we'll switch you out for Terry."

"Shoot, Chief, that's hardly nothing."

Evidently Chief likes his boys cocky. Clarence is going for coffee when an Apache loops in ahead of the flotilla, spins around and hovers a hundred feet above the river, aligned and angled in position to fire on the boats. *No way* he thinks as everyone stops what they're doing and stares at the helicopter. They are, Clarence realizes, as disbelieving as he is, which seems to suggest anything is possible. Scoot takes a step toward the gun locker, and Chief stills him with a whistle. Clarence wonders if they're still in America, or have they entered a region apart, a mutant America where a homegrown My Lai would be as natural as a July Fourth parade.

He can't catch up to it. All he knows from second to second is that they're still here as of a second ago. Five, six, seven, eight—he'll count it off when he watches the news video—and at last the Apache streaks up and away as if swept by the hand of God. Everyone turns to Chief, who seems not so much alarmed as intensely curious, a chess master confronting an unorthodox move.

"Nicko, you ready?"

"Ready up."

"All right, let's do it. Let's get this over with and go home."

"Should I tell him about the . . ."

"Nothing to tell. Go."

Nick dives over the side and catches up with Rasputin in a few strokes. Clarence's phone is blowing up—the news feed, texts and calls from Renfro, Faith, Nelson. Scores of videos are being posted with various heart-thumping taglines—"Showdown on the Potomac," "Dramatic standoff," "Will they really pull the trigger?"—and the flotilla looks utterly helpless in every version, their gaggle of boats proverbial sitting ducks as the Apache takes aim. As witnessed by thousands, viewed by millions. The optics are scandalous, but someone up the chain of command is clearly past caring about optics. It takes multiple views for Clarence to realize that the Secret Service boats aren't in the frame.

"What the hell is going on?" he asks Dave, who meets his eye for a long moment, shakes his head for an answer.

"Should we be worried?"

Now Dave speaks: "They aren't going to fire."

"You sure about that?"

"They aren't going to fire," Dave repeats.

"How do you know?"

Dave points to the Sea-Doo off their bow, Chief leaning over the gunnel to speak to the kayaks. On Clarence's phone there's a voicemail from Renfro: "Are they insane?" And a text: Your safety is paramount. Take whatever steps necessary to protect yourself. Then a text from Nelson: Not believing this shit. And one from Faith: News going bonkers over that helicopter. But the Candidate looks better with Nick pacing him. They clock mile thirteen in thirty-six minutes and change, and during the break Clarence watches video taken moments ago in Iowa. "I don't know anything about it," the president huffs in an on-the-fly interview with CNN's Dana Bash. "Helicopters, sure I called up the helicopters, to keep order. Or would you prefer a bunch of radical-left lunatics running wild in our nation's capital."

The Apache appeared to take direct aim at Mr. Rasputin and his escort.

"Appeared, whaddeya mean *appeared*, what does that even mean? Somebody says they saw something?"

We have it on video.

"Video! Does anybody even believe that anymore?"

Sir, the First Lady is there. In the line of fire, if you will.

█████ goes blank. "What First Lady?"

Clarence thinks this might be as cold-blooded as anything he has ever heard. He shows the video to Dave, who tells him to show Scoot and Terry. They're a hundred yards into mile fourteen when Rasputin has to stop and throw up. Dave waves Clarence over and points at the dashboard screen.

"See that? His body temp, 95.1."

"Okay?"

"That's borderline hypothermia."

By six p.m. it's full dark and they have the rising tide against them, and as the river bends to the west the wind delivers a sideways wallop. Rasputin's stroke rate falls to forty-four, and he clocks his slowest mile yet. At the break, with the Sea-Doo and kayaks tending Rasputin, Nick swims over to *Waterboy* and rests his arm on the port pontoon.

"He's got a real bad sound in his lungs," he confides between slurps of UCAN. "Croupy. Claggy."

Dave murmurs, "You think he's done?"

"I don't see how he's still going. But, man."

"What."

"I'm not doing this so he can kill himself."

"You want out?"

Nick shrugs. "I'll do another mile. If he wants it."

"All right. I'll have Terry start suiting up."

Nick nods and pushes off. Majority shareholder of Slumdog Trillionaires is Box Canyon Private Bank of Del Rio TX, Renfro texts, and Clarence resolves to investigate, assuming he ever gets off the river. He can feel his brain descending to a lower state, the action slower, duller. A mud mind. He's cold to his core, and thinks this day might be the end of him. Now a Black Hawk parks directly above them, treetop height, and proceeds downriver at the flotilla's snail pace. The noise is simply deafening, can't hear yourself talk—Clarence tries—then a blinding white spotlight beams down from the Black Hawk's belly, standard psyop move. It has great fun bopping from kayaks to swimmers to boats, lingering here, giving a quick blast there, and how petty and simultaneously evil it manages to be.

Clarence marks how all expression has been wiped from his shipmates' faces. They are pure function, their personalities subsumed within some deep behavioral groove. It seems impossible that the helicopter would just stay there, but it does. Like being in a gale, a giant blender, and with all the racket they don't hear the gunfire onshore. Clarence has to see it on his news feed, multiple shots fired in Fort Hunt Park, details pending. He shows it to Dave, then texts his nephews, Leave. Nelson replies, Not without you. Then, Cops wilding out. Then, They're blocking the trail we're going back to car.

See you at hotel, Clarence answers, though it's hard to imagine he'll be getting there anytime soon. Rasputin has to stop twice before they complete mile fifteen, and at the break he refuses nourishment. The Sea-Doo, the kayaks, and *Waterboy* are all snugged in close around him. He's draped his arms over the cap of one of *Waterboy*'s pontoons and seems insensible to everyone talking over him. Clarence realizes if he just stands here he might watch that man die. He moves forward and opens the front deck gate and sidles along the narrow outer deck, and with one hand gripping the rail he squats and puts his face within an inch of the Candidate's.

"Grishka, it's Clarence. Fake News."

It takes several tries before Rasputin lifts his head. He doesn't recognize Clarence at first, and when he does he very nearly bursts into tears.

"Ah, Clarence. My friend."

"I'm here. Tell me what I can do for you."

"Pray for me."

"Of course. What else."

Rasputin shakes his head. "This is the hardest thing I have ever tried to do."

"I believe it. It's a very hard thing."

Rasputin's eyes fix on his, and under the blasting spotlight Clarence sees in them something more than doubt, more than dread or pain or physical breakdown. It takes him a moment to realize that what he's seeing is terror, and he wonders: Is the facade about to crack at last? After all the months and years of bravura performance. As if only death could undo the enduring character, and what will be revealed?

"You don't have to do this," he says. "You've come so far, nobody will fault you for stopping now. It's not worth killing yourself for."

"No."

"Grishka, man. Listen to me."

"Either I finish or I die. That is my destiny."

"You've got hypothermia. Your pulse rate's all over the place."

Rasputin closes his eyes and lays his head on the pontoon.

"Grishka."

"Just let me rest for a minute."

Clarence calls for hot tea. The crew scrambles, and within moments Scoot is handing a cup over the rail. Clarence squats again and coaxes Rasputin into raising his head.

"Here. Drink this."

Clarence feeds him a sip, and the Candidate groans. Then another sip, and a third. A sob works its way up from deep in his chest. "Clarence," he wails, twisting his face toward the Black Hawk, "I am so weary of that sound!"

"I know. It's awful."

"Make them stop."

"I'll work on it."

He gets a UCAN tube from Scoot, puts it to Rasputin's lips, and squeezes. Rasputin swallows. Clarence squeezes again, and again he swallows, and it goes on, the Candidate feeding like a baby from a bottle. Clarence starts to feel like he's on the verge of something, some rare grace or mystical tenderness, and he slips out of time, nearly out of consciousness, and comes to just before losing his grip on the rail. As Rasputin continues to feed, Clarence feels it happening again, that aching tenderness, grace like a brush of the divine. He thinks he might be having a genuine spiritual experience, or maybe he's simply out of his head with cold and exhaustion.

"I have to go," Rasputin says, pulling away.

"Really, you don't."

"It is my destiny." With a last grim look at Clarence, he settles his goggles over his eyes, slides off the pontoon, and instantly disappears underwater. Terry is there to take him under the arm and get him swimming in the right direction. Two miles to go. Scoot is tending Nick, who's slumped cross-legged on the forward deck with his back to the console, wrapped in a cone of thermal blankets like a human teepee. Helicopters are sweeping the shoreline with spotlights, and the bitter chemical smell of tear gas reaches the boat. Clarence suspects the crowd has broken through the police barricades, and the news feed confirms as much. Police from multiple jurisdictions are being called to the Fort Hunt area. Clarence is texting his nephews when the signal drops, and the next moment the phone goes dead. Not a freeze-up. He half wishes it was.

"They're jamming us!" Dave shouts, pointing at the Black Hawk. Clarence writes this down, along with the time. The Sea-Doo is on their right and *Capitol Gains* on their left, with the remaining press boat farther out to the left. Clarence writes this too. The shoreside Zodiac suddenly bolts sixty yards ahead of the swimmers, holds steady for a minute, then races off into the dark. Clarence puts his mouth to Dave's ear and shouts, "Where's he going?"

Dave shakes his head. The trailing Zodiac moves in tight with the flotilla. They do mile sixteen in forty-six minutes, and the swimmers keep going. Rasputin has now been in the water for twelve hours and thirty-three minutes. Clarence moves to the bow for a look, and walking back to the console, he sees two inches of rifle poking from the top of Nick's blanket teepee. When he pauses, Scoot lifts a blanket just high enough to reveal the other long gun next to him on the lounger. Of course, Clarence thinks, they're going to kill him. At this point it's the only thing that makes sense. The next moment the notion strikes him as absurd, the same moment that his legs give way. Dave grabs his arm and pulls him onto the seat, then points to a blurry string of lights on the horizon.

"Mount Vernon!" he yells. "The wharf!"

The Sea-Doo runs forward and swings ahead of the swimmers and abruptly slows, gathering them into the smoother water of its wake. They enter a small bay, and with the wharf on their left the Sea-Doo leads them toward a thin pale crescent of beach. At last the Black Hawk peels away, which is a shock; it has come to seem like a permanent condition. Clarence sees the lead Zodiac sitting on the beach. The Secret Service and a handful of police officers are gathered around it, and several dozen more police form a kind of salient or perimeter. The cops are waving a TV news crew back from the perimeter. Several more news crews are jogging this way from the wharf, and in the near distance helicopters are circling and jabbing their spotlights at the ground.

It dawns on Clarence that Mount Vernon is being overrun. Ten feet from shore the Sea-Doo swings about to make way for the swimmers. Terry touches bottom and comes to his feet, but Rasputin keeps swimming and ends up grounded on his hands and knees in the shallows. People, civilians, are emerging from the dark of Mount Vernon's grounds onto the beach. The bow of the shallow-draft pontoon boat scrapes bottom, and Dave throttles down. Scoot and Nick are standing in the bow, their long guns hidden within easy reach. Terry is bending over Rasputin with his hand on his back as cops and Secret Service start to converge on them. Clarence becomes aware of a deep rumble, a kind of volcanic surge or warp in the air, and he's struck by how helpless Rasputin is at this moment, slumped in the shallows with all the uniforms coming at him. Some basic impulse gears the reporter into motion, and he crosses the deck to the bow and opens the gate and steps off the boat into water up to his thighs.

The ferocious cold barely registers. As Clarence sloshes toward Rasputin, the Candidate digs at the mud with both hands and comes to his knees with an animal howl. He throws out mud balls like grenades, then grabs his goggles and cap and flings them aside. From the dark inland, people are storming the beach—his people, his army bearing banners and flags and here they come in their fearsome multitudes. The police line quickly buckles and the beach becomes a melee, bodies colliding and reeling, cops swinging their batons like men possessed. A helicopter gyres overhead, its spotlight crazily raking the crowd, and camera flashes and the videocams' hot lights shiv up the dark like flying glass.

"Grishka!" Clarence yells, though he's right here with him, he's wrapped his arm around the wrestler's chest in a protective clench. "Grishka, come with me. We've got to get you on the boat."

They're going to kill him, he's thinking. Either somebody will gun him down or his people will rip him to shreds out of love, adoration, primal goat-god frenzy. Cops and Secret Service rush the shallows and Clarence is pushed aside, then takes a blow to the kidney that knocks the breath out of him. He glimpses Terry on all fours at the water's edge, bleeding from the head. The helicopter turns and turns, gyring outward, now it's blaring an idiot loudspeaker drone that no one understands.

Clarence staggers onto the beach. *Waterboy* and the Sea-Doo are still there, just off the beach; *Capitol Gains* stands off in deeper water, and the press boat is pulling up to the wharf. He scans the crowd for Rasputin and spots him crouching in water up to his chest. As Clarence watches, he slowly stands and unzips his wetsuit to the waist. He frees his arms and lets the top dangle around his legs, and steam fumes off his skin in silver waves. For a moment he doubles over, then gradually, with wild-eyed effort, he pulls himself erect, a slouching Sasquatch slowly rising to full height. With a dragging gait he powers through the shallows toward the beach and raises his arms.

"I am here!" he bellows. "The Wrath of God has arrived!"

The answering roar seems to lift Clarence off his feet. With his arms still raised, Rasputin lumbers onto the beach and the crowd collapses around him. Clarence can see only his upraised arms as he crosses the beach and heads for Mount Vernon, and his people are moving with him. Clarence watches them and wonders, Where are they going? Inland, into the crowded and chaotic dark, but where are they going?

Ben Fountain has received the Joyce Carol Oates Prize, the National Book Critics Circle Award for Fiction, the PEN/Hemingway Award, the Los Angeles Times Book Prize for Fiction, the Barnes & Noble Discover Award for Fiction, the Center for Fiction's First Novel Prize, and a Whiting Award, and has been a finalist for the National Book Award and runner-up for the Dayton Literary Peace Prize. A former practicing attorney in Texas, he now lives in eastern North Carolina.